STRIKE

Killers Incorporated Book 2

by Stuart R. West

Smoke irritated his eyes. A cough erupted from his chest. He fought it, conserving his oxygen. He'd need it. Taking huge leaps, he ran the length of the bed. At the tip, he sprung up. He grabbed his knees, cannon-ball style, the briefcase pinned into his lap. Flames licked the bottom of his tennis shoes, his souls hot through the rubber.

Use the momentum, don't stop, outrace the fire. Feet down, hit the target.

His toes kicked out small glass shards from the window, then balanced on the sill. Fighting the constricting bedspread, he brought his elbows back, punched the air. Jumped up. Heat grazed his back, hungry.

Leg muscles strained. A knee wobbled when he landed on the railing. He used it to his advantage, dropping his other knee to join it.

One more jump, the biggest, life or death. With a grunt, he sprang, shooting off the railing. Flying. Not the arc he'd hoped for, too low.

Not gonna make it.

Behind him, the fire combusted. Intense pressure, a steaming wind, shoved him. A desperately needed boost. His chest thrust out, shoulders and legs reflexively thrown back. Arms flailed until he struggled back into a diving position. The bedspread burned, wrapping him in a funeral pyre. He shook the spread off. It caught on his foot. Flames licked his ankle. One more kick, it dropped. The smell of burning synthetics filled his nose, the odor of singed hair revolted him.

Wisps of smoke peeled from his body. He cleared the iron fence surrounding the pool. The briefcase fell, bouncing safely onto a narrow strip of grass. But he was plummeting fast, too fast. He kicked out, swimming in the air. Striving for distance.

Just a little farther, push, push.

He descended toward the pool deck. The cement rose. Closer, closer...

Dedication

This book goes out to my pals Flip, Jeff, Scott and Joel. Accountants all, and to my knowledge, not a single serial killer amongst them.

And, as always, a huge dedication to my wife, Cydney and daughter, Sarah. My own team of experts.

Chapter One

Leon knew exactly what to expect next and he didn't like it; hated it, in fact. The thing is he couldn't do anything to stop it. Not yet at least.

As Leon rinsed out margarita glasses—something he could now practically do in his sleep—he kept a discreet watch on the tourist and his family. He flipped the glasses upside down onto a towel about the same time the tourist patriarch started flipping out.

Sunburned, the man sank into his lounge chair, gulping down his sixth drink. Whiskey with beer chasers, not the typical tourist beverage of choice. Yet he wore the traditional "hey, look at me, I'm having fun" vacationer Hawaiian shirt. It draped open, exposing a fur-covered belly protruding like a birthing baby. Even though the man's sun damage date had expired, anger baked him redder. Leon knew the signs well.

The man's wife sipped out of a coconut shell. Unlike her husband, she had the sense to cover up with a floppy hat, bug-like sunglasses, a sundress, and a towel turbaned around her legs. All of which just seemed to press her husband's buttons more. He scowled at his wife, his top lip upturned. The man's son, though, really got to him. Possibly five, maybe six years old, the boy circled the table, strafing his parents with a nonsense song, occasionally punctuating it with a "Daddy, Daddy, Daddy!" Clearly bored out of his mind, the idea of watching his parents get their drink on didn't fulfill the boy's idea of paradise.

"Shut up." At first, the father's words simmered low. But they reached a boil fast. "Shut up, dammit." He chugged back the rest of his beer. Didn't cool him down a bit. "Shut up! Jesus

Christ." At one of the boy's passes, the man swung out, missing his target. Undeterred, the boy continued his attention quest, now running backward. Taunting his father. Not a smart move.

Leon gripped the edge of the bar, knuckles white as bone.

Keep cool. Don't give up your game. You're here for a reason. Hiding at the end of the world.

The boy's mother did nothing, casually shook her head: *happens all the time.* A half-hearted gesture, she uttered "Carl" into her coconut shell. Carl, "Mr. Wonderful," didn't hear her; or more than likely simply ignored her. Abusers have a strangely acute sense of selective hearing.

Carl wiggled out of his chair, not an easy task. Once he stood, he appeared winded, his chest expanding and constricting. Turning blustery. "Goddammit, Kyle, stop it!" Carl snaked his hand out, latched onto the boy's neck. Gave him a shake, followed with another. Kyle squealed, just once, then closed his mouth. Learned behavior.

Then it happened, the inevitable. The man pulled an arm back. His hand opened, fingers silhouetted by the blistering sun.

Smack.

Kyle didn't cry out, didn't look stunned. Instead, he ran just outside of striking distance and calmly said, "Hate you." Business as usual.

But Leon wouldn't—couldn't—tolerate this type of business. Someone had to stand up against the tyrants. The only problem? He needed to maintain his low profile. Had to stay hidden from Like-Minded Individuals, Inc. Even though he and Cody, his unlikely ally from last year, had decimated LMI's Los Angeles headquarters, he knew they were still looking for him. He'd stabbed a sword in the beast's belly, but the head remained intact, living, still breathing fire. Disposing of an abuser—Leon's modus operandi—would certainly draw unwanted attention.

Then again, it'd been some time since he'd plied his trade. Not only did the monkey on his back want to be scratched, it demanded to be fed and coddled. Put to bed with loving care before the inevitable headaches started tearing him up.

While sipping from a glass of water, Leon glanced back

at the table. The boy had vanished. The mother had likewise vanished into her phone, tap-tap-tapping at the keys: *What a wonderful time we're having, Marge.* Carl sat seething, burrowed into his chair, his energy spent. And just like some people do after a robust round of sex, he fired up a cigarette. Miniature clouds rose. A tropical breeze fluttered the poolside umbrellas like kites stuck in trees.

Don't do anything rash. Not now. Wait.

Leon relaxed or at least gave it a solid effort. He'd been on his toes, ready to spring over the bar. His fingers ached from the grip he'd held on the bar.

The gust died. So did Leon's burning need.

The last men he'd killed had been LMI employees: hit men, assassins, security guards who'd meant to kill him if given the chance. A king corporation of abusers, LMI had arrogantly lied to their contracted employees, using them to further their own greedy needs. Thanks to LMI, Leon had killed people who didn't necessarily deserve it.

Yet, to be perfectly honest (something he constantly struggled with these days), Leon realized he was trying to vindicate his actions. Undoubtedly a therapist would applaud his progress, but if Leon thought about it too long it curdled his stomach. Long story short, he was a killer. That's why he'd vowed to take out only LMI from here on out; no more abusers.

But as he watched Carl, the prototypical abusive family man, he realized vows were meant to be broken. Like an addict, he told himself he'd stop later, just not today. Quite simply, he wanted to kill Carl. End his abuse. And rejoice in doing so.

Leon smiled, pleasant warm tingles riding his spine. Yep. Just what the doctor ordered.

It took Carl three attempts to hoist himself up from the lounge chair, his wet trunks creating a ripping sound. The path he took toward Leon zigged and zagged, a serpentine affair. Drunk on alcohol and high on power over those physically weaker than him.

Leon looked forward to balancing those odds. Later. Tonight.

"Close my tab," demanded Carl.

Leon nodded, avoiding eye contact. Not that Carl'd even

recognize him after the gallon of booze he'd downed. Still, better safe than jailed.

After tallying up the damage on the *Conch Getaway Resort* pad, Leon asked, "Charge it to your room?"

"Yeah. Do that." Carl hitched up his trunks and stuck his refrigerator chest out, obviously empowered by Leon's subordination. Power games with these guys, always the same. "Room number 112."

"You got it, sir. Thank you and enjoy your stay at the Conch Getaway Resort."

And, thank you, sir, for making my work much easier.

At the prices the Conch charged, Leon couldn't afford to stay there. Definitely not on a bartender's hourly wages (plus tips which usually never materialized; the general rule being the wealthier the drinker, the less they tipped). Even with the employee discount, the cost soared, clearly meant to keep rooms available for the paying "one percent." Which suited Leon just fine. No need for flashy digs, unnecessary perks (who really needed warm towels delivered daily?), poolside service and ocean access; everything *Heaven before your time*—the Conch's motto—apparently implied. Which was kind of ironic, really, at least in regard to Carl. *Your time is up, welcome to Hell* seemed much more appropriate.

People resided in Key West, Florida for very few reasons. Tourists came to fish or relax by the ocean. Paradoxically, the locals serviced the wealthy tourists yet hated them, a mind-set Leon understood after working a short time at the resort bar. Didn't take long, either.

At times, pangs of regret and guilt bothered him when he wondered if he'd displayed the same rude, superior behavior in the past. After all, he'd been one of the privileged not too long ago, a corporate hot-shot living the dream.

The final reason to flee this far South? To hide at the edge of the world. Sometimes Leon felt ready to slip right off. And some of the locals looked like they wanted to do exactly that.

On the other side of town, Leon had set up shop at the run-down Poinciana Motel on Truman, a place tourists avoided.

Blending in with the other tenants had been a snap, most of them head-in-the-sand and haunted looking. Everyone kept to themselves, holed up in their rooms, never to be seen. A drug den, so rumors had it. On the rare occasion Leon'd pass one of the other tenants, they didn't speak, wouldn't even glance his way. *Perfect.*

Living on the second floor was less than perfect, though, at least for Leon's tastes. He'd inquired about the first floor, much easier to escape should the need arise. Apparently, everyone else had the same idea. For the foreseeable future, all first floor rooms were booked. The second floor, however, remained fairly vacant.

He hopped up the stairs, two at a time, less sludge headed than he'd felt in some time. Funny how anticipation reinvigorates.

The paint-flaked steps wobbled beneath Leon's footfalls, inducing a case of "sailor's legs." He gripped the railing to settle his stomach just as much as the steps. Once Leon reached the second floor landing, ghostly reverberations still tingled through the souls of his shoes.

His room overlooked the Poinciana's pool, if you could call it such a thing. A rusted fence surrounding it gave it a semblance of privacy, he supposed, but wouldn't discourage non-paying visitors. The pool sat just beyond a small lounge area. For good reason, he'd never seen anyone so much as dip a toe in the water. Algae murked up the water, resembling the area's surrounding wetlands and swamps. Only one man, covered in hunting greens and a cap much more suited for Midwest winters, ever visited poolside. Constantly he hunkered down in one of the weathered chairs, chain-smoking. Fidgety. Some nights, through a sliver in the curtain, Leon watched him. Looking for anything out of the ordinary, anything that smacked of LMI surveillance. But LMI wouldn't delay, waste their time on surveillance; they'd kill him in an instant.

Next to his room's doorjamb, Leon's finger caught on a chipped piece of white stucco. Years ago, the white stucco walls probably spruced up the motel, exuding a happy, bright, seaside image. Now, where the walls weren't fragmented, the white had aged into grey, the color of despair.

He ran a finger across the piece of scotch tape at the top of the door. Unbroken. An old trick, but sometimes you can't beat the oldies. Entering the room, he grimaced. Home, ugly home. Fifties-era wallpaper bubbled and peeled. A large charcoal-black spot blemished the wall behind the bed, reminding Leon of the horrific Hiroshima nuclear "shadow" photos he'd seen as a child. If shadows could talk, he imagined this one had a helluva story. The room smelled musty, the windows permanently sealed. But leaving the door open to air the place out wasn't an option. An invitation to disaster.

While the room provided a decent hideaway, the more time he spent there, the lonelier he felt. And not just because of the confining walls. Thoughts of Rachel, the one woman he'd ever considered settling down with, tormented him. He abhorred the room, a dark symbol of everything that had gone wrong, the reason why he'd been forced to live this way.

Best to stay busy, not dwell on what could've been.

But, in keeping with his newly adopted policy of self-honesty, he realized there could be no other option. It'd be easy to travel ninety miles to Cuba, passport and false identity ready to go. A fresh start. But he had unfinished business with LMI in the States. For the time being, he had to keep off the radar, hide in relative squalor until it came time to strike.

And, of course, the pressing matter of the job he needed to attend to tonight couldn't be ignored.

He fired up the cheap laptop, one of two he possessed. The other he'd buried beneath the spare tire in the trunk of his car. Wyngarden's computer, the one holding LMI's secrets and agenda. The one he hadn't been able to crack into yet. No matter, it'd happen with time. Eventually everything comes to those who wait, something his mother used to tell him.

But now, Leon couldn't wait.

As he scoured the internet for anything on Carl Johanssen, successful stockbroker and abhorrent parent, his heart performed a rapid-fire drum solo.

Happy days are here again.

Leon knocked on room number 112's door. Scratch that, not

really a room. One of the Conch's luxury "cabanas," a stand-alone, incredibly over-priced miniature cabin. Proving once again, money can buy anything but good taste. And common decency on Carl Johannsen's part.

Leon's research had paid off, easing him into the night with peace-of-mind. Johannsen's pool-side manner hadn't been a random incident of ugly, drunken behavior. Last year, Kyle Johannsen's kindergarten teacher had reported strange bruises on her student's arm. Clumsy to a fault, Kyle'd previously suffered a sprained wrist and a broken arm. Except clumsiness wasn't to blame.

Of course this information wasn't privy to just anyone over the web. Over the years, Leon had acquired certain hacking talents, taught by the IT guys at various accounting firms. Leon long suspected if computer experts ever banded together, inspired to do so, they could easily take over the world. Scary, really, what they knew. For the cost of an armload of bagels and a lotta' "atta-boys," they'd been more than eager to share their knowledge with Leon. To succeed in the corporate sector, you had to treat your resources with respect.

Leon's excitement faded after the first round of unanswered knocks. As he prepared for another volley, the door yanked back. Still wearing his same afternoon outfit, Carl frowned. Red as dawn and ready to fight. He gave the beer bottle in his hand a little shake, a cowboy showing off his six-shooter.

Leon detected no recognition in Carl's eyes, hadn't expected there to be any. The new dark-framed glasses changed Leon's appearance drastically. His long hair, freed from hair gel and a ponytail, hung down to his beard-covered cheeks. Before Leon had left his motel room, he'd hardly recognized his mirrored image. Laid-back, aging hipster chic.

"Whaddaya' want?" Carl swaggered a bit, catching the doorknob for support. His liquid gaze wandered, eventually zeroing in on Leon.

Good. Still drunk.

"Ah, sorry to bug you…but the front desk told me—"

"What the hell you *want*?"

Leon jacked a thumb over his shoulder. "Is that your town

car in the parking lot? The Lincoln? The blue one?"

Carl's eyes widened, fear over something he actually cared about. "Why?"

"Well, crap...I nicked it." Before Carl detonated, Leon quickly added, "The damage isn't bad. Really. But...I wanted to track down the owner. Exchange insurance information."

"Goddammit! Probably texting or some shit!"

"No, I was just—"

"Hang on." Carl disappeared into the adjoining bedroom. His voice rose, yelling, the only way he knew how to express himself other than with his fists. Leon waited at the open door. That old feeling of exhilaration and danger—interchangeable, can't have one without the other—electrified him. He'd missed it.

Then the boy, Kyle, stepped into the doorway. The flesh around his eyes looked swollen from crying, his cheeks splotched. He stared at Leon, apathetic yet curious. Unnervingly quiet. After a lifetime of abuse, not much could rock his world. Innocence lost. Leon knew from experience.

Leon swallowed, a dry click. "Uh, hi there. I just..." He stopped. He had no words for the boy. Actually, he did, but he wouldn't say them. *It's a harsh world out there, but the sooner you distance yourself from your family, the better off you'll be. Your father's an animal, your mother's an enabler. Run.*

Leon considered running too, just packing it in. Because he was about to kill Kyle's dad, add to the boy's world of anguish. Someday Kyle might understand the nature of abuse, but he couldn't now. In his eyes, the monsters who raised him also loved him.

But Leon changed his mind when he carefully studied Kyle's face. A purple welt blossomed beneath one of the boy's eyes.

Bastard. Back to business.

Carl returned, slippers slapping against his feet. He dropped a hand on Kyle's mop-top of hair and shoved him back, a man kicking his dog away from the front door. As he barreled past Leon, he left a sickening odor of sweat, alcohol and too much cologne behind. "Let's go." Still taking charge, always the one in control.

Big mistake on his part.

The sidewalk wove between man-made fountains, oddly placed coconut trees and more fauna than a greenhouse. Leon offered apologies and mundane conversation. Carl responded with an occasional grunt, a disgusted shake of the head.

Sparse lighting draped the parking lot in shadows. Small globes poked up randomly amongst the cars, nothing more than a night light's worth of illumination. Apparently the resort's architect thought security cameras might sully paradise as well. An architect's idea of a romantic getaway. Great for lovers, even better for what Leon had in mind.

Carl's car slanted across two parking spots, a man who didn't adhere to any rules. Now Leon wished he'd done some actual damage to the town car.

On his knees, Carl inspected the back end. With a gentle touch—much more than he ever showed his family, no doubt—he caressed the bumper. "Can't see nothin. But that don't mean anything, not as goddamn dark as it is out here. Give me your insurance info."

Carl's size worried Leon. He'd had trouble in the past with large men. Although not tall, Carl definitely packed extra weight, muscle hiding behind the blubber. But challenges build fortitude.

Leon reached into his shirt pocket and withdrew a hypodermic. Carl looked over his shoulder. The needle's tip disappeared into his neck. "*Shit*! What the *hell're* you doing?"

Quickly, Leon pocketed the needle. He clamped a hand around Carl's mouth. His other arm wedged beneath Carl's chin, attempting to leverage him down to the pavement. Carl stayed planted in his squat. Rather than fighting the laws of physics, Leon improvised. He wrapped both hands around the obese man's neck and squeezed.

Fingernails bit into Leon's hands. Leon tightened his grip, waiting for the drug to kick in.

Come on, dammit.

Carl straightened from his crouch, dragging Leon up with him. He tottered, windmilling his arms. Leon held on, clutching the larger man's throat until the drug finally took effect. Carl twisted and tumbled down to the ground, pinning Leon beneath him. Air blasted from Leon's lungs. Leon wrapped his legs around the man's back, trying to roll him off. Carl beat Leon's shoulders, his arms, unable to put much power into the blows because of their proximity. Teeth snapped next to Leon's ear, dangerously close. A fist exploded onto Leon's temple. The dull pain dropped Leon's arms to the cement.

Carl's fight slowed, now gentle taps. With one last heave of his chest, Carl collapsed onto Leon. His snores rattled through Leon's chest.

Spent, Leon slumped as well. Three hundred pounds of dead weight nailed him to the ground. The fall, the fight, dizzied him. Almost like he drugged himself. Dread filled his barely lucid mind. He worried his pocketed needle had pricked his chest. Then he remembered he'd capped it. Yet, his eyelids tugged down, stubborn. He forced them open, flexing the eyelids again and again.

Have to stay awake. Can't get caught in a romantically dark parking lot, in a lover's embrace, a bear of a man lying on top of me.

Hardly the time for it but Leon laughed. The needed adrenaline boost to kick him into gear.

He heaved back and forth, rocking both their bodies. Inch by overweight inch, Carl slipped off him. For a crucial second, Carl teetered on his side, undecided what direction to take.

Fwump. He flopped down beside Leon.

My God.

Leon mentally slapped himself, added a physical one. He crawled up on shaky legs. Either from Carl's blows or renewed migraines, his head pounded. Time to worry about a possible concussion later.

Several deep breaths psyched him up for the demanding task ahead. As he dragged Carl by his wrists to his car, he seriously considered investing in a wheelchair.

Traversing the wetlands by car took care and time, but dragging a damn big body through the woods proved even more harrowing. Every time a nocturnal creature trilled or twigs snapped, Leon froze. Listening for human (or otherwise) intruders. Still, the wetlands suited Leon's requirements for body disposal. Icing on the cake if a particularly ravenous crocodile eats the remaining evidence.

After leaving Carl a couple feet deep in a watery grave, Leon sloshed through the mud to his car. He slumped down in the seat, exhausted, mentally and physically.

The euphoric high he used to experience while disposing of an abuser hadn't changed. Oddly enough, it made him feel alive. It dredged up rare emotion, an emotion he couldn't put a name to. Simply didn't have the life experience.

However, the remorse he felt once he'd finished Carl Johannsen was something new. Sort of akin to masturbation guilt; everyone knows it's a sin, enjoys it anyway, what the hell, pay for the consequences later.

Maybe it wasn't remorse, not really. He didn't particularly feel tormented by disposing of Johannsen. The world would be a happier, safer place without him. But he kept thinking about the son, Kyle. The look in his haunted eyes, a look Leon recognized from his own shattered childhood. When his dad murdered his mother in front of him.

Leon fired up his car, chunked it into reverse. The tires sucked at the mud, spitting muck onto the windshield. Trying to stay ahead of his thoughts, he drove fast.

Cruising down Truman Avenue, virtually on autopilot, he mentally replayed the past several hours. Wondering if he'd made any errors. Fully aware he'd hung up his "Back in Business" sign, ready to keep the shop open whenever opportunity rises. Supply and demand. Abusers supply, Leon demands.

But. He acted stupidly, impulsively. A missing abuser practically screamed Leon's M.O. Not that the law even knew Leon existed. But LMI would red-flag it, no doubt about it.

He pulled into the parking lot behind the motel, his car dripping water from the carwash. By the pool, the chain-smoking man carried on his lonely vigil, quietly muttering to himself.

Leon crawled into bed, but he didn't sleep. Eventually, he pulled the plug, got up. He sorted through his emergency briefcase, counting his money, memorizing his latest falsified documents (procured for a hefty sum by a rather frightening Cuban man he'd found). Everything good to go at a minute's notice. Except for a gun. As much as he hated guns, he might be better off with one. His new Cuban acquaintance would be thrilled to help him out.

With the briefcase tucked beneath his pillow, Leon lay back down again. This time in his jeans and shoes, not comfy whatsoever, but feeling a whole lot safer.

The guard, ferociously smacking his gum, opened the gate. He handed Cody a folded pair of khakis and a button-down shirt; old man clothes.

"What the hell am I supposed to do with these, yo?" Cody shoved the clothes back at the guard. "You keep 'em. More your style."

The guard sneered, got up in Cody's face. Onion peeled off his breath, but, damn, if it didn't smell good. "Like I care. You'll be back, you losers always come back. But next time? It'll be a nice, long stay at Leavenworth."

Cody really wanted to deck the guy, but probably not the best idea, not on his first day of freedom. "Yeah, whatever. Only loser I see here is you. I'm leavin' this shithole. You're still stuck here, making what, nine bucks an hour?"

Cody hit the sweet spot, one of his talents. The guard pinched his lips tight. He patted the gun at his side, showing off his pocket cock. "I'll remember you said that, Grainger. Next time…next time."

"Whatever." Cody brushed by him, bumping Johnny Law's shoulder. "And guess what, dumb-ass? My real name's not even Grainger. But you guys are too stupid to figure that out."

As the guard pulled the gate closed, he hooked his fingers through the chain-links. "Doesn't matter what your name is. 'Punk-ass bitch' suits you just fine. We'll meet again…*bitch*."

"Yeah, in your dreams, dick-head. In your dreams…" Cody kicked the fence. The guard hopped back, forcing a laugh. But Cody knew he'd scared him, straight up.

As Cody walked down the drive, the guard's laughter

receded. Sure, the guard pissed him off, but he wasn't gonna show it. Sacking up, he tossed his shoulders back, dug his hands into his hoodie pockets. It didn't take him long to find his rhythm, his strut; you never forget things that come naturally.

All in all, he felt pretty damn good, no sense in letting an asshole rent-a-guard bring him down. Four months in Leavenworth had been easy-peasy, a cakewalk. It could've been a lot worse. Especially if they'd found out he was the "Denver Decapitator." But these Kansas clowns couldn't find an elephant in a circus. Instead, they stood around pissing in the wind, wondering why the stream kept coming back on them. *Idiots.* All they got him for was jacking a car. Him, Cody Spangler, the goddamned Denver Decapitator. Friggin' Jack the Ripper in their hands and they just patted him on the back and let him mosey right out the door. With old man clothes. *Laters.*

He fired up a fresh cig. Not the usual stale ones he had to settle for on the inside either, but a gift from his crew. The smoke filled his lungs, tasted great, almost as great as freedom.

In prison, it hadn't taken him long to get his crew on board. A few days in, a couple jackasses tried to make him their bitch. Several broken noses later, all romantic notions went out the window. Eventually, everyone started sucking up to him, giving him food, turning to him for protection. Hell, had he been inside longer, he'd be running the place. Cody Spangler, Prison President. Had a nice ring to it, really, but one he didn't care to hear toll. He preferred to live in the here and now, none of that fantasy crap for him. Especially now that freedom beckoned.

Down the driveway, a soot-covered bus stopped and parked along the curb. Smoke coughed out of the exhaust pipe. The dark, grey windows looked less than inviting, hardly a new beginning worthy of him. And, really, he didn't have any plans, let alone a new beginning. Just fifty bucks in his pocket, a half-pack of smokes, and the clothes he had when they locked him up. And they smelled pretty ripe at that. Hardly babe-bait, the first thing on his mind.

Maybe the time had come to ditch Kansas, leave the backwoods state far behind. He wouldn't miss it. Hell, he'd never wanted to be in Kansas in the first place. Goddamn Wyngarden put him here for his own reasons. But he'd put Wyngarden in his place, a six feet under place. Cody grinned at the memory.

The bus driver chuffed open the door, an asthmatic wheeze. "C'mon, kid, get in already. I might be gettin' prettier but I ain't gettin' any younger." What a joke. The driver looked anything but pretty. Saggy and dumpier than a bag of potatoes, maybe. And probably a mother. A familiar sensation crawled over Cody, marching ants from head to groin. He bet the driver was a bad mother. They all are. Mistreating their kids, only caring about themselves. Like his mother, the dog killer. Killer of his beloved pet and only friend. Even his miserable childhood of orphanages, foster homes and nasty nuns was better than ever seeing his mother again.

Inspired, Cody imagined the bus driver's detached head, tucked under his arm like a bowling ball. So warm, so wet with blood, so…

Down the road, a long black bullet trailed dust. A limousine soared into the prison drive, bouncing to a halt several hundred feet from Cody. The engine clicked and tinked. From the driver's side, a guy stepped out, dressed in a crisply black suit. Tall, thin, possibly Asian, hard to tell with his face-hugging sunglasses.

"Mr. Spangler?" The driver fussed with his jacket's buttons, attempting to hook a loose runaway.

"Who's askin'?"

He flashed a dentist-bought smile. "My employer would like to have a word with you." He stepped toward the back of the limo and opened the door.

What the hell? Ever since the LMI throw down, Cody'd been wary of strangers offering gifts. Then again, most of his life he'd ridden a streak of good luck, always had. Maybe the rep he'd nurtured in prison had reached beyond the walls. Someone recognizing his talent, his artistry.

Behind him, the bus driver called out, "You comin'?"

Easy choice. "Not today. Treat your kids good or karma's gonna bite you in the ass, yo."

She snorted, shook her head, and closed the door.

With windows black as night (no doubt intentionally so), Cody couldn't see inside the limo. The driver didn't say a word, just stood there. Looking waxy, a mannequin with a permanent smile.

No problem, whatever. Cody knew he could take the driver if he had to. And any guy dainty enough to be chauffeured in a limo probably had never thrown down in his life. Afraid to scuff up his manicure or something.

Cody feigned a punch at the driver's face, hoping for a reaction. Nothing, not a flinch, just his damn smile. "Goddamn Buckingham Palace guard, yo."

As Cody slid into the limo, the fully stocked bar snagged his attention. Priorities. Then he noticed the passenger.

Summers. "Goddamn son-of-a-*whore!*" Rage propelled Cody across the seat. His hands found Summers' thin neck. "Gonna *kill* your ass!" Blood colored Summers' cheeks, his forehead, heat practically emanating off him. But it didn't come close to Cody's fire.

Summers. The LMI dick who'd first recruited Cody last year.

Like a cat hacking up a hairball, Summers coughed. He yanked up his ever-present briefcase, an ineffectual shield. Cody clutched harder, wringing tears from the gaunt man's eyes. "Son-of-a-bitch! I'm gonna—"

Something clonked Cody's temple, returned a second time. Cody tumbled back onto the bench seat facing Summers. The driver folded into the limo, gun butt raised in his hand, primed to deliver another crack. "Cool it, hotshot."

It didn't deter Cody. Roaring, he elbowed the driver back outside. This time he'd finish Summers.

"*Stop.* Wait, Mr. Spangler!" Summers' voice pitched high. His briefcase batted at Cody. "*Stop!*"

"*Kill* you! Gonna—"

Swump.

Another bash of the gun butt to Cody's head didn't slow him. His fingers tightened around Summers' throat.

Click.

The cold metal pressing into his skull, however, did the trick.

Cody shoved Summers back onto the seat, raised his hands.

The driver prodded the gun, tapping Cody's head. "You done now?"

Cody flumped down in the seat, his arms folded. He spat at Summers' feet. "What the *fuck* is this? You gonna kill me, Summers? Good luck with that, bitch!"

Still coughing, Summers raised a hand. The driver held the gun steady. Cody thought about rushing him. But bullets trump human speed every time, something he learned last year. Wait for an advantage, play it cool for now. Like he always does.

"No, Mr. Spangler...I'm not here...to kill you." Reclaiming his balls (part of them, at least), Summers straightened, slowly caressing his tie. "I...we...have a business proposition for you."

"A business...what the hell you talkin' 'bout? Leon and me, we *crushed* LMI." Cody smacked a fist into a palm, then waved finger shrapnel. "*Boom.* Out of bidness!"

"Well...yes and no."

Cryptic as always. Cody hated Summers' type, much preferred an in-your-face attitude. Damn buzzard never said anything straight up. "Just say what you want, Summers. Quit beatin' 'round bushes." Cody jerked his head toward the driver. "Call off your boy."

"I don't think so. Not yet anyway." Summers positioned his briefcase beneath his pointy chin, a security blanket. A slow grin burned, his cadaverous cheekbones rising. Back in his element. "Call it...insurance."

"Quit the damn drama, yo. No commercial breaks here."

Summers leaned back, shadows obscuring his eyes. "Same charming manner as always, Mr. Spangler."

Cody nodded in agreement.

"All I ask is five minutes of your time. Hear me out." The tip of Summers' tongue crawled out, licked his lips. Hungry for carrion. "Then should you choose to leave, you'll be free to go." He gestured toward the door, rotating his hand, voguing like a damn model.

"Bullshit, Summers! It's the same crap I heard last time you hooked me up with LMI. And how'd that work out for ya'?"

"This time things are...ah, how do we say..." He tapped a finger across his bottom lip. "Let's just say things are different.

I believe you'll like what I have to offer you."

Still grinning, the driver slid onto the seat next to Cody. So close Cody could snatch his gun. But some daredevil heights are too tall to climb. "Hi there. I'm Bob."

"Damn, Bob, if we're gettin' all cozy here, the least you can do is buy me a drink." Cody gestured toward the bar.

With a sigh, Summers' said, "Go ahead."

Bent over, Bob hobbled to the bar. Apparently, the selection stumped him as his hand wavered over the line of bottles.

"Just give me a damn bottle, don't care what. Been a while since I had a drink."

Summers nodded. Bob handed Cody a bottle of whiskey. Cody chugged a good portion, knowing he'd need it. A dying man's last supper. Upon release, the bottle made a hollow *flump*. "That's the shit, yo. Now what kinda' shit you tryin' to sell me?"

"Not selling. *Buying*. Mr. Spangler, you and Mr. Garber perpetrated a lot of extensive damage to our corporation last year. Rather than considering it a loss, we seized it as a business opportunity. Our management consultants weighed the pros and cons, considered the black and red options. We've…shall we say, restructured. It's still the fine, lucrative organization it's always been. Only stronger, *better*. Now, I'm the first to admit that Mr. Wyngarden and his, ah…'game-playing'," Summers' finger quotes looked about as natural as Astroturf, "were detrimental to our long-range goals and twenty year plan. But…you put an end to his personal agendas and amusement."

"Damn straight, yo."

"Yes, well…for Mr. Wyngarden's actions, you have LMI's deepest, most sincere apologies. Wyngarden acted as a loose cannon, a free agent. What he ordered was not dictated by our board of directors or president." Summers' hands spread, palms up: *all cards on the table*.

Cody didn't buy it, not for a minute. "Yeah, eat it, Summers. You guys were using us, having us kill people to—whaddaya call it—further your political deal."

"That may've been so in the past. But I guarantee you we've tightened our scruples, formalized a new business model, secured stronger benefits and higher security for our clientele, adopted an extremely stable vision plan—"

Cody dropped his eyelids, fake snored. "Wha? Damn, sorry, musta' dozed off. You say somethin'? All I remember is a buncha' buzz words meanin' nothing. What's any of this crap got to do with me?"

Summers sagged into the upholstery. "I'm trying to reach that salient point."

"How 'bout you reach a little faster?" Swig. *Tumph*. The alcohol burned nice and toasty in Cody's chest. Stoking his fires with a shovelful of liquid courage. Amping him up to make a move.

"Let me ask you this, Mr. Spangler..." One of Summers' eyebrows raised. "...did we ever ask you to eliminate someone you didn't want to?"

Actually, a damn good question. Last year, Wyngarden had admitted that's what LMI was all about: tricking the Like-Minded Individuals into whacking people for the company's personal gain. But, really, during the short time Cody'd been with LMI, they'd never once told him who to take out. Well, they told him to kill Leon, but that he understood. Just business. Maybe they'd used Leon (dude was way gullible) and the others; never him. Nobody ever takes advantage of Cody Spangler. Impossible, no way. Still, Summers was laying the whole blame at Wyngarden's fat and blood-covered feet. He smelled bullshit and told Summers as much.

"Of course we'd never be so brazen as to ask someone of your stellar talents to eliminate someone not of your choosing. I'm telling you the truth, Mr. Spangler." Summers held up three fingers, a scout salute or something. Cody doubted Summers had ever camped anywhere not artificially climate-controlled. "And to demonstrate that LMI has a new face, a new corporate model, I've been instructed to make you an offer."

Showtime. Now or never. In two quick moves, Cody could smash the bottle over the chauffeur's head, swing around and cut a second mouth into Summers' throat.

All in, Cody whipped the bottle up.

Snack, snick.

Bob released the latches on a second briefcase. Cody dropped the bottle.

The briefcase held more green than a forest, all planted in nice, neat rows of riches.

Cody tried to be cool. His audible gulp sounded embarrassing enough, strictly amateur hour. "What? You givin' me mega-bank?"

Summers grinned with baited teeth, trying to reel in Cody. "Precisely. And there'll be more…much more…where this comes from."

"Yo, Santa Claus, check it…I've been on the naughty list. As in 'bad ass' list. Maybe you didn't check it twice. What's the 411?"

"Yes, well, assuming by '411,' you're asking me why we'd grant you this cash reward? We want to offer you a position with LMI."

"Say that again."

"You heard me, Mr. Spangler." Satisfied, Summers settled back, crossed his legs, tented his fingers beneath his chin. "We'd like to offer you a position, a very well-paying, highly respectable position."

"Yeah, right. You dicks 'hired' me last year to—"

"It's very different this time. Our last unfortunate…ah, business collaboration proved disastrous. But that's because we underestimated you, hired you as a means to an end. Whereas you are now the end."

Cody understood none of this. He suspected Summers still hid behind the truth, camouflaging it with fancy-ass business-speak. But one thing Cody did understand: *Respect.* Finally, LMI wanted to give up the proper respect he'd rightly earned. Damn straight. "What I gotta do?"

"It's quite simple, really. We need you to find Mr. Garber. And eliminate the problem."

Boom. Finally Summers said it, not that it really came as a shock. LMI always plays games, pitting everyone against one another. Predictable as hell. "You're outta' your fuckin' mind, yo." Bob snorted. Summers shot him a look, a *wait 'til I get you home* look. "This is the same damn 'job' Wyngarden wanted me to do last year. And it ain't as easy as it sounds. The old man's tricky, more damn lives than a cat. Besides…why the hell would I wanna' do it anyway? I got no grudge with Garber. You got a ton of other guys. Get one of them to do it."

"Ah, but, Mr. Spangler, we need someone with your specific set of skills, your talent. And, yes, your art."

Not only did that scratch Cody's itch, it soothed like a salve. Music to his ears. Good music, too, not that tired jazz crap Garber likes. Head-stoking metal rap.

"No one knows the mind-set of Leon Garber better than you do, Mr. Spangler. You've spent more time with him than anyone."

What, a week? But Cody knew all Like-Minded Individuals were lone wolves, the only way to howl. A week was probably a long time in LMI years.

"You know what Mr. Garber thinks, how he reacts…where he's hiding."

"I got the chops to take Garber down, fo' realz, but, again, why would I want to?"

Summers fluttered his eyebrows, his face drawing down into phony empathy. Not a good look. "Honestly, Mr. Spangler…have you forgotten what Garber did to you? Why you spent the last four months in prison? That's not how friends treat one another."

True, Garber manipulated the situation to get Cody busted. Basically planted a gun in Cody's hands and cried wolf until the mall's rent-a-cops took notice. But, while locked up behind prison walls, Cody'd spent a lot of time wrapping his head around Leon's actions, justifying them. Seeking sunshine where it couldn't possibly shine. For a while, he thought Leon (in his own crazy-ass way) believed he was actually helping Cody. The postcard Leon had sent, the one with the dog, had sealed the deal. But now, outside in the free world, none of it made sense. Bastard sent him to jail, no denial. Even with this realization, though, Cody still trusted Leon more than Summers.

"The old man said he was trying to help me, yo. He—"

"Really, Mr. Spangler…" Summers pursed his lips, a holier than thou approach that pissed Cody off. "…how can you say he was trying to help you? He framed you. And where did he go? He's somewhere living very comfortably, playing you for the fool. He's certainly no friend of yours. Whereas, we at LMI, take you very seriously. We admire your formidable talents. It takes quite a man to inflict the damage you did. We're offering you a new home, Mr. Spangler. One where you'll be respected, treated as a valuable commodity."

The magic word again. *Respect.* Something Garber clearly had none of for Cody. Old man gave him a one-way ticket to jail. Why? For kicks? Laughs?

Cody felt the game starting again. *It's so on, Garber. Feel me comin' for ya?*

"Well? What say you, Mr. Spangler?"

"I'm thinkin'." Cody wasn't quite ready to sign on board just yet. Unlike last time, he wanted everything straight up. "What happens after I do Garber for you? You guys gonna kick me to the curb like a hooker or something?"

"Not at all. As I said…we consider you an extremely important commodity, one we want to place in a full-time position."

"How much green we talkin'?"

Summers slipped into shark-smile mode again. Maybe Cody needed to brush up on his poker face. "Five hundred thousand dollars in the case is yours now. Just for saying 'yes.' After that, you'll be supplied a very, ah, comfortable monthly salary of $100,000."

Now Cody felt his poker face melt away. A smile tugged at his cheeks, impossible to stop. No wonder the chauffer wore a permanent dumb-ass grin. LMI was offering more cash than he'd ever seen before. He wanted to swim in it like that rich, comic-book duck, what's his name. "Tell me again why you want the old man gone. Why not just let him hide the rest of his life. He's probably got, what, only ten years left anyway."

"Yes, ahem, he's only forty, Mr. Spangler. Regardless, to answer your question, he's a liability. One who we, at LMI, don't suffer lightly. He's already shown, along with your help, naturally, what he can do. And we have reason to believe he's not done seeking vengeance upon LMI. Misguided though it may be, of course."

"Yeah, whatever, of course." Cody rattled the words off

just to say something. His mind wandered, already mentally spending the money.

"He's the kind of man our research shows doesn't give up. The kind who—"

Bla, bla, bla. Summers blathered on about the wonderful qualities of Leon Garber who Cody now considered less than wonderful. He sure as hell wasn't a half million dollars worth of wonderful. That serious cash could buy a shit-load of wonderful.

First, though, Cody needed certain conditions met. Not because of feelings for Garber or anything pussy like that. No, this time LMI was going to play by his rules; his way or the highway.

"Fine, Summers, you got a deal. But..." Cody stuck an imposing finger up. "...we're gonna do things differently. My way. And I've got some, whaddaya call 'em, terms you gotta' meet."

Summers dragged out a long sigh. Taking Cody seriously as he deserved. "What might these 'terms' be?"

"Okay, first, no more of your damn games. No more lies. You want me to find the old man for you? Fine. But I ain't doin' it alone and unlike last time you guys need to have my back."

"But, of course. We've already chosen several of our best— well, surviving, that is—'business process outsourcers' to aid you in—"

"Fine, whatever. Just make sure they know I'm boss. No cowboy crap from them."

"You're the boss."

It sounded good, spine-jinglingly great. Cody'd never been the boss before. Sure, he'd been self-employed, but ordering his own minions around? *Heaven.* "Bet yer ass I'm the boss. Okay, two more conditions..."

"I'm waiting with eager anticipation, Mr. Spangler." Frankly, he sounded less than eager, the smarmy dick. Didn't matter. He'd have Summers sucking up soon enough, practically worshipping at the altar of Cody's ass. Because Cody had mad negotiating skills. The way he did everything. With killer style.

"I want a kick-ass office with a bar, my own bathroom, the works." Bob tittered, but Cody shut him down with a stern glare. Time for his day of *respect*, yo. "And I want a hot blonde for a receptionist. Nothing too milfy, though."

Summers groaned, no doubt blown away by Cody's professionalism.

Chapter Two

Water lapped at Leon's feet as he pounded the surf. Troubled thoughts chased him, paranoia riding shotgun. It'd only been a day since he'd dispatched Carl. Any time now, the investigation would sweep in like one of the Keys' unexpected tropical storms. Fast, fierce and yielding catastrophic results.

Out of breath, he stopped and bent over. Every day he strove to belt out five miles along the beach. Some days he even hit the target. Physically, he'd never been in better shape. His legs had become sinewy, muscular. His encroaching middle-aged spread had vanished. But emotionally he felt vulnerable and weak. He shouldn't have killed Carl, a stupid risk not worth the fleeting pleasure. Even if the guy deserved it.

Several minutes after Leon clocked in for the afternoon shift at the Conch, the parade began. Carl's wife, hiding behind a large hat and sunglasses, had already fallen into the role of the shell-shocked, mourning widow. She moved slowly and stiffly, possibly medicated. Kyle, shuffling behind at his mother's flats, displayed a child's natural curiosity, everything fascinating. Too young to understand the unfolding drama, possibly relieved dear Daddy had taken a runner. Bringing up the rear were two men, sweltering in their sports jackets, very much out-of-place at pool-side. Very much detectives.

They weren't the only ones feeling the heat. Leon attacked the bar's dirty glasses, polishing them with fervor. Occasionally he glanced at the table where the entourage had settled.

Mrs. Johannsen's voice rose, high-pitched and dramatic. She honked into a detective-supplied handkerchief, her hand throttling the air with operatic flair. Hunched over the table, the detectives spoke quietly, in compassionate mode. Kyle's gaze wandered, seeking distraction. He found it in Leon.

Earlier, Leon had worked hard to change his appearance. His long hair was now gelled back, a shade darker courtesy of a box of hair dye (not trying to cover-up the specks of grey, of course). He'd ditched the heavy-framed glasses he'd worn while paying Carl a visit.

But children see things adults often overlook.

The boy raised his hand, the tiniest of casual waves. Leon knew, absolutely so, Kyle recognized him.

He debated waving back. Considered ignoring Kyle. He split the decision, nodded and smiled at Kyle. Just enough to get him to lower his hand.

If the detectives saw the interaction, they paid no notice. Mrs. Johannsen's theatrics held them in thrall.

Regardless, Florida was getting too hot this time of year anyway. Scorching hot. Leon felt a sudden stomach bug crawling his way, quite a shame. His boss, an easily irritable kid fresh out of college, wouldn't like it. Tough.

His mind made up, Leon plucked the money from the register to hand in along with his resignation.

Not fast enough. One of the detectives caught Leon's eye and stood. He walked slowly toward Leon, obsessively tucking his shirt tail into his pants.

At the bar, the detective slapped a hand down and sighed. "Evenin'."

"Hey. What can I get you?" Playing ignorant usually worked. Not so much with cops, though.

"Just wanna' have a little chat." He flashed a badge, snapped it shut before Leon could see it. "What's your name?"

"Oh. Mark Slater." Sweat greased Leon's palm. He offered it anyway, something he hated doing but recognized as a necessary evil to maintain cover in a touchy-feely world. His hand practically slid off the detective's upon contact.

"Yeah, anyway..." The cop inched a photo across the bar. "Seen this guy?"

The photo showed Johannsen with his arm around his wife; grinning in a "Call me Carl!" manner. Husband of the year, irredeemable abuser. Leon's regrets dissolved. No matter the consequences, the monster deserved his fate.

Leon cocked his head, Mr. Indifference. "Yeah, think so. He was out here...what, yesterday, maybe...or the day before." His shoulders pinched up in a half-shrug. "Hard to say. These guys all look alike after a while."

"But you remember him?"

"Sure, I guess so." Never offer too much info. Cops are suspicious of people who're great at remembering details. "Why? What'd he do?"

The cop smirked, impossible to decipher. "He didn't do anything. Think hard. When was he here? At the bar?"

"Two days ago, I guess."

"'You guess.' That the best you got?"

"Okay, yeah, sure, I remember him."

"Why?"

"Huh?"

"What was it about him you remember?"

"Well...he drank a lot. I mean a *lot*. He was pretty hammered. But, hey..." Leon stuck his hands up, surrendering. "...not that there's anything wrong with that. Not my job to judge." But he certainly wanted the detective to judge Johannsen. Establishing Carl's drunkenness could lend credibility to the notion he stumbled off into the wetlands and fell into a swamp. Leon just needed to lead the detective there.

"Uh huh. Afternoon? Evening? Night?"

"Afternoon. Yeah...afternoon."

"You said he was hammered. Exactly how many drinks did he have?"

"I dunno. Lots. He was ordering 'em two at a time. Here, wait..." Leon pulled out his receipt copies, thumbed through them. "Here. That's his tab."

The detective whistled, impressed. Saying a lot for a cop when it comes to alcohol consumption. "Yep. I'd say he was righteously hammered."

"By the time he left, he was staggering around, bumping into things. Looked like he didn't even know where he was."

"Thanks, you've been a big help." But the detective sounded

bored, a rote dead-ending of his interrogation. Which pleased Leon. "Anything else you remember about the guy? Any odd behavior?"

"Well...yeah..."

The detective raised his eyebrows.

"He didn't tip."

Summers dropped Cody off at a hotel parking lot, gifting him with a set of keys and a pissy smirk. Cody stared at the Prius, just couldn't believe it.

"What? A damn hybrid? How about somethin' with a little kick beneath the hood, yo?"

Summers said nothing.

"Fine, whatever."

Bob, the chauffer, stood next to Cody, tapping his foot impatiently, the briefcase of cash in his hand.

Cody ignored him and spoke into the limo's open window. "So what's next?"

Summers stuck his hand out, a business card between his fingers. Except for an address, the card was blank.

"Topeka? What the hell's in Topeka?"

"Mr. Spangler, because of the events that, ah, transpired in Kansas City last winter, you're long overdue to leave town. Wouldn't you agree?"

"Yeah, guess so. But couldn't you've picked somewhere cooler like Vegas or something?"

"Just show up there tomorrow afternoon, two o'clock. The car's equipped with a GPS. Don't be late. You'll meet your team and then we'll conduct our business. Here's a phone. You are not to use it for your amusement, Mr. Spangler. No calling old girlfriends, no ordering pizzas, nothing. Do you understand me?"

"Damn. Uptight much? Yeah, I get it." Cody grabbed the phone, an old-school flip-style joint.

"Mr. Spangler...do you know where Mr. Garber's current whereabouts are?"

"Got a pretty good idea, yeah."

"Where, pray tell, might that be?" Summers finally looked

alive, his tongue running over his teeth.

"Tell you tomorrow." Always leave 'em wanting more. Job security.

Summers dredged up another sigh, dismissed Cody with a back-handed wave. "Very well. Tomorrow. Oh, and do not, under any circumstances, tell anyone about this meeting."

"Yeah, got it already. I'm a professional, yo."

Bob slammed the door, inches from Cody's face. "Watch it, dick!"

The driver grinned, everything an inside joke.

"Gimme my money already." Cody reached for the briefcase. Their hands met on the handle. Bob yanked back, playing tug-of-war.

"Ya' wanna' play grab-ass? Just give me my damn money before I get your sugar daddy involved."

Bob released the case with a jerk. Cody's arm flung up into the air. The briefcase clunked to the ground. "What's your *problem?*"

Again with the silent treatment. Bob strut back to the driver's side. Before hopping behind the wheel, he lowered his glasses. Winked.

"Asshole," yelled Cody over the screech of tires. Eventually, he'd have to get the driver in line, teach him some respect.

As Cody drove toward Topeka, the thought of the driver dissing him still burned. That and the sour pit that used to be his stomach. Probably his fault, but what the hell, no way was he gonna stay in last night. Not with all that money screaming to be wasted. Naturally he got wasted right alongside the dollars.

And he'd made it rain like crazy, showering down the green. After the second strip club he couldn't remember where he went. But one stripper stuck in his otherwise muddied memory, clear as day. She'd mounted a pole, her stretch marks prominent as sun-baked cracks in the earth. A *mother*. When he thought of her abandoned kids at home, waiting while Mommy whored herself for cash, he went ballistic. He'd clenched his beer bottle so tight, the glass exploded. The bartender bounced him after that, probably not a bad idea in retrospect. Otherwise he would've taken the head off of more than just a beer bottle. And he knew Summers wouldn't appreciate his plying his trade; not a good way to start a business relationship.

Overall, though, fun night.

Except for the hangover.

Even though the sun had long ago vanished behind clouds, Cody wore his sunglasses. If eyeballs could develop headaches, his suffered the mother of all migraines.

Topeka thoroughly killed his residual buzz. Endless industrial buildings blurred together, nothing but bland grays and utilitarian rectangles. Stacks chuffed out black smoke, smearing the already dreary afternoon. A tattoo parlor sat on every corner, numerous Chinese restaurants and bail bondsmen shops nestled in between. The capitol of Kansas looked more like the armpit of the Midwest.

Not too far from the Capitol building, he found his destination. An office building that had seen better days, it stood ten, maybe twelve stories high, too hard to count with a hangover. Everything gray, gray, gray.

Usually he'd opt for the steps. Not today. The elevator stopped on the third floor with a head-splitting ding and deposited him in front of suite number 322. *Gladhand & Associates.*

Cody bypassed knocking, partners didn't need to knock. A tall suited guy, scrunched up behind a desk, stared at him. Cody suspected he had guns instead of sticky notes and staplers hidden in the desk's drawers.

"You've been expected, Mr. Spangler." The guy pressed a button and hissed into his phone, "Your two o'clock is here." He leaned back in his chair, yawned. Serious attitude problem. "Down the hall, last door on the right. You'll be buzzed in."

As Cody shuffled down the hallway, he wondered if he'd saddled up with a loser. This set-up was a far cry from the up-scale LMI offices he and Garber had destroyed last year. The floor sounded hollow underfoot. The odor of rot and paint nearly made him gag. And LMI couldn't even spring for a hottie receptionist.

A fingerprint I.D. gizmo sat next to the last door, a half-assed nod to security. A green light sparked, a lock clicked, the door swung open and Cody stepped into his first corporate meeting.

Summers sat at a nearly barren desk, the downtown skyline looming behind him. "You're late."

Two guys rose from their seats in front of the desk. One of them was built like a gorilla, his massively wide chest tapering down into a thin waistline. The buttons on his short-sleeve shirt tugged over his muscles. Easily six-and-a-half feet tall, he hung his head slightly, clearly used to navigating places built for shorter men. The light gleamed off his shaved scalp. Beneath one eye dripped a single tattooed tear. And he sneered at Cody.

Except for the sneer, the other man was the exact opposite. Thin and short, dark crescents rimmed his sad cow eyes. Strands of greasy hair stuck to his forehead as if painted on.

Hardly the crackerjack team of experts Summers had promised Cody.

Big and bald turned to Summers. "This kid? *He's* the one?"

"That's the way our business plan has—"

The giant roared, bounding across the room in two leaps. Hardly the welcome Cody expected. He snagged Cody's hoodie collar, hefted him up and pinned him against the wall.

"Whoa, *whoa*! What the *hell* is—"

Baldie thrust a cigar finger into Cody's face. "*You*...you killed Donnie and Marie! You took—"

"What? Those assholes who tried to kill me last year? Hey, kill or be killed, yo! They—"

"Shut your *mouth*! They were my friends...they were... they..." His voice turned sloshy, drowning in sobs. *Blubbering.* A fist slammed the wall next to Cody's head. Reluctantly, the big man released Cody, hovering over him like an eclipse. Until he folded, burying his face in his hands, shuddering.

"Jesus Christ! Summers, call off your dog before I call off our deal!" Still shaken, Cody tried to man up. Hard to do when a scary-as-hell, huge-assed cry-baby wanted to take his head off.

"Ned...Ned, settle down," Summers said in a soothing tone. "We're LMI's chosen team, selected by the president himself. Take a minute to gather yourself."

"Sorry...sorry...I'm so sorry..." Baldie gulped up his waterworks, hiccupping out a final sigh. "Sometimes I just think about..." Then round two rolled out. The guy's shoulders shook like a volcano on the verge of eruption. "Sometimes my emotions...get to me..."

Cody sidestepped the ape, careful not to look him in the eye. "What the hell, Summers? This is what you're giving me?"

"I assure you, Mr. Spangler, when I say they're the best, they're absolutely the best." Summers gestured toward the scrawny guy, who seemed to be taking it all in stride, nothing new under the sun. "This is 'Bug,' one of our most successful business process outsourcers."

"The hell kinda' name's 'Bug'?"

Bug made a *click-click* sound from the side of his mouth. "If the name fits, wear it."

Cody thought he looked kinda' like a bug, a real dirt dweller. He considered fist bumping the guy, then sacked the idea. All sense of professionalism had long flown out of the room. "I'm Spangler. Cody Spangler. Maybe you heard of me, yo. I'm the Denver—"

"The men have already been brought up to speed on your, ah, accomplishments, Mr. Spangler. No need to rehash yesterday's headlines."

"Hey, the Denver Decapitator's forever! No one's ever gonna forget—"

"Let's proceed, shall we, gentlemen?" Summers lifted a palm, a high five left hanging. "Time is of the utmost urgency."

"Whatever." Cody glanced at the crying elephant in the room and carefully positioned a chair between them. "Who's the weeping willow?" As soon as he said it, he regretted it. The man adjusted to his full height, clenching his fists. Knuckles cracked hard, the sound of a nose breaking.

"Enough name-calling, Mr. Spangler." Summers whacked his hand on the desk. "You *will* get along with your team. Bug, please see to Ned."

Bug readjusted himself like he had arthritis, inching out of his chair at a granny's pace. If Summers was in such a hurry to nail Garber, Cody thought he should hire somebody who could at least move. Then Bug slapped a hand on the big guy's shoulder, stretched up on tiptoes and whispered into his ear.

Finally, the giant nodded and drew his shoulders back. His bald super-dome barely cleared the ceiling.

Summers ignored Cody's not so subtle eye roll.

When the big man came toward him, Cody flinched, hated himself for doing so. Cody Spangler didn't fear anyone, straight up, yo.

"Sorry we got off on the wrong foot." The large man dug his hands into his pockets, toeing the carpet with a foot. From psycho killer to chastised schoolboy in nothing flat. "My friends call me Ned."

"Yo, Ned, bygones and all that shit. It's—"

"You are *not* my friend. Donnie and Marie were my friends." His voice chirped, a goddamn bird. Cody didn't want to see him lose his shit again. The big guy closed his eyes, tilted his head back. Probably counting or some stupid therapy crap. Regaining his balls, he opened his cold, blue eyes. "*You* call me by my company name…Mr. Sensitivity."

"You're shitting me, right? What, am I being punked or somethin'?" Cody looked around, searching for cameras he knew didn't exist, but sure as hell might've leant some structure to his new world order. "Come *on*, Summers. You gotta' be kidding me!"

As Mr. Sensitivity tensed up again, all muscles and murder, Summers intervened. "Everyone has a personality, Mr. Spangler, everyone's human. Isn't that right, Ned?"

Sensitivity nodded, his chin dropping to his chest.

"Ned's a bit sensitive, a truly lovely person." Summers words didn't hold much weight. "But I can assure you, he's one of the best."

Like some sort of freakish superhero, Sensitivity thrust his chest out, the buttons threatening to pop off.

"Now is everyone happy?" asked Summers.

Cody said, "Yeah, shit, whatever." But he realized he wouldn't be making easy money, not with these ass-hats in tow. He commandeered the seat Sensitivity had abandoned, a show of dominance. Best to get 'em in line up-front.

With a look of relief, Summers said, "Glad we have that settled. Now, down to business—"

"Summers, what's with the digs?" Cody spread his hands. "This office sucks, yo. You guys hurting for cash or what?"

Summers exhaled loudly, his favorite expression. "Mr. Spangler, this is by no means our office. This is merely a temporary meeting place, a sham acquired for essential privacy. We are by no means bankrupt. We're extremely solvent, so much so that LMI practically defines the term 'solvency'. The office you laid waste to—"

"Damn skippy."

"Yes, well, that location was just a drop in the ocean. We have global offices, entire corporate—" Abruptly, Summers shut up as if he'd said too much. Whatever. Cody didn't want to hear another boring corporate lecture anyway. "Back to the business at hand. Mr. Spangler, you said you have an inkling as to where Mr. Garber may be. Please enlighten us." Summers leaned back, his chair squeaking.

"Yeah, I got a, whaddaya call it, inkling."

"Well?"

"I think he's in Florida."

Summers smiled, the happiest Cody'd ever seen him. Which wasn't saying much. The guy made morticians look like game show hosts. "Oh? Why do you believe this?"

"First, Garber always talked about Florida. Said it was nice, warm by the ocean. He also said his old man—you know, before Garber's ol' man offed his mom—used to yammer on about Florida. Some shit about spending his youth there or somethin'." Cody paused, building anticipation before dropping his bombshell. "And…when I was in Leavenworth, I got a post card. Postmarked from Florida." *Boom.*

"*Where* in Florida?"

"Don't remember. I pitched the card."

Summers eyelids fluttered like wings preparing for liftoff. "I suppose it's a start. But, as you may or may *not* know, Florida's a large state."

"No shit, Summers. We narrow it down."

"And how do you recommend we do that exactly?"

"What, you guys stupid or something? Look for missing guys. Abusers, yo."

"We *have* been doing that. There haven't been any missing—"

"When's the last time?"

"Excuse me?"

"When's the last time you searched? Garber won't hold out forever. Guy's got a mad itch to scratch. Look in Florida."

Silence. Except for Sensitivity's rhino-like huffing. Summers' face strained, wrinkled from some serious mental lifting. Then he pressed a phone button. "Get our IT associate on the line now, please."

Pulling up his temporary roots seemed like a great idea. But now Leon needed to wait a while before quitting his job, couldn't look too suspicious. Over the past couple of days, the detectives continued to swarm the Conch. The same detective stopped by the bar and asked Leon if he remembered anything else about the missing man.

"No...no, sorry," he'd said with a sympathetic smile. After a long enough pause for serious consideration, naturally. Never be too hasty, but don't take too long. A fine art, dealing with police.

This time the detective had been less than cordial, walking off swearing.

But the boy really put Leon on edge. Like a beaten dog wary of humans, Kyle circled Leon at the bar, each time drawing closer. And every time, he waved. The mother camped out at her usual table, crying, occasionally moaning out her husband's name, all while knocking back Mai Tai's and the Conch specialty, "Blossom Fire." Pool attendance had dropped, no real mystery why either.

Leon'd suffered through a restless couple of nights. He slept (or tried to) half dressed, perfect for the man-on-the-go. The briefcase beneath the pillow offered rocky support. Every time a tire screeched or a random shout rang out on the street below, he bounced out of bed and pinched back the curtain. Other than the lone drifter, forever maintaining pool watch, he saw nothing. Just fading taillights zipping by the motel, red-eyed and lonely. Yet in his mind, he imagined plenty.

His body, his mind, needed sleep.

On the rare occasion he'd drift off, something always clicked in his brain, an intrusive thought tugging him back into the waking world.

The job that lay ahead frightened him. Destroying LMI. Procrastination can be a powerful dissuader. He'd barely made it out alive last time.

Finally, exhaustion caught up to him. In bed, his thoughts slowed to a nonsense scrawl. Hit and miss images collided together. His breathing regulated. One step closer to shutting sleep's door…

As far as new jobs go—especially since Summers had promised Cody the world—this one sucked. Cody hadn't been given anything to do, not yet. After he'd told the LMI idiots how to find Garber, it seemed his usefulness had ended. Still, once LMI found a "hit"—a missing, suspected child abuser—in the Florida Keys, Summers insisted Cody go with the two losers. Cody'd have it no other way. He enjoyed the chase. And, hell, he was no charity case; he earned his cash.

When Cody found out they'd be driving, though, he threw a bitch-fit.

"Summers, why the hell ain't we flyin'?" he'd asked.

"Because these days any flight can be traced and tracked. It's of the utmost importance that LMI maintain complete management invisibility in today's marketplace. We simply can not—"

"Yeah, yeah, whatever. But, really, why aren't we flying?"

Summers had answered with more of the same bullshit, no real info. Like pulling teeth with that guy. The idea of driving just didn't make any sense. LMI had the cash, so Summers said, so why not go first class? Besides, Cody didn't really want to road trip with "Big and Bawling" and "Sickly and Psycho."

But that's what they did. Sheer agony. Bug drove straight through the night, Cody relegated to the backseat. Not where the boss should be riding, but at least he could stretch out his kicks.

During the trip, not much was said. Cody didn't exactly want to buddy up, but anything beat twenty-four hours of silence in the damn car. Lousy, cheap bastards couldn't even spring for a limo like Summers' car. Stuck in a Cadillac, hell on wheels.

No hotel stops either. Sensitivity got mad when Cody had to take a leak, but finally gave in when Cody threatened to drop trou in the car. Easy listening, for God's sake, provided their music of choice. Guys were as tightly wrapped as a chick in skinny jeans.

But the worst thing? They wouldn't let Cody smoke. Freaked their shit when he lit up once. Immediately, Bug had slammed on the brakes. He pulled the Caddy to the shoulder and jumped out like the car had caught fire. Sensitivity dragged Cody outside, slapped the butt from his lips. But not before Cody blew one last good puff into Sensitivity's face. Showing 'em who's boss.

Still, Cody wondered if he'd made a huge mistake accepting the job.

But everything fell into place once they reached the southern keys of Florida. LMI phoned with Garber's location, his room number, his new alias, even the car he rented. Excitement stirred Cody, hands-on fun his dangled carrot. Outta' the car and into the action.

Problem was these guys—his "support team"—hardly seemed in a hurry.

Bug parked the Caddy in a motel lot across the street from Garber's hideout, a real shit-hole. There they waited, an eternity and a day. Hardly how Cody imagined spending his first days of freedom.

For at least an hour, Cody watched the lights snap off in the rooms at the Poinciana Motel.

"What're we waitin' for, yo? Most of the motel's out."

Sensitivity said, "We're waiting for the right time."

"What's that, like some Zen crap or something?"

"Yeah, Spangler, something like that." Sensitivity turned around, a muscular arm slung over the seat. "You'd be smart to watch what you say about Zen. I've found it very...helpful in alleviating stressful and unpleasant situations."

Cody slumped back, defeated. He couldn't talk to these guys. No middle ground, nothing in common. Sensitivity proved smarter than he looked, sometimes saying crap that flung over Cody's head. Half the time, Cody thought he might be bullshitting him, but at the same time, he knew it'd be stupid to underestimate him.

Bug, on the other hand, was about as open as a stuck-up country club. He said next to nothing, kept his glassy, creepy eyes locked straight ahead. Cody suspected he chose to drive just to avoid talking. Occasionally, Bug'd reach into his pocket, pull out a golden lighter, fiddle with it. *Flick, flick, flick,* the flame drew Bug's eyes toward it. It just made Cody want to smoke more.

Weird guys. The first thing Cody planned to do once Garber was toast? Fire their asses.

"Let's do it," Sensitivity said to his partner.

Bug slid out. Almost as an afterthought, he turned back to Cody and said, "You stay here."

"What? *Bullshit.* Why the *hell* I have—"

Like a cannonball, Sensitivity shot out of the car, wrenched Cody's door open. Grabbing Cody by the hoodie—apparently his favorite new hobby—he shook him. "Listen, Spangler, do as you're told. LMI brass said you're to stay *out* of the actual operation." He throttled Cody again, one for show, then released him. Sensitivity studied his hand, turning it over and back again, as if it baffled him. "I'm sorry…so sorry…" He gulped. "It's just…look, our bosses said you're the brains of the operation and—"

"Hell yeah, I am. So I call the shots."

"No. They said to…keep you safe." Sensitivity took in a deep breath and tucked his spine back in. "LMI has…plans for you. They realize you're an important commodity."

Good enough or at least it'd do for now. Cody sat up, smoothing his hoodie front. "Just don't forget that, yo."

The trunk popped open. The two men mumbled behind the open lid. Bottles clinked. Weight shifted and something clunked. Cody lowered, peering through the gap below the trunk lid. Sensitivity captured Bug's gloved hands in the glow of his flashlight. Pouring something into a bottle. It took forever, more of the waiting game.

Sensitivity slid back into the passenger seat. He'd traded up his white button down for a black one. Bug's matching black attire made him look like an ant next to the bigger man.

"Ready?" asked Bug.

With closed eyes, Sensitivity stuck his hands up, the thumbs meeting the fingertips. A low hum vibrated from his chest. Meditating or some crap. These guys took forever just to get out of a car. Cody would've been all "wam, bam, later, man" by now. A bullet for Garber, a gold star for Cody.

At last, Sensitivity clapped his hands and hopped out of the car.

To Cody's surprise, Bug stayed in the car. Cody looked around, couldn't see Sensitivity anywhere. Not like he's hard to miss, either, a vanishing act worthy of Houdini.

"What're we doin', yo?"

Bug lifted a finger to his lips, remained quiet. Then he slowly crept the Caddy out into the street, headlights off, and idled into Garber's motel lot. They stopped next to Garber's crappy rented sedan.

Cody spotted a flash of white behind a palm tree. Sensitivity's bald head and arms glowed under the moonlight. His hand crawled up the motel building's edge as if trying to scale the stucco-covered wall.

"What the hell's he doin'?"

"He's taking out the security cam. Old school type, stupid, insufficient. Now shut up. I need to concentrate."

Bug left the Caddy. *Click.* The trunk lid levered up. Sensitivity jogged toward them, staying low, dodging between parked cars. Armed with a box gathered from the trunk, Sensitivity followed Bug around the corner of the motel.

Sick of waiting, Cody slipped out, fired up a smoke. First one in over twenty-four hours and it weighed like Heaven in his lungs.

Behind him, a sound swelled, a crowd's mass roar. Above the Poinciana's roof, the sky lit up. Orange lightning flickered, rising instead of striking down. Smoke curled off the roof, a massive cloud.

"Goddamn…" Cody flicked the butt away, climbed back into the Caddy. Seconds later, his subordinates raced around the corner like fire nipped at their heels. It pretty much did, too.

Bug jumped into the car, said, "That was fun." He offered Sensitivity a sweet smile.

Cody finally figured out why they called him "Bug."

Drenched in sweat, Leon bolted up in bed. Glass cracked like breaking ice. *Floomph.* Fire circled the room, a blazing tide. Intense heat seared his face. Behind the inferno, he saw a figure on the walkway. Tossing something into the room through the shattered front window.

One chance, don't think, just do it.

Leon snatched the briefcase from beneath the pillow. Standing on the bed, he tugged the bedspread up, the tail already catching fire. The fire accelerated around the room, unnaturally fast. The curtains vanished into black smoke and winking embers. Larger flames devoured smaller growing ones. The bed remained untouched by fire, an island of safety. But not for long. He wrapped the bedspread around his shoulders, pulled it tight. Clutching the briefcase to his chest, he backed against the wall. He'd committed the measurements of the room to memory before. Now he just had to hit the marks.

Smoke irritated his eyes. A cough erupted from his chest. He fought it, conserving his oxygen. He'd need it. Taking huge leaps, he ran the length of the bed. At the tip, he sprung up. He grabbed his knees, cannon-ball style, the briefcase pinned into his lap. Flames licked the bottom of his tennis shoes, his souls hot through the rubber.

Use the momentum, don't stop, outrace the fire. Feet down, hit the target.

His toes kicked out small glass shards from the window, then balanced on the sill. Fighting the constricting bedspread, he brought his elbows back, punched the air. Jumped up. Heat grazed his back, hungry.

Leg muscles strained. A knee wobbled when he landed on the railing. He used it to his advantage, dropping his other knee to join it.

One more jump, the biggest, life or death. With a grunt, he

sprang, shooting off the railing. Flying. Not the arc he'd hoped for, too low.

Not gonna make it.

Behind him, the fire combusted. Intense pressure, a steaming wind, shoved him. A desperately needed boost. His chest thrust out, shoulders and legs reflexively thrown back. Arms flailed until he struggled back into a diving position. The bedspread burned, wrapping him in a funeral pyre. He shook the spread off. It caught on his foot. Flames licked his ankle. One more kick, it dropped. The smell of burning synthetics filled his nose, the odor of singed hair revolted him. Wisps of smoke peeled from his body.

He cleared the iron fence surrounding the pool. The briefcase fell, bouncing safely onto a narrow strip of grass. But he was plummeting fast, too fast. He kicked out, swimming in the air. Striving for distance.

Just a little farther, push, push.

He descended toward the pool deck. The cement rose. Closer, closer...

Not far from the pool water, the life-saving filthy water.

His head cleared the pool's edge, his face close enough to smell the stagnant water. Too soon to celebrate. He jabbed his arms out. Cold water skimmed his belly.

Go, push, reach.

Dive, don't fall. Not at this angle.

His arms landed flat on the pool's surface, stinging. Water submerged his head, cold and shocking. A sound like sizzling bacon surrounded him. Shoulders, torso followed, knees dropping. A foot caught the pool's edge, pivoting him forward. His head cracked on the bottom of the pool. Confusion enveloped him, near unconsciousness. He thrashed, clawing away thick masses of algae. For a panic-stricken moment, he forgot where he was, why he was. His lungs ached. Murk colored his vision. Yet above, he saw light, just a glimmer. Climb toward it, basic survival instincts.

As soon as he broke the water, cool air slapped him. So did awareness. Above, his motel room raged, fire clawing out the window. His head still throbbed, his ankle felt dead and frighteningly fragile, perhaps sprained. But he made it. *Alive.*

He wanted to rest, couldn't. Every second could be his last.

Spitting out water, he paddled to the pool's edge. Smoke rose above the water like fog. He brought a knee up on the cement, felt his left ankle twinge once he put weight on it. And that was with an underwater cushion.

"Rough night?"

The voice jolted him, nearly pitching him back into the pool. Then he saw the speaker. Immobile in his chair and unmoved by Leon's plight. The poolside watcher.

"Might say that." Leon scrabbled out, shirtless. His pants trailed a path of water behind him. Wet squelches accompanied each step. He patted down his face, his hair, everything, taking a quick inventory of body parts. Surprisingly, the only casualty appeared to be his left ankle. He had to work with it. Time to go. Now. Discreetly so.

"Reckon you got some folk don't like you much." The man said it matter-of-factly as if Leon's death-defying dive seemed like no big deal. Maybe not too uncommon a sight at the lovely Poinciana Motel.

Leon hobbled toward his briefcase, turned to his spectator. "Friend, you have a car?"

"Nope. Got a pick-up."

Even better. "Good shape?"

He shrugged. "Gets the job done. Got a few years on 'er, but hasn't let me down."

The fire cast an apocalyptic orange light over the pool area. Sirens cried, whining closer. Negotiations needed to be wrapped up.

Leon shook the briefcase. "Give you $30,000 cash for the truck right now."

Nothing. The man's cap cloaked his face in shadows, just a patchy beard and a bouncing toothpick visible. Impossible to read his expression. After an intensely long silence, the man countered, "$40,000."

Leon looked up at the spreading fire, back at the man. The sirens grew louder. "Tell you what...toss in your cap and your coat and you got a deal."

Digging into his camouflage coat's pocket, the man pulled out a ring of keys, a zookeeper's amount. With shaking fingers, he rolled two off and tossed them to Leon. "Treat 'er well. She's parked out back on the South end. Can't miss it."

Leon quickly counted out four stacks of $10,000. The man stripped off his jacket, plucked off his cap. Apparently, Leon'd made his day. His face-wide grin told a story of many drug-fueled nights in his future.

The parking lot looked as lively as a cemetery. Anyone still awake, and not in a self-induced drug coma, had gathered on the flip side of the motel, watching the fireworks. No conspicuous LMI appearing cars. Just a bunch of the motel occupants' broken-down vehicles.

Adopting an old man's step, Leon hunched over. It didn't take much acting. Every time he crunched down on his bad ankle, a bolt of electricity zapped him.

The truck had at one time been dark blue before cancerous oranges and browns ate away at its body. Still it looked sturdy. Mud splattered the back end, drying in thick chunks on the tires. Four-wheel drive, tough enough to haul through the wetlands. Should it come to that.

And, yet, there sat his sedan. He had no love for the car. But the treasure in the trunk was his grail, the means to win the battle: Wyngarden's computer. Another look around confirmed the lot was empty. Cars passed by on Truman, slowly gawking at the motel tragedy. His lone parking lot stroll couldn't compete for interest. He still had the sedan's keys, heavy inside his soaking jean's pocket.

A fire truck pulled up by the pool. Firemen yelled, scrambling, adding to the confusion. Perfect subterfuge. But the army of cops he soon expected scared him nearly as much as LMI. Too risky to grab the computer.

Leave. Be thankful for your life, your freedom.

The hell with it.

He'd come this far, wouldn't leave without the computer. And to hell with the old man ruse. Just a waste of energy and time.

Running (more like hopping) through the lot almost did him in. He didn't wait for the left leg to settle upon footfall, hoisting it up fast as possible. Yet the water-soaked jeans and shoes slowed him. Hop, skip, squish, *grimace.*

He opened the trunk, wrestled the spare aside, grabbed his ultimate weapon.

The truck turned over first time, grumbling with reassuring power. But his poolside auto salesman had lied. Not a full tank; half. It'd have to do for now.

Inching out of the parking spot, he tested the rev, the pull, the brakes. All good to know. Once on Truman, cop cars sped by him, heading toward the burning motel.

"Hold up, hold up, hold the hell up! We're leaving?" Cody couldn't believe they thought they'd finished the job, not without proof.

Sensitivity said, "Yeah, we're leaving, dumb-ass. Sorry… shouldn't have said that. But you hear those sirens, bright boy?" He cupped a hand around his cauliflower ear. "You wanna' stick around, welcome them?"

It didn't make any sense to Cody. Especially after they'd just put in a good solid five minutes watching the blaze, Bug's choice.

"But I know Garber. He's a tricky bastard, yo. He ain't dead 'til you see his head."

"Trust me…" In a rare mood, Bug turned around to face Cody, grinning and happier than a pig in shit. "…after the job I did? No one's gonna live through that."

"So, what, you set the motel on fire?"

"Not the motel. His room. With him in it."

"And you think that's enough? Why the hell didn't you just put a cap in his ass? Easy, old school."

"Listen and learn," said Sensitivity. "Word came down the job was to look like an accident. That's what it'll look like. An accident."

"How the hell you do that? I mean…they can check for arson and crap."

Bug fired up the engine, started backing out. "I'm an expert.

It'll look like a meth deal gone bad. The ol' 'shake 'n bake'."

"What? You plant a meth lab in there?"

"These days that's overkill. Now tweakers just shake everything—pseudoephedrine, lithium, fuel, whatever—in a plastic bottle. Boom!" His hands went wide. "Instant fire. Even dropped some evidence outside the room. No way it'll look like anything other than a meth burn."

"And I'm tellin' you Garber ain't dead 'til you see the body."

The two men laughed, good times, good times.

As the Caddy entered the street, a swirl of red and blue approached in the distance, a sight that chilled Cody. A crowd of lookie-loos had gathered in front of the motel, their phones lit and held high.

But Cody still had doubts. These idiots hadn't butted heads with Garber before. On a whim, he grabbed Sensitivity's binoculars and scanned the crowd. Nothing. Swung back to the parking lot. Garber's car was still there, the parking lot empty. Then a figure, a limping man, hobbled through the lot. Cody focused the binocs, zoomed in. A grim mouth-set, all serious and no play. Cody knew the look well enough, having been stuck with it for a week. *Garber*. At the sedan, Garber popped open the trunk, snagged something, and then climbed into a truck.

Cody hooted, stomped a foot and slapped the back of Bug's seat. "Better turn the car around."

"Why the hell am I gonna do that?"

"There goes our boy." He jacked his thumb behind him. "In the crappy-lookin' blue pickup. Told you, yo, I tried to tell you! Dumb-asses!"

As the car ripped through a U-turn, Cody bounced back onto the seat, laughing. *Game on, old man, game on.*

He'd missed it.

The rear-view mirror claimed Leon's attention more than the road ahead. Reckless. But after escaping a near incineration, false bravery buoyed him. Adrenaline plus miraculous luck, a dangerous equation.

Headlights blurred and bobbed behind him, typical

nighttime traffic. He considered driving through town, making numerous turns and loops just in case he had a tail. Yet the Overseas Highway ramp sat a half-mile away, beckoning him. It'd always bothered him there was only one escape route from the Keys: the Overseas Highway. Unless he wanted to swim to Cuba, of course. No thanks.

Best to get going.

Once he reached the highway, he relaxed. His shoulders sagged, his teeth stopped grinding. A deep breath in, then out. *Calm down.* Only 127 straight miles, then he could vanish in Miami, probably where he should've stayed in the first place. Yet, in a way, he'd felt more sheltered at the southern-most tip of the States, a child hiding under covers. Stupid in retrospect.

The highway stretched out ahead. The moon's reflection rippled in the ocean beneath him. Freedom Highway might be a more apt name than the Overseas Highway. Because that's what it felt like. He'd barely escaped an attempt on his life from LMI's army of killers. The only explanation, clearly a professional job. They'd tossed some sort of chemical bomb into his room, fast spreading and evidence obliterating. Sealing the deal by making it look like an accident. Anything to take eyes off of LMI. *Bastards.*

Pinpricks of light brightened his rearview mirror. Growing, gaining on him. He swallowed, his throat still sore from smoke inhalation. Already hauling fifty, five miles faster than the posted speed, Leon pressed down on the pedal, just a bit. Early on, he'd learned from the locals the highway was a notorious speed trap throughout its 127 mile length. You had to know where to expect the police. So, either his tail was a cop, a damned foolish tourist, or something far worse. For once, he hoped for a policeman.

The car sharked toward him, swimming through the darkness. Accelerating. Brights flashed, dazzling in the rearview mirror. Leon flipped the mirror up. Stepped on the gas. His heart paddled a series of quick, short bursts.

He flew by Rockland Key, only about nine miles out of town. Embankment trapped him on both sides, the one-lane highway appearing to narrow. For a moment, he considered pulling over onto the slight shoulder, letting the speeder pass. A huge gamble. But if it wasn't a cop or a tourist, if he made a wrong choice, he'd be a stationery target. No second chances, not with LMI. His gut won the argument. LMI'd already made one attempt on his life tonight, a daring one. Prepare for round two.

Sixty, sixty-five, the speedometer's needle tugged to the right. The car following him picked up its pace, further closing the gap. Once it lapsed back, then barreled up on his tail again. Toying with him. Bright headlights blazed in the mirror. Leon averted his eyes, residual twin stars twinkling in them. The Boca Chica Road exit was one mile away, his goal. He had a better chance to shake his pursuer there rather than proceed down an endless straightaway. If he could make it that far.

The car roared, then tapped his bumper, a light kiss. Leon gripped the steering wheel, arms locked, knuckles white. He kicked it up to seventy. Tremors started in his hands, worked up through his arms, a combination of fear and bad alignment. Dangerous on the narrow highway. One minor slip and he'd plow through the embankment and into the ocean depths. Soaring twenty miles over the speed limit, he hoped a cop's radar gun would ping him. Bring 'em on. Better a speeding ticket than certain death. But Lady Luck apparently had kicked him to the curb; cop's night off.

His pursuer held tight. The speedometer reached eighty, still climbing.

If he slammed on the brakes, the car would back-end him, sending them both rolling into the ocean. Unless the truck ignored physics, staying solidly planted by virtue of its weight. A desperate and deadly ploy, one he wouldn't risk.

If he could pull ahead far enough, he might be able to whip a U-turn. Throw them off guard. Clearly the truck could take the smaller vehicle in a game of chicken. But the thin highway allowed for nothing less than a slow six-point turn. The car would crash into him, grinding him into shark chum.

The truck had edge, though, able to handle sharp, precise turns. Boca Chica Road remained his best—his only—option.

His speed mounted. Ahead, the exit sign glowed within his headlights.

Take it at the last minute. Don't slow. Fly down the ramp. Keep going.

Behind him, the car lurched left into the oncoming lane. Tearing up alongside him. A dark Caddy, the perfect LMI vehicle; bland enough to blend in and built to kill.

Perfect. Right where he wanted them. As long as they rode alongside him, he could hook the exit. They'd overshoot it, wouldn't bash into him. Give him a small advantage.

Unless, of course, they drove him into the ocean. Or shot him, always an option.

The Caddy swerved in, inches from the truck. And kept coming. Metal scraped. His truck the bigger beast, Leon fought back. He wrenched the steering wheel left, driving the car toward the left embankment. Sparks flowered as the Caddy scraped across the wall. The tail end of the truck whipped. Leon reined in his ride, tamed it back in line. The Caddy centered again in the other lane, speeding neck and neck, bumper to bumper.

A quick glimpse showed a large bald man riding shotgun. Sunglasses at night, grim, calm. But who Leon saw in the back seat sent him spiraling.

Cody. Laughing. Hanging out the window, the wind buffeting his hair. Banging a fist on the car door. *Screaming.*

Dammit! Think about it later. Survival first.

Leon whipped right. The truck's back left tire bounced off the exit ramp, slicing into gravel. Pebbles hailed into the bed, skimming off the windshield. He swerved, corrected course. Charged down toward Boca Chica Road.

He heard the Caddy's tires screech. A roar of an angry engine.

Leon blew through the stop sign at the end of the ramp. Headlights bounced down the exit after him.

Take advantage of the lead. Straight into the wetlands.

He raced along Boca Chica Road. An unhealthy amount of smoke plumed from the exhaust. A smoke screen; also a glaring, attention-gathering flag. The truck was a monster, no denying it; strong yet stubborn. It harnessed power, speed; just took a while to obey its master.

The Caddy jetted down the road after him. It advanced quickly, too fast for some of the wildly curving turns. Several times it left the road, burning up roadside grass.

Leon hesitated pressing the truck's speed on the road, fearful he'd lose control, launching him into the surrounding jungle-like foliage. But he had to get closer toward the ocean; the better his chances.

Just ahead, to the right. A small, unmarked road—more like a path—barely wide enough for one car to traverse. Straight into the wetlands. But even with the four-wheel drive, he had to be careful.

The Cadillac gained on him. Leon practically felt the heat from the headlights burning into his neck.

Leon slowed. Instead of smashing into him, the car slid across the road to avoid him. Tires screamed, laying down black tattoos on the pavement. Leon yanked right, the truck's tires slaloming over the dirt road. The Caddy's engine revved. And Leon swore he heard Cody howling above it.

The road dragged the truck down over ragged terrain. Leon's head banged into the ceiling. Slowing, slower, the only possible way. The Caddy pushed it, attempting to keep up. Dirt flowed into mud over the road. Water filled entrenched tracks. His pursuers lost ground, the car's back end fishtailing. The truck grumbled, briefly stalling once in a deep pocket of standing water. But it pulled through. The palm trees and foliage dwindled, finally dumping Leon onto Ocean Front Road, a true road.

One look into the rearview mirror showed the Caddy stuck. Leon rolled down the window, listened. Tires spun, whizzing like a dental drill. Voices shouted, arguing, Cody's unmistakable laughter loudest of all. Enjoying the danger like the psychotic kid Leon knew him to be.

"Why didn't you give me one of your guns? I coulda' capped the old man's ass easy." Cody sullenly hung an elbow out the window. The car jacked up and down, Sensitivity getting in a workout at the back bumper. Bug worked the pedal. Cody grinned, enjoying his "told you so" moment. Maybe now they'd finally listen to him. "Lissen up, yo, I want my own gun. Maybe one of—"

Cody started when a fist banged the door. Sensitivity's bald head lowered. Mud spattered his formerly spotless white button-down. "Shut your damn *mouth* for once and get out and help!"

"What? No way. Ain't my job, brah. You're the hired help. Just get—"

His arms thrust inside the window, white lightning. "I'm *not* asking." Cody's hoodie bunched tight as Sensitivity yanked him forward. Cody braced himself at the window, refusing to be pulled through. "Hold up, hold up, yo! Leggo, goddammit! You're gonna ruin my hoodie. Christ, relax…I'll help."

Sensitivity tossed him back inside. *Goddamn King Kong.* But Cody'd just as soon get the hell out of the sticks, even if he had to sweat to do it. He slid out and sneered at the big man. "You better lay off, chief. Before I give your boss the low-down on how you're treating me."

Sensitivity's knuckles dug into his waistline, elbows straight out. He leaned over Cody, trying to intimidate. "And who exactly are you gonna call, punk? Huh? Tell me…should be good for a laugh."

Cody considered his options, realized he really had no idea who he was truly working for. "Um…Summers."

Sensitivity rocked back his head, howling at the moon. "That's a good one, kid. You go right ahead. Here…" He offered his cell-phone to Cody. "Here ya' go. Want me to dial it?"

For a minute, Cody thought about calling his bluff. Then again, Cody'd never signed any damn contract, wasn't really sure what the terms were.

Sensitivity's phone rang. He stared at it as if in awe at the all-knowing powers of the mighty LMI.

Hesitantly, and paler than usual, Sensitivity answered. "Yes?"

Cody couldn't hear the voice on the other end, just a rasp and several staccato coughs.

The big man turned, as if trying to block Cody from listening. "Yes, sir…. That's correct, sir… I see… I'm sorry… So sorry…" Predictably, Sensitivity's shoulders started shaking. He pinched the bridge of his nose, his hand covering his shame. His baritone voice rose into a whine. "It won't happen again, sir… I promise… No, no… We're the men for the job…" He turned back toward Cody and sized him up like he was the blue-light special. "I understand… We won't let you down again, sir. Goodbye."

With a huge inward sniff, Sensitivity wiped his tears away with the back of his hand. Then he pointed toward the Caddy's bumper. "You take that side. I'll get the other."

But Cody wanted answers. "Who was that?"

"Our boss. Get over there."

"I wanna' know who the hell I'm workin' for."

Cody swore he heard Sensitivity's bones interlocking with snaps and crunches as he drew up to his full height. "You'll know when it's time to know. Now, I'm not gonna tell you again. Get on that side."

"Shit, whatever. But I'm gettin' sick of the run-around. Why the hell ain't I got no gun anyway?" At the bumper, Cody took his time, stretching first.

"You're not gettin' a gun. Bounce it up and down, same as me."

"What? That's bullshit! Why can't I have a gun?"

Sensitivity bent over, muscular arms rigid on the bumper. Cody thought he could probably lift the damn car's back end on a good day. "Everything we do has to look like an accident. We don't need a clown like you pulling a Wild West, shooting up everything in sight."

"Yeah, yeah, total black-out visibility, whatever. Still I want a gun. Promise I'll be good." Cody snapped an imaginary trigger toward the large man, cooled his finger with a breath.

Sensitivity ignored him, whirled his hand around the air, and yelled, "Hit it!"

Bug stepped on the gas. Mud flapped up onto Cody's face, some of it into his mouth. Just a reminder of the shit he'd already been fed.

After doubling back through some of the lower keys and crossing several bridges, Leon landed back at his departure point, Key West. It'd been an escape route he'd long planned, an exacting one. One that had paid off. No one could've possibly followed him. If anything, once his pursuers had dislodged their car, he'd be tailing them. Highly doubtful they'd consider looking back.

He found an all-night convenience store, gassed up, and stoked himself with coffee. With a pat to the trunk's hood for luck, he entered the Overseas Highway again. Every time headlights approached, he watched them pass, checking out the automobile. No ominous Cadillacs.

The coffee cup shook on its way to his mouth. Hot liquid spilled over the side into his lap. He welcomed the stark heat, a wake-up call.

Cody Spangler. The Denver Decapitator. He couldn't believe it. The insane kid who'd made his life hell last year. The one who he'd forged a very unlikely alliance with to confront LMI. And who, against all odds, he'd grown rather fond of in a short period of time. Stranger things had happened, he supposed, but he never expected a friendship to develop, tenuous as it had been. Almost a mentor/protégé relationship, something he'd never experienced. Leon had even concocted a harebrained scheme to get Cody the mental help he needed. Didn't work out so well.

But none of that explained why Cody had allied with LMI now. Completely contrary to logic. Cody despised LMI as much as Leon did. Maybe Cody was working alone, exacting revenge on Leon for getting him arrested. But that didn't track. Fresh out of prison, Cody wouldn't be able to acquire two goons, a Cadillac, and the means to find Leon. Definitely the work of LMI.

But Cody...

Unexpected grief struck Leon, a sense of mourning. He knew if LMI had its hooks into Cody, he was as good as dead. If not exactly in body (and he knew LMI would soon see to that), Cody's remaining humanity couldn't be resurrected. A lost cause. Everything LMI touched, they shattered, the destroyer of worlds.

Wartime had come and Leon needed to dig deep into the

trenches. Go on the offensive. Bring the battle to LMI. But he couldn't do it without an army.

Suddenly his phone shrilled, startling him. Obviously LMI. They found him, tracked his phone number. He cursed himself for not having pitched the burner. But he hadn't had time to consider it, other things on his mind.

With the window down, he drew back his arm, preparing to pitch the phone into the ocean. The caller was insistent, ten rings and counting. Morbid curiosity clawed at Leon. *Unknown,* the phone read, as portentous as it gets.

Against his better judgment (which, lately, had admittedly become less reliable), he pressed the button, held the phone to his ear. Listened. He heard a slight whistling on the other end, nose hair chimes. Leon surrendered. "Hello?"

"Mr. Garber." A statement, not a question. The speaker's nasally, weak tone sounded vaguely familiar. Hardly the voice of doom.

"That's right. Which you already knew. Who's this?"

"Why, Mr. Garber, is that any way to greet an old colleague? It's Albert."

Leon said nothing, stunned. Not who he expected, not by a long shot.

On the other end, Albert sighed. As if strong-armed, he reluctantly said, "Perhaps you remember me better as…'The Mad Doctor'. Very unfortunate name."

Chapter Three

Of course Leon remembered the Mad Doctor. Hard not to. But he didn't trust his ears, couldn't rely on his instincts. Not when pitted against LMI. He wouldn't say too much, stay on the phone too long. Directly to business. "Prove who you are. What did you tell us about yourself when we met?"

The caller inhaled deeply. "I told you and Mr. Spangler about my lost love, Gretchen. Cancer took my wife from me, too soon, too cruelly. I do what I do out of love. A deep, abiding swan love."

Last year, Albert had been quite garrulous while talking about his wife. Now, he rattled his tale off quickly as if the explanation exhausted him. Been there, done that.

Leon didn't agree with Albert's methods—killing innocents to conduct covert cancer studies—but at least it supplied a reason to his barbarity. If you could call it "reason." Still, Albert was definitely the lesser of two evils. "So…you're Albert."

"Indeed I am."

"How'd you find me?"

"I'm not at liberty to divulge our methods, Mr. Garber. Not yet, anyway. When we meet—"

"Who says we're meeting?"

"Surely you realize meeting with us is in your best interest. LMI is after you. You need our help."

"Like you 'helped' last time?" Albert's help had consisted of driving Leon and Cody to LMI's headquarters, dumping them at the front door, patting them on the head, and peeling out with a "God speed!" Leon didn't trust the man. In Leon's world, trust tasted bitter, a food he no longer ate.

"I gave you all the help I could at the time."

"What do you want?"

"We're assembling. We have a team. I would like you to join us."

Headlights streamed toward Leon, blurring around the edges. He held his breath as the car passed, a Mustang. It also bought him time to think.

In a way, what Albert offered seemed like a blessing, too good to be believed. Safety in numbers. He felt less alone, no longer a sole person taking on a murderous corporate giant. "Tell me more."

"Last year I told you we were gathering. Disgruntled Like-Minded Individuals, past and present, joining forces to fight LMI. Against all the injustices they've subjected us to. We plan on—"

"And how do I know LMI hasn't enlisted you?"

Leon held the phone away while Albert laughed. "Surely you jest." Albert paused, waiting for corroboration. Leon stayed quiet. "No, I can absolutely assure you that isn't the case. Mr. Garber, we can help one another. You've been black-marked. You have no other options. Join us."

"Why?" A simple question, the type Albert never answered head-on.

"'Why?' 'Why' what, exactly?"

"What do you want from me?"

Silence. A click, one of those damned, nearly imperceptible telephone clicks he'd heard too many of during last year's nightmare. A recording, possibly another party on-line. "Mr. Garber, you've proven yourself quite adept at hitting LMI where it hurts." Still dancing. And Leon was sick of Albert leading. Leon knew there was more to it, could hear it in the way Albert's voice pitched higher, ran faster. "And…we understand you've come into possession of something that could be very valuable in our disagreement with LMI."

No doubt Wyngarden's computer. Leon intended on holding onto his prize. At least for the time being. Insurance in case Albert had ulterior motives. "Your 'disagreement' with LMI. Is that what you're calling it now?"

"For reasons I'm certain you're well aware of, sometimes it's best not to be to explicit over the phone." A reminder that Leon had been on the phone for too long. "Ah, Mr. Garber...do you still possess this particular item?"

Let Albert sweat. God knows he'd amped up Leon's anxiety last year with his frustratingly vague doublespeak. "Maybe. Maybe not. But I'm willing to talk."

"Splendid." Yet Albert sounded less than assured. "As it happens, we have impending business in Miami. That's where we'll contact you. It's quite fortuitous you're heading there now."

Leon's skin grew clammy. Albert knew as much as LMI. Possibly more. His phone achieved a venomous nature, something he considered heaving away before it bit him. "Not saying that's where I'm going. But what makes you think I am?"

"Put your mind at ease. No worries. All will be explained in due time." Albert's nonchalant attitude infuriated Leon. Always in the background, Albert had an uncanny talent of staying invisible as radiation. Possibly as dangerous, as well. "Here's what I need you to do...find temporary residence in Miami. Don't tell me where! And, of course, I don't need to tell you to acquire a new alias. You're a resourceful man, shouldn't be a problem for you. And...I'm afraid you're going to have to keep your phone. At least for a while longer."

"*What*? Obviously, that's how you found me! If you did, LMI sure as hell can!"

"That's not necessarily true. Again, all will be explained later."

"So if you're not worried, give me your phone number. I'll contact you."

This time the phone razzed, a sound Leon'd not heard before. "I'm sorry that's not possible, Mr. Garber."

"Thought as much. Just like last time, you want me to take all the risks while you sit back reaping the benefits."

"It's the way it has to be I'm afraid. Please keep your phone. We'll contact you soon. It's—"

Leon cut him off. He'd heard enough. The phone weighed like a brick in his hand, a grenade waiting to blow. The window rolled down. He held the phone outside, releasing one finger

at a time. He derived satisfaction from it, the way he imagined
rappers felt when they dropped the microphone onstage.
Brazenly illustrating his finished status.

Dammit.

He tossed the phone on the floorboard, rolled the window
up.

Simply, he had no other choice. Even though the lifeline
Albert held out to him might unravel, it still might hold.

Extreme caution. Lay low, burrow deep like a mole. Hope
Albert and his team can supply a solution, not a quick trip six
feet under. As they say, hope springs eternal. Leon attempted a
smile. Just to see if he could do it. It hurt.

Bleary-eyed and wide awake, Leon headed down the
highway. One hundred straight, laborious miles into Miami, his
destiny.

A brilliant sun rose, dappling the sky flamingo pink, welcoming
Leon to Miami Beach. The truck had been running on fumes,
the way Leon felt. Before it overheated, Leon needed to give
his getaway vehicle an overdue rest. If only he could sleep as
well. Exhaustion muddied all rational thought. Yet live wires
coursed through his body, charging him with nervous energy.
Too amped to sleep. Maybe an ocean-side jog would quell his
anxiety. Not exactly keeping a low profile, but he knew he
wouldn't be alone. No matter the time of day, large beach-side
cities always hosted a marathon's worth of runners.

Out of all the Miami cities to choose from, he'd picked
Miami Beach and didn't really know why. At least that's what
he told himself. Actually he knew why; it just pained him to
admit it. One of the few things Leon remembered about his
father—other than his murdering his mother, of course—had
been his tales of Miami Beach. On the rare occasion his father
was in a good mood (just enough drink in him to enliven his
spirits, not enough to uncork the demon), he'd cajole Leon with
tales of his youth: nights playing on the beaches of Miami, days
spent toiling beneath boats, scraping off barnacles. Leon had
sat at his knees, enraptured, willing his father to love him. Had
he known how things would end, he wouldn't have bothered.

Inhuman bastard. But affection-starved and abused children know no better.

Which made his destination a bittersweet one. As much as Leon loathed admitting it, Miami Beach had drawn him in. Maybe to get closure, seek enlightenment as to what had made his father the son-of-a-bitch he was.

Slowly, Leon drove through the outlying areas, getting acquainted with the city's character. Important for someone with his lifestyle. Like all big cities, the quality of neighborhoods varied wildly, upscale and downtrodden coexisting within blocks of one another. A powder keg of social tension.

The Oceanside resorts and hotels were too pricey, of course. And much too showy for a man laying low. He compromised. He found a ramshackle motel within walking distance of the beach, neglected by everything but cockroaches.

The surrounding streets comprised a microcosm of a "bad neighborhood," the kind parents warned children away from. Dazed vagrants wandered the sidewalks in front of shuttered pawn shops. Tweekers sat on curbs, legs stretched out in the street, soaking up the sun and frying their brain-cells. Blatantly, dealers and hookers displayed their wares, surely the most profitable business now in the once-thriving downtown district. After staying at the Conch, it almost felt like home to Leon.

The motel clerk didn't bat an eye as Leon peeled off $225 in bills to pay for two nights. Clearly used to seeing cash, plastic a rarity at shady motels. As if to solidify his discretionary policy, the kid avoided looking directly at Leon, his gaze settled on a small desktop TV set. A policy Leon wished everyone would adopt.

When asked for a name, Leon gave "Chris Hampton," his new alias. *R.I.P. "Mark Slater" and welcome to the world, Chris, make the best of your time on earth.* After last year's events, Leon vowed to always be prepared: a backup set of papers, ID, the works. Back in the Keys, he'd made his Cuban ID guy very happy by tossing him double the business. To celebrate, his contact had busted out huge cigars and an even larger smile.

Unlike in the Keys, Leon had no trouble securing a ground-floor room. No more midnight swims, not that there was a pool anyway. Still, small comforts, take 'em where you can.

A hole, foot high and foot sized, decorated his room's door. Next to him, a door squealed open. Leon turtled his head, hurrying, the key stubborn in the lock.

A blonde woman with dark roots and even darker raccoon eyes stepped into the sunlight. A large purse kept slipping off her bony shoulders. Her jeans were well-worn, peeling at the knees, probably a wear-it-till-it-rots fact of life for her. "Oh. Hi." Not an enthusiastic greeting, just a weary, no way around it societal necessity.

"Hi." Leon shot her a fleeting glance, looked back down, twisting at the key.

"Yeah, sometimes they stick. Here let me try." She lassoed her head within the purse straps. Withdrawing enormous white sunglasses from her purse, she slipped them on. Ready to go to work. "The trick is...you gotta' rattle, turn at the same time, put some shoulder into it." She did, the door obeyed. "Ta-dahhh." Her hand swayed over the threshold. "Welcome to paradise."

Leon chuckled. Then he stopped once he saw his new living quarters. Even more drab and unkempt than the awful Poinciana.

Amused by Leon's grimace, she chuckled, fingers flying to her lips. "It's not much, but it's home." She stuck her hand out, the purse threatening to strangle her neck. "I'm Theresa. Terrie."

"Chris." No last names exchanged; another person happy with the privacy policy of off-the-grid living. Her grip surprised him, solid and belying her slender nature. Yet her severely dehydrated hand felt like a shed snake skin. A hard life, each callous representing a bump in her journey. He wondered what secrets drove her here. "Thanks for the tip."

"Welcome." Walking backward, she appraised Leon with an obvious head to toe scan. Apparently found him worthy of getting to know better. Leon preferred she didn't. Too late. "I've lived here a while. Hope not to in the future. I can tell you where to avoid, what to avoid. I mean, like food wise. Basically don't walk anywhere around here at night." She shrugged, the purse rising and slumping against her body. Could be a formidable weapon. Something probably needed in the neighborhood. "Just sayin'."

"Thanks, appreciate it."

Impatiently, she looked inside her open door and yelled. "Gavin! Come on, already!"

Footsteps thumped, small and swift. A teenage boy with dark brown hair—Leon imagined Theresa's original hair color—rushed outside. Like his mother, he shared a natural struggle with accessories. His weathered backpack slipped from his thin frame to the sidewalk. He tossed a casual nod, a half smirk, toward Leon. Trying to be tough, the defensive instincts of the small. "Hey." His voice squeaked, on the cusp of changing.

"Hey yourself."

"Gavin." A real cowboy move, he slapped his hand on his jeans, wiping it before offering it to Leon. Good manners, strong in spirit, frail in body. Possibly malnourished. Immediately, Leon liked the kid. And it scared him.

"How you doin', Gavin? Chris." Another strong shake, practically a clone of his mother.

The three of them stood in silence, trading awkward glances. Too much attention already. Apparently schooled in diffusing uncomfortable situations, Gavin grinned. "Gotta' bounce." And he bounced like a ball off the walk, chugging toward the parking lot. "Cool meetin' you," he called.

"Same here, Gavin."

Theresa followed her son to an old Celica, the front bumper glued together with hipster bumper stickers. Before she slid into the driver's seat, she flashed a yellowed smoker's smile.

Leon watched them drive off and dropped his smile. Definitely no more socialization, already far too much for comfort. Worse, a familiar tide of sickness swelled in his stomach.

Both of them looked sickly, pale by Florida standards. Rail thin. The kid looked like he never ate.

They lived in a dump. The only reason for doing so is to escape something, past or present.

She showed signs of dehydration, little sleep, inadequate nourishment. Possibly alcohol or drug abuse.

God, he hoped she didn't abuse her son.

Leon pondered the world map of stains covering his bedspread, "Africa" the most prominent. He wondered if each stain represented DNA from a multitude of people or if one individual had a particularly tough time corralling his bodily fluids. Either way, he knew he wouldn't sleep on those sheets, that bedspread. Even fully clothed. He'd have to buy some sheets tomorrow.

That had been the extent of Leon's business since arriving. Watching TV washed out; he couldn't focus on any show. The local news depressed him too much. The mere thought of firing up his laptop frightened him, much too easy for LMI to track. LMI and Albert had him jumping at shadows, some real, some imagined.

And sleep wouldn't be visiting tonight either, no doubt about it.

But the *rap, rap, rap* at the door announced an all-too-real afternoon visitor. A reflexive habit, Leon scanned the room, looking for a makeshift weapon. Nothing, just a lousy lamp.

Leon waited, hoping to hear retreating footsteps. Maybe just the woman next door. He didn't believe it for a moment, though. Another knock, this time stronger and demanding. Time stood still as he held his breath. His heart kicked into overdrive, his pulse throbbing in his ears. But LMI never knocked, impatient as death.

Leon hedged his bets (and he never used to gamble), snagged a capped hypodermic of Azaperone from his briefcase. Palmed it.

Quickly, he looked out the peephole. A short, young black woman and a slovenly middle-aged man stood outside. Both in suits, hers tailored, his not so much. *Detectives.*

Impossible. There hadn't been time for the Key West cops to even realize "Mark Slater" was missing, let alone connect him to "Chris Hampton" in Miami. Something routine, had to be. Not answering would just open up a world of scrutiny.

Pocketing the syringe, Leon mussed his hair, stripped down to a t-shirt, kicked off his shoes, yelled, "Just a minute!" When he opened the door, he dropped a yawn. Narrowed his eyes. "Yeah?"

"Mr. Hampton?" The female detective stared up at him, eyes

brown and piercing. Obviously, she already knew his name, now just going through police formalities.

"That's right." Another yawn, then Leon shook his head. "Sorry. Was asleep. What's goin' on?"

The larger detective placed a hand on the door above his partner's head, declaring his self-imposed alpha dog status. Leon imagined he struggled constantly trying to keep the façade up. "We'd like to have a word with you. I'm Detective Bellup..." While he reached for his badge, the woman had already flashed hers, snapped it shut, replaced it in her pocket. "My partner here is—"

"*I'm* Detective Keats." Feisty, used to fighting for her place in a world dominated by male cops. Clearly the detective to worry about.

Bellup on the other hand looked bored. Heavy eyelids suggested the end of his beat or plain middle-aged burn out. Leon thought it likely a combo.

"Can we come in?" Bellup's nostrils flared every time he spoke, an odd habit Leon couldn't help but focus on.

"What's this about? As I said, I was sleepin'." He jerked his head back toward the bed.

Keats leaned in, one foot poised several inches off the ground behind her. "Doesn't look like your bed's been slept in."

Dammit. "Yeah, you blame me? Check out the bedspread." He went for a smile, one that twitched at the corner of his mouth. "I was so tired, I crashed at the desk. Neck hurts." For the detectives' benefit, he rubbed it. "Look, I'm not tryin' to be a pain. I'm just really tired. I was up all night and then some."

"Why were you up all night, Mr. Hampton?" Keats asked all the tough questions, the ones that unnerved Leon. Adding his two cents, Bellup snorted.

"Just got in from six months on the sea. On a trawler. Do it every year." And he had the fake documentation to back it up. As long as someone didn't look into it too closely. After last year's close call in Kansas City, Leon made sure every new alias came with a history with corroborating papers. He thought Chris Hampton had a particularly compelling back story, bonus points for hard to pin down sea-faring adventures. "What can I say? Love the life." His smile meant to disarm. Yet Keats tapped her hidden gun, the bulge obvious beneath her blazer. Nervous habit, nothing more, Leon hoped.

"Oh yeah?" Bellup came alive, his lids raising half-mast. Maybe he dreamed of a sailing life. "Whaddaya' do?"

"Cook, fisherman, skinner, basically a glorified deckhand. I do it all. But it's the water that matters. Hey, again, what's this about?" Get them back on track. Enough about him.

"Sorry, yeah…" Bellup squared himself, tugging his trousers and shoulders up. The belly stayed out, though. "There was a shooting here couple nights ago. On the second floor."

Great. The wrong motel. "Huh. As I said, didn't get in till this morning. The guy dead?"

"Not sure yet. You heard anything? Seen anything?" All bluster now, Bellup assumed the lead. Fine by Leon. Clearly a less thorough cop than Keats.

"Guys, I got here this morning, went straight to sleep. Ask the clerk."

"We did," said Keats.

So much for Leon's analysis of the clerk's "see nothing, hear nothing, say nothing" motto. "Um…is there anything to worry about? I mean…staying in this motel?"

Bellup said, "Probably nothing more than the usual. Keep your door locked. Don't answer the door if—"

"But I answered the door to you guys." Leon knew better than to bait him, he really did. But the stupid hypocrisy of it all, compounded by lack of sleep, had taken its toll. And he suspected there was more to their visit than they were telling him. Typical cop procedure.

"Yeah, well, we're the police." Bellup stammered a bit, almost shrinking down in size.

"Do you ask every new tenant here questions? The local welcome wagon?"

"Not everyone," answered Bellup. "Just the white guys."

Bellup's reply astounded Leon. Thankfully, Keats' expression was visibly worse. Poisonous eyes glared at Bellup. Holding her partner in her hypnotic sway, she attempted to commandeer the ruined investigation. "What my partner *means* to say, Mr.

Hampton, is that you're the only new tenant since the shooting. We just thought, being new, you might've noticed something the others take for granted."

Again, Leon practiced a brooding appearance, one he'd perfected in Key West. "Nope, sorry, only thing I've seen is the back of my eyelids."

"Fine, we've taken up enough of your time." Bellup to the rescue, big man in charge. Nostrils expanded. Shoulders up again. He bumped into Keats while strutting outside.

Keats wasn't having it, though. She stood her ground. Determined to fire one last salvo. "What are your plans now, Mr. Hampton?"

"Dunno. This time of year, I sorta' just kick around 'til I find something local. I'll wash dishes if I have to. Not afraid to work."

"Uh-huh. And what trawler did you come in on?"

Meticulous, smart. Entirely dangerous. *"Finnegan's Mate.* Don't ask me what it means. I've asked Cap and he ain't talkin'." Leon had nothing but time in the Keys, plenty of time for homework. Finnegan's Mate, a real boat, had recently sailed out for another six month tour. "You may have to wait another half year 'fore you get hold of 'em, though. Cap never sits still for long. No phone either." Leon framed a "sorry" face, held up a faux phone.

"C'mon, Keats! Time to go!" Bellup stood behind her, sighing, tapping a foot. Tossing a real hissy fit. But Leon sided with him all the way.

Keats' smile felt anything but friendly. Tight and controlled and meant to loosen Leon's nerves. She offered her hand toward Leon. A quick up and down, then Leon dropped it. "Thank you for your time, Mr. Hampton. I might wanna speak with you again." She snapped around, stormed past Bellup.

"Call first next time," hollered Leon.

He shut the door, leaned against it. Dark patches of sweat rimmed his t-shirt's underarms.

Clearly he'd picked the wrong motel. But he couldn't bail now, not yet. Too suspicious.

Albert had better call damn soon.

Fuming, Keats slid in behind the wheel. Of all the damned foolish things she had to put up with from Bellup, this time he'd crossed the line. She waited patiently, maybe not so much, until Bellup finally acknowledged her.

"What?" His hands flew up, pretending ignorance. Or maybe he was truly clueless. Keats knew Bellup flew his racist flag high and racists generally denied such labels.

"You know damn well 'what', Bellup!" She dropped her voice, imitating Bellup's grumble, "'Only the white ones'. Reverse discrimination much?"

"Oh, sack the liberal shit." It took him a while to shift his girth so he could face her. Of course the mini-mountain of trash at his feet also impeded his movement. A cornucopia of fast-food wrappers, styrofoam coffee cups, soda cans (*always* crushed in half), and wadded up cigarette packages covered the floorboard. At least she'd succeeded in putting an end to his smoking in the car.

Keats, on the other hand, kept her side of the car spotless, a fitting metaphor for their partnership. Every morning it pained her to look at the trash. Just one more reason she disliked Bellup.

In fact, she'd disliked him upon their first encounter. He'd said, "Call me 'Belly', everyone else does." *Yeah, never.* She'd looked him in the eye, defiantly called him "Bellup." Let him know how things would be. No adult should call himself "Belly."

And, now, this last bit of immature, not to mention unprofessional, behavior stoked her fires high.

"I was just bustin' the guy's balls a little," Bellup said, his defense so weak it sounded like he even doubted himself. "He's harmless."

"The next time you try some of that racist crap, leave me out it." She fired up the Crown Vic's engine, gunned it with a heavy foot of aggression. "Not gonna go down on my record."

"It's not goin' on your record. I've been at this a lot longer than you have and—"

Bellup blathered on, in love with the sound of his own voice. She'd heard all of his tales before, his unwarranted reputation not impressive in the least. Fact is, since she'd been partnered with Bellup—three-and-a-half very long years—she hadn't seen him do a single impressive thing in that time. The fairy tales he reveled in came off as phony as his toupee. Accorded the golden halo of all aged, experienced cops, the rest of the men's club gave him a pass on real police work. Felt he'd earned it. Truthfully, though, he was an anchor tying Keats' ship down in dry dock. The only one looking forward to his retirement more than Bellup was Keats. Another year, then she'd step up; hopefully with a better, more ambitious partner.

She let Bellup gab on, tuning him out. She'd become quite good at it.

But something bothered Keats about Hampton, something she couldn't pin down. She needed to talk it out, even if Bellup provided the worst sounding board in town.

She interrupted Bellup. "I don't think he's harmless." At a stoplight, she tapped her lip, thinking.

Bellup jabbed a yellowed thumb toward the windshield. "Light's green, Keats. Whaddaya' waiting for?" When Keats hit the gas too hard, the car lurched. "Jesus, take it easy. Now, what'd you say?"

"Hampton. You said he's harmless. I'm not so sure he is."

"The hell he ain't. He's just some poor schmuck, tryin' to make ends meet. Leave the guy alone."

"Yeah, whaddaya' base that on? The fact he's white?" Keats didn't really believe it, not even Bellup would be that ignorant. More than likely late-afternoon laziness sealed Bellup's findings. But she'd found the only way to reach what little cop's brain Bellup still had was through confrontation.

"Good Christ, here we go again with the racism crap." His eyes rolled, something Keats hated with a passion. More animated than a cartoon and twice as juvenile. "Everything's a soap-box with you. Everything's a goddamned cause. Should've never let people like you…" He stopped himself, a rare occasion.

"Excuse me? People like *what*? Black people?" If Bellup wanted to be a dick, she'd match him point by point.

"No! God, no, that's not what I was gonna say. I've known a lotta' great black cops." Bellup flew into action, his hands waving. Trying to quell the situation, no doubt sensing his pension on the line.

"Oh. You mean women." Of course that's what he meant. He'd made it no secret he thought only those equipped with a penis should police. *Sexist jackass.*

Bellup sighed, said nothing. Suspicions confirmed. Jerks like Bellup made her job so much tougher than it had to be. It didn't help that the other detectives looked down upon her, literally and figuratively. Shorter than any of her squad's other detectives by nearly four inches, her height compelled Keats to climb the promotional ladder higher than any man. She knew the other detectives considered her a three striker—female, black and short. One of the reasons she projected a shield of bitchiness.

"You're a goddamn dinosaur, Bellup. Get out of the stone ages already. You know women vote now, right?" Sure he pissed her off, but she didn't want to derail. Not while all cylinders were sparking. "Whatever. But there's something about Hampton I don't like."

Clearly relieved to be leaving uncomfortable topics behind, Bellup seized the opportunity. "Okay, super-cop...what's got your panties in a bunch?"

Keats chewed it over. She certainly didn't want to hand Bellup a loaded gun by saying she felt it in her gut. It sounded like a tired cop cliché, even though a foundation of truth formed most clichés. She imagined Bellup laughing it off, calling it "girly, not how a real cop thinks." But she had to work it out, listen to her own voice until the puzzle pieces fit.

"First of all, he seemed too smooth. He—"

"'Smooth?' You think Hampton's some sorta' bad guy 'cause he's smooth? If 'smoothness' is your criteria, what am I, a criminal mastermind?"

Keats laughed. "Yeah, right, in your dreams. Anyway, Hampton had an answer for everything. We didn't shake him, not once."

"Christ's sake, Keats, that's 'cause he's got nothin' to hide."

Keats ignored him, his thoughts didn't matter. "And if the guy was so damn exhausted, up all night on a trawler, he woulda' slept on anything, no matter if the bedspread was dirty."

"He slept. Crashed at the desk."

"So he says." The Crown Vic's front tire visited the oncoming lane. A passing driver blasted a horn.

"Dammit, lemme drive if you're not gonna pay attention."

"I don't think so." Then it hit her. All the talk of "smoothness." "His hands," she said.

"What the hell you talkin' about?"

"When I shook his hand...it felt smooth."

"Big deal, guy lotions. Whaddaya call him, a metrosexual." She shook her head. "Definitely not a sailor's hands."

"Jesus Christ! Guy has smooth hands. Lock him away and call the judge." He cuffed his wrists together, offering them toward Keats.

"Bellup, you know how hard working on a trawler is?" She knew he didn't. "His hands should be calloused, hard. They were soft. He wasn't working on a trawler."

"He's a cook. Making soup don't bring on calluses." He rubbed his mouth with a swishy, wet sound. "Leave the guy alone, already. He's just some down on his luck slob."

"Maybe he is, maybe he isn't. Wouldn't be much of a cop if I didn't follow up on my instincts." *Sorta' like you, Bellup*, she wanted to add. But that was a given.

"Instincts. Pfft." He made short spitting sounds, the kind he always made while digging at the remnants of his lunch with a toothpick. "Woman's intuition and all that bullshit, right?"

"Yeah, something like that." He'd never get it, too old a dog to learn new tricks.

"Just let it go, Keats, let it go." Melancholy colored his words. Which surprised Keats. Maybe her partner had a soft spot for sailors. Still it confused her. Usually Bellup was as easy to read as a "Jack and Jill" beginner book.

"Bellup, at first you had a hard-on for the guy. *You're* the one who wanted to go shake him down. For no real reason. Well...hell, hate to say it, but maybe your instincts were right. For once."

As if deep in thought (a mighty big void, thought Keats),

Bellup looked out the window, swaying with the jolts of the Vic. Finally, he said, "Yeah, well...you gotta' admit it's weird for a white guy to check into that motel." One hand shot up, an anti-racist shield. "Don't mean anything by it, don't mean anything by it. I'm just sayin'...white guy checks into a motel in a hugely ethnic 'hood like that. Raises my suspicions. But...he put my doubts to rest. Nothin' to do with our shooting. Guy's a sailor. He is what he is. Like Popeye. Nothing more."

The Zen lifestyle according to Bellup. Fine. He wasn't going to help. Shocker. She'd handle it on her own. Her way: quiet, close scrutiny. End of topic.

Still, she couldn't help but get the last word in. "Guy's hidin' something. I know it."

"And I told you to let it go! Guy's just tryin' to live his life... like we all are."

Actually this was the true lifestyle according to Bellup. *Just get by.* He wanted to perform the smallest amount of work necessary. Comfortably watch the seconds tick by on his retirement clock.

Have at it, champ. Hope I never end up like you.

But she fully intended on investigating Chris Hampton further.

What the hell was that all about?

The question looped through Leon's mind as he ran along the beach. Instead of rejuvenating him, the jog brought on a bout of nausea, every footfall pumping it up a notch. Yet he couldn't stop. He pushed himself harder as if running for his life. The cops may as well've been pursuing him on foot.

Leon's new strict exercise regimen served a two-fold purpose: he had to be in tip-top shape with LMI on his trail and it gave him clarity of mind. Both essential defenses. But tonight the cork stayed stubbornly plugged into his brain. It sealed his fears deep inside, an airtight jar of paranoia and neuroses.

Absolutely a shooting could've taken place at the motel. But for the cops to single him out, harassing him over an event that he, for once, had absolutely nothing to do with begged the question, *What's really going on?*

Bellup, the tired and lazy detective, had lost interest as soon as he swaggered through the door. But the other cop, Keats, grilled him with rapid-fire questions, doubting him with searching eyes. Leon thought—*hoped*—his back story would hold. Unfortunately, his back story only travelled as far as the sea. Scattering a historical-fiction trail since birth had proven next to impossible. Hard to believe his best hope lay in the lazy cop, Bellup, giving up on the case.

Which again, led him back to the beginning: *What the hell was that all about?*

On the other hand, the cops' visit could very well have been routine. Most likely, the motel clerk had speed dialed Bellup before Leon had even made it inside his room. Maybe they checked out every new tenant, especially "a white guy" as the racist cop pointed out. But the more Leon thought about this theory, the lower the rock in his gut sank.

Leon stopped, his chest heaving. On weak legs, he dropped onto an isolated section of beach. Not too many people out tonight, possibly because the locals found the seventies unseasonably chilly. They'd never survive a winter's night in the Midwest. He missed Kansas City, missed his life there.

Slowly, the ocean absorbed the sun, the sky turning a fiery orange. It looked angry and mean, very unlike that morning's welcome mat of a sunrise. Pulling his knees to his chest, he wrapped his arms around them. Tethering himself to reality.

He checked his phone again for missed messages, ensuring the unit was fully operational. Nothing.

Where the hell is Albert?

His knees cracked, a distressing sound. His muscles, his bones hurt more than usual. Perhaps he'd been punishing his body, pushing it too hard.

With both the cops and LMI hot on his heels, it felt like old times again. Maybe not such good times.

He strolled across the beach. As he lifted heavy legs onto the ramp leading to the boardwalk, he suddenly felt very old.

Darkness fell fast. An unexpected cool breeze blew between the buildings on the boardwalk, a warning of something cold coming.

Raymond kept on the move. From experience, he'd learned not to stay in one place for too long. Shop owners frowned upon it; cops called it loitering. But people gotta eat. The good Lord created man's natural hunger, after all, a top-of-the-food-chain need to survive. So Raymond had no doubt God would turn a blind eye, maybe even favor him with a holy wink, if he resorted to picking a pocket or two. Possibly bring down a few minor scams ("minor," though, mind you). Maybe even indulge in a bout of gambling if he felt Lady Luck shining him on. Just stayin' alive, the way God wanted him to. No matter if the weak fell victim to him.

Plenty of lost souls wandered the boardwalk. They stumbled and bounced into candy-colored touristy stores until flustered clerks shooed them away. Some folks were downright vocal, cursing and harassing frightened tourists.

Not Raymond, though. Sure, he didn't have a place to hang his hat, not at the moment. But he certainly didn't consider himself homeless, no sir. Just currently between places of residence. And unlike the rest of the bums, he didn't mind working. In fact, he liked dirtying his hands, taking pride in hard work. Figured he'd just wait for the right opportunity to come along. It always did. The good Lord provides.

Stretching with a monumental yawn, Raymond towered over everyone on the sidewalks. His mostly skin, bone and muscle physique added a few extra visual inches. He knew he projected an imposing figure and always used it to his advantage. Mostly he attributed his healthy build to clean living. No matter how you cut it, no one messed with him. Although in his early sixties, he felt in the prime of his life.

Miami had changed since he'd last visited. Lots more "color." And not just the gaudy ocean's worth of Hawaiian shirts or the tight (pleasantly so) and shockingly bright (not so pleasant) colors of women's skimpy dresses. Nope, the entire mix of faces had changed so drastically he didn't even recognize the place. Hispanics, Latinos, whatever they called themselves these days, used to be the minority. Not so much now. But Raymond excelled at rolling with the changes, always had. No moss on him.

The crowds began to thin out, at least the smarter folks. Only the most foolhardy of tourists remained, unaware of the after-dark dangers that lurked around the Boardwalk. Chinamen in suits snapped phone photos of everything in sight. Frat boys wearing backward ball caps jostled one another. Drunken, bovine women shrieked while tossing money around at over-priced seashells. Get just as good free shells down on the beach. If you had the patience. A God-granted virtue, patience. And Raymond had patience in spades. Looking for his next prey.

Sometimes God worked in mysterious ways, something Raymond firmly believed, rightly so. Usually if despair comes callin', you ignore it. Because, soon enough, God's always waiting to answer your prayers. And he never calls collect, either, not like despair.

A rousing hallelujah in the form of a man brushed by Raymond. At first he couldn't believe it. He rubbed his eyes like in the old cartoons, practically heard them squeaking with disbelief.

Leon.

Unbelievable. Then again, Raymond knew better than to doubt a miracle.

At a distance, Raymond followed Leon. Not too closely. He danced around nighttime stragglers, strategically positioning himself on the streets like a chess piece. His prey turned often around corners, down alleys, in a hurry. Constantly looking over his shoulder. *Nervous.* Raymond knew the signs well, someone on the run.

Whenever Leon glanced back, Raymond sunk his head, rounded his shoulders. Painting a more delicate, older picture of himself.

Time hadn't favored Leon. He possessed the same features, but older, rougher, sharper. Flesh chiseled away by worry. A life roughly lived.

Not that it mattered much, not one iota.

Carefully, Raymond continued to follow. Always ten feet behind and a little closer to the answer to his prayers. Big money. No matter what happens to Leon.

Chapter Four

"Yes, sir... I understand completely. If that's where you want us... I know that, sir." Kissing long-distance ass, Sensitivity tossed out more "yes sirs" and "no sirs" than a Marine Boot Camp trainee. Obviously upset (not that it took much), the big guy's shoulders rocked back and forth, his hand roving over his shining dome.

Cody strained to listen in, curious as to who could make Sensitivity squirm. The mysterious big boss. All Cody could hear was a squawking. Frustrated, he gave up. Accepting his secondary citizen status—for now, at least—he slid down into the back seat, arms folded. His excitement had drained away anyhow. Last year, when he and Garber had battled it out, it totally rocked. No wussy breaks. No waiting.

The Cadillac's tires thumped rhythmically across the bridge. The motor hummed. Little clicks and tics dinged up against the outside of the car, nearly lulling him to sleep. *Boring*. If he saw any more of the damn bridge, he just might hurl. Earlier they'd spent hours along it; now they'd reversed the same path. And Garber's path had long frozen over. The old man had vanished.

Of course Cody tried to tell these guys the next best place to look for Garber. *Miami*. It was on their way, anyway. And, truth be told, Cody thought it'd be a kick-ass place to meet some ladies.

"Yes, Spangler says Miami. Apparently, Garber's father talked a lot about it... On our way, sir. I'll keep you posted. I understand, sir." Sensitivity tapped a button on his colossal iPhone. Big man, big phone. Big show off. To Bug, he said, "Boss says Miami."

The fact that Sensitivity ran everything by the "boss" pissed Cody off to no end. Cody's operation, after all, his idea to look for Garber in Miami. If the asshats would've listened to him earlier, they could've saved hella' time. Instead of getting bedsores in the back of a car.

And, seriously, what the hell about Miami thrilled Garber? Cody didn't get it, not at all. Yeah, his old man told him how cool it was. Big deal. Garber's old man was a colossal dick. Offed Garber's mother in front of him. Why would Garber want to hang there based on that prick's recommendation? But Cody knew Garber, knew how he thought. Knew that's where he fled to.

Didn't matter. Cody wanted to go to Miami, call it a company perk, yo. He'd seen the Spring Break shows with the hot Miami chicks, looked forward to some hands-on training. Leaning back, he interlocked his fingers behind his head and fell into a nice daydream. Only thing better than his fantasies was the real thing.

"Headquarters is havin' problems pinning down Garber's phone. Guy's tricky, pinging his signal to third world countries and back again." Sensitivity's info-drop provided nothing new under Cody's sun. He already knew Garber was as careful as a student driver. But since these LMI idiots never consulted Cody, he wouldn't make it easy for them. Especially since they'd been busting his balls the entire trip.

"How come Skeeter can't nail him down?" asked Bug. "Guy's a genius. 'Sposed to be able to do anything."

"Yeah, I thought so too." Sensitivity wiped a handkerchief over his sweating scalp. *Who the hell even owns handkerchiefs anymore?* "But Garber's invisible. Guess he learned a lot since last year. He never holds onto a phone for long. Goes through 'em like paper tissues."

Paper tissues? Jesus Christ.

Fed up with amateur hour, Cody whacked the back of Sensitivity's seat. "I tole you idiots what you was facin'! I *tried* to tell you. Hellz yeah, the old man's invisible. Shit, you already saw he's unflammable!"

Sensitivity snorted. "Someone like you calling us

'idiots'. That's rich." He turned around to face Cody. "It's not 'unflammable'. That's not a word. Use proper grammar. It's 'nonflammable'. Goddamn kids today."

Specks of life lit under Bug. "I believe the proper term is 'inflammable'." Speaking the language he loved: anything fire related.

"That right?" Sensitivity lifted an eyebrow. "Huh. Always thought it was nonflammable. How come there're two words, Bug? Don't they mean the same thing?"

"Well, technically, both are right when used in the proper—"

"Shut the fuck *up*, already! Garber's *anti-flammable*, all that matters! Dude doesn't burn, a human torch, yo! Now quit schoolin' me and get on with it!"

Jesus Christ.

Leon knew some tricks, Raymond granted him that. As Leon wove through the boardwalk, he fell in with clusters of people. Easily blending in, a human chameleon. More than once, Raymond thought he'd lost Leon. But like a bloodhound, he quickly regained the trail.

Leon slithered into the seedier side of Miami, a dying couple of blocks more despairing than the boardwalk. He hurried around whores, pimps and addicts, jagging worse than a man on a three day bender. And Raymond knew a thing or two about benders.

It seemed impossible Leon'd spotted Raymond, but it'd explain his erratic roundabouts. They went down alleys, circled around blocks. Leon strolled within spitting distance of the worst-looking denizens, no doubt dropping a warning of sorts: *Beware you who follow.*

Raymond tossed out some tricks of his own. Over the years, he'd developed a knack for fading into the shadows, becoming forgettable. Here he looked right at home in his sodden denim, just one of the street people. To embellish his disguise, he developed a drunken wobble, favoring one foot over the other. The criminal element didn't spook him either. He'd seen worse. Besides, every mugger knew drunks had no money. Yep, he'd mastered the art of subterfuge. A right handy talent. Especially when he could drop the weak act when it came time to strike.

Leon, on the other hand, looked scared enough to piss his pants. His head darting back and forth, afraid of his own shadow. Some things never change.

The moon loomed bright above Miami. Residents appeared pale, bodies leached dry of color. Cars bounced up and down, bass notes blasting from car trunks. Raymond felt the music throbbing in his chest. Voices shrieked in Spanish, English, other languages he didn't recognize. Dealers sold drugs openly, pitching them louder than a carny barker. The streets swarmed with lower life forms, everyone trying to survive. Just like prison.

Raymond also knew a few things about prison.

With one last look over his shoulder, Leon vanished down an alley. A long alley, dark as a tunnel. The graffiti-covered buildings blocked the moonlight, a natural criminal habitat. Raymond broke stride, racing across the street to catch up to Leon. The alley was empty; just a small rectangle of moonlight at the opposite end.

A light breeze carried an odor of rotten produce, hell on the nose. To Raymond's right, an open dumpster sat in a garbage nook. Something skittered across his foot. Then a hand slapped over his mouth, an arm locked around his neck. Raymond froze, didn't struggle. Had to understand the game first before playing.

"Who are you?" Street-life sounds nearly drowned out Leon's whisper. But his breath blew hot, angry against Raymond's neck.

Given the proper leverage, Raymond could easily overtake Leon. But that was no way to begin their relationship anew. He let his body slump within Leon's hold. His hands raised: no harm, no foul.

Slowly, Leon dropped his hand from Raymond's mouth. But the arm stayed around Raymond's throat, unyielding. Untrusting.

His voice ragged from Leon's grip, Raymond croaked, "That any way to greet your daddy, Leon?"

Apparently not. The blow to the back of Raymond's head

appeared to be Leon's preferred how-do-you-do.

Oh my God, no, no, no, no...
    Leon'd first spotted his tail back on the boardwalk. Impossible not to, really. Awkward, sloppy, trying too hard to look inconspicuous. Clearly not a professional, not up to LMI standards.
    But he never expected *this.*
    Anything but this...dear God, no...
    A tic developed in Leon's right eyelid as he stared at the son-of-a-bitch lying at his feet. His heart-beat raced. Even in the dark, Leon recognized the thick stock of hair, untouched by time except for the chalk-white overcoat. Same hateful jutting jaw. Identical crooked nose, more prominent than a hawk's beak. The face he'd hated for years, the face he'd never forget. A little more wizened, weathered. His childhood fears given physical essence. *Again.*
    This isn't real, can't be. Why, why, why...
    Like a shattered mirror, reality broke. Leon couldn't trust what he saw, felt. He thought his mind had snapped, his migraine swimming into a full-on, hallucinogenic inducing brain tumor. Yet he *smelled* the bastard. Cheap after-shave mixed with rancid body odor. Lava burned up from Leon's belly, coating his throat. Leaning into the trash nook, he expelled the little food he'd consumed in the last twenty-four hours. Not much, mostly bitter bile. The way his emotions ran—bitter and out-of-control. Dizziness threatened to drop him. Angry specks of orange and flashes of violent red painted the alleyway. He heaved again. And he thought his mind just might swim out next.
    This isn't real, not real, not...
    Yet—somewhere deep, someplace very dark—he knew this was no nightmare. A frayed strand of reality tugged at him, persistent.
    But insanity seemed easier. Reality terrified him. He couldn't deal with the man in the alley.
    Not a man. A hellish demon. And Leon'd been dropped into hell.

He never thought he'd see the bastard again. Even though he'd fantasized about taking his life. But he figured his father would be in prison for the rest of his miserable life. Hell, Leon pretty much thought he'd died a lonely, deserved death behind bars.

But he couldn't deny the truth. As much as he wanted to.

Leon drew back a leg, smashed his foot into his father's ribs. Welcoming reality back.

Raymond groaned, rolled onto his side. Undeniably real. Here. *Now.*

Leon knew what he wanted to do. A no-brainer: kill Raymond. No sugar-coating it with nice metaphors either. *Murder* him. Something Leon'd been training for his entire life. Ever since the day his mother died in his arms. In fact—and as much as Leon hated to admit it, but surely knew it—every abuser he'd disposed of had been a proxy for the miserable bastard he knew as his father.

Yet if he killed Raymond—right here, right now—he couldn't drag his body away, not without notice. The streets were crowded. He needed an optimal disappearing point.

And if the police found Raymond Garber's body? Leon may as well wear a flashing neon sign around his neck, reading, *I give, LMI, come get me.*

What do I do, what, what, what?

Leon dangled his foot above Raymond's head, ready to guillotine the killing blow. Several blows, actually, much more preferable. Even though the sight of blood turned Leon's stomach, his subconscious had given him the all clear he'd weather through it this one time; take one for the team.

But the consequences…

Swaying, Leon fell back against the brick wall. Cold sweat chilled him. His headache lashed with the force of a leather belt. Like the belt Raymond had always used. Triggering thoughts of…

Blood bubbling from his mother's open throat. A red fountain splashing onto his face, wetting his shirt, his arms. Her dying breath, warm on his face, then slowing, cooling. Wide eyes full of fear, regret, horror. Then...nothing. Glassy eggs, nobody home. No more. Ever.

Son-of-a-bitch, you miserable, vile...

This time he gladly gave into his foot. It arced out at his father's face, the way Raymond had kicked Leon's nose so many years ago.

Raymond rolled toward the opposite wall. The tip of Leon's shoe caught his shoulder.

"Leon? Son, *stop*...I just want—"

A scream struggled to escape Leon, but he locked it down. Too many people around. Although, in a strange way, he wouldn't have minded spectators, an appreciative crowd. Applause at the end of his life's work, his career-ending goal at long last achieved.

Leon gave his father's back another kick, nothing more than a tap. Moments like these should be savored. The thud sounded good, very rewarding.

"Please, son...let me talk to you." Raymond's voice broke, a preview of other body parts to follow. "Stop. Please, I wanted to...wanted..."

Leon hesitated, disgusted. Pathetic, simply pathetic, Raymond's pleading for his worthless life. After what he did. An act that had changed Leon irreparably. Made him the man— the monster?—he is today.

"Leon...I've changed." Sobs lengthened Raymond's words. His hands flew to his face. "I never meant to... I was sick. I *loved* your mother...please, listen..."

A trick, Leon knew it. After committing such a heinous crime—on someone Raymond professed to love, no less—there could be no lenience. A judge's gavel pummeled Leon's brain: *guilty, guilty, guilty!* Leon, the self-appointed executioner, would see the proper punishment doled out.

"Oh my God, son...if I could just take back..."

But...again, Leon hesitated. Something he thought he'd never do given an opportunity he thought he'd never get.

Enlightenment struck Leon. The insight offered a brief respite, small yet soothing. Just enough. His entire life, Leon'd sought to understand why his mother's murder happened. It's what drew him to Florida, a strong emotional magnet. He wanted—*had*—to understand Raymond, his actions.

Leon knelt and whispered, "Shut up, Raymond." A foul odor rose from the old man. "Get up." Leon wrenched the back of Raymond's tattered work shirt. Before a crowd amassed, he had to get Raymond on his feet. But the idea of touching the old man, extending a helping hand, sickened him. Instead he nudged him with the back of his hand as if touching his father would burn him. Not that it hadn't already. "Get the hell up. Now."

Raymond crawled to all fours. Using the wall as a ladder, he dragged himself up. Shadows obscured Raymond's eyes, his true intent.

With a hand over his ribs—the most tender touch Leon'd ever seen his father administer to anything—Raymond said, "Thank you, Leon…son…I—"

"Shut up. Just shut the hell up. You don't get to call me that." Raymond opened his mouth. Then he shut it.

Leon leaned in close. Struggling not to be intimidated by the monster, his childhood boogeyman. "*Listen* to me. Don't say a word until I *tell* you to speak." Raymond jerked his chin, a one-and-done militaristic nod. "I don't know why you're here. How you got out of prison. What you want with me. You're dead to me, understand that. You always have been." Leon smiled, trying to cement it in place. An impossible task. "You're going to walk in front of me, go where I tell you to. Then I'll decide what to do with you." Leon waited a beat, then barked the order, "Go!" And hated how his voice sounded weak, shaky.

He shoved Raymond ahead of him. Kept pushing him down the length of the alley, sometimes hard. The old man stumbled, obviously playing up his frailty. Attempting to elicit sympathy. Something he'd never get from Leon. Neither man uttered a word as Leon prodded him the next several blocks to his motel. Every time they'd come within sight of anyone on the streets, Leon stepped in close behind Raymond, his driving hand hidden. Shove, walk, shove, avoid eye contact, walk, stall; repeat.

Thoughts burned through Leon's mind.

Just because Leon wanted to understand, didn't mean he wasn't going to kill Raymond. And enjoy doing so very much.

Ten o'clock. The action was just heating up. South Beach had its party on in full swing, a carnival of neon, throbbing music and hot women. Restless, Cody watched, hypnotized by the street life. A window stood between him and instant gratification. That and the two hit men playing babysitter in the front seat.

"Where we goin', yo?"

"A motel." Sensitivity seemed oblivious to the revelry around him. The guy had the testosterone of a eunuch. "We'll get to work in the morning."

Cody had no idea what the "work" entailed, but it sounded less than thrilling. Particularly while a hurricane of fun whipped by him outside. The night-time traffic had stalled, bumper to bumper. Partygoers on foot passed them, adding to Cody's frustration. What the hell, Cody reached for the door handle. Face the consequences later. *Locked.* Asshats childproofed his door.

A group of girls, connected at their mini-skirted hips, peeked into the Caddy. With a giggle, one of them tossed Cody a flirtatious finger wiggle. He thumbed the button, lowered the window, flexing his arms on the sill. "What's up, ladies? Room for one more? Ain't a party 'til Cody's on board." They tittered into cupped hands. A brunette flung him an air-kiss from flame-red lips.

"Damn it." Sensitivity swung around, his arm held back like a parent ready to smack a car-antsy child. "Keep your mouth *shut.*"

Bug rolled up Cody's window from the driver's panel. A battle of buttons, Cody defied him. The window rose and lowered along with Cody's libido.

Zzzz, tump. Zzzzz tump....

Cody didn't see it coming. A flash of flesh, an open-handed slap. But the force of Sensitivity's blow sparked stars across Cody's vision. He slammed back against the seat, lowering himself more out of humiliation than pain. Rubbing his cheek, he said, "Dick, you bitch-slapped me!"

"I'll do more than that if you don't shut your mouth. Keep the damn window up. We don't need any—"

"Yes, Dad." Cody sulked, embarrassed. No way to treat the boss. Especially in front of the babes. "Fuckin' bitch-slapped me. Wait 'til I tell—"

"Yeah, yeah, yeah, sing me a new song, wonder boy. Gonna tattle to Mommy? Wah, big bad man hit Cody." Sensitivity screwed his face up, his fists coiled into his eyes. Bug let loose an uncustomary giggle.

Cody envisioned wrapping an arm around Sensitivity's neck, crushing his wind-pipe. *Sweet.* But reason, a pest Cody rarely listened to, said, *you probably can't even get past the cords of muscle on his neck before he'd pulverize you.*

"Lissen up, asshole. You forget who's callin' the shots here? LMI needs me, yo. Next time you lay a hand on me," he leaned forward, dropped his voice, "you're gonna regret it."

Sensitivity looked at Bug. Then trumpeted his lips, spraying spittle onto the windshield. "Oh, that's rich, kid. Tell you what…" He shifted around. To avoid hitting the roof, he angled his head. "…when this is over, after we get Garber…you name the place and time. I'll be there. Hell, I'll even wear a blindfold to make it an even fight."

Cody knew it was all talk. They'd never hurt him, couldn't do it. But to gain respect, he had to walk the walk. "Don't need no blindfold to take you out. Shoulda' seen what I did to Wyngarden. I—"

Sensitivity dropped his chin to his chest, closed his eyes, pretended to snore.

Cody flumped back. *Dicks.* He'd get them. Just like Sensitivity said, once they completed their business. But Cody needed to reassert himself. Now. Nobody respects a top dog who runs away with his tail tucked between his legs. "Let me off here, yo."

"You're outta' your goddamn mind," said Sensitivity. "No way we're gonna—"

"I said let me out! Pick me up in three hours. I need to stretch my party muscles, yo. Feel the night."

"Not gonna happen."

If he had a gun, he'd cap them both. One, two easy shots. Then bounce out of the car and into the party. But he had to make do with verbal bullets. "If you don't, I'm gonna roll down the window, start screamin' like a bitch about how you guys kidnapped me and—"

"You don't wanna' do that, kid." Again Sensitivity pulled back a threatening arm.

"The hell I don't." When the window rolled down a few inches, Cody cocked his face sideways, his mouth at the gap. "Hey! Yo! Hey, these guys—"

Smack.

This time Sensitivity didn't kiss him with an open-handed-love slap. Cody bounced off the seat, dropped to the floorboard. Electric gears hummed. Sensitivity scooted his seat back onto Cody.

Gnnnnnnnnn....

Time to play hardball. "If you don't let me get my party on...I'm gonna quit helping you with Garber. I know more info...where to look...but you ain't gettin' *dick* 'til you let me outta' this car."

With his arm pinned against his cheek, Cody's words slurred. But the seat stopped. He got their attention, all that mattered.

"He's bullshitting," said Sensitivity.

"Maybe. Probably." Bug paused, always careful with words. "But you wanna take that chance? What if Mr. R. gets pissed?"

Mr. R. Names popped into Cody's head then slipped away, a whack-a-mole phone book. Razmatazz. No, Rasputin. *Rasmussen. Shit, yeah!* The name Wyngarden gave up before Cody'd whacked him. Now he had the name of their boss, a step up. "Call Rasmussen. Tell him my demands."

Silence dropped over the hit men. Cody risked it, gambled, won, aces up. *Rasmussen:* the magic word to keep these clowns in line. "Move your damn seat up. Let me outta' here."

Cody heard some clicks, big fingers tapping on a small keypad. "Sir? It's Sensitivity. We have a problem..."

Halfway through the conversation, the seat ground up.

Cody crawled out of his foxhole, splayed out onto the backseat with a contented sigh. *Victorious.* The tide had turned, South Beach style. Already he imagined macking on a hot chick, grinding with her on a crowded dance floor. Maybe even doing something a little more.

Finally, Sensitivity said, "Yes, sir. Absolutely." After Sensitivity hung up, he remained quiet. But Cody knew the answer already.

"Looks like we're goin' partying." Sweet, sweet defeat sucked all the threat out of Sensitivity's voice.

Surreal didn't even begin to describe Leon's situation. He felt disconnected, a stranger in his own body. As in a childhood dream, he imagined his soul (if he had such a thing) hovering above, an uninvolved observer. Distancing himself emotionally seemed to be the best coping tool he had. If only he could manage it.

Leon pushed Raymond into the motel room, kicked the door closed behind him. Vertical slats of moonlight poked through the curtains, the only light in the room.

"Lay down."

"What?" The corner of Raymond's mouth twitched. Amusement danced in his eyes, not taking Leon seriously. Leon meant to change that. "Lay down where? On the bed?"

"On the *floor*. Now! Lay down!" Leon swept a foot under Raymond's feet and shoved his chest. Raymond clumped down. Motes of dust swirled in the moonlight's rays.

"Son…why… What—"

"Shut up. And *stay* down there. I want you to know how it *feels*. If you can feel anything. The floor's where you last left me."

Raymond perched up on his elbows. "Son…Leon…I just want to talk to you. I…"

Uncontrollable rage simmered within Leon. Not a good place.

Leon walked to the desk, struggling to reclaim reason. He sat in the desk chair and yanked the lamp chain. A small arc of light spiked above the shade, a larger oval spread out beneath it.

He scooted it toward the edge of the desk, away from himself. He didn't want Raymond looking at him. In the dark, wearing a black hood of shadows, Leon felt like the Grand Inquisitor.

"Why are you here, Raymond?"

"Son, I—"

"Don't call me that."

"What? But, son, I—"

"I swear to God, Raymond, if you call me 'son' one more time, you'll find out what I'm capable of."

Swathed in shadows, Raymond's face remained a mystery. But Leon thought—imagined—he heard his father's lips part in a moist smile. Probably thinking: *a chip off the old block.*

"Fine, then. 'Leon'."

"Again. Why are you here?"

"What? In Miami? I grew up here. Remember the stories I used to tell you? How I always wanted to come back?"

"No." Of course Leon remembered. But letting Raymond know would give him power. Power Leon feared. By virtue of the past, Raymond was already the most powerful person in Leon's world.

"No? Shame. We used to spend hours, days—"

"We're not reminiscing. We never shared a good day. You were never a father. Just a murderous bastard. Don't say a damn word unless it's in direct answer to my questions. The last time I'm asking...why are you *here*?"

"I tole you...this is my dream city. As soon as I got outta' stir, I hightailed it—"

"Why are you out of prison?" Fifty years had been his sentence. Time wasn't up, not by a long shot.

"Hm? Well, good behavior had a lot to do with it. Also, there was some issue, something to do with a foul-up in my case—"

"The judicial system means nothing to me." It quit mattering a long time ago. Now only Leon's brand of justice mattered. "You shouldn't be out. You're an animal. A butcher. Inhuman."

Silence. More than likely, Raymond was weighing his words carefully, planning them for maximum impact.

He doesn't wield the power.

"Leon...I've had a long time to think about things. I thought about you. About… I thought a lot…about your mother. Your… dear, sweet mother… I loved—"

"No you didn't." Leon's stomach turned over, warm bile souring his mouth. But he kept it in check.

"I did, boy, I did! I loved her with all my heart and—"

"Don't even *say* it. You *never* loved my mother. You beat her every chance you got. And you enjoyed it, a hobby. Until finally you let the monster completely out…when you killed her…"

"I know…I know what I did. But, you gotta' understand…I was *sick*. Sick in the head! I was outta' my—"

"No excuse." Not in Leon's world. Some people control their mental illness.

"But it's what the prison doctors tole' me, it is! They said I had a sickness, a—"

"Bullshit. You knew what you were doing. Knew it all along. I saw it in your eyes. Awareness. You'd planned it. You—"

"No! No, boy, that's not true. Somethin' inside…somethin' evil…took over, made me…do to your Momma what I did."

Raymond couldn't even say what he'd done. Sidestepping it. *Bastard.* More reason for him to pay. "*Say* it."

"Say what?"

"Say what you did."

"I don't know—"

"Say it, goddamn you, *say* it! *Admit* it! *Say* what you did!" Leon's fist hit the table. The lamp shook, shuddering light throughout the room. "For once in your *miserable* shitty life, own up to what you did!"

"Honest to God, I got *no* idea—"

"Say you killed my mother!"

"Is that what this is about?" Sarcastic. Bordering on glee.

Leon tipped. He jumped out of his chair, raced across the room, growling. Up on his feet fast, Raymond beat him to the punch. He caught Leon's fist in his. And squeezed hard.

"Boy, I already gave you a crack at me. It's all you're gonna get. I'd think mighty long and hard 'fore you try it again." Raymond's grip tightened. Still incredibly strong even after all these years.

Leon wrenched his hand away, averted his gaze. "I just want

to understand," Leon muttered, a terrified child again.

"You...you want to...*understand*? What do you wanna understand?"

Before Leon's legs turned to jelly, he returned to the desk chair. He took his time, gathering himself. He wouldn't let Raymond win again. Too much of his life had already been formed by his father's actions. "You knew what you were doing, Raymond. I saw your...exhilaration. Every time you beat Mom. You weren't sick. That's a lie. So I want...I need to know *why* you did it."

"Leon...I'll be glad to talk to you. But I gotta' go get patched up first." He coughed, not too convincingly. "Think you might've broken one of my ribs back in the alley, maybe my nose. Might have a concussion, too."

Raymond shuffled toward Leon. Shadows, then light, played over him, making him look larger than life and twice as terrifying.

"I'll be back. We'll talk then." The lamp's beam illuminated his father's bloodied grin, worthy of the devil. "Need some money, though. For the doctor. Ain't like I got insurance."

Don't let him turn this on me. Even though I haven't seen him for thirty years, he still wields the power.

Leon stood, tossed his shoulders back. "I'm not giving you any money. Can't afford a hospital visit? Too bad."

Raymond spat a nickel spot of blood on the carpet. Challenging him. "We'll talk money later. Plenty of time for that. Because I can see it in your eyes, boy, you want something from me. You wanna' pick my brain. I'll be back. Soon. To finish this."

A threat.

"No. You'll be in front of the *T-Shirt Tiki Store* on the Boardwalk every night at 8:00. When I'm ready, I'll meet you there." Two dogs, challenging one another. Leon moved around the desk, intending to show the beast the door. Raymond countered, blocking him. Grinning. "I mean it...don't come here again. Forget my name, you don't know me. You haven't seen me." Leon tried to hold Raymond's gaze, then his eyes shifted downward. All Raymond needed to press his advantage. The nature of war.

"We'll just see 'bout that. We'll just see." Raymond poked Leon's chest with an iron finger. "You want information, you're gonna pay. And I know the look, I know the talk. You're hidin', maybe from Johnny Law. Maybe someone else. And, usually—something I learned in prison—whenever folks are hidin', money's involved. You got money. Can smell it on you. And if you wanna' buy my silence, you're gonna pay. Least you can do after I let you beat on me. I'll be back."

Raymond pulled up to his height, hardly the simpering, beaten old man Leon'd encountered in the alley. With one last contemptuous look, Raymond strutted out the door.

Leon's headache flared. His hands trembled, his legs shaky. He aimed for the chair, crashed to the floor.

He wanted to kill his father. End the nightmare. More than anything. But before he could do that, he needed answers, knowledge. To understand himself, the things he does, Leon had to understand his father first. But he was afraid, deeply terrified of Raymond. He hoped when the time came he'd be able to rise above it. End Raymond, all of it.

He moaned.

Then someone pounded at his door, louder than gunshot.

Chapter Five

"Chris? It's Terrie." Leon heard the woman's voice clearly, couldn't quite place it. Nothing fit. For a brief moment, he couldn't remember he was "Chris." "Is everything all right? Come on, I *know* you're in there."

His neighbor, Terrie. Battering the door like an adamant woodpecker. Leon stood, wiped the cold sweat from his face with a shirt sleeve. Turned the lamp out. At the door, he took three deep, sobering breaths. Even though he knew Terrie stood outside, he peeked out the curtain anyway. His senses couldn't be trusted, not now.

Leon jerked the door open. Terrie's fist shook, knocking at air. Immediately, she plunged her hand into her purse. Reaching for something, possibly protection.

"Hi Terrie." Leon cleared his throat and repeated the greeting louder. Then stepped back into darkness. "What can I do for you?"

"Nothing. I mean...what's going on with you? Gavin and I heard shouting. More like screams." On tiptoes, she looked above Leon, peered around him into the room. "You okay?"

"I'm fine. I, ah...was just on the phone with my ex. You know how it is." For a spur of the moment lie, it sounded decent. And Leon suspected she had a less than stellar ex, one she'd been happy to leave behind.

"Yeah, been there, done that." She relaxed her guard, withdrew her hand from her purse. "But...you *sure* you're okay? I really thought I heard two voices."

"Hmm? Oh...well the walls here are thin and there's not much in the room. Probably just my voice echoing."

With a slight tilt to her head, she looked at him with untrusting eyes. A human lie detector. "Yeah, right. Look, Chris, I'm the last one to get all up in someone else's business. But I had to make sure you weren't, like, dead or something." She paused, clearly uncertain whether she should speak her mind. "And to be honest, my kid's next door. *Safe.* I want to keep him that way. If you bring danger into his world, I'm all over it."

Terrie's thinly veiled threat actually made Leon feel a little bit better. She appeared to be a concerned, good parent. He crossed her off his "to-do" list. "I understand that, Terrie. You don't have anything to worry about from me. It's just...it's been a hard night."

Sympathy drew down her mouth. In mothering mode, she took a step toward Leon, then gasped. "Oh my God, Chris...you look like you've been steamrollered. What the hell happened?"

Leon turned, hiding. At the same time, he welcomed her compassion, an affirmation of humanity when he needed it most.

"The usual. My ex makes everything tough. Sorry for the noise. But, Terrie, I'm—"

"Damn, son, you look like you could use a drink. You want a drink? I only got coffee and crappy tap water, but sometimes it's the company that counts."

"Rain check?"

Still scrutinizing him, she finally relented and gave him a jaded nod. Way too curious for comfort. But Leon felt a kindred spirit. He absolutely knew she'd travelled from a world of trauma, a fellow commuter along troubled highways. "Okay... cool, cool. If you ever need to, you know, talk or something, you know where to find me." Her smile brightened, all worry temporarily snuffed out. But it fired right back up again. "You *sure* there's not somebody else here? I know what I heard."

"I'm sure."

"Okay, fine. Have it your way. Just wanted to see if you were alive or whatever. 'Night, Chris." She clawed a key from the depths of her purse.

"Night. Thanks, Terrie."

She shook her head, puzzled. "For what?"

"I dunno. For seeing if I was in trouble. For caring, I guess."

"De nada." She flourished a hand over her purse, took a small curtsy. Flashed a smile. All suspicions on hold once again. Then abrupt sadness eclipsed her. "I know about trouble."

Trouble. Leon knew about trouble, too.

The cigarette butt flipped through the air. Sparks bounced as it hit the parking lot pavement.

So Leon's got himself a little girlfriend. A little worn around the edges, but a looker nonetheless.

Raymond smiled as he watched the woman vanish into her room. Things were definitely looking up, getting better over time just like a fine wine. He could use the woman to his advantage if necessary. It never hurt to have leverage, any way you force it. God supplied him with this new tool. It'd be a crying shame, practically an insult to God, not to use it.

While his son still lacked the backbone of a slug, he'd definitely changed. Raymond noticed a new coldness in the boy, definitely not the simpering pup Raymond had spawned. Which made Raymond wonder what exactly had happened to him.

No matter really. What happened in the past stays in the past. All that matters is the good ol' here and now. Raymond knew he'd stumbled onto something. Something good and rewarding. His money train.

Didn't take a brain surgeon to realize Leon had secrets to hide. If Raymond dug a little deeper, he'd be in the money. Knew it like he knew the back of his hand.

The rules Leon laid down were half-assed, insulting really. Rules Raymond had no intention on following. Telling his father to wait around a store every day like he had nothing better to do with his time. Boy needed to learn some respect. Apparently he'd forgotten who brought him into this world.

Raymond studied the dark motel, watched the flickering *vacancy* sign. Not much to look at, but it sure beat sleeping in an alley or a half-way house. He still had a wallet of cash; took it off a drunk in an alley. Wouldn't last long, but as a wise man once said, *to make money, you've got to start with money.*

Yes sir, the money train was whistling for him. And he needed to make damn sure he'd be there to board it.

Keats couldn't get anything done, not with Bellup's constant griping. He'd circle her desk, complaining about his latest and greatest body ache. He questioned her every move. Watching her with unnaturally keen detective eyes. Unusually restless. Frankly, she wished he'd just go home. Sure they had a growing skyscraper of paperwork to level, but she handled most of it anyway.

"Christ, Bellup, just leave already. I'm sure you got a hot date with a bottle of scotch." Keats flipped a folder onto her desk, leaned back. "It's not like you're doing anything."

"Hey, on the job, on the job." He kicked up scuffed shoes onto the desk. "No one's ever gonna say Arnie Bellup's lazy."

"Yeah, keep living the dream." Her sarcasm lost on Bellup, she plunged into the next file. She couldn't concentrate, rereading the top sentence several times. Making matters worse, Bellup kept humming some old tune, Cole Porter. Trying to get under her skin. "Make yourself useful and go on a donut run, Bellup."

A much more melodic Sinatra tune jangled from Bellup's cell phone. His feet crashed to the floor, the backwind knocking a Styrofoam cup over. Frowning at the phone's face, he said, "I gotta' take this." As he hurried from the squad room, Keats heard him say "hello" in a tentative, hushed voice. Another one of his secret phone calls. He'd been getting a lot of them lately. Bookies are a dogged bunch.

Now maybe she could get to work, real police work. Since that afternoon, Hampton had been making her skin itch like a mosquito bite. Something about the guy seemed too clean, too transparently innocuous. Everybody's got secrets, just a difference in magnitude. What had started as Bellup's bullying of the week had turned into Keats' obsession.

She started big. The National Crime Information Center database featured several Chris Hamptons, a delightful looking bunch of sex offenders and petty criminals. None of them squared up with her guy. No crimes listed for handsome Chris Hampton; at least none he'd been busted for. Oddly enough, instead of feeling disappointed, giddiness stoked her. On the chase. If her perp went down easily, what was the fun in that?

Yet, according to the more dependable sites, the guy was as bland as iceberg lettuce. A Florida issued driver's license, not a single speeding ticket. How could someone live to be forty without a ticket? Keats cringed at the thought of the two unpaid tickets in her glove box. Not that she considered herself above the law; sometimes the law simply got in her way to uphold the law.

Social security number, check. No marriages, no children (at least reported). No surviving family members.

In Miami, Keats had crossed paths with a fair amount of ocean-faring roustabouts. Most of them had left a rowdy trail of drunken brawling and shattered marriages in their wake. Bad credit loved these guys. But Hampton had no credit rating. Nothing. The guy'd never heard of plastic. Or banks. *Odd.*

And how convenient for Hampton's employer to be out of touch. A career criminal couldn't have planned it any smoother. Not that she suspected him of being a super-criminal; the feds would've been keeping hefty notes on him in that case. But everything on Hampton seemed perfect, right down to a cleaner than a new-born babe's rap sheet.

Hampton's driver's license photo smiled at her. Not a jolly grin. The smallest of smiles, taunting and superior: *I'm so pulling one over you, Keats.*

Usually, Keats could smell Bellup coming. But this time, preoccupied, she dropped the ball. He stood behind her mouth breathing, red as an apple. Keats failed to hide the computer window in time, ineffectively clawing at the mouse.

"What the *hell*? Keats, I told you to quit chasing this guy! There's *nothing* there."

"Yeah, that's what the database shows."

Satisfied, Bellup sat down before he keeled over. The cushion whiffed beneath his weight. "What'd I say? I *knew* there was nothin' hinky about the guy. Now let it go. We got bigger things on our plate."

"Only thing on your plate's chili dogs."

"Jesus...shoulda' never...wish I never dragged you along to see the guy."

"Too bad. You did." She tapped her fingers on the desk, thinking. Buying time with a finger-nailed drumbeat. "And I still think it's weirder than hell you were so fired up about him, then just as suddenly kicked him to the curb."

"What can I say, Keats? Got a sharp mind." With a pencil, he thumped his sharp mind. "Instinct's right up there with good police work. Guy's a zero, not worth my time. Quit wastin' yours. We got a shooter to catch."

"*Fine.*" That one word killed Keats. Gutted her like a rabbit in a bear's jaw. Conceding to her nemesis, her "partner." But Hampton was well worth her time, she knew it. Arguing with Bellup wasn't. So she lied. "No more Hampton."

Tomorrow, though, she planned on getting chummy with her new best friend, Chris Hampton. Maybe on her lunch break while Bellup bellied up to the bar.

As far as "wingmen" went, Mr. Sensitivity really scraped the bottom of the barrel. He sat at the table, wearing his ever-present sunglasses, pretty much ignoring the stripper in front of him. When one particularly nasty dancer had offered him a lap dance, he folded his arms, zipped his lips. Looked dead ahead. Pretty much sucking the fun out of the air.

Cody tried to get his rave on anyway. Of course it sucked hard Sensitivity didn't take him to a dance club, something cool like that. Instead they ended up at a skeevy strip club far from the real action. Still, it beat sitting in the Caddy, dying a slow death by boredom.

Five brews in, Cody's bladder hit the panic button.

"Gotta' go," he yelled to his bald babysitter. Over the '80's arena rock blaring out of the speaker, no one could really have a conversation. Not that he wanted to chat up Sensitivity, but he had some choice words he'd like to lay on the ladies.

Sensitivity sat up at attention. "Where?"

"Gotta' drain the lizard. You wanna' hold it or somethin'?"

A vein popped out on Sensitivity's temple. Stressed-out guy. For a minute Cody thought he might take him up on his offer to accompany him. Finally, he said, "There and back. Don't do anything stupid."

"Hey, cool and easy's my middle name." Cody stood, stretched, taking his sweet time. Making sure the blond on stage checked out his abs when his T-shirt rose. Not that his bodyguard would let him go home with one of the honeys. Winking at her, he flagged a twenty between his fingers. She wiggled toward him, her pelvis undulating near Cody's face. *So close.* He slipped the bill into her g-string. Even though he knew it was against the club's policy, he couldn't help himself. Gave her ass a quick light slap.

A bouncer in the corner (also wearing sunglasses, apparently protocol for beefy jerks) shot off his stool and stormed Cody's way. Sensitivity stood, fists curled, shoulders back. Battle of the beasts. Cody thought it might be worth a few laughs. But when Sensitivity blocked the bouncer's path, the guy stood down, weakly said, "No touching." Retreated to his stool, his head retracting into steroid defined shoulders. All of which made Cody feel like the *shit.* A damn kingpin, protected by his minion. *Respect,* yo.

Near the john, Cody spotted several plates piled up on the bar's counter. Chicken wing bones, some other unidentifiable carcass. And a steak knife. The serrated edge gleamed beneath the bar's low lighting, a twinkle in a black sky. He leaned over the bar, pretending to study the beer taps. Palmed, then pocketed the knife. Smooth as silk moves, cool as hell. *Protection.* Not much of a weapon, but should things go south with Sensitivity and Bug, he now had a fighting chance.

When he turned around, a stripper startled him. "*Shit.* Damn, woman, scare the *hell* outta' me."

"Had something different in mind than scares." Clownish makeup obscured her face, hard to tell what she really looked like. But the skimpy, sequined dress generously displayed her curves. Old school figure eight.

"What's that, yo?"

"For a lil' extra somethin', somethin'..." She rubbed her thumb and forefinger together next to her ear. Her impossibly long nails came close to severing a neck artery. "...I can give you a lil' somethin'."

Not really Cody's type, but what the hell, he hadn't seen any action in a while. And what "Dad" didn't know, wouldn't kill him. Cody heard opportunity knocking and was eager to knock boots back. "Sound's cool, baby, I'm all in. You got a room or somethin'?"

She snorted, bit of a turn-off. "Yeah, sure. Hotel Royale here." Her thumb hitched behind her toward a dented gray door. A burned-out emergency sign hung above it. "You want the deluxe suite or the imperial bedroom?" Before Cody could answer, she nudged open the door, her backside swinging like a pendulum.

Outside, a blanket of humidity enveloped Cody. The moon rode high above the alley, a welcome spotlight. Best to see what he'd be getting into. Several blocks away, the roar of the party—the *real* party—sounded full-on. He felt uninvited, the wallflower at the dance. Until the stripper hitched her dress up. Her lips parted, uncovering a green smile. Leaning back against the brick wall, the short skirt shimmied up to her belly. No underwear. Ready for action, Cody style.

"First things first, honey," she said. "One hundred bucks. Up-front." Still clutching her dress up, she extended a fist. Her fingers slowly unfurled a condom, giving it the red carpet treatment. "And you gotta' use this."

"Hellz yeah, my kinda' woman! Don't want no little Codys runnin' around out there." He pinched a handful of twenties out of his wallet, made the swap with the condom. His shorts dropped, his manhood straining at his briefs. Seeking freedom.

In his excitement, he couldn't tear the condom wrapper. Tugged at it with his teeth.

"Shit!" The condom pack tore, his hand reflexively jerking up. The condom flipped, then plopped down in the alley. Distracted while counting her financial windfall, the stripper hadn't noticed. Quickly, Cody snatched it up. *Ten second rule.* Good enough for food, good enough for condoms. Nothing mattered now more than getting his party on. Pulling down his briefs, he set his big man free. Rolled the condom on in a second. Approached the hooker, his divining rod leading the way.

He thought about kissing her. Deep-sixed the notion. Her

lipstick would end up all over him, no need for two clowns in this circus. Grabbing her dress, he pulled it up to her chest. Slipped a hand over her belly, sliding his fingers over her skin. Intending to travel south. Then he stopped. His fingertips found ripples, imperfections that shouldn't be there. *A C-section scar.*

He stepped back, wilting like a rain-sodden flag. "Jesus Christ! You got *marks*! You're a *mother*!"

She barked out a laugh, climaxed with a cough. "Kiddies don't come from the stork. Your momma never teach you that?"

The alley turned on its side. The ground beneath Cody shifted, then slanted like a fun-house floor. An electrical charge crackled through him, rising. Light-headed, dizzy, drunk on hatred. And it felt *good.*

A *mother.* She had to be a mother. Worse? She'd joked about *his* mother. His mother who'd murdered his dog, sent him on a mother-killing path of retribution.

With his shorts binding his ankles, Cody bobbled back toward her. Her freak show laughter stopped when he wrapped a hand around her throat. Pinned her head to the wall. Through gritted teeth, he said, "Where's your kid, *slut*? You leave him home alone? While you're out screwin' around for cash?"

"Let me *go*, dickhead! My kids ain't—"

"You got more than one kid? You're *shit.* You don't *care* about your kids! You don't *love* 'em! You're just like the rest! All you care about's *yourself*! Worthless *whore*! *Bitch*!" Cody knew what came next, no denying it, no stopping it. Frankly, he'd missed it. Maybe more than sex.

Then an odd serenity calmed him, healed his fury. Detached, he went about his business. Still holding the stripper against the wall he leaned over, tugged his shorts up with his free hand. A quick zip-up. And the knife felt nice in his pocket against his thigh, very reassuring.

He brandished the weapon in front of her before pressing the tip against her neck. Held it there for a moment. Teasing her.

"What're you…? *Help*! Somebody, *help*—" His hand jumped from her neck, latched onto her mouth. She struggled, bare shoulders heaving. Stronger than she looked. No doubt years on the stripper pole had strengthened her muscles. But she couldn't overpower Cody. He raised the knife over his head. Ready to take the plunge.

Behind him, a door cracked back against the wall. Cody felt the explosion reverberate into his balls. His butt clenched and his teeth clacked together. *Crap.*

"What the *hell?*" *Sensitivity.* Always the spoil sport. "God *dammit,* Spangler! What the *hell've* you done now?"

Cody wouldn't have his fun taken away, not this time. His hand jagged down. Before metal ate flesh, a steely claw wrenched his wrist to a stop. Sensitivity twirled him, shoved him against the opposite wall. Cody slipped down from the impact. His shirt rolled up, his naked back scraping across brick. As if watching a movie—safely tucked far away from reality— the events unfolded before his appreciative eyes.

Cradling the stripper with enormous arms, Sensitivity rested his square jaw on top of her big hair, softness in his touch. He rocked her, cooing into her ear. "I'm so sorry, sweetheart. So, so sorry..." His voice climbed. Tears—like acid—dissolved his words into nonsense. "...for all of this, honey. Truly, really..." It only took a second. Sensitivity trapped her throat in the crook of his arm. His other hand whipped up, gave her head a sharp turn. No louder than a breaking twig, her neck snapped. She slumped in Sensitivity's arms. After he dragged her into a trash nook, he tossed a cardboard box on top of her. A burial too good for her. And like a funeral goer, Sensitivity mourned her by crying.

Planting log-like legs in front of Cody, Sensitivity rounded his shoulders like an ape. His paws nearly hung to the ground. He growled. Seriously pissed off.

Cody attempted to stand. Uneasy, tingling legs made it a chore, not entirely unpleasant. He'd never had anybody kill for him before. Even better than doing it himself.

Apparently his proxy felt otherwise. The big man flung Cody back down, treating him like the rest of the alley trash.

"*Liz?*"

Sensitivity whirled around at the sound of the voice. Light from the open door backlit two men, one unmistakably the burly bouncer. They stepped out, dropping into defensive stances when they saw Sensitivity. "What the *fuck* you do with Liz?"

Sensitivity dabbed at his dripping nose, wiped tears away with his forearm. "Sorry, fellas. Wish it didn't have to be this way." With a deep inhale, Sensitivity's chest expanded. Cody swore he grew a couple of inches. *Hulk smash.*

Speechless, the two men gawped at one another. Undoubtedly waiting to see who would rush King Kong first. *Flick.* A switchblade materialized in the shorter man's hand. With a battle cry, he rushed Sensitivity.

Sensitivity caught the man around the chest. In one swoop, he lifted him, twisting with blurring speed—a buttoned-down tornado—and rammed the bouncer's head into the wall. The knife clacked down onto pavement. The dead man followed. Sensitivity extended a leg behind him, an incredible span. Waiting for the next bouncer. The bouncer obliged. Sensitivity hopped, turning in midair, switching legs. Perfectly timed, a black-shoe tip caught the rushing man in the throat. Force catapulted him into the wall. With an "ugh," he fell face forward to the ground. Sensitivity jacked a foot down on the back of the man's head, finishing the job.

It had all happened within seconds. A beautiful ballet of carnage. Cody seriously reconsidered challenging Sensitivity to brawl.

"It's me," Sensitivity said into his phone. "Big-time snafu. A *bad* one. Emergency clean-up." He raised an eyebrow, squinted at the moon. "South-East alley behind the club. Make it fast."

Pocketing his phone, Sensitivity dropped onto his haunches. Red-rimmed eyes glared at Cody. "You stupid, *stupid* son-of-a-bitch. You've jeopardized *everything.* And you made me... you *made* me..." Again with the blubbering. Cody imagined whoever bullied this guy in school to make him such a pansy probably regretted it later.

At the end of the alley, the familiar Caddy jerked to a stop. Sensitivity grabbed Cody, hefted him up. Gave him a sharp shove. "*Go.* Get in the car *now.*"

Back to prison. Still, Cody's afterglow stayed. Another evil mother wiped out of existence. As he approached the Caddy, his lazy grin grew. Bug greeted him with a disgusted shake of the head. But Cody ignored him while he melted into the backseat. A van pulled up alongside them, screeching to a halt. Emblazoned with bland black letters on the side, the logo read *Dorian's Carpet Cleaning.* Beneath it, in a jauntier, smaller script: *We get the tough stains out. You'll never know we were there.*

LMI being cute.

Like SWAT members, men in black jumpsuits leaped out of the van. Gung-ho in movement, they rushed toward Sensitivity in well-rehearsed silence.

Cody relaxed, closed his eyes.

Better than sex.

Such was the nature of Cody's ecstasy, the ride to the motel played out like a hazy, pleasant dream. Kaleidoscopic night colors swirled together, a trippy light show. While LMI's men remained quiet, he drifted off into a gentle sleep.

Upon awaking, the first thing Cody saw was Sensitivity in his face. Major buzz kill. He hovered over Cody, shaking him, jabbing him with girder-strength fingers. Cody sat up, rubbed his eyes. The motel sign brought him crashing back to dreary reality.

After parking the Caddy, Bug ran inside the office. Key in hand, he led the way to the room. Sensitivity manhandled Cody from behind.

Moments later, a rollaway bed arrived, steered by a hot Latino maid. Immediately, Sensitivity blocked Cody with his arm. He flicked the girl a tenner, sent her on her way. With a scowl, his usual look, the big man vanished into the bathroom. Whiny pleas filtered through the door, obviously Sensitivity freaking out over the phone with Rasmussen.

Cody hopped on a bed, his kicks up and off. Clearing his throat to catch Cody's attention, Bug gestured toward the rollaway. Grumbling, Cody obeyed, unfolded the thin mattress. Springs poked up in Cody's back. Not fit for anyone to sleep on.

The bathroom door thwacked open. Sensitivity huffed out,

his bull-like nostrils expanded. He stared Cody down.

It delighted Cody, knowing he got a rise out of Sensitivity. Not finished yet—not by a mile—he couldn't resist inching Sensitivity's thermostat up even higher. "Yo, big guy! Was it as good for you as it was for me?"

His speed scared the hell out of Cody. A white streak, he crossed the room and snatched Cody by the throat. Holding Cody at arm's length, Sensitivity flattened him against the wall. Cody's legs dangled, his hands wrenching at Sensitivity's arm.

Sensitivity's finger—the one Cody now knew by heart—jabbed into his cheek. "You listen to me and listen *good*. Don't say a *damn* word. Your little *antic* back there may've cost us our mission. Thanks to you, we're going status '*red*'. Visibility blown sky-*high*. One more mishap and I'm gonna enjoy destroying you. No tears. And I don't care *what* Rasmussen says."

"Get the hell *offa'* me, bitch!"

To reinforce his point, Sensitivity brought Cody forward, yo-yoed him back again. "You just don't *get* it, bright boy! You're *not* calling the shots. No matter *what* you're told."

"And I said get the hell *offa'* me!" Kicking his feet into Sensitivity's legs had no effect. Made him smile as if it tickled. Cody pummeled his stomach, like hitting cement. His knuckles burned, the pain zipping through his arm. Sensitivity just kept on smiling. "Let me *down*."

Smack. A slap to his cheek. "You gonna behave? Gonna listen to the *adults* in the room?" *Swap.*

Too humiliated, too pissed off to say anything, Cody looked to Bug for support. Pretending to be asleep, Bug rolled over with a fake-sounding snore. No way would Cody give Sensitivity satisfaction, though. Instead he delivered more ineffective jabs to his gut.

"Tired yet, bright boy? I can do this all night. What about you?" Gracefully, Sensitivity swung around. Dizziness rushed up on Cody as he flew through the air. When he hit the rollaway, it buckled, dropped. The halves snapped like a mousetrap, sandwiching Cody. Sensitivity guffawed. Piss poor sense of humor. "Now that I've got your undivided attention, Spangler, let me tell you something. Mr. R. gave me permission to do with you as I see fit if you step out of line one more time. You're an LMI liability. Mr. R. ain't gonna save you."

Managing to crawl out between the upended bed, Cody flumped to the floor. "You wanna' find Garber or what?"

"You can only play that card so many times, bright boy. Now get the *fuck* to sleep."

Jesus. Surrounded by lunatics.

Mercifully, Sensitivity vanished into the bathroom again. Time for his evening constitutional, no doubt.

Cody crawled into bed. Worried for the first time. What if LMI *had* turned against him? Just like last time. And, hell, it wasn't even his fault. Not really. He wasn't the one who offed half the strip club staff.

Through the door, Sensitivity's whining carried far. On the phone again, or just way jacked up and talking to invisible people.

"I miss you, baby... No, they're not picking on me...but something happened, something bad... I'll tell you when I get home..." Crying a river, same ol' shit. "...kiss the girls good night for me... I need you... can't believe what I had to do..."

Cody wrapped the pillow around his head, drowning out the sobbing. Retreating to a happier place: the look on the stripper's face as she died...

At best, Leon had managed four hours of dream-deprived sleep. Massaging his aching back, he grimaced at the filthy sheets he'd slept on—didn't bother him last night—and stumbled into the bathroom, his bladder full.

Midstream of relief, his cell buzzed in the bedroom. Quickly shutting down the waterworks, he raced to retrieve it.

Unknown caller. Could be Albert. Might be LMI. Go for broke.

"Hello?"

"Good morning, Mr. Garber."

"Albert."

"It's time we meet. Let's say later this afternoon, 2:00. Be at *Seashells* on South Shore Drive and Ninth Street. It's a most delightful—"

"I know where it is." He'd driven by it. A little hole in the wall, specializing in rock shrimp. "I'll be there."

"And, ah, Mr. Garber?"

"Yes?"

"Please do bring the item we're interested in." *Wyngarden's laptop.*

"Fine." *Absolutely not.* Leon turned the phone off without saying another word, just not in the mood for social niceties.

Now he just had to stay out of trouble and lay low until this afternoon.

Hard to do when you're suddenly the most popular man in Miami.

At all costs, he wanted to avoid Raymond. He needed a good prepping before his next inevitable meeting.

But he had to get out of the motel room.

Head down, he jumped in the truck and took it to the derelict neighborhood's streets. Already the inhabitants were out, selling wares of addiction and vice. At a stoplight, a homeless woman snapped her dentures at him, cursing. A drug dealer hassled him for not having the good taste to buy.

At the end of the block, a swirl of bright colors and long legs caught his attention. Several women, dressed in gaudy form-fitting leather and denim, stood on the corner. Their miniskirts rode high, barely covering their money-making goods. One of them sashayed up to a crawling car, leaned into the window. At the back of the prostitute gang, a woman guarded her own niche. Struggling with an over-sized bag, *Terrie*, his neighbor. Dressed in little more than a slip of a dress. Clothes he never saw her wear around her son.

It didn't shock him, not really. Intuitively, he knew she was running from her shadow, hoping to escape its reach. Trying to make ends meet any way she could. But it concerned him. Terrie's son, Gavin, counted on her. In her dangerous line of work, what would happen to Gavin if she picked up the wrong customer?

After a two mile jog on the beach, Leon packed it in. He stopped, hands on his knees. Stared into the surf. Wishing to burrow into it like a crab.

Incoming laps of water washed over his feet. The receding tide left behind shells and half-devoured fish bodies, a seaside burial. Around him, younger joggers zipped by. Showing off and smiling at Leon: *You're old, face it. Move over.*

Behind him, someone laughed.

Gavin, Terrie's son, lay stretched out on a blanket. He tossed a book beside him and drew his knees up. A bottle of sunscreen, his backpack, and a Big Gulp surrounded him. Survival kit of the young and pale.

"'Sup, Chris?" Gavin smirked, a look all teens bestow upon everyone outside of their age range.

Still winded, Leon strolled over. "How're you, Gavin?"

"Livin' the life, livin' the life." He scooted over, patted the blanket. "Chill. Looks like you're gonna drop if you don't."

Leon accepted the offer. Not the best idea, but he needed the break. "Skippin' school?"

"Nah. Parent-teacher conference."

"Your mom going?" A fishing expedition even though Leon suspected Terrie'd be on the no-show list. Currently, she was deeply ensconced in a conference of a different kind. Leon had no idea if Gavin knew what his mother did for a living, but he wouldn't be the one to shatter him with the news. Not his business.

"Nah, she's gotta' work." Gavin grabbed a seashell, pitched it out into the ocean. "Really don't need her to go anyway. Straight A student."

"Good for you. What're you reading?" Leon gestured toward the book: *Greek Mythology Tales and Beliefs.*

"Ah, some stupid crap about Greek gods punishing humans. Gotta' write a paper on it. How's this gonna help me in the 'real world'?" He hooked finger quotes, heavy with sarcasm.

Leon shrugged. "Dunno. Just enjoy it as fiction, I guess. Consider the tales parables. Compare it to the world today. You know…like the Bible."

"Yeah, right. The *Bible*. There's something else that's helpful in the real world."

Leon remembered his foster home peers' similar attitudes all too well. Adopting irony as a lifestyle, a protective tool. "Not a fan of the Bible, huh?"

"No. You?"

"Suppose not. But I don't discourage other people from their beliefs." Not that he ever had the chance. Rarely did he get to know anyone that well. "You read the tale about the guy who went to Hell to find his wife?"

"Yeah. Orpheus. Kinda' cool. But I still don't see how that's gonna help me once I'm outta' school."

"Maybe…it's an allegory about people climbing out of hell. Trying to better their lives."

"Yeah, well, when you live in hell…anything would be better. Show me the shortcut outta' there." He fell silent. Flipped on sunglasses, possibly to hide tears.

Leon let the silence linger, more effective than anything he could say. Waves pounded the surface. Seagulls glided overhead, cawing. A small toddler waddled ankle-deep into the water before his panicked mother reclaimed him.

Against his better judgment, Leon empathized with Gavin.

Not my concern. Plenty problems of my own.

Yet, like it or not, it had become his concern. The dysfunctional family had somehow needled their way into Leon. "You think you're living in hell, Gavin?"

"It's not exactly Disneyworld."

"Guess not." *Dammit.* Goodbye low profile, hello involvement. Something fate had seen fit to throw his way lately. In buckets.

"I mean…I pretty much keep it a secret from everyone at school that we live in that shitty hole. Can't hang with anyone, can't date. *Nothing.* That's all I need, right? Everyone knowing we're poor. Finding out what happened to us. High school's tough enough already."

One step farther. "Yeah, high school's tough. But…things get better." *For most people.* "What happened to you that was so bad?"

Another shrug. Tough guy posturing. "Dad went crazy. Drinking, whatever. Beat the shit outta' Mom one time too many. We took off. No money. No car. Nothing, really. Guess we're hiding."

Too close to home. But at least Gavin's mother made it out of their abusive situation alive. Down the road, once things cooled off, Leon might just look up Gavin's father. "Sorry to hear that. Is your, ah...dad looking for you?"

"Don't think so." Gavin nibbled the end of his drink's straw. The equivalent of biting down on leather to numb the pain. "Looked him up some time ago on the 'net. Far as I know, he's in prison. Some kinda' fight. Killed a guy. Or something."

"Huh. Sounds like that's where he belongs. Ah, sorry, Gavin. I know it's tough. You—"

"You're right, though. No love lost there. Let him rot."

Good attitude, Leon wanted to say. But he refrained. "Still, I know it's rough."

"What? Same thing happen to you?"

This time Leon shrugged, hoping to bury the issue. "More or less. But enough about me. We're here to talk about you, right?"

Gavin returned Leon's grin. "Finally an adult who gets it."

"Well...your mom seems decent, a good mom. Right?" Leon was definitely pushing it. But he had to know.

"Guess so. She tries. But...I don't like what she's doing. She doesn't..." His voice trailed off. Leon couldn't supply the comfort—a simple hug—Gavin needed. Not in his DNA.

Gavin rolled his shoulders, turning away feeling. "Anyway... whatever. She thinks I don't know what she does. You know what she does?"

Reluctantly, Leon nodded, said nothing.

"Yeah, world's best kept secret, right? I'm not stupid, the clues are all over the place. It's kinda' like how she and I kept up the ridiculous Santa Claus routine. Back in better times. Even though we both knew I didn't believe that kiddy crap." He smacked the sand, digging his fingers in deep. "But...I also know she does it for me. She's got no job experience, no education. Dropped out of high school. She tried a waitressing job. We couldn't even afford the cheap motel on her salary. And she's...doing her crazy shit... Doing it for me. Determined like hell to get me into college. Crazy-ass dream. She's never gonna make the bank. No matter how many guys she..."

This time Gavin let the tears flow. Leon forced a hand onto Gavin's shoulder. Squeezed. Kept it there until Gavin ran dry.

"No matter what your mother does, Gavin...she does it for you."

"Yeah, but I don't want her to..."

Leon let go, shook his hand as if it burned, working the coldness back into it. "I know you don't. And if you want it enough...to get into college...you'll make it somehow. I did. And I had nothing."

"Really?"

"Yep. You know there're scholarships and—"

"Whatever. They're not gonna give me a scholarship. I get good grades but I'm not exceptional."

"Says who?"

"I'm realistic. My dad forced me to grow up fast. As soon as I'm outta' high school, I'm going to work. To help Mom out. Get her away from her...crap."

"You'll make it into college, Gavin. You will." As Leon spun his hollow promise, he could see Gavin didn't buy into it. Not one bit.

Leon couldn't dive any deeper, though, way too emotional. He needed to bail. He slapped sand from his hands, his work there finished and stood. "Gavin, I gotta' go. Keep your chin up, alright? Things have a way of working out. You'll see."

"Whatever." Gavin's smile faded. "Later."

"'Bye." As Leon ran, he called out, "Put on more sunscreen."

Gavin didn't respond.

Leon jogged back toward his shirt and towel, cursing himself. Just like last year, he'd opened the door again to "involvement." Something more frightening than his father, more worrisome than LMI. At least all they might do is kill him.

The neon yellow post-it note stood out on Leon's door like a flag down on a football field.

He raced toward the door, apprehension building. His hand shook as he snagged the note.

Sorry I missed you! Been thinking about you a lot. Detective Keats

She'd flourished the note with a big smiley face, cute little wink on top.

Damn.

He'd have to deal with it later, though. Now he had an important date to make.

Crumpling up the note, he tucked it into his pocket. He'd look for a recycling bin on the way to the *Seashell* restaurant. Maybe doing his part in keeping the world green would negate some of his other sins.

Couldn't hurt.

Chapter Six

Perched on a stool in the *Seashell*, Leon's nerves jangled like a caffeinated timpanist. Per his usual cautious custom, he showed up early. Checking out the lay of the land. With his back against the wall—in both senses—he watched the front door. He sat close to the rear exit. Just like numerous thriller films, the way out was through the kitchen. Just about the only thing movies ever got right regarding his line of work.

Peanut shells scattered the bare-wood floor, plucked and discarded from a large oak barrel by the front door. A tip of the hat to rusticness, he supposed. Instead the sloppiness seemed somewhat appetite killing. Not that he had much of one any way.

Located fifteen miles away, the restaurant was well outside of his jogging radius. Or ability. He'd parked the pickup blocks away, stashed in the middle of a crowded business parking lot. LMI knew what the truck looked like and he didn't necessarily want Albert finding out what he drove. New transportation climbed to the top of his agenda.

He'd managed to keep the waitress at bay for a while, nursing an iced tea. Couldn't last forever. Albert needed to hurry the hell up. The longer Leon waited, the deeper paranoia staked its claim. Albert could be setting him up, secretly working with LMI. Frankly Leon just wanted to get the show on the road, his curtain call or not.

The vibration in his pocket made him jump. A text message: *Leave cash now. Come outside. A.*

Leon peeked out the restaurant spanning front window. Saw nothing. He slid off the stool, plopped down five bucks and stepped out onto the sidewalk.

He half expected a car to come roaring up; men exiting with guns, forcing him inside. Instead a red Chevy Malibu hybrid crept up, idling. When it finally stopped, he heard the transmission clunk. The window rolled down slowly, the way Albert did everything.

Albert's mild-mannered, clerkish face poked out the window. "Get in if you want to live. That joke never gets old." A high-pitched shriek of laughter supplied the drum lick. "Hello, Mr. Garber. Do get in, please."

Leon slid in and may as well have slipped into a time warp. Inside, the car remained as identical and spotless as it had last year.

"I do so hate texting," said Albert. "I've been told my phone's a dinosaur. Tap-tap-tap, space, repeat. But, alas, it's the favored way of communicating these days." Albert pinched his lips in a tight bow. "I see you didn't bring the laptop."

"No."

"Is it safe?"

"Yes." *Not really.* Leon had tucked the computer beneath his pillow, hung the *Do Not Disturb* sign on his room's door. Not that the motel even employed a maid. But it was dangerous scattering things too widely, best to keep the computer close. The crucial element that might win the war. "I'll give it to you soon."

"That *wasn't* part of our deal, Mr. Garber." With force, Albert chocked the gear into drive. After checking all mirrors repeatedly, he moved into the traffic.

"Albert, we don't *have* a deal. You told me you want the computer. Nothing was offered in return. I haven't been out of the corporate sector so long I've forgotten how commerce works."

"I see. Fair trade. How about this? You said you want protection, asked for shelter… Deliver the computer and we'll offer you safe harbor."

Before last night's events, Leon would've jumped at the chance. Now, dangerous or not, he had reason to stay put at his motel. *Raymond.* "Not yet. Maybe later."

In a rare move, Albert swung his gaze from the road to

Leon. "'Not yet'? I thought that's what you desperately needed, Mr...may we dispense with formalities? May I call you Leon?" His entire face lit up when he smiled, little "Mr. Sunshine."

"Call me what you want. It's not like you've ever divulged your last name." And apparently still not forthcoming. Albert just offered a reconciliatory nod. But if Albert wanted to play, Leon was happy to toss the ball back to him. "As I said, you'll get the computer later. Now how about telling me what's going on? I mean, I know your goal is to take down LMI...but how? I want answers."

"All good things come with time, Leon."

"Yeah, so I've heard, never experienced. But if I'm putting my life on the line, I need you to *level* with me. Where? When? *What?*" Albert's grin failed to disarm Leon. Instead, tension locked and loaded as surely as if Albert held Leon at gunpoint. "Give me *something.*"

"I believe that's best saved when you meet the rest of our team. Not too much longer now." Their conversation ended, Albert tapped on his stereo. A cassette player. Big band music, everything about Albert pretty old-fashioned. Except, of course, his predilection for murdering innocent people.

Farther down the road, buildings aged, a time lapse photographic effect. Gentrification swept into dilapidation. Palm trees struggled to thrive as if understanding the neighborhood's poisonous nature. Discarded cups and wadded up hamburger wrappers rolled like tumbleweeds. It reminded Leon of some of the shabbier locales in Kansas: full of cold, sterile one-level buildings.

Albert flipped the left-turn signal up. The car's metronome ticked away long seconds until Albert finally deemed it safe to turn. A large parking lot separated *Kearney's Body Shop* from the road. Nearly deserted, only one beaten down Chevrolet occupied a space in front of the building. Albert drove around back. Leon heard loud whizzes, hydraulic pumps, clanking tools; a body shop symphony. Much too lively sounding for the business "Mr. Kearney" appeared to be lacking.

Albert finagled his car into a tight spot. The automobiles next to them originated from deep pockets, a Mercedes and a foreign sports car amongst them. *Very* out of place.

At the garage door, Albert tapped out an exacting pattern. An electronic pulley rolled the door up and it clattered to a stop. Leon squinted, adjusting his eyes to the garage's dark interior. Yet the sound of invisible mechanics working continued. "Sorry for the noise pollution, Leon." Scuttling toward a workbench, Albert adjusted a knob on the wall. The sound lowered. A recording. *Overkill.* Then again, maybe not. "One can't be too careful these days," Albert said with a small grin. Another button lowered the door behind them. The overwhelming smell of rubber tires and oil permeated the garage. Cutting a path through the darkness, Albert led Leon to a door. Dim light bled through the rippled glass.

When Albert opened the door, the sudden brightness dazzled Leon. At the end of the long narrow room, several people sat around a table staring at Leon.

Next to Leon, a voice shrieked. A familiar voice Leon thought he'd never hear again. "Leon, my friend! How good to *see* you!" The little person, Gustav. Wealthy European immigrant and serial killer. "I'm so *ecstatic* you survived that nasty little business last year!"

While Gustav disturbed Leon—his actions, his joyous attitude toward his work—he had to admit he welcomed the small man's presence. Someone who actually liked Leon, someone who'd helped him last year. A frightening yet friendly face in the crowd.

Leon leaned down, offered his hand. Gustav bypassed the gesture, let his arms fly wide and launched into a hug. Cutting the embrace short, Leon said, "Nice to see you too, Gustav."

Stepping out of the shadows—her favorite place to lurk—Gustav's girlfriend, Delilah, jut out her hand. Together, Gus and Delilah comprised the "Good Samaritan Killer" team, even though law enforcement considered their work that of one entity. Their M.O. consisted of Gustav dressing as a baby. Delilah would swaddle him in a blanket, carry him down rarely traveled roads until an unwitting driver—a "Good Samaritan"—stopped to pick her up. Gustav always sealed the deal with a knife. And Leon would never forget the pleasure Gustav shared in relating his hobby.

When he accepted Delilah's hand, Leon had forgotten her strength. With a powerful grip, she shook several times, ended contact. The way Leon preferred it, quick and out. Leon noticed her features hadn't changed, she hadn't grown taller. *Good.* Maybe she was older than Leon had first guessed, already fully grown when they'd met. Hard to tell really. Beneath the teenage goth makeup, she remained elusive, a mystery served up only to Gustav.

She broke a wide smile, unusual for her. "How's it goin', Leon?"

Leon shrugged. Social niceties of lying about your welfare just didn't seem to apply. "I'm alive. Good to see you again, Delilah."

She smirked, once again reminding Leon of a teenager. He'd rather not dwell on it.

"Leon, Leon, Leon, *come!*" Gustav clapped his hands in magnanimous fashion. "We absolutely *must* catch up. Tell me everything about yourself. What you've been doing, how you managed to destroy LMI's Los Angeles headquarters, everything about—"

"I'm sorry, Gustav," Albert interjected, "but we really must get down to business." He shot Gustav sad puppy-dog eyes, hanging jowls to match. "Plenty of time for pleasantries later."

Leon didn't think he'd be staying for "happy hour," though. The more he associated with these people—these serial killers— the more he worried about himself. Their insanity could rub off on him, a contagious mental disease. At least that's what he told himself. But in all honesty, Leon questioned if he might be one of them already.

Gustav tugged at Leon's wrist. "Come, come, you *must* sit by us." Conspiratorially, Gus leaned in, whispered in a voice everyone could hear, "I'll catch you up to the speed."

Delilah shot Leon a look, loving amusement over Gustav's slaughter of English slang.

But Gustav's presence struck Leon as odd. "Gustav, why are you here? I thought you were happy with LMI."

Gus' tailored suit jacket pitched up at the shoulders. "What can I say, Leon? Delilah swayed me to her side of politics. Isn't that right, dear?" She nodded. "LMI became much too right-wing for my newly awakened sensibilities. Viva the *revolucion!*"

Gustav played everything as a game, a grand party. Despite his diminutive size, his larger than life persona projected the vitality of several men. Leon bet he always slept well, able to shrug off every worry. He probably wouldn't remain so happy-go-lucky once he entered the frontlines of battle, though. Fighting for your life's hard to casually dismiss.

Impatient, Albert waved his hands. "We really must get started. Time is everything. Please have a seat."

As Leon approached the table, the others sat in sulky silence, defensive with folded arms. If Gustav played the host of the soiree, the rest of them looked like party goers who'd rather be anywhere else. Gustav dragged out a chair, the legs scraping across the floor. With a formal bow, he gestured for Leon to sit. Delilah plopped down next to Leon, waiting with open arms. Gustav crawled into his love seat.

At the end of the table, Albert said, "Introductions are in order, ladies and gentlemen. You all know me. And, of course, you've heard of the, ah, accomplishments of Leon Garber." Leon cringed upon hearing his real name. The fewer people who knew it, the better off everyone would be. Albert appeared to be waiting for applause that wasn't forthcoming. His enthusiasm dropped along with his smile. "Yes, well…Leon, sitting across from you is Teddy."

A stick of a man, Teddy jerked his head with bird-like movements. He'd pop up a shoulder, tilt his head as if to hear better. Briefly he looked at Leon, then his contemplation fell to his navel. Clearly lacking self-confidence. His appearance didn't help matters, a computer geek stereotype. Oil drenched his slick, black hair. His shirt, buttoned to the top, choked his constantly bobbing Adam's apple. As if lacking a spine, he slithered around in his chair, melting into the contours.

Gustav leaned over, cupped a hand, and whispered into Leon's ear. "Don't be fooled by how Teddy looks. He was one of the lucky ones during the dot-com boom. Made his fortune, then got out at the right time before everything went head's up. Oh, he's also the 'Doberman Pincher'."

Nausea swelled in Leon's stomach. It stunned Leon that Gustav didn't lead with Teddy's alias, a pretty important fact.

Last year, the "Doberman Pincher"—a particularly nasty serial killer—brought terror to Detroit. After every kill, the Pincher sent letters to the media. Baiting them. Eventually signing them as the "Doberman Pincher."

Very proud of his grotesque atrocities, an appropriate nom de plume. Before the Pincher stabbed his victims to death, he bit them in various places. Repeatedly. Teeth marks and bruises were left behind, his depraved signature. When Leon envisioned Teddy biting into a woman's leg, he looked anywhere but at Teddy.

Teddy emitted a low growl. At first Leon thought he was emulating his canine namesake, but then realized he was clearing his throat. After what seemed like an eternity, the phlegm finally cleared his passageway. "Hello, Leon." Leon nodded, his gaze cemented onto the tabletop. "I understand you have issues with LMI. Me, too. LMI wanted me to quit sending notes to the press. Said I was attracting too much attention. I mean...I'm the one paying their dues! The customer's *always* right. Yet, they told me to *stop*. Can you imagine?" Leon tried not to. Teddy's voice rose. So did his hands, waving about with acrobatic ire. "It was good enough for Jack the Ripper, wasn't it? What about the Zodiac Killer? How about—"

"Mmm. Yes, well...let's do try to stay on point, shall we, Teddy?" Albert patronized him with air-tapping hands. Just in time, too. Leon'd rather not see Teddy turn over into full-on rabid.

Redness tinted Teddy's ears, flooded his cheeks. Humiliated, he hung his head. Gustav just stared at Teddy, shaking his head with dramatic empathy. Delilah, on the other hand, grinned. Clearly, they didn't share Leon's shock, his apprehension at being in the company of this man.

Albert waited a moment—making sure Teddy's tantrum had finished, no doubt—before moving on. "The gentleman next to Teddy is Robert. Leon meet—"

"*Bobby.*" A gruff voice huffed out from behind a grizzly bear's worth of facial hair.

"Please excuse me. *Bobby*. Leon meet Bobby."

Bobby, wearing a vest over a flannel shirt, stood up abruptly, thwacking his chair against the wall. He stuck out his hand, an "I dare you" look in his eyes. Reluctantly, Leon accepted it. Bobby grinned, crushed Leon's hand, then sat back down. Leon suspected both Bobby and Teddy would be vying for "pack leader" status.

"Pleasure," Bobby grumbled.

Gustav continued his entirely too loud commentary. "Bobby's the 'I-35 Vampire'. No one's certain where his money comes from, but he has it. *Insane,* yes? After all, he *is* a truck driver!"

Leon sized Bobby up and there was a lot of sizing up to do. Beneath Bobby's John Deere cap, a wreath of hair encircled his head, all the lumberjack oranges and reds of autumn. From his lips, a toothpick defied gravity, rolling back and forth. He tossed back massive arms, interlocking fingers behind his neck. Appraising Leon with a smirk: *He's not all that.*

Again, Leon knew about the I-35 killer. Pays to keep up on the competition, his peers. Mainly so he could avoid them. But unlike Teddy, Bobby looked exactly how Leon imagined the I-35 Vampire would look. His alias said it all, succinct and to the point. The unknown killer drove up and down the long stretch of I-35, state to state, truck stop to truck stop. Picking up hitchhikers, snatching people from parking lots. Then he'd leave their blood drained corpses at rest-stops—generally in bathrooms—down the road. His methods baffled the police. Blood was never found around the corpse, on their clothing. And based on the mileage covered, the law surmised the blood draining occurred while on the road, the only timeline that possibly worked. They just didn't know how.

But some things are best left unknown. Besides, curiosity didn't do too much for the proverbial cat. And Leon certainly didn't have nine lives to squander.

"Heard about your beef with LMI," said Bobby. He tipped his chair back, his booted toes acting as the front legs. "Got my own problems with them a-holes." He tipped his hat to Delilah and the other woman at the table. Exposed a tobacco-stained smile. "Pardon my French, ladies." Delilah rolled her eyes. The other woman sat still, partially hidden in shadows. "LMI done tole me to quit goin' state-to-state. Tole me to settle. Can't do that. I reckon I got a travellin' spirit in me. I tole 'em as much. They threatened me. Said if I didn't toe the line, they'd pursue other options. Readin' between the lines, they was aimin' to put a bullet between my eyes." He poked his index finger between red eyebrows, brought the thumb hammer down. "*Bam!*" Teddy jumped. Bobby's chair came down, his fist following on the table. "*Nobody* threatens Bobby Muller! *Nobody!*"

He carried the weight, the stage presence, the over-the-top acting skills of a television wrestler. A lot of big talk, told in an even bigger voice. Still, Leon imagined he had the strength to back up his intimidation. He certainly didn't intend to challenge the I-35 Vampire.

"I'll *get* those bastards! They made me go on the *run*! *Nobody* makes Bobby Muller go—"

Purple fingernails flew to Delilah's lips, barely covering a snort.

Albert shook his head, complete with a magnificent eye roll. "My, we're certainly a volatile bunch this afternoon, aren't we? Finally, Leon, meet Nanette." Silence dropped—even Bobby chopped off his violent diatribe—as all eyes turned toward the woman owning the corner of the room.

She leaned forward. A hanging lamp highlighted Nanette's delicately fragile features. An almost imperceptible smile—a Mona Lisa smile—proved unreadable.

With gusto, Gustav whispered, "I don't know much about Nanette. Just what I hear on the olive vine. But do not underestimate her, Leon. Her count is *extraordinary*." Leon knew exactly what kind of "count" Gustav referred to. "Somewhat of a black widow killer, I suppose, she targets men from all walks of life. Using various methods, of course. Law enforcement doesn't know she exists. She's a *marvelous* ghost!" Gustav slapped his hands together. Nanette looked at the small man, unnerving in her lack of emotion. Leon really wished Gustav would stop his commentary. Like an over-excited child, he couldn't manage his "in-door voice."

Nanette turned back to Leon. "Hello."

"Hi."

Blue eyes—so blue they almost had no tint—swam behind face-hiding-black-rimmed glasses. Inquisitive eyes, intently studying Leon. Strong, high cheekbones held her glasses in place. Lipstick free and fairly colorless, her lips formed a small heart, a bloodless pout. A bun of blonde hair pulled tightly at her scalp, almost as tight as the personality she projected.

Nanette could've passed for a dowdy librarian. Intentionally so, thought Leon. Within her frumpy cocoon, an alluring butterfly waited to take flight. Her method of staying in the background. Smart. And deadly.

Enthralled, completely intrigued, Leon's mind drifted to places better not visited. To send them packing, he dug fingernails into his palm.

Still, Nanette stared at him. Out of the corner of his eye, Leon saw—more like felt—Delilah grinning. A flash of black leather, her elbow jabbing into Gustav. The lovebirds possibly already planning a double-date.

They'd be disappointed. Never again. Leon had come too heart-wrenchingly close to Rachel last year.

Finally, Nanette let Leon off the hook and included everyone in her sweeping gaze. "I also have my reasons for leaving LMI." That's all she said. Another thing to admire about the woman. No explanation, no bragging rights. Keep your mind on business.

"Very well, Nanette." Albert gave her a smile, almost a paternal one. "We're waiting on one other to—"

Outside the room, Leon heard the garage door grinding up. Then it came down with slow, mechanical inevitability. Tension tightened inside Leon's chest.

"Ah! That would be him now." Albert flattened his hands on the table. His lips trembled through a smile. Slowly, his command of the room leaked away.

For whatever reason (no, reason had nothing to do with it; call it gut instinct), Leon knew the worst was yet to come.

If these gathered lunatics couldn't faze Albert, what sort of person could?

Inside the garage now, a methodically paced *tic-tic-tac* of footsteps echoed. Unhurried, ambling.

The door opened. A tall, lean man stopped briefly in the doorframe as if posing for a photo. Moving with cat-like agility, he fluidly strolled into the room. Head up, eyes straight ahead. Ignoring everyone.

Dressed in a clearly tailored overcoat, he moved very deliberately. Even though the coat looked like overkill for the Miami weather, sweat seemed to be an alien concept to him. Gaunt, yet old-world handsome, his eyebrows pinched down over deep-set eyes. He pinched an expensive—no doubt handmade—leather glove off one hand, finger by finger. Painstakingly repeated the process with his other hand. Wing-tipped—handcrafted?—shoes chocked out even steps. Robotically, he lifted a hand to his fedora, took it off. His slick, black hair appeared unruffled, unbothered by the constraints of a hat. A very slow grin unveiled alabaster white teeth. Teeth long and straight, vicious and hungry. A shark-worthy smile.

Beneath his other arm, he clutched a shoebox to his chest.

He held thrall over the occupants of the room. Gustav gasped loudly. Then chugged out a locomotive's worth of whispers into Leon's ear.

"I can't believe my eyes! It's the 'Man with the Shoebox'! Personally, I'd always thought of him as a lone badger, not a company LMI gentleman. Never, in all my days, did I expect to meet him! Why, Leon, he's absolutely *legendary!*"

The Man with the Shoebox. Gustav wasn't far off the mark regarding his legendary status. Working in the field for close to twenty years, he remained one of the FBI's most wanted criminals, baffling multiple task forces. And he had the strangest work peculiarities. Saying a lot considering everyone else in the room. A true mystery, he gained entrance into his victims' homes, never leaving signs of forced entry. Like a shadow in the night, he'd slip away, never spotted by anyone, invisible to cameras. One flustered detective was infamously quoted as saying, "Shoebox *has* no DNA." Shortly after that, the cop retired. Gone fishing or fired. But the oddest thing was how Shoebox's victims always appeared peaceful in death, some even beatifically smiling. Except for the fact their feet were cut off. Nice, precise, medically thorough dismemberments. And, every time, at the end of the bed, the killer left behind a shoebox like a demented Santa Claus. Now Leon understood why the other killers were humbled before him. Or too afraid to say anything. Look him in the eye, you might turn to stone.

The Man with the Shoebox stood before the seated killers, studying them in turn.

Gustav continued. "Rumor has it, he's *fabulously* rich. Beyond the wildest imaginations. Even has a private jet plane. No one knows where his money comes from either. A true gentleman, by all accounts."

A gentleman who cuts off innocent people's feet. Solid judgment tossed to the curb, morbid curiosity claimed Leon. He whispered to Gustav, "What's in the shoebox?"

Gustav's eyes grew round, his mouth followed suit. "No one knows, my friend. No one knows."

Even Albert put his impatience on hold while the newcomer settled in. Carefully, the Man with the Shoebox set his fedora, then his shoebox onto the table. He slipped off his overcoat, folded it, minding the creases, and draped it over the back of his chair. When he sat, the chair apparently knew not to make a sound, reverent in its silence. Remarkably, his three piece suit didn't wrinkle. He grinned at his shoebox, then nudged it an inch, frowned. A finger tapped his lips. He scooted the shoebox back to its original position, again unhappy with the results. With a knuckle, he inched it, pushed it again. And smiled again. A leg crossed over another, his hands folded in his lap. "Ladies. Gentlemen. Hello. I'm Bartholomew. It's very much my pleasure to meet with you toward our common goal."

An evenly measured voice; erudite, quietly demanding, enunciation that comes from good breeding and even greater money.

"Let's get started, shall we?" Bartholomew turned toward Albert, nodded, signifying he was ready.

Clearly flummoxed, Albert had forgotten where he'd left off. He stammered before finding his reedy voice. "Very good."

Leon didn't blame Albert, not really. Nothing could compare

to the Royalty that had just breezed in. Even if he was a foot-chopping King, more terrifying than anyone else in the room.

Albert unfolded a laptop, set up a projector box next to it. He snapped his fingers at a day-dreaming Teddy. Perhaps the only one Albert felt comfortable barking orders to. "Teddy, would you please get the lights?"

Startled, Teddy looked around. Self-conscious of every move, he backed out of his chair. On his way to the light switch, he looked back as if ensuring he wasn't the butt of some cruel joke. Leon imagined he'd had a terrible high school tenure.

The lights dimmed. With clicker in hand, Albert turned on the projector. A rectangle of white blinded Albert until he moved out of its range. A couple of clicks, several blank images, then a pie-chart materialized on the wall. Albert had gone to town with his PowerPoint presentation.

"Ladies and gentlemen, as Bartholomew so eloquently stated, our mutual goal is to correct the wrongs that LMI has perpetuated on us. The pie-chart to my right...ah, that'd be stage right...shows the odds we're currently facing. As you can see..." He pointed to a needle thin slice of charted pie. "...we're in the minority. Those of us in the room represent a little over one percent of LMI's otherwise misguidedly happy clientele. But our numbers are growing. Already I'm hearing of—"

After a loud guffaw, Bobby said, "Hell's bells, the only pie I got any use for is..." He paused, clearly remembering there were women present. Redirected course toward less choppy waters. "...um, my momma's apple pie. What's all this shit, Al? I want *action*! Not charts! This ain't school! You know what they *did* to me, those bastards? *They—*"

Leon didn't see it happen. But once Bobby suddenly stopped barking, he saw the reason why. Bartholomew held two of Bobby's fingers, pinching them back at an angle. Bobby's eyes were shut, his mouth screwed into a figure eight of agony.

"Bobby, you're being extremely rude," said Bartholomew. "Let's let Albert finish his presentation." He smiled at Albert. "After all, it looks like he put so much time into it."

With his free hand, Bobby pounded the wall behind him, the way wrestlers do on the mat. It seemed odd Bobby, after all his bluster, didn't fight back. But, Leon knew all too well, looks can be deceiving.

"Alright, alright, dammit! Just havin' a little fun. Jesus, let up!"

Bartholomew released his grip. Caressing his fingers, Bobby settled into a funk. Frankly, it astonished Leon that Shoebox could intimidate, let alone overpower, the bigger man. Something he stashed away in his mental danger files.

Mortified, Albert hurried through several more charts of various styles. The wall locked onto another block of light. "*Fine.* We'll move this along. For various reasons—ah, ones we've already covered in depth…" He shot a stern look Bobby's way. "…we've gathered to formulate a strategy to take down LMI. It simply has to be done. Not only are they impeding our rights, but they're stealing from us. All to their own personal ends."

"Albert, how exactly are we going to achieve this?" asked Teddy. "We're not much of an army."

"Good question." Teddy beamed, proud of his verbal gold star. "I know for a fact, more of LMI's constituents are growing disgruntled. From such small beginnings…" He opened his hands to the room. "…armies can be built. And we have several top-notch…let's call them 'secret weapons' at our disposal. Bartholomew has donated all of his resources to our cause."

Ah, Leon thought, *money.* Still it couldn't hurt. LMI certainly had extremely deep pockets.

"And Mr. Garber is in possession of the late Mr. Wyngarden's laptop. Which could prove *immensely* rewarding and revealing with the information it contains." This time Albert's sour puss snagged Leon.

"'Could?'" said Nanette.

"Excuse me?"

"Albert, you said, 'could.' I take that to mean so far the computer's yielded nothing valuable."

"Well, ah, yes, that's true, I'm afraid."

"Why?" A woman of few words, Nanette still made each word count.

"Hmm. Oh, yes, well, simply put, we haven't been able

to break through the security." Which told Leon Albert was lying to his own troops. What the top military brass do to their grunts. Sighs and murmurs of discontent flowed through the room. "But we're *working* on it. Soon, my friends, soon." Albert aimed empathetic nods to everyone in the room. Except Leon. Hard to miss.

Albert reacquainted himself with his security clicker and pulled up a grinning photo of an aging man. Well built, full white hair. Hard lines riding his face. Cop badge pinned to his belt, proudly displayed like a Texas-sized belt buckle.

"Meet August Schroeder. Augie. Until now, presumed dead. At least that's LMI's take on his, ah, current condition. And it's my belief they still believe him dead. But he's not. Recently, I found his whereabouts. Living under an alias. Right here in Miami."

"Dead or alive, what the hell we want with a cop?" Bobby had reclaimed his manhood, bulling his way back into the conversation.

"Not just a policeman, Bobby. Augie was a well-respected beat cop, then detective. Received his pension with highest honors." Albert looked around, waited a few beats. Building to a crescendo although Leon'd already guessed the final note. "He's also the first LMI member to be black marked." Again, Albert waited for dramatic gasps. "That's correct, ladies and gentlemen. During his proud years as an upstanding law enforcement officer, he was also known as 'The New York Vigilante'. He doled out his particular brand of enforcement— with an unmarked gun—on criminals who evaded the judicial system."

Finally, someone with a motive Leon could get behind.

"Not only did he successfully evade the FBI and other law enforcement divisions, he escaped the wide net of LMI. They wanted him dead. For some reason—maybe LMI just gave up, believing he'd died a natural death—LMI no longer considers him a threat. A *living* threat. But he very much is. And that's why we need him."

"What exactly was he black-marked for, Albert?" asked Bartholomew.

"We don't know." Every time the news was good, Albert claimed it. When not so good, he brought up the ubiquitous "we." Leon wondered if there actually was a "we." Or just another of Albert's shams. "But, as I said, I've located him and the information he holds could prove the downfall of—"

"Like Wyngarden's laptop?" Nanette directed the question toward Albert. But her eyes locked onto Leon. Tapping her fingers; one-two-three-boom. *Gotcha.*

"Yes, Nanette. But soon, very soon, we'll contact him. If he's willing to help, excellent. If not…we'll simply have to take him." And Leon bet Albert wouldn't be participating in any of the taking.

Once again, Bobby unwisely decided to play devil's advocate. "That's your big damn plan, Al? I traveled all the way down to this miserably hot hole to hear you wanna' talk to a cop? Some retired, snowbird, son-of—"

Bartholomew cleared his throat, all it took to stop Bobby.

Albert's chin seemed to withdraw into his neck a little bit. "What else would you be doing now, Bobby? LMI's *after* you. Without our help, I imagine you'd already be *dead*."

Bobby shrugged.

"Okay, that about wraps up our business for today, ladies and gentlemen. I'll be in touch soon with—"

"Wait. That's it?" said Leon, breaking his silence. He'd never been much for public speaking. "Nothing's been accomplished! You called us out here…gave us a half-plotted idea of a plan. Then send us on our way?" Across the table, Bartholomew grimaced at Leon.

Gustav slapped Leon's back. "Why, Leon, my friend! We can now go out for coffee—"

"Why don't we do something *now*? We're all here. It's *unsafe* continuing to meet. With everything going on."

Behind tented hands, Bartholomew sighed. "Albert, perhaps Leon has a point. Meeting often is risky."

Thank God.

Albert raised his voice, throttled his fist like a hammer. "That's *exactly* right. *Everything's* risky! I, for one, don't want to spend the *rest* of my life behind bars. Or *worse*." Everyone seemed to agree on this point, confirmations all around. Solidarity in survival. "You better *believe* LMI's looking for every one of us! Not to mention law enforcement! One mistake—one small drop of DNA, one wrong word—it could be over. For all of us." For the first time, Leon saw strength in Albert's leadership abilities. Rallying the troops. Giving them something to fight for: their lives. "The plan's in motion. Believe me. If I'm *vague*, tight-lipped, I'm sorry, but it's *intentionally* so! Out of necessity, we'll move at the last moment. And the less you know about the plan, the better off you'll be. Just in case LMI catches up to *any* of you." He tossed finger darts at everyone. "I need to check on a few last details. See where LMI is—"

Delilah asked, "Albert, how do you know anything about 'where' LMI is?"

"Because...because, Delilah, I have an inside contact. Who must remain anonymous. I think you all understand the necessity of that."

Leon did. And he had a strong idea who that insider might be.

"But even his hands are tied as to how much information he can slip out. Or that he actually knows," continued Albert. "We don't really know where to—"

"Rasmussen."

Albert's eyes grew wide. "Excuse me, Leon?"

"Rasmussen. That's where we need to start. He's LMI's top dog, their leader."

"How do you know this?"

"We got the name out of Wyngarden before he... I'm sure of it. He's the leader. We get to him, we cut off LMI at the knees."

"Splendid, splendid..." Albert entwined his fingers. "I've heard the name volleyed about, heard rumors, but have never had anything substantiated. And where might this 'Rasmussen' be found, Leon?"

"Dunno. That's up to you and your mole. I've looked. Man's a ghost, doesn't want to be found. Doesn't even want to be photographed. He's why I was black-marked in the first place.

I had a couple photos of him in my possession. Wouldn't have thought twice about them, either, if he hadn't started showering love onto me. Do something, Albert. Find him…then we can end this."

Leon looked around, studying his comrades. His stomach swelled with nausea again. "I've…I've gotta' go. Get some fresh air."

He didn't belong here. Not with these maniacs, monsters, serial killers. What bonded them together? They were mad at LMI for throwing a wrinkle into their "hobbies." And, from what Leon could tell, none of them had a good reason to rid the world of people. *Good* people. He didn't belong, didn't *want* to belong. Didn't want to be categorized as one of them.

He wasn't that bad. *Was he?*

A small part of him, his hen-pecking subconscious, said, *yes, Leon, yes you are.*

He jumped to his feet, dizzy. Ready to escape. The walls had other ideas. They dipped, shadows swooping in, wrenching him down, down, down. As he zagged toward the door, Albert called out, "I'll be in touch within two days. With all of you. This I promise. Um, Leon? You need a ride?"

A stomach full of vomit was his answer. Clearing his mouth with his sleeve, Leon fought his way through the dark garage, trying to stay ahead of everyone. He opened the garage door and felt like he'd stumbled through the gates of hell. Fiery sunshine baked him, lashed at him with rays sharp as pitchforks.

Blinded, he toppled. The last thing he remembered? *Dust tastes terrible, cement feels even worse.*

Chapter Seven

Jumbled voices overlapped. Leon pried his eyes open.

"There you are, Leon! You gave us all quite a fear, I'm afraid," said Gustav.

Sprawled out in the passenger seat of a car, Leon shook himself fully awake. Nanette sat behind the steering wheel. Amusement swirled within her blue eyes. Gustav stood outside the car, Delilah hunkered down behind him.

Fire ravaged Leon's throat. "I'm alright." But he didn't *sound* alright, his voice sludgy.

"Nanette, are you certain Delilah and I can't take our friend Leon back to his automobile?" Gustav patted Leon's knee. "We would be delighted to do so."

Nanette hitched up a corner of her mouth. "He's in my car. No sense moving him again."

"Don't need a ride." Leon dropped a foot out the door. Quick as a whip, Gustav shot out a hand, levering Leon back into the seat.

"You're not going anywhere right now, my friend. The lovely Nanette will escort you. When you're feeling more over the weather, you give us a call." He whisked a business card into Leon's shirt pocket, tapped it. "But now you're in *very* good hands."

"Come on, Gus, leave 'em alone," said Delilah. "Later, Leon, Nanette."

"Yes, farewell for now, friends." After a gallant bow, Gustav reached his arms up toward Delilah. She lifted him and scooted across the parking lot, her Doc Martin's kicking up a cloud of gravel dust.

A little humiliated and a whole lot mortified, Leon attempted another escape.

"Whoa, whoa." Nanette gripped his arm. "You're not going anywhere. You're in no shape. Just get in, accept a helping hand."

When Leon looked down, the ground moved, shifting like a teeter-totter. The horrible taste of gravel came back to him. Resigned, he closed the door. Welcomed the cool vinyl of the seats, the rejuvenating air conditioning. "Fine. Thank you. Which way're you going?"

"Where'd you park?"

"About twelve miles or so down the main drag."

"Then that's where I'm going." She dropped the gear down.

"Sure know how to make an exit, Leon." Another slim smile, economically inexpressive. She dropped her glasses into a cup holder and replaced them with slender sunglasses. "Don't think the others knew what to make of your getting sick."

"Always leave 'em wanting more."

"That's one way of looking at it, I guess. Anyway, after you took a nose dive in the parking lot, Delilah and Gustav helped you into my car."

"Thanks."

"Little guy's stronger than he looks. But the real surprise was Delilah. Girl's got abs. Practically did all of the heavy lifting."

"Guess she gets a good workout carting her boy-friend everywhere."

"That would do it. So, tell me, Leon...why *did* you get sick?"

Leon couldn't very well tell her he threw up because of the company in the room, Nanette included. Yet she seemed different. Possibly more understanding, maybe more compassionate. A little more human. He caught himself, realized he was projecting. She remained a mystery. Was she trustworthy? *Doubtful.* No matter how much he wanted her to be. "Must've been something I ate at the *Seashell*. You know where that is?" She nodded. "You can drop me there."

"Fine. You don't wanna talk, I get that." She looked at him, her eyes hidden behind her dark glasses. Usually Leon excelled at reading people. But he couldn't get a take on Nanette, a blank book.

"Appreciate that. I assume you value your privacy as well. Everyone else in the room pretty much reveled in their life story."

"Yep, I'm a private gal."

Leon massaged the back of his neck, working out a kink. Back and forth he debated, wondering if he should confide in her, express his concerns. "So, Nanette...I won't ask about your past. I respect that. But...let's talk about now. What do you think about our group? About the reality of tackling LMI? Do we stand a chance? Honest opinion?"

Fingertips rapped the top of the steering wheel. "I'm not sure what I think. *Yet.* How about Albert? You trust him?"

Game playing, feeling him out. Unwilling to commit until he did. Time to volley the ball back into her court. "Don't know him well enough to judge one way or the other. How about you?"

"Same, I guess." *Of course.* "I know I don't trust Bobby. Guy raises more goose bumps than a geese farm. Big time jackass. And Teddy seems like a wild card. Potentially dangerous."

"Yeah, I agree. I'd feel better with someone other than them watching my back." Leon knew, absolutely so, he'd be leading the group into battle. Albert pretty much made that clear last year. But he needed allies, a necessity of wartime. "What about the 'Man with the Shoebox'? You know him?"

"I don't know any of them, Leon. Only what I've heard. Bartholomew's a strange one. 75 percent charm, 25 percent terror." She flashed a lightning quick grin. "My kinda' guy."

"Good luck on that first date. Wear nice shoes." She laughed, brief but contagious.

"So...about this computer of yours..."

Ah. Now we're finally getting to it. "What about it?" Disappointed, Leon gazed out the window. He expected better of Nanette. Now he considered the possibility she might be a plant of Albert's, anything to get at the computer. A very alluring plant, indeed, but one he didn't intend to water.

"What's the deal? I mean...why didn't you bring it?"

"Look, Nanette...it is what it is. You know about the computer. It's not exactly like I'm keeping secrets. It seems like everyone knows *everything* about me. And I don't know you or most of the others. That already puts me at a disadvantage. So I need to keep something for leverage. Maybe keep me alive a while longer. I don't know who to trust. Learned the hard way last year."

"Think I might've heard something about that." She grew fidgety, constantly in motion like she couldn't get comfortable. "Hmm."

"'Hmm,' what?"

"Nothing. Just thinking. Where's the computer now?"

"In a safe place."

"Yeah?" Her eyebrows rose.

"Yes."

As they approached the *Seashell* restaurant, she slowed the car. Then kept on going.

"You passed it."

"I know. You're in no shape to drive. Where're you staying?"

Suddenly, Leon wanted out of the car. Gustav's succinct description of her echoed in his head: *black widow*. "A motel. And the hell I'm not ready to drive. Nanette, pull the car over. Now."

Hesitantly, she wheeled into a taco stand lot, jerked to a stop. "Hey, just tryin' to help a teammate, that's all." She draped an arm over the back of the seat, whipped her glasses off. *The better to seduce you with, my dear.* Her sharp blue eyes cut right through Leon's confidence.

"Appreciate the ride, Nanette." Leon avoided looking at her while he slid out. But like a metal shaving attracted to a magnet, he leaned back into the car. "Really. Thanks for the ride."

White teeth dazzled in her smile. Her eyelashes batted. She pushed back her shoulders ever- so-slightly, accentuating the curves she strove to previously hide. The demure librarian had instantly transformed into a tantalizing seductress. "No problem, Leon. Hope to get to know you better." Her hand lifted from the seat, fingers wiggling. A tilt of the head. She even shot him a bullet hole of a pout, absolutely shameless.

Now Leon knew exactly who she was. "See you soon."

Numb from the day's events, Leon staggered through the

lot. One foot malfunctioned, tripping up the other. He bounced until he righted himself. Embarrassed, he looked back to see if Nanette had seen his near pratfall. She had. Still smiling, now looping a lock of hair around a finger. Wanting to entangle him in her web.

He knew better, but the idea tempted him more than he wanted to admit.

Leon took a long route back to the motel, driving in circles, retracing his tire tracks. When a stoplight turned yellow, he slowed, then, at the last moment, barreled through it. He watched the rearview mirror, looking for a tail. Particularly a Lexus, Nanette's car.

Maybe he was just being paranoid. But Nanette wanted Wyngarden's laptop, the reason why she asked where he was staying.

But what if she had other ideas?

Foolish. Get a hold of yourself.

Still it took an extra hour for Leon to arrive at the motel. There were no new yellow post notes—no new visits from Detective Keats—on his room's door and everything sounded quiet next door. *Good.* He sorely needed some downtime.

After checking the safety of the laptop everyone desired, he sat down at the desk, pen and paper in hand. Corporate accounting had taught him the importance of miniscule details, how to ledger them into columns. Torturous to a point, it was a habit he'd since applied to his life. He listed everyone in Albert's renegade group, scribbling out their weaknesses and strengths. Trying to decide who he could trust. One problem, though. Ordinary human behavior couldn't be applied to the band of killers.

In a strange way, he welcomed the pounding at the door. Expected it even. Detective Keats said she'd be back. He wanted to get her interrogation behind him, one less problem to deal with.

But it wasn't Keats at the door. Someone far worse.

"Hello, boy." Raymond grinned like a barracuda and swam right past Leon. The filthy sheets on Leon's bed didn't deter him; he stretched out onto the bed, cracked knuckles behind his head and crossed his ankles. Brazenly, he said nothing, smiled like he had the world by its tail. Challenging Leon.

"What the *hell* are you doing?" Leon kept his voice low until he closed the door. "This isn't part of the rules. You're *not* supposed to come here—"

"Why, is that any way to treat your old man? And your new neighbor?"

Leon backed up, steadying his legs against the desk. Afraid to take his eyes off the man in his bed. Slowly, Leon scooted the chair out and sat down. "What'd you say?"

"You heard me. I'm your new neighbor." He shut an eye, pointed a finger and lined up Leon's window in his sites. "Right across the way. Room number 242. Ain't you gonna welcome your own kin?"

Don't let him get to you. He's goading you. It's what he wants.

"You *can't* stay here. You're not supposed to come to my room, goddammit. I told you how things are gonna be now. I *told* you—"

Raymond waved his hands in mock surrender. Between splayed fingers, a vicious grey eye peered out. "Just wantin' to get close to my son. Ain't no way to treat your daddy." His tone was as close to playful as Leon'd ever heard. But malice dripped like rotten honey.

"Get the *hell* out. Leave this motel. Even talking to you was a mistake. I should've—"

"Aw, shoulda, woulda, coulda *shit*. What're you gonna do about it? Can't go cryin to your mama, Leon. Not like you used to do."

The mention of his mother—from the cracked lips of the man who stole her life—sent Leon into a spiral. Snapshots of violence flickered through his mind, wishful thinking, his father mashed to a pulp beneath his fists. But he couldn't move, couldn't say a word. He struggled to speak, instead let out a tiny mewl.

"What's that?" Raymond sat up, cupping a hand around his ear. "Speak up, Leon. The ol' hearing ain't what it used to be.

Oh let's cut the crap, son, how 'bout I just call you by your new name. *Chris*. Chris Hampton."

"I don't know what you're—"

"Son, save the shit for someone dumb enough to fall for it. I know damn well you're goin' by a fake name now. Lad down at the office tole me as much. Hell, it was easy. Kid didn't even hold out for a twenty."

Change of plans. Leon had to eliminate his father immediately. He slipped open the desk drawer. Quietly, he rummaged through it, his fingers searching for a weapon, a letter opener. Anything. Because Raymond was lying on top of Leon's weapon of choice: the syringes sandwiched safely between the mattress and box springs.

"Fine. That's the name I registered under. So what?" Leon spread his hands, showing he had nothing-to-hide. "I've got reasons."

Raymond perked up, his eyebrows flying high. "Oh? And what might those reasons be, boy?"

Leon never considered Raymond discovering his alias. He should've known better, stupid of him not to. The bastard always had a way of coming out on top. "None of your business. *Why* are you here?"

"I'm askin' the questions now, boy. Why are *you* here?" Raymond looked around the room, appraising it with a bird's darting view. "Last time I heard, you was doin' really good for yourself. Some big shot accountant or something."

"So?"

"Well, now, how the mighty have fallen!" Raymond roared, swung his legs over the bed. Clapped his hands the way he used to do when listening to the radio in a drunken stupor. "Look at this shithole, boy! Gotta' be a reason you're here. Hiding out. Using a fake name. I wanna know why. And I want cash." His fingers rubbed out an imaginary dollar bill. "Lots of *cash*." He stood tall, straighter than he had before, the smell of money performing miracles on his arthritis.

"If I had money, do you really think I'd be living like this?"

"Already thought about that." *Scitch, scitch, scrutch.* Dirty fingernails scraped at his five o'clock shadow. "You're livin' off the grid, hidin' from someone, I'd reckon. Somethin' big's goin on here, boy. I just know it. Now. You gonna be smart and fess up? Or you gonna make me pay a visit to the local police?"

"You're insane. Always have been. I have *nothing* but this room." Leon knew Raymond wouldn't buy it. Time to try a different angle. "Fine...loan sharks are looking for me. That's it. Lost all my money in bad investments. Tried my hand at gambling. That's—"

"Don't shit a shitter." He backhanded a violent gesture, reminiscent of the many blows he'd delivered to Leon as a child. "Money's around here somewhere. Maybe under the bed." His knees cracked when he dropped to the floor, but he moved fast. On his side, he reached an arm beneath the bed. "Ah! Dumb, boy, real dumb. First place anyone'd look."

Before Raymond dragged the laptop out, Leon charged across the room. He fell on his father's back, tugging at his arms. "Leave it *alone*, damn it!"

The impact of the laptop upside Leon's head made no sound, none he was aware of. Just created a nightscape of stars. He rolled over with a groan, helpless until his vision cleared.

His father towered above him, brandishing the laptop. "You don't jack with your *daddy*, boy! Thought you'd learned that lesson by now!" A boot kicked at Leon's face, the tip splitting his lip. "All this *shit* over a damn computer? What the *hell's* matter with you?"

Leon said nothing, gave Raymond nothing. Stared up at the beast through blurred eyes. Spat a trickle of blood.

"Goddamn computer. *Shit*."

"I told you...I don't have any money." But Raymond was close to finding the briefcase lodged under the mattress. *Too* close. The case containing Leon's cash stash and syringes. "It's just my lap-top. Not worth anything." Leon knew he couldn't over-power the son-of-a-bitch, so he had to outsmart him. Downplay the importance of the computer.

"Goddamn, boy, I knew you was a pussy. But keepin' a diary or some shit? Maybe hidin' gay porn? Startin' a fight over that?" Disgusted, Raymond whipped the computer across the room.

Leon watched it drop to the carpet, inches short of impacting with the wall.

"Guess so."

"Damn, so *stupid*. Same way you always been. But I *know* there's a cash cow somewhere. Just *know* it!" Raymond planted his feet around Leon's waist, then dropped in a squat. Leon didn't flinch, staring directly into the face of madness. And wondered if he shared the same crazed look when he took someone's life. Because that's what it felt like, the end of the road.

Raymond grasped Leon by the armpits, pinching his flesh. Without straining, he hefted Leon up to his feet. A long breath hissed out between his father's clenched teeth. "You tell me what you done. Tell me *right* now or I'll wreck your precious computer, wreck it but good."

"I *told* you the truth. Loan—"

Raymond roared. He twisted, slamming Leon down onto the bed. Leon crossed his arms in front of his face, anticipating a blow. Instead, Raymond forced him over onto his stomach. Pain shot up Leon's spine as his father punched his back. He muffled a scream into the mattress. The bed bounced from more blows, the springs groaning. Leon turned his head, gasping for breath. A hand pressed down on Leon's cheek, burying half his face into the mattress. Raymond climbed onto his son's back, his weight nearly unbearable. Knees locked tight around Leon's arms.

"You *listen* to me, you little shit, and you listen *good!*" A rush of memories cascaded through Leon's mind. He remembered the voice Raymond had used in the past. The same voice as now. "I want the goddamn *truth!*"

Leon struggled. An impotent effort. Pinned down tight, he couldn't uproot Raymond. Probably a move his father learned in prison.

Raymond wrenched Leon's arm behind his back. His breath grew heavier, deeper, the rhythm of violence carrying him away. Thoroughly enjoying the ride.

His father smacked his gums next to Leon's ear. "How 'bout I tell you what I think you done, Leon? You like that?" Sharp bone cut into Leon's shoulder, Raymond's chin. For a minute, Leon thought his father might take a bite out of him, swallow it whole. Just like an animal. Something dead, a foul odor, rolled out of Raymond's mouth. He whispered, "I think you killed someone, boy. Only explanation."

Leon rocked his shoulders, hoping to spark adrenaline. Another twist to his arm put a stop to it. "Ah! Hit a nerve, didn't I, boy? Tell you what, you little piss-ant. You wanted to know about me. What makes me tick. Why I killed your momma. Let's start our little lesson." He yanked up on Leon's arm. "Just wanted to make sure you're awake. First of all, I killed your momma 'cause she was a lying, cheatin' whore. But, fact is, I'm not so sure she was. Think I was just lookin' for a reason to be done with her. Divorce was too expensive and I wasn't about to pay no child support. Not for a little shit like you. But you know what, son? The *best* part? That was when the kitchen knife slid deep inside her. Cutting into her so cleanly, so easily. Like hot butter. *Swish, swish, swish...*"

The sound resonated with Leon, driving him back to the kitchen of his childhood. Hearing, seeing the knife tear his mother apart. While he lay battered and beaten, helpless on the floor. *Again and again and...*

Leon shut his eyes, straining to vanquish the memory. The pain, the memory...his mother's life leaking away, her blood coating him. And the old bastard delighting in it. The *knife...*

Leon envisioned the same knife carving into his father.

"...so much fun. And so easy. Surprised it took me that long to do it. But enough about me. What about you, Leon? You kill somebody? I know you did, feel it in my gut. You look different. Colder, I suppose. The look of a man who's killed. And don't regret it, not a lick. Like me. Like a lotta the fellas in prison." Raymond smashed Leon's face down into the mattress, held it there. Leon kicked, sputtering for breath. His father let up but leaned even closer. "Let's talk about how you *felt* when you killed, boy. Did you feel a rush to the head? All warm and fuzzy, hot tingles fingering your body from head to toe? Better than goddamn sex. And a lot cheaper. Hell, I thought I could fly, lighter than air, take on the world! And you know something, son? It's all about the *power*. Knowin' you can end someone's life like that. And by God if I didn't feel my body, my mind, suckin' up your momma's life energies. Goddamn, it felt *great*!" He released his grip, only for a second, raising his hands in victory. "*Great*! And so damn easy. How 'bout it son? You like killin'? Give you a kick? Admit it boy, go on, tell the truth. Ain't no one here but us Garbers. Like father, like son, a chip off the ol' block. You love to kill. You get a sexy rush outta' it. Turned on, maybe, by the power. Come on, son...you get a hard-on from endin' someone's life? Asking you a question, *boy*!"

His father *knew* him. Described some of the sensations Leon'd experienced. Something he'd never admitted to himself before, tried not to dwell on it.

But he wasn't like Raymond. Refused to turn into him. He wouldn't succumb, physically or mentally.

"*No*!" Anger primed every muscle. With renewed strength, Leon bucked, his back arching up. Raymond rolled off, thumped to the floor. Leon seized the moment. He looped an arm around his father's neck and brought an elbow down onto the back of his head. Raymond countered, bringing a hard-knuckled fist into Leon's ear. Leon dropped. The boot, Raymond's favorite tool of torture, rose over Leon's head. Leon rolled, didn't stop. Raymond's foot came down on the carpet hard. He bobbled as if his ankle caught, then teetered back with arms out. On all fours, Leon scrabbled toward the computer. But his father was faster. The all-too-familiar boot crunched down on Leon's hand. Lightning struck Leon between the eyes. He tried tugging Raymond's leg, couldn't find the strength. With all of his weight on Leon's hand, Raymond swooped down and scooped up the computer, the spoils to the victor.

Raymond stepped off Leon's hand. Not out of compassion; his balance was clearly faltering. "Lissen up, you little bitch. The way you got all pissed told me what I need to know." Leon massaged his hand, lightly kneading for broken bones. But he wouldn't show pain. Never again to Raymond. "You're a killer, boy. I know you feel that itch in your chest. That hollow sensation like when you're needin' a smoke. And nothing satisfies like the real thing. Gotta do it, no other way round it. Got the killer gene in you, boy. Got it from me." For a moment, a far-away look in Raymond's eyes swept him away, a look of fatherly pride. "Tell you what I'm gonna do…I'm gonna hang onto this computer for a while. Since it's so near and dear to your precious little heart. Give you forty-eight hours. Plenty of time to get your ducks in a row. I don't really give two hoots and a holler 'bout what you done, boy. Your business. But you don't meet my needs, I start singin' like that ol' canary in a coalmine. To anyone who'll listen, startin with the cops."

"No you won't. You broke your probation by leaving Wyoming."

"You ain't been listenin', dumbass!" He bent down, hands on knees, in full on mocking mode. "I told you there was a foul-up in my case, something some money-grubbing lawyer found. Case was dropped, time *served*. I got the upper hand, boy, always will." As if to make his point, he joggled the computer above him. "You can never be as strong as me, boy. Or as smart."

"You're a bastard."

"Gonna hurt my feelings. Too bad you can't write about it in your lil' diary. You know what I want."

"How much?"

His shoulder lifted in a casual shrug, a little blackmail between father and son no big deal. "How much you got?" Leon said nothing.

Thwack.

Leon rocked back. The computer swung in Raymond's grip, ready for another strike. Blood trickled down from Leon's forehead. "That one's just to show you never forget your betters, boy. You can't beat me, so don't even try. See you in a couple days. And you want your computer back? No funny shit. I'll be keepin' my eye on you. Remember…live just across the way." He cradled the computer beneath his arm and strolled out, leaving the door open. Leon heard him whistling a jaunty tune, the sound receding until a door slammed across the way.

Welcome to the neighborhood.

Leon sat on the floor. The circulation in his legs crawled to a standstill. He closed his eyes, seeking escape, anywhere but the present.

An ocean draft carried to Leon's room. His sweat cooled, the blood from his lip and head dried, his cuts now tolerable.

But he couldn't stop his painful thoughts. Raymond had forced him to confront his own dwindling identity, an identity he thought he understood, accepted. Now he didn't know who he was. Nothing more than a shadow of his heinous father. He'd learned much more than he'd bargained for.

And now the bastard had the computer.

Outside, something ratcheted along the sidewalk, coming closer. *Chak-chit, chak-chit, chak-chit...* Mechanical, evenly spaced. Wheels.

Backlit by the moon's rays, a figure stepped into the open doorway. With liquid finesse, Leon's visitor kicked his taxi, a skateboard, up into his arms. Gavin.

"Chris? Hey, man, you in there? Your door's open. Chris?"

"Everything's alright, Gavin. No worries. Just lettin' the breeze in."

"You don't sound so good, dude." Gavin stepped in, flipped on the light. "Dude! What the hell happened?"

"Just a little dustup. No broken bones." As Leon tried to stand, he doubted his self-diagnosis. Tender muscles pulled him back down. His hand throbbed, his chest ached, his head burned. Dried blood tightened his forehead, nature's Band-Aid. "Go home, Gavin. Sure your mom's waiting for you."

"Whoa. You're *bleeding*. Hang on, I'll get Mom!" Gavin dashed off. Shouts of excitement rose next door.

Dammit. Leon clawed his way up, pulling at the bed like a cat on drapes. Several stilted moves and he stood straight. Bone on bone ground, pain screaming from body parts that had never hurt before. His bastard father still had the strength of three men.

"Chris?" Like a waitress, Terrie walked in, carrying a small plastic box perched atop her fingers.

"Hey, Terrie. I told Gavin there's nothing to worry about. Just a...family squabble."

"Yeah, right, whatever." Jutting out a hip, she glared at Leon. Behind her, Gavin peeked in, curious, probably looking for grim thrills. Terrie turned, raised her voice. "*Gavin.* Go back inside. Finish your homework."

"Already done."

"I said *go!*"

Gavin didn't talk back. Quiet as a shadow, he flit away. *Smart kid.* Terrie, on the other hand, looked primed to fight. She closed the door, strut toward Leon, snagged his hand and dragged him to the bathroom without saying a word. Turned on the light switch. The fluorescent bulbs waffled, finally took on life. "Sit." She pointed toward the toilet. Leon obeyed. "Let's have a look." Gently, her fingers probed his forehead. As she worked, he studied her mouth. Tiny life-lines drew around her lips, scars of smiles and frowns. Beneath the light, her eyes sparkled, green but angry. "Jesus Christ, Chris." She opened the plastic box, pecked around for a bottle of iodine. Well prepared for living in a combat zone. A cotton swab dabbed at his cut. Impatiently, she sighed. "Hold still, dammit. You're lucky you don't need stitches." A Band-Aid combined with her magical touch diminished the pain.

"Thanks." He avoided her judgmental stare. Clearly she wanted more from him, an explanation.

She leaned back against the sink, one ankle wrapping the other. "Chris, you'd have to be deaf not to have heard the commotion. I know you want your privacy, God knows I'm trying to respect it...but when there's a full-on battle going on next door, I can't turn a blind eye. Had Gavin been home, I woulda' been over sooner. I don't *care* what happened...but look me in the eye and tell me my kid's not in danger. I mean it, Chris. *Say* it!"

Honestly, he didn't think Gavin's life was at risk. Then again LMI had practically torched the entire second floor of his last digs. Still, he couldn't tell her the truth. "No, Terrie, Gavin's not in danger. I just had a scuffle with...a cousin. Mean guy, we've been fighting over money issues since—"

"Seems to me you get in a lot of fights with family members."

So much for her not wanting to dig deeper. "Wouldn't

consider my ex-wife 'family' at this point. And, as for my cousin, well...he started it."

"Really, Chris? *Really*? Even my son's not that immature."

"You should see the other guy." Her lack of amusement told him to derail that particular train. "I'd never do anything to hurt Gavin. He's a great kid. We had a nice talk—"

"Whoa, whoa, *whoa*! You talked with my son? Without my knowing it?"

"Terrie, it's not like I'm a sex offender." *Just a repeat murderer.* "We talked, that's all. He's a really well-adjusted kid. He told me about..." He'd said too much. *Stupid. No involvement.* But lately involvement seemed to orbit him, an inescapable law of nature.

"About what? About...me?" She darted her gaze away. But hardened by life, she pursued the topic. "Did you talk about *me*?" Palms pressed down, she lifted up and sat on the sink, anchoring in. Leon expected a long night ahead.

"Ah, it's really none of my business, but—"

"He knows. Gavin *knows*, doesn't he?" Her heels banged into the empty cabinet, counting down her patience.

"Yeah. He's known for a while."

She said nothing, just tapped her heels into the wood. *Wap, wap ,wap...* Her feet slowed, a mournful drum beat. *Bam... bam...* She dropped her head. Waves of blond hair veiled her face. A sniff, a deep breath, then a cleansing one. "My *God...* what he must *think* of me. He *hates* me, I know he—"

"Terrie...*believe* me, it's not like that." Her vulnerable side caught him off guard. He'd thought her husband had beaten it out of her. Leon struggled to his feet. Gently, he took her hand, guided her down to the toilet.

"Listen. Gavin's a smart kid. He understands. Kids grow up fast, learn the truth the hard way..." Leon paused, carefully considering his words. In over his head, he knew nothing about well-adjusted children. But he couldn't go wrong by emphasizing the positive. "He's bright, Terrie. He knows you're doing...what you do for him. No, he doesn't like it. And he worries about you. But...it is what it is." Words he'd used earlier in a much different context. "He'll make it into college some day. And you—"

"I doubt he will. Not on the money I'm making. And how much longer do you think I can keep it up? It's not like guys want geriatric…" She waved her hand, snorted, unable to label herself.

"You're far from geriatric." Time to bail. Too close, too attached, yank the rip cord. "Anyway…you know Gavin'll be alright. I'm sorry but I've really gotta—"

"Shit. No, I'm sorry. I came over to patch you up, maybe give you hell. Ended up crying on your shoulder. Lame. So damn lame…" She offered a weak but heart-felt smile. Her eyes pleaded for a hug, a touch of humanity, something Leon couldn't deliver.

"You're not lame." Before he knew it, he'd boarded the plane again. Didn't even pack a parachute. "Terrie, Gavin's right about one thing, you know…you should quit. It's dangerous and—"

"Yeah, says the guy bleeding all over his bathroom."

"Point taken. But for Gavin's sake, if not yours, find a different line of work."

"I can't *do* anything. I don't have any skills—"

"You fixed me up like a pro. How about nursing school?"

"Right. Takes education. Education takes money. Things I don't have."

"Anything's better than your current occupation." Like her, he didn't give the world's oldest profession a name. Keeping it at arm's length. Similar to how he'd regarded his life's work.

"Dream on. Anyway…I'll get going. Sorry again."

"No need for apologies. And thank you. For the patch-up job, I mean."

"De nada."

"Don't worry about Gavin. He'll make it. And so will you. You'll see."

"Okay." Her downturned mouth showed she didn't believe it, though. "Chris, if there's anything I can do for you, just holler."

"Well…no, never mind."

"What?" Curiosity stopped her at the bathroom door. Leon regretted baiting her even though he knew she'd bite.

"What's your ex-husband's name?"

Her face crinkled with bemusement, clearly the last thing she expected. A sardonic smile, a shake of the head, then she asked, "Why in the hell do you want to know that? I'm hoping to forget the bastard's name forever."

"Hm? Oh, no reason, really. Just curious, I guess."

Detective Keats breezed down the sidewalk. For once it'd been easy to shake Bellup's shadow. He'd been preoccupied by other matters. No doubt anticipating a night inside the bottle, planning his nightly itinerary. When she tossed him a "see ya'," he'd hardly acknowledged her.

But the anticipation of cage rattling really set wind to Keats' sail, Chris Hampton her bird of choice. She couldn't wait to watch him jump, see him squirm. Granted, she was officially off-duty, having punched out, the whole nine yards. It didn't matter. Good police are always on the job.

She knew she was onto something. Something big. *Felt it in her craw,* her late grandmother's favorite pearl of wisdom. With a smile, Keats jabbed a finger to the sky, thought, *this one's for you, Grams.* Childish, maybe, but appropriate. Grandma'd been married to a cop, so by extension, she'd been wed to the law, too.

Her footfalls clattered across the mostly empty parking lot. She kept her gaze straight ahead, focused on the prize. Room number 113, Hampton's room. Barely audible shouts stopped her cold. The room to number 113 swung open. Out stalked a tall, older man, a laptop tucked beneath his arm. Left the door open, too. Keats backed up, blended in with the shadows behind the brick office building. And watched.

At first, she thought the old guy might be homeless, his wardrobe pretty despairing. But he carried himself with vigor and energy, the kind you don't see in alleyways. Beneath the man's denim shirt, lean muscle rolled in his shoulders. Confidence boosted his strut. She couldn't place the song he whistled, not that it mattered, but he was definitely experiencing a roll-out-the-barrel moment. With long strides (hell, his legs practically came up to Keats' chest), he passed her, heading toward the opposite side of the U-shaped motel. Hopped up the steps two at a time. Finagled a key out of his pocket and opened the door to room number 242.

Interesting. Hampton has some strange friends. And what's with the computer?

Even more interesting was Hampton's next visitor. A kid (mid-teens, she guessed) zipped down the sidewalk on a skateboard, his long hair flying back like a scarf. He stopped at Hampton's door, said something into the darkness. Soon he raced next door, grabbed a woman (his mother?) and tugged her toward Hampton's room.

Keats stayed glued in her makeshift auditorium, watching the production unfold until all players had left the stage. Then she rounded the corner, walked into the office, wanting to put names to the actors.

"Help you?" The kid ("young man," probably, but once you hit thirty, Keats figured you earned the right to call everyone younger a "kid") was leaning over onto the counter, chin in hands. Glued to a small TV. No interest in Keats, at least not until a commercial break. Already she hated him.

"Detective Keats with the…" Once she realized she was wasting her time, she stopped her rote introduction, snapped shut her wallet. She reached over, turned off the TV.

"Hey! Hey, I was watchin' that!" Despite the humidity, he wore a beanie, the kind hipsters wear no matter the weather. The cap somehow managed to stick to the back of his scalp, defying gravity.

"I've seen the movie, save you some time. Guy's wife's the killer."

"Ah, shit—"

"Yeah, too bad, real sad. Listen, I want you to watch me for a few minutes. You know, real life?" She turned pitch-forked fingers from her eyes to him. "I need info on a couple of your tenants. Who's the old guy in—"

"Where's your partner…Bellup?" Beanie smirked. Apparently under the misimpression his presence mattered in the conversation.

"Probably at a bar. Tell me—"

"Bellup. I only deal with Bellup. Guy oils the palm." He

jammed a finger into a palm, rubbed it out like a cigarette into an ashtray.

"Yeah, I'm not gonna pay you anything."

"Then I'm not talkin'." He switched the TV back on, changed the channel.

Keats followed the power cord leading out the back, yanked it away from the wall.

"God *dammit*! Tole you how it's gonna be!"

"Let me tell *you* how it's gonna be, numb-nuts. You're gonna give me the names I ask for or I'll be back here with a warrant, toss the place, look at everything with a goddamn microscope if I have to, and make your life *very* unpleasant."

"Have at it. I ain't the owner. No skin off my back."

Keats tried playing nice, always did. It turned her stomach whenever Bellup played "bad cop," abusing the law. But he managed to teach her one thing: sometimes "bad cop" gets good results. She jacked her hands out, latched onto Beanie's t-shirt. Jerked him forward. Startled, he fell across the counter, arms splayed out in a clumsy dive. His chin snapped onto the counter-top, his eyes clamping shut. "God *damn*, lady!"

"It's *Detective*. Okay, Beanie Baby, you don't care about your place of employment? That's fine, whatever, don't expect anything different from you lame 'Millennials.' But how 'bout your background? What'll I find if I look into it? Maybe follow you around, spread the word you're a snitch. That sound like a good deal?"

He paused, weighing his future options. Stood up, straightened his t-shirt. "Hey, I wanna do my civic duty. Whose name did you want again?"

Chapter Eight

Jasper Rasmussen rolled into the boardroom, jockeying his wheelchair with the hand control. Directly behind him bounced his newest nurse (he couldn't ever remember their names, but always insisted they be lookers), steering his urine drainage bag on an IV pole. The catheter line snaked out beneath his robe, his dark orange urine coursing through it. Probably not an ideal color, but it didn't worry him. He'd made it into his mid-90's, discolored piss sure as hell wasn't going to kill him.

Rasmussen's wife, Sheera, brought up the rear (*and my God, what a rear!*). Her name was as phony as her breasts and skeletal cheekbones, but he'd have it no other way. A trophy wife in all regards, she stood tall, shoulders back, bosom hefted out, perfect posture, more statuesque than any inhumanly formed Barbie doll. Young enough to be his granddaughter, dazzling enough to start wars over. And all his. Of course he couldn't get it up anymore, especially with the damn plastic tubing hijacking his pecker. But behind closed doors, she put on a helluva show.

He'd seen the lust in his staff's eyes, overheard his employees whispering about his wife. If they were blatant about it, naturally, he fired them on the spot. And that's if he liked them. Actually (and he'd never admit it to his lackeys) their awe filled him with secret pride, the kind money and power commanded. And even though Sheera claimed the contrary, she was, without a doubt, in it for the money—his money. The secret was to string his wives along, then kick 'em to the curb before they got too comfy. And never sign a pre-nup, a preposterous idea valid only for fools and love-struck schoolboys. He imagined he'd toss Sheera by the wayside soon enough. By his estimation, he had a couple more wives left in him yet.

His money was his, only his. He'd made it the hard way, transforming a germ of an idea into a global empire. And he did it without the benefit of going public, marketing, or applying any of the attention-grabbing business tools that drew curious eyes upon him. Nope, he'd been the man behind the curtain and he damn sure wanted to keep those curtains drawn tightly. Never had a problem either until that damn Garber upstart came along making trouble.

Rasmussen took his sweet time arranging his wheelchair until he slid into place at the head of the table. Making his audience wait. The table shone too brightly, the overhead lights rippling waves down its length. He'd have to fire the maid for waxing it too frequently.

The gathered suck-ups, kiss-asses and sycophants sat in reverent silence. His way or the six feet under way. Sheera latched onto the chair next to him, inched it out just enough so her crossed legs would show at the edge of the table. Most of the men knew better than to ogle her, rigidly locking their eyes onto Rasmussen. Disappointed by the lack of lechery, Sheera kicked a high-heeled foot, setting her legs as a hard-to-miss focal point. At the far end of the table, a toadie—someone Rasmussen vaguely remembered—took the bait. His Adam's apple moved up as he swallowed, a not-so-subtle gawk fixed on Sheera's legs. Rasmussen loved it, best way to start off a day.

"You!" He pointed a gnarled finger down the table. All chairs swiveled toward the branded man.

"Ah...yes sir?" The man drew a finger around his collar, looked around for support. His compatriots stared down upon their folded hands as if in prayer. No fools, they knew who their God was. Made it all the sweeter.

"See something you like?" Every word came out a struggle, a wheeze, a noise Rasmussen hated. It made him sound weak. More the reason to let his actions speak louder than words.

The convicted man attempted a smile. Rasmussen didn't return it. "Um...no sir?"

"What?" *Smack.* Even though it hurt like hell, Rasmussen brought his hand down on the table like a gavel. "You mean...

you don't think my wife's *beautiful*?" Sheera smiled, thrilled, picking her kick up a notch.

"No sir! That's *not* what I meant at *all*. She's stunning and—"

"*What*? So you wanna' screw my wife?" Rasmussen had the man on the hook. Around him, the school of fish squirmed, wishing to swim far away downstream. Power's a beautiful thing.

"No sir! Nothing of the sort! I just—"

"Now you're insulting Mrs. Rasmussen." When Sheera grinned at her husband, only her lips flexed, the rest of her face permanently set in stone. "You're fired. Gaines! Gaines, where the *hell* is that—"

Like a genie, Rasmussen's man, Gaines, materialized at his shoulder. "Sir?"

"Jesus *Christ*, Gaines! Quit sneaking up like that! Gonna give me a heart attack!" While Rasmussen caught his breath, Gaines stood by his side, hands folded in front of him.

Funny man, Gaines, thought Rasmussen. Slight of build, receding hairline, the demeanor of a hen-pecked husband, not formidable looking in the least. Everyone was nonetheless terrified of him. *Rightfully so.* Rasmussen's enemies constantly underestimated Gaines. Part of Gaines' power was the element of surprise. Beneath that docile façade lurked a body composed entirely of rock-solid muscle. His forgettable face and reticent manner disguised a shrewdly sociopathic mind. He could turn anything into a weapon. And he delighted in doing so.

"What can I do for you, sir?" Gaines beamed, one gold tooth (his only concession to vanity) sparkling. Rasmussen appreciated Gaines because the man truly loved his job. Not afraid to toil, he upheld an excellent work ethic. A real American.

"Fire this jackass." Rasmussen swept a liver-spotted hand down toward the troublemaker. "Make sure he gets his severance."

"Sir." Gaines lips spread wider. Everyone in the room knew what LMI's version of "severance" was, Gaines the deliverer of the exit interview.

"Mr. *Rasmussen*! No, *please*, give me another *chance*!" As

Gaines yanked the man out of his chair, the doomed man sniveled. *"Please,* sir, I meant no disrespect! Just *give* me—"

"Oh, for God's sake, be a man! Gaines, get him out of here!"

"With pleasure, sir." And there wasn't a man in the room who didn't believe Gaines wouldn't derive the utmost in pleasure out of delivering severance. LMI's a business, after all. *Big* business. Once your contract is terminated, so is your life.

"Anybody else?" Rasmussen probed the rest of the board of directors with hoot-owl eyes, his bushy eyebrows twitching. A few of the table's occupants snuck a glance at the screaming man being escorted from the room. But most of them knew the protocol, shaking their heads in proper veneration. As she always did, Sheera basked in the spotlight: enjoying the show her killer curves had induced. "Let's get started then… Where in the *hell* are we with this *damn*…'Operation Renegade' business?"

Billyews, always bucking for a promotion, spoke up. "Sir, I'm afraid Operation Renegade is still in the red. The corporate raider has maintained low visibility since Key West. But—"

"Goddammit!" *Flick.* Rasmussen winged a sharp pencil toward his Operations Director. The missile fell far short of its target and clattered onto the table. Rasmussen's muscles weren't what they once were. Back in better days, he used to throw darts. But that had proven too much of a strain on human resources. "That's *not* what I want to hear, Billyews. Give me some *good* news!"

Unshaken, Billyews launched into more placating nonsense. "As you know, our best business process outsourcers, along with the Spangler project, are on top of the situation. They're currently in Miami Beach. After Spangler's little, um, snafu—"

"Has that been handled? Better damn well *better* be!"

"Yes sir. I held an emergency 'mydeation' meeting and our best 'smarketeers'—"

"Holy hell in a handbag! What the *hell* are you talking about?" Rasmussen looked at Sheera, astonishment in his eyes. She pouted her lips, but with all of her work, it looked like someone had shot a hole in a blow-up doll. "What've I *told* you about using all those damn foolish made-up *words*? God damn it! Speak *English*! We're in *America*!" Quickly, he scanned the room for questionable people from questionable backgrounds. Never hurts to be safe.

"My apologies, sir. Ah, 'mydeation' is an ideation...that is, *brainstorming* meeting we held to solve our immediate crisis. Our clean-up crew expertly diffused the physical aspects of the problem. The smark...*marketing* team decided to launch a newsjacking—"

Shwift. Clickety-click-clack. Again the pencil rolled across the table, this time making it as far as Billyews' lap. "What did I *say* about those stupid words?"

"Sorry sir, won't happen again. The marketing team implemented a larger, more newsworthy story to derail attention away from a missing stripper and two bouncers. They decided to—"

Rasmussen lifted his hand. "Spare me the details. That's why I'm paying you. Just tell me it's handled."

"It's handled."

"Which doesn't get us any closer to resolving our goddamn problem."

"We're working on it. Unfortunately, Mr. Spangler has once again proven to be a liability. I would highly recommend—"

Rasmussen leaned over, coughed into his hand, did it again. His nurse stepped to his side, her hand wavering over his bent back. "Mr. Rasmussen, are you—"

"Get offa' me, god*dammit*, woman! I'm not a little baby you have to swaddle. Jumping Jesus on a jet ski!" He waved her back, his hands flapping like wings. "Billyews, you don't recommend things. You *ask*. I built this company on my business savvy. Not your *damn* stupid recommendations. Spangler stays. For now. He's not ideal, no, but no one knows Garber better. He almost led us to him in Key West, he'll do it again. And I've already put into motion his exit interview. Now tell me something new. And make it *good*."

"Ah...our Chief Culture Officer has advised me—"

"What're we *running* here, a goddamned *museum*?" *Whisk.*

The pencil barely got airborne before it dropped. "Why'm I paying for a 'Chief Culture Officer'? What the *hell* do we need culture for?"

"Again, I apologize, sir. Mr. Summers is our Chief Culture Officer. He—"

"Then why didn't you say so!" Rasmussen's hands curled into tiny, misshapen tree trunks. His face turned red, swam into a deep purple. Quickly, the nurse tapped out two pills from a bottle, handed them to Rasmussen. With a noticeably trembling hand, she chased it with a glass of water. As Rasmussen lapped at the glass, water trickled down from his mouth. His board of directors sat up, watching, some of them no doubt hoping he'd taken his last breath. Not a chance. He intended to outlive them all. His heart rate normalized, his breathing settled into the usual wheeze.

Billyews' hand hung midair, an imperative finger pointing up, frozen through Rasmussen's fit. Acting as if nothing had occurred, he continued. "Yes, sir. Mr. Summers has informed me he's currently opening negotiations with another renegade. Someone with information regarding Garber. But he wants to be paid, contractually so. And he's withholding information in small info-bytes. He..."

Rasmussen glared at Billyews until he stopped talking. If his blood pressure hadn't just sky-rocketed, he would've launched a classroom's worth of pencils. "Billyews, give the informant what he wants. Anything to find Garber. Can't believe I have to tell you this *shit*. Then once we finally end Garber, take care of the informant. No one negotiates with me, lousy ingrates!"

"Yes sir."

Behind Rasmussen, the door opened. He twisted—tried to, at least—wanting to see who was so brazen to interrupt his meeting. Gaines glided up beside his boss. Blood spots decorated his usually pristine white shirt. Around the table, the others averted their eyes.

Gaines whispered into his employer's ear. Rasmussen waved him back. Like a ghost, Gaines floated back toward the door, leaving without a sound.

"Well, God *damn*! You buncha' *pathetic* incompetents!

Gaines just told me Garber's father was sprung from prison a *month* ago! And the last trace of him was in Florida." He sprayed finger bullets around the table. "Why in the *hell* are we *just* finding this out? We're one of the *biggest* covert operations in the country! With the best technology, the best people money can *buy*! At least that's what you sorry idiots keep telling me!"

The spineless grouping ostriched their heads, hoping the buck wouldn't stop with them. But it did, every last one of them. After the Garber screw-up was finally handled, Rasmussen planned to conduct a good housecleaning.

But, right now, excitement surged through him. He had a lead, a damn good one. From what he knew about Garber, the man wouldn't be able to resist killing his father.

Rasmussen leered at his wife. She'd been filing her nails, bored with the business end of things. With her hand up, she admired her fingertips, waggling them for everyone to see. Her bountiful cleavage drew his eyes in. For the first time in a while, he thought a trip to the bedroom was in order. Hell, maybe he'd even try to join in this time.

They'd done absolute *jack* for a day. Just sat in the damn motel room. Sensitivity told Cody to stay on the rollaway, treating him like a little kid. Getting pretty rank in the room, too. At least Sensitivity showered. Bug hadn't even looked at the sink. Just slept and coughed. Besides starting fires, his hobbies, Cody supposed.

Cody turned the TV on. Sensitivity snatched the remote away, slapped it off, then crashed back down on his bed. Over the top of his yoga book, he looked at Cody through Granny glasses. Giving him a pissed off parent's face.

Damn prisoner of war. That's how Cody felt. Not for the first time, he wondered if he'd chosen the right side to fight on. These asshats had treated him like crap from day one. Wouldn't even talk to him now.

His dream job was tanking, going balls up.

Not like last year when he'd had a killer time with Leon. Sure it'd been dangerous, but he couldn't deny the kick he got out of it.

Leon. The old man had been his bud. Gave him shit for a

while, but, hey, just part of the game. Frankly Cody thought that's why he'd signed up again with LMI. Another game, a fun time killer. But this didn't ride like last year's rollercoaster, not by a long shot.

With a chesty snort, Bug rolled over on his side. And Sensitivity still glared at Cody.

"Jesus. Got the hots for me or somethin'? Take a picture, yo." Cody flung his shoe toward Sensitivity, making sure it didn't reach the big guy. No sense in riling him up again. Not after he saw what he could do back at the strip club.

Sensitivity didn't blink. Dude's not even human. The way he studied Cody made him uneasy. Like he was a primo steak Sensitivity couldn't wait to bite into. And Cody had a pretty good idea that's what these two were going to do to him. As soon as the Garber job was done. Summers had been blowing hot air up his ass. It sucked, but Cody had to man up and admit it: he wasn't the boss.

Cody weighed his options, each one pretty lame. He could take off tonight, escape the motel. Except Sensitivity damn near slept with his eyes open. Guy'd be on him like a dog in heat. Of course he could purposefully botch the Garber gig, stretch the job out until something better came along. Yeah, how long could *that* last?

Or maybe he'd switch sides. Team up with the old man again. Garber'd welcome him with open arms.

His stomach warmed, tingling like he'd touched a live wire. The idea felt right. But how could he pull it off?

Sensitivity's phone blared out. Cody rolled his eyes at the easy listening tune the dude programmed as his ringtone. Still *any* sound—no matter how crappy—was better than sweating total silence.

"Yes?" Sensitivity sat up, scrawled something on the back of his magazine. "I see." A black eyebrow hefted up. He held a hand over his mouth, muttering something. Gossiping like a little girl. "Got it. We're on it."

He tossed the phone on the bed, stood up. As he tucked the back of his shirt in, he said, "Got a new lead. Get your ass up."

"Yo, you gonna fill me in or what?"

"Garber's father. He's here. In Miami."

"No shit?" Cody sprang up, retrieved his shoe. The game just got exciting again. "So what're we doin'?"

"We're gonna find Garber's pops, bright boy, what the hell you think we're doing?"

"Yeah, check it, Mr. Clean…Garber ain't exactly on cuddling terms with his old man. They ain't gonna—"

"How 'bout you leave the thinking to me." Sensitivity shook his head, then shook Bug's shoulder. "I know what Garber's father did. But I also know Garber's type. Nothing's gonna keep him away from a family reunion. *Nothing*. Just gotta find Garber's daddy before Garber kills him."

"Raymond Garber?"

The sun struck Raymond's blood-shot eyes with the force of railroad ties hammered into hard ground. He held up a hand to block the offending rays. His visitor was black, small, pretty. Dressed in a cheap cop suit. Raymond could smell her a mile away. "Who's askin'?"

"I'm Detective Keats, Miami Police. Like to ask you a few questions." She peered around him, nosy as cops can get. Raymond wasn't in the mood. He'd tied a major one on last night, celebrating his good fortune. Soon, he'd be out of this rat hole, living the good life on his ungrateful son's dime. Still she was a looker, even if she was a little on the scrawny side, no meat on her bones. Actually Raymond hadn't even thought of the fairer sex in a while. His soon-to-be financial fortune apparently worked on him like Viagra.

"Depends on what this is about, lil' lady." Although he had a pretty good idea what it was about.

"Yeah, you can call me 'Detective'." She stepped in as if she owned the place, queen of the cops. Brassy, this one. She sneered at the empty bottles cluttering the table and lying on the floor. With a dainty kick, she toed a tequila bottle across the floor. "Big night?"

"Woulda been a lot better with some company. How 'bout you let your hair down and join me for a drink?" He leaned toward her, grinning.

"While the offer is terribly tempting, I'll pass." Stubborn as a mule, she held her ground. Tried to square up her bony shoulders, putting on airs.

"Your loss, lil' lady."

"I'm sure. And it's 'Detective'. Not 'little lady'."

"Now don't get your knickers in a bunch. Just havin' some fun." Raymond tossed last night's clothes into his suitcase, covering the laptop computer. He shut the suitcase, dragged it off the bed and sat down. Boldly (nothing could ruin his day), he patted the mattress. "Have a seat, get comfy."

"I'll stand. Mr. Garber, what's your business with Chris Hampton?"

He knew it was coming, couldn't be about anything else. After all, he'd served his time. The parole board practically fell over apologizing about the cop screwing up his arrest report. Only in America, rah, rah, rah and praise the Lord.

Raymond scrunched his face up, faking dim recall. "Hampton...huh. Chris Hampton, you say?"

The detective sighed, tapped a foot. "Mr. Garber, I saw you leaving his room last night. Number 113. You gonna play games with me?"

"Hm? No, no game- playin'. Just took me a minute. Yeah, Hampton. Didn't even know his first name."

"Yet you knew him well enough to be in his room."

"What can I say? Met the guy down on the Boardwalk. He owed me money and I was collectin'."

"Why'd he owe you money?"

"Poker game. Didn't have it on him at the time."

"And you just happen to reside at the same motel?"

Raymond's hands opened, offering truth. "Hey, it's a small world."

"Not really. How long have you known him, Mr. Garber?"

"I tole you I just met the guy...lessee, when was it?" He closed one eye, lifting the other up to the ceiling. "Couple days ago."

"Uh huh. Tell me about him."

Of course Raymond didn't want to protect the little shit. Call it protecting his retirement plan. His best interests were to keep his son out of jail. For now. "What's this about? What's he done?"

"I'm just inquiring. Nothing you need to worry about."

"Do I look worried to you?" Raymond's head pounded. Too many cigarettes had shortened his breath. His generous patience fizzled away. With her patronizing attitude and endless questions, the detective had drained his good-time buzz.

"Please answer the question, Mr.—"

"I already done answered it, goddammit! I don't *know* the man from Adam. Told you everything I—"

"Mr. Garber, I know about your past. Checked you out last night. You murdered your wife."

"*What*? Lissen up, lil' lady, I was fully exonerated of—"

"No you weren't."

"*Excuse* me?"

"You're excused. But you weren't exonerated. You did the crime. Due to some bureaucratic screw-up, they tossed you."

"Call it what you want, but I don't see how my past is any concern of yours, no way, no how!" If she didn't have a badge in her pocket, Raymond would've tossed her out. Just like all women, all holier than thou. Rage set him on edge. He cracked his knuckles, soothing the beast. Even though he'd like to teach her a lesson, he didn't cotton to spending any more time behind bars either.

"It's been my experience criminals run together like pack rats."

"The hell you sayin'? You *judgin'* me? Who the hell are *you* to judge me? Standin' there all big and tough. Why you ain't nothin' but a little—"

She stopped him with an upheld hand, probably learned it at crossing duty. Where Raymond wished she'd return to. "Settle down, Mr. Garber. I don't want you. I'm interested in Chris Hampton. I find it odd that a recently released convict is so…chummy with him. You know the man well enough to know where he lives, play poker with him…collect money from him."

Raymond popped off the bed, felt a vein in his temple throbbing. "We're done here, missy. Told you everything I know 'bout Hampton. Which is *nothin'*. Guy don't talk about himself, neither do I. Now get your high and mighty *ass* outta' my room."

Her smirk really pissed him off. Knowing and condescending. "We're just having a friendly little chat, Mr. Garber. Seems to me it's your knickers in a bunch now."

Damn uppity woman. Slandering him with her feminist crap. Thinking she's better, stronger than him. But he wouldn't give in, give her what she wanted. Best to get her out of the room before she felt what *real* power was all about. "And I told you to leave. Now. *Little lady.*"

"Fine. But we'll chat again, count on it." She whirled, her ponytail slapping her back. "If I were you, I wouldn't go anywhere. Thanks for a very enlightening interview." She tossed him a goodbye wave, not even affording him the courtesy of eye contact.

"*Bitch!*" Raymond scooped up a bottle, hurled it. It smashed against the door, shards raining down onto the floor. He grabbed a large jagged piece, drew it down over his tattooed bicep. The inked angel wept tears of blood. Something he desperately wanted to make Detective Keats do.

He had to light a fire under Leon. Before a more potent fire consumed him.

Another sleepless night. Leon expected it, the norm these days. Even as bad as things were last year, he'd never felt more on edge. Raymond put him off his game. He was acting out of character, not thinking straight. He knew what he had to do, the only possible thing. Kill Raymond. Get back the computer. But how? And when?

His phone interrupted his planning.

Unknown caller. Of course.

"Hello?"

"Leon, it's Albert." Albert paused, waiting for acknowledgement. "Ah, are you there, Leon?"

"Yeah."

"We're moving tomorrow. Extracting August Schroeder."

Another pause. "Um...did you hear me?"

"Yes." Leon heard, but didn't connect, not really. The absurdity struck him how everyone involved with LMI used code words to hide behind. He wished Albert would call it what he meant: *kidnapping.*

"Mr. Garber...Leon...are you feeling well? You sound rather...I don't know, distracted."

"I'm fine."

"I...see." But the way Albert said it, he may as well have been blind. "Will you be able to meet at our same rendezvous tomorrow at, say, 2:00?"

"I suppose."

"And, um, will we be seeing the laptop?"

The laptop. The damn computer everyone wanted. Which Leon really didn't care about any longer, that ship had long sailed. But better it dock with Albert and company than Raymond. Not that he trusted Albert. But he didn't want to give his father anything.

"Albert, I'll give you the computer tomorrow. But I need to talk to Nanette. Have her call me. Now."

"I see. And may I ask why—"

Leon hung up.

Five minutes later, another unknown caller rang in. But Leon knew the caller's identity.

"Hello, Nanette."

"You develop mind reading?" He envisioned her smiling, a pleasant image for a change.

"Something like that. Hey, I need your help."

"And why would I help you?"

"Because of my boyish ways and charm?" *Flirting, for God's sake.* Totally ludicrous, but he couldn't help it. She brought it out of him. "But...there's something else in it for you."

"Be still, my beating heart. This just gets even better," she purred. Her formidable flirting blew his amateur status away. If Gustav's "Black Widow" analysis was accurate, no doubt she'd had a lot of flirting field practice.

"You want the computer? It's yours. But you have to do a little work for it."

"I'm listening." And she did while Leon told her about his father. Ordinarily he wouldn't have told a soul. Too painful, opening himself up too much. But he'd reached a crossroads, a marked change in direction. He just didn't care. And he imagined his new mind-set might strengthen him, transform him into an unfeeling killing machine. *Thanks, Dad.*

For the most part, Nanette handled the information bomb with restraint. Nothing moved her to judgment, not Raymond's murder of his mother, not his father's emotional and physical abuse from the past two nights. Not even Leon's losing the computer. It felt good to put it all on the table.

"Sounds like your family's as bad as mine," she offered.

"Kinda think it runs in our line of work."

"Want me to teach your...*Raymond* a lesson?"

More metaphors, although Leon had no doubt what her "lesson" entailed. "No...I'll take care of him. Thanks anyway."

"Okay, I'm in. Sounds fun. Tell me where and when. And how. Anything I need to bring?"

"Yeah. You got a maid's costume?"

While Bellup trotted outside for a smoke, Keats fired up the NCIC database. With department cutbacks running rampant, she'd been reduced to sharing a terminal with Bellup, a terminally awful situation. Not only did she have to deal with his constant badgering and watching her, she had to take canned air to the keyboard on a daily basis. White crumbs and unidentifiable debris flurried around her while the can grew cold in her hand. She had about fifteen minutes to work; Bellup knew how to make a smoke last.

Raymond Garber. Basically the same story she'd found last night on her home computer. But more detailed. His mug shot displayed an even leaner (not so much meaner), younger man scowling into the camera, eyes glassy and cruel. Age hadn't tempered his demeanor. While she'd enjoyed rubbing salt in the creep's wound, the anger he flared seemed disproportionate. Why'd he get so pissed?

Easy. Because he knows more about Hampton than he's letting on, protesting way too much. One of the first things she'd learned on the job: some clichés are true.

Garber had stabbed his wife. Left behind a son, a young child. Other than technical information about Raymond's early prison release, the NCIC database ran out of steam.

Her fingers flew across the keyboard, her eyes charting the computer clock's progress. She dug deep into the Gillette News Record archives (out of Wyoming, the state of Garber's crime) and struck gold. Gillette was apparently a boring, scandal-starved town; the newspaper had played out the story for all its worth. Some muckraker managed to snap a photo of the surviving son, Leon, in a police car. The details were hard to make out, the picture muddy and dark. But the child looked shaken, lost. Staring down into his lap. Dark splotches dotted his face, possibly blood. And his nose looked swollen. White puffs of tissue stuck out from his nostrils. With no living relatives, Leon was proclaimed a ward of the state and shipped off to a foster home, the worst possible place for hurting kids. Keats sped read through the trial proceedings, focusing on photographs. With the determination of a reporter, she scratched deeper.

There. Another photo of young Leon. Leaving the courthouse, still understandably frazzled. The swelling on his nose had gone down. But his nose held a distinct crook to it. The aquiline nose skewed slightly to the left, a flaw in his otherwise handsome features. One she'd seen before.

Son of a bitch! Keats' heart sped up. Another glimpse at the clock, only a few puffs left for Bellup. As a girl, she'd read many Sherlock Holmes tales, wondering what in the world the detective meant when he proclaimed, "the game is afoot!" Now she knew. Which quickened her pulse even more.

No more pics of little Leon. A global search uncovered brief mentions (no photographs) of an adult Leon Garber's quick rise in the high-end business accounting sector, a true star amongst bean counters. One blurb mentioned Leon's Gillette, Wyoming origins. Then nothing. Like the man died, dropped off the face of the earth. But not with a boom, more like a whiff. For someone rumored to be making seven figures a year near the height of his career, it seemed unusual he quit making financial headlines. Unless he died. But she found no such obituary. He simply quit existing.

Except Keats had found him.

Sure, with a new alias, supposedly a new career. But it was her guy, no denying it. Her excitement escalated when she anticipated dropping the bomb on him. Finding out why a wealthy man of corporate America was now living amongst rats, hookers, and tweekers. Her computer screen reflected her smile. Hadn't even realized she'd been grinning like an idiot. Then it just as suddenly vanished when she saw the pasty head reflected beside hers.

Shit. Her heart stuttered. Her fingers trembled until she closed the search page.

"God*dammit*, Keats." Bellup thrust his fists down, tossing a surprisingly hushed tantrum. "You're *still* on this Hampton shit? What's your *damage* with this guy?"

She should've smelled him a mile away, a walking ashtray. "Why the hell do you care anyway? Ever since I've been stuck with you, you haven't given a damn about anything I do. Now, you're, what...taking me under your wing?"

"Yeah, best place for you, locked under my wing."

"The hell's that supposed to mean? You're not the boss of me, Bellup, even though you've been tryin' to be from day one. Just...go do your crap, whatever it is you do all day." Red and sweaty, the man looked ready to stroke out. She turned back to the computer and continued her search for Leon Garber.

"I'm tellin' you, Keats, leave him be. Guy's innocent."

Her chair swung around fast. "Well, I'm gonna find out, how 'bout that? Go get a chili dog. God knows you're probably goin' through withdrawal. Let the real police...*police*."

He stalked off, phone glued to his ear. Watching her. If she could read lips, it likely might even embarrass her. Or make her proud. Probably both.

Then she turned back to the only man who currently captivated her, heart and soul: Leon Garber.

Chapter Nine

As stubborn as pulling teeth, Nanette had finally given Leon her cell phone number. Before leaving on her mission, she'd batted her eyes and raised the act of being coy to an art form. He knew she was playing him, expert at it, really. But he wondered if they might have an actual connection, something beyond her usual games. Which he wished she'd stop playing. Even though largely frustrating, he couldn't deny she was also intoxicating, addictive like a dangerous drug. But he couldn't consider romance now.

It was time, however, to put his plan regarding Raymond into effect. Past time. Even if the plan had changed at the last moment. He'd wanted to dispose of his father, make him suffer, fantasized about it for an unhealthy long time. That plan had gone out the window. It surprised him, too. Yet a new realization struck him as surely as a bolt of lightning. Instead of leaving behind a charred corpse, though, hope rose from the ashes.

He closed his eyes, murmured a yoga mantra, one to give him strength. Took three loud, cleansing breaths, braced himself. *End game.* He called room number 242.

"*What?*"

"I've got something for you," said Leon.

A rusty chuckle. "Knew you'd come around, see it my way. Better be *good*, boy."

"You're going to get what you deserve." Leon ended the call. No sense fighting over the phone. Not when he knew he had a fight ahead of him.

He peered out the window, watching Raymond rush out his door. Two steps and his father stopped as if hitting an invisible wall. He turned back, double-checked the door knob, gave it an extra jiggle. Making sure the laptop was secure within.

Leon rang Nanette, said, "You're on."

Earlier, Nanette thought it cute when Leon'd asked her if she could manage the lock.

"Please." She'd said no more, basking in the aura of mystery she'd carefully cultivated over the years. And Leon's perplexed look had been priceless, the way she liked her men. Always keep 'em guessing.

"So…you have a maid's dress?" He looked her over head to toe. She suspected he was gaping at more than just her utilitarian blue work uniform. Looks are free.

She tapped his chin, smiled. "A girl's gotta be prepared."

It took no time at all for Nanette to jimmy the lock. Old motels were still operating in the dark ages, especially regarding security. The tension tool released the plug, the pick moved the pins aside and she pushed open the door to room number 242.

With one last glance down the motel's walkway, she closed the door behind her. Quickly inventoried the room. Musty, rank, filthy. Empty bottles on the floor, crowding the desk. Unmade bed, not that she expected anything else. Dust swirled, trapped in a beam of sunlight burning through the window. Rings scraped across a rusty rod as she yanked the curtains closed.

Cute. There were many "cute" things about Leon besides his adorably befuddled schoolboy behavior. Handsome, smart, witty. Not so good at handling pressure but not everyone's perfect. Possibly wealthy. She felt a corner of her mouth curl up, dimpling into a grin.

It'd been some time since she'd allowed herself a lover for fun. Other than the fun of disposing of them afterward, of course, and the requisite cash reward for her hard work. Most of her past marks had been rich, ghastly men, the way it had to be. Money never rained down upon salt-of-the-earth, good-hearted men. For what she had to deal with over weeks, months (and in one miserable case, a year and some change), she worked hard for her money. No one should have to go through the humiliation they subjected her to. Not without pay.

She had her reasons.

Any childishly romantic notions she harbored about Leon dropped as suddenly as a change in the wind.

Business. Keep your mind on business.

She dropped to the stained carpet, dirt particles adhering to her knees. Other than dust bunnies and cobwebs, she found nothing under the bed. A quick scan of the small room showed no suitcase, not in plain sight.

Her mind wandered again, a troubling new tendency she couldn't shake. With so much going on, she felt scattered, not operating at full capacity. She had no idea what to expect regarding the war on LMI. When Albert had first approached her, she'd played indifferent. Shrugged it off without a second thought. Once Albert told her about LMI's ulterior motives she changed her mind. The irony bulldozed her. It pissed her off that she'd been duped by LMI, killing people of their choice to further their political agenda. People like them were responsible for turning her into who she was today. The war was *so* on.

She rolled her eyes at Raymond Garber's idea of subterfuge. In the closet, several natty shirts hung on wire hangers, in such bad shape she imagined they'd never met a hanger before. Clearly out of place. She pushed the shirts aside to unveil an equally battered suitcase crammed onto a shelf. *Ta-daaa.*

Whether the kamikaze war on LMI would succeed seemed like a moot point. Frankly she thought they didn't stand a chance in hell. But she had to try at least, no way around it. And more than that, Leon Garber kept her interested. Again she felt her lips involuntarily tugging upward. She felt foolish crushing on a man, a guy she'd end up using for her own needs. Just the law of the land, the way of nature. The way it had to be. But, damn, if a girl can't dream.

The suitcase came free with a couple of tugs and clumped to the floor. No lock, probably didn't even make them when Garber'd bought the suitcase. *Clack, cluck.* The latches snapped like mousetraps, the top folded back. She parted the wadded up clothes and found the grail, a scratched mechanical marvel that could turn the tides of war.

A small part of her felt bad about what she had to do, just

a smidgeon. She'd made a tenuous agreement with Leon that they'd hand the computer over to Albert together. But, then, she'd have to split the finder's fee (of which she was absolutely certain Albert would dole out). Lately, her funds had been running low. She needed a windfall. She couldn't keep living at her high standard without unwitting help from easily duped men. *Sorry, Leon, but at least you escaped with your life.* When she realized her silly, girlish crush would remain unresolved, her mood again turned dour.

With a sigh, she flapped open a large plastic trash bag. She rifled through Raymond's sodden clothing, snatched a flannel shirt and wrapped it around the laptop. Then slipped the treasure into the bag.

A sharp knock at the door brought her to her feet. Her heart skipped a beat. Quickly she closed the suitcase, replaced it, drew the shirts back into place. Shut the closet door. The knocking rose, louder. Impatient. A quick glance around the room, everything back in place.

She breathed deeply. Considered looking out the window, discarded the notion as too obvious. Her fingers caressed the knife in her bag, one of her favorites. She wanted it close, a trusted ally, but realized she might be jumping the gun. For all anyone knew, she was a maid. She cinched the bag shut, clutched it like a lover, and pulled open the door.

Two men crowded the doorway, a bald bear and a grizzled bunny.

"Excuse me, I'm looking for Raymond Garber." The big man's mirrored sunglasses smacked of a cop's favorite accessory, but the rest of his wardrobe didn't follow. His button-down, precisely pressed white shirt suggested a manservant. Or an enforcer. The little guy was definitely anything but police, not in his skid row chic. He coughed into a fist, closed his eyes like he hurt. Then glared at her through tired eyes.

LMI, her gut told her. Always go with the gut.

"Sorry, nobody here. I'm just finishing up." She pulled up the trash bag, prepared to swing it if necessary. "You might wanna leave a message at the office."

As she tried to step around them, the large man blocked her

path. "Hold it, ma'am. You're the maid? At a dump like this?"

Nanette shrugged. "Girl's gotta work. If you'll excuse—"

"Kinda odd this place even has maid service. Whaddaya' think, Bug?"

The man who looked like his namesake dug hands into his pockets, cracked his neck. "Odd."

"S'what I think."

"Yeah, okay, glad we got that cleared up. Now if you'll kindly get the hell outta' my way, I've got other pleasure suites to clean." She lifted a plunger, a last minute grab from Raymond's bathroom.

The large man chuckled, but yielded to the germ-ridden weapon and backed up. "Fine, miss, go about your work. You have any idea when Mr. Garber might return?"

She snorted, playing up the underpaid, overworked act. "Do I look like his personal secretary? Let me do my damn job already."

She came at Bug strong, giving him no choice but to move. Outside, she started to pull the door shut behind her. The large man rallied, halting the door with one solid finger. "Miss, we're old friends of Mr. Garber. You don't mind if we wait for him inside." Not a question, a demand.

She brought a hand up, smacked it to her side. "Hell if I care. Do what you want. Take a bath, give each other manicures, whatever. Enjoy."

The larger man laughed. No doubt at her "spunk." But had he called her "spunky," she'd have gone for the knife and gutted him like a fish. Some things women shouldn't have to tolerate.

But she'd made it, no sense in blowing it now. She looked back over her shoulder. The door closed. She breathed a sigh of relief, ready to descend the steps to freedom. Until a younger guy blocked her passage. Sprawled out across the stairwell, he sat on the right handrail, his legs forming an impassable bridge to the left. Smoke billowed from his mouth, a chimney's worth. His lazy gaze rolled over her, then he hopped to full height.

"Yo, what's up, what's up?" He sucked on his smoke again, flipped it around. "Want a drag?"

She didn't know why she did it, but she grabbed the cigarette anyway. Stupid, she'd given up smoking years ago. Maybe it was the tense situation she'd narrowly escaped. Or perhaps it was the guy; young, brazen, cocky, muscular, good looking, and probably more than a little dumb. The prototypical bad boy. She needed to have sex soon to clear her mind. Her primal urges were taking their toll, making her sloppy. "Thanks." She inhaled. The nicotine immediately struck her brain, rendering her lightheaded. "Needed that."

"Hey, s'all good, s'all good, mama." Nanette nearly giggled when he flexed his muscles for her benefit. "What's a hot piece of awesomeness like you doin' in a shithole like this?"

Ordinarily talk like that would've set her teeth grinding. But something about this kid seemed sincere, not just spouting off ludicrous pick-up lines. Like an animal, he was merely following his instincts. "Work here. What's your excuse?"

His broad shoulders straightened. "Just chillin'. Waitin' on some dudes upstairs. My boys, yo, followin' my orders."

Damn. This guy's with LMI? "Think I might've run into them. Big and bald and his sidekick, Buggy?"

He snorted. "Yeah. Chill dudes, right?"

"'Spose so." She sucked deeply on the cigarette. The ember brightened, then ashed over. She exhaled the cloud of smoke into his face, then handed the butt back to him. "So what kinda' business are your boys taking care of?" Risky, she knew, but she also had no doubt she could wrap this kid around her finger. And the idea of making him her slave tickled her.

Suddenly, he turned serious, pulling down thick eyebrows. "Why you axin', yo?"

She took it as a personal challenge, a speed challenge. "Just curious." She smiled, demurely at first. Making him feel he's in control. *Too easy.* Then she unleashed body language to deliver the true message. Slowly, she gave him a once-over, brought her eyes up, locked them on his. Tilted her head, thrust out a hip, hand placed delicately alongside it. "I like things that make me curious." She swayed, not too much, just enough. Her finger teased her hair, entangling a lock around it.

Boom. Four seconds top. He stepped closer, his breath heavy. Placed strong hands on her shoulders, gazed down at her with stupid, but definitely soulful eyes.

Her finger zipped up his chest, breaking the spell. "Whoa, tiger, put it back in the cage. For now, at least." This time she gave him a flirty smile, but only playfully so, an end gesture. "I've got work to do."

"God *damn*! Whaddaya say I, like, escort you to one of your rooms or somethin'?" He backed off, edgy and uptight. Maybe she'd moved too fast for this live wire.

"Hey, I don't wanna lose my job, handsome. I get off at nine. I can meet you at the office." She stepped around him, leaving him with his jaw hanging open.

As she made her getaway down the steps, he called out, "Yo, what's in the bag?"

She stopped, turned around. Guy's attitude changed faster than Midwest weather. He jogged toward her, banging down the steps. He glared at her out of untrusting eyes. Maybe she'd underestimated him. "Sorry?"

"Your trash bag. What the hell's in it?"

Instinctively, she clutched it tight to her chest, a protective mother of her cub. "Dirty sheets, linens."

"Looks like it's kinda'…I dunno…saggy or heavy or somethin'." He pointed at the bag. The computer indented one edge, a very definable rectangle.

"Yeah, you really wanna' look?" She held the bag toward him. "You won't believe the shit I have to clean up. I mean, *literally*."

He took the hint, grimaced. Waved a hand as if he could smell the imaginary fouled linens. "Nah, it's cool. Whatevs. Hey, don't know if I can make it tonight." He looked disappointed. She didn't know if she wanted to fix the bad boy. Or maybe sexually ravage the hell out of him. Possibly kill him.

"Aw, if you want to badly enough, you'll find a way." Without waiting for his response, she scuttled off, smiling all the way across the parking lot, around the motel and to her Lexus.

All in all, a fun day.

The room's windowpane shook as Raymond banged on Leon's door.

Leon opened the door. Out of breath and trying not to show it, Raymond heaved his chest out. His nostrils flared, tiny grey hairs retracting and dropping. Bloodshot eyes lanced Leon. His lips parted with an apprehensive smack. Big man on campus. *Not for long.*

"Got my money?"

Leon stepped back, gestured for his father to enter. For the last time.

Impatiently, Raymond bumped Leon's shoulder as he brushed by him. Leon closed the door, gave the knob a squeeze to bolster himself. His father waited with open arms. Not for a hug, of course.

"Well? Where the hell's the money?"

Leon walked over to the desk, opened the drawer. Grabbed the cold metal of the tire iron. Patted the hypodermic in his shirt pocket, comforting reassurance. The weapons were for worst case scenarios. Frankly, he remained indifferent as to whether he'd use them or not.

"You're not getting any money, Raymond."

"Come again?"

"I'm not giving you any money. I'm not giving you anything. Not a penny."

"What the hell is this, boy? You think you can *fuck* with me? Guess again!" Raymond's finger stabbed the air. "I'll burn your ass. Real good! I'll tell the cops, call the newspaper, fix—"

"Go right ahead, old man." Leon'd never called him that before. He knew it'd sting; he had firsthand experience after Cody constantly called him "old man" last year. "I don't care anymore. You do whatever the hell you want to do."

Raymond's hands unclenched. He sputtered, tossed for a loop. For the first time, Leon had the upper-hand, didn't intend on losing it. "I'll get you good, boy. You ain't afraid of the cops? I'll take care of you myself then." Fast as a bullet, Raymond shot toward the desk. He reached to his back pocket, pulled out a switchblade. *Skit.* The blade flashed inches from Leon's face.

"I'm gonna carve you up. Cut you 'til you bleed out like a stuck pig. Just like your—"

But this time Leon was ready. No hesitation. The second

Raymond pulled the blade back, Leon thrust out, latching onto his father's ears. Shocked, Raymond froze, knife arm hanging in air. Leon yanked down. *Crack.* Raymond's face went onto the desk. The knife dropped, clacked onto the desk. Leon brought Raymond's head up. The white of his father's eyes glowed through seeping blood. The only way to handle an animal's attack: be proactive.

Never again.

Leon grabbed the knife, then brought his father's head back down to the desk. And kept him there. Dazed, his father slithered to his knees, held aloft by Leon's grip. Probably the closest the man had ever come to praying. "You had enough, Raymond? This is how you treated me last time. How's it feel? You like it?"

Weak fingers scrabbled at Leon's arm. Feeble like an old man. "Son-of-a-bitch. I'll kill—"

Leon pressed down on his skull. "Shut up. I *don't* like it, you know. *Torture.* And I *don't* like to kill."

"Bullshiff…"

"Couldn't quite make that out. Here's the deal. You actually helped me, Raymond. More than you can imagine. You gave me something to think about, something dark I didn't want to tackle. You made me confront myself."

"Kill you…"

"Hardly in any position to do that. No, if I wanted to kill you I could easily do it right here, right now." To prove his point, he pressed the blade tip against Raymond's throat. A small poke, not enough to break the skin. Raymond whistled a sharp breath. "But I'm not going to kill you. You know why? You know *why?*" Leon shook his father's head for him since he didn't answer: *no.* "Because I'm not you. You tried to convince me I am, but I'm not. To kill you…well, that would mean you'd win. I'd be just like you. Giving in to my dark side. Enjoying it…like you do. Hell, you'd win in death. I'm not going to give you that victory."

"*Pussy…*"

"Whatever. You're sick, a twisted *monster.* Not worth my time. I still have compassion, a soul. What do you have? *Nothing.*

You're gonna rot in hell." As if giving him a head start, Leon leaned in harder. "I *wanted* to kill you. I was going to. But then I thought, what's even worse for you? What would you hate more than death? How about returning to prison, Raymond?" His father bucked, screaming into the wood. "Thought so. Now…I have no doubt you'll end up back there by your own accord. You have nothing, no money. You won't…*can't* get a job. Sooner or later you'll break. But…you also might break innocent people in doing so. So I'm going to hasten your journey back to the state pen. How's that sound?"

"*Nrrrrrr.*"

"Eloquent. You won't see it coming, Raymond. I want you to taste fear for a while. But one of these days, you'll get a visit from the local authorities. They'll search your place, here, maybe somewhere else. And they'll find what I've planted on you." It made sense, a beautifully sound logic. As paranoid as Raymond was, Leon knew he'd be afraid to leave his room now, unable to hurt anyone. Die a lonely death in a flea-bag motel. And if it didn't happen fast enough? Leon would follow up, keep his word, tip the scales of justice out of Raymond's favor.

Satisfied, Leon let up. He hovered over his father, feeling taller than the pathetic man for the first time. "So, Raymond… watch your back."

Raymond pushed himself to his feet, breathing wildly. "You son-of-a-bitch, no-good, pansy-ass piss-ant! I'm gonna call the law afore you get the chance! I'm gonna—"

"You don't get it. I've already beat you." Leon shook his head, sighed. Yet inside he felt on fire, thrilled. "Soon…very soon, Leon Garber's going to 'die'. I'll arrange it so there's no doubt. The police won't believe you, think you're crazy. Maybe lock you up in the mental ward where you belong anyway."

"I'll call now." He turned his head, spat. A projectile of blood stained the carpet, probably not the first time.

Leon offered his phone. "Sure. Go ahead. But how do you know that during our little meet and greet, I didn't have someone plant something in your room? And maybe I called the cops on you already?"

"You didn't do that." But doubt sucked the bravado, the tough guy, out of Raymond. He looked less like an unconquerable boogeyman and more like a pathetic, beaten bully.

"Maybe. Maybe not."

"I still got the computer, dumb-ass. You're not gonna risk that!"

"Oh, really?" Leon couldn't help his grin. It spread like wildfire. "You checked your room lately?"

Raymond's eyes glazed over, far away; back at his motel room. Where he kept Leon's laptop. "You're lying."

"Better go check then. Go on." Leon flicked fingers, an inconsequential gesture. "What're you waiting for, Raymond? Get your ass out of here."

Raymond said nothing, at first. Just stood, mental cogs grinding. Finally, he turned, nearly stumbling over his feet. "*Fuck* you." He kept it low, barely audible.

"Is that any way to talk to your kin?" A little childish, Leon realized, but the big kid in him enjoyed tossing Raymond's words back at him. His father hurried for the door. "Last time you'll ever talk to me, Raymond. But…you'll feel me all around you and never see me coming." Turning the fear back on the fear monger. "Thanks again, you bastard, for making me the man I am today." The odd thing was Leon really meant it. If not for his father, he would've leapt right off the precipice of sanity.

Leon slammed the door after Raymond stalked off. Couldn't believe he'd vanquished the demon. On his own terms. But he'd have to celebrate later.

He suspected Raymond wouldn't do anything, not right away. Maybe come running back for blood once he saw the computer'd been taken. Or maybe call the police as he said he would. Or just sit in the dark, cowering at every shadow. The latter prospect sounded good to Leon, but he couldn't chance it. He had to leave. Arrangements had been made, time to end the latest chapter on his life.

Because he'd been serious about burying Leon Garber. Forever. He no longer associated himself with that person's past, his sicknesses, his fears.

He gathered his clothing, tossed them into his suitcase. Snapped on disposable gloves and gave the place a thorough wipe-down. Didn't take long. The visual grime had limited what he'd touched in the room. Seconds later, the call he'd been expecting came through.

"Hello?" Leon couldn't keep the pleasure out of his voice, speaking through a grin. For once, the stars were aligning in his favor.

"It's 'Sly Fox'. The goose has dropped the golden egg."

"Funny. Alright, swing by and get me. Fast, please."

"Sorry, Leon. No can do."

"Seriously, Nanette, I've gotta get outta here." Leon's celebration came to an abrupt halt. The phone slipped a bit in his hand. He wanted to believe Nanette was playing another of her flirting games, but in his gut, he knew better.

"Leon…I *like* you, I really do. But this is business. Don't take it personally." In the background, he heard tinny salsa playing through a car radio, her celebration going strong.

"Dammit, Nanette. I'm serious. If it's about the computer—"

"But it *is* about the computer, that's the whole point."

The longer the conversation continued, Leon felt his life's clock ticking away. "You can *have* it. I don't care about the damn computer. I need you to—"

"Whoa, hold up, son. First of all, you don't *need* me to do anything. I already *have* the laptop. And I'm not some little subservient girl to your needs. I'm disappointed in you, Leon. I thought you were different…different from other men…" Her voice lost all playfulness, a vocal hurt freezing over it.

"That's not what I meant and you know it. We had a deal. We were going to give it to Albert *together.*"

Her shrill laugh may as well've been a slap. "Sometimes plans change, love."

"What're you going to do with the laptop?" His right hand tingled so badly he had to switch the phone to his other hand. "Are you working with LMI? You gonna give it back to them?"

"Of course not." Another laugh, but her heart wasn't in it. "I hate them more than Albert. I'm just gonna sweat Al for some cash, that's all. Girl's gotta make some bank somehow. In case you haven't heard, it's a man's world."

"Jesus Christ, Nanette, I have nowhere to go! Please take me in! I left myself hanging just now with Raymond, everything's at risk. Because I trusted you! I put my—"

"You should know better than to trust me, Leon." Her voice lowered, contemplative. As if fate had been taken out of her hands, impossible to change course. "That's your problem."

"Nanette, please—"

"Oh, one last thing, Leon…while I was in the room, Raymond had some visitors."

"What?" He didn't like where this was going and already knew the destination.

"Not what, Leon 'who.' Two guys, one large and impressive, the other the opposite. LMI men, I'm pretty sure."

An invisible fist knocked the air out of him. "Nanette…was there a third person?"

Clearly surprised, she said, "Yeah. Young kid, cocky, good looking—"

"Did he say 'yo' a lot?"

"Come again?"

"Did he say *'yo'*?" Her pause gave him his answer. "Nanette, *please*! You've got to get me *out* of here. Now! They're going to *kill* me! Raymond will give me up if he hasn't already! I can't take my truck, LMI knows it! I'm *begging*—"

"Don't beg, Leon. It's unbecoming. You—"

"You're *not* hearing me! Who do you *think* has a better chance at stopping LMI than I do? I've *already* gone up against them! I can't do it if I'm *dead*. Just come get me! Please—"

"Sorry, baby. But if you're gonna keep yelling at me, I'm gonna let you go."

"This isn't a goddamn game, Nanette! In a few minutes, they'll be on me! It'll be—"

"Now you've gone and offended my tender little heart, Leon. Later."

"No! Don't hang up on me! Don't…" Screaming in the wind. No sense trying to call her back.

God damn it.

He pinched the curtain back, looked across the courtyard. No activity near Raymond's room so far. He'd have to make it to the truck, switch autos somewhere. Pay with cash. Then what? The computer'd been his ticket to safety. Now he couldn't even be certain Albert wanted—needed—him on the team.

The noose tightened like a familiar, uncomfortable necktie. With shaking hands, he grabbed his briefcase, visually swept the room one final time. He had minutes tops, seconds before—

Blam, bang, blam…

The big one. A heart attack. No other explanation. His heart yanked at the sound of the knock on his door, rebelling against his chest. It caught, stuttered, leaving sore chest muscles behind.

Kak, kak, kak…

The visitor had switched from knuckles to something metallic. A gun. Leon's hands trembled over the briefcase. His fingers wouldn't steady enough to accurately roll over the combination, pull out more syringes. *The tire iron.* Still in the drawer. His only choice, last call for the living. He tucked it into the back of his jeans, beneath his shirt.

Clak, tak, chak…

"Open up, I know you're home. I can see your shadow moving inside."

Outside, a dark silhouette darkened the curtain. Hands were placed around the intruder's face, peering in. A female's voice. Familiar. *Detective Keats.* Queen of great timing.

Relief flowed through him, temporarily so. Keats wasn't much more comforting than LMI. But he might survive her. He called out, "Just a minute." Buying time, time he didn't have.

How could he use her, turn her presence into a positive? Ask her for protection, worry about the fall out later? Get the jump on her once in her car? No. He'd never hurt police, not innocents. Besides, LMI's hunger for anonymity wouldn't allow their hit men to take him out while in the presence of a detective. He hoped.

Leon opened the door. "Detective. Sorry, ah, you caught me on my way out. Just—"

She stepped in, giving the room full appraisal. "Hm. Looks like you're going *way* out." She whirled to face him, hand on hip. Gifting him with a smile he didn't want to accept.

"Sorry. Don't know what—"

"Suitcase." She pointed toward the obvious. "You're leaving?" Blatantly, she pulled back her jacket flap, exposing her holstered weapon. Ready to use it.

"Yeah. You know us drifter types. Can't stand still in any port for—"

"That go the same for accounting firms, Mr. Garber?"

Leon tried to play dumb. Numb, absolutely, but his face wouldn't cooperate with 'dumb'. His chuckle rattled like a last gasp of desperation. "I'm sorry, Detective…I don't under…" He ran out of steam, too much coal in his engine. He fell onto the bed, the tire iron prodding him in the back. A weapon he lacked the energy to wield. A thick layer of detachment settled over him.

Impossible. Keats had uncovered his identity. While his would-be killers lurked across the parking lot. *Impossible.* He laughed. Laughed at his situation, his struggle, mostly at himself and the joke his life had turned into. And to keep tears of hysteria at bay.

"Something funny, Mr. Garber?"

"No, not really. Well, yeah, everything, actually."

"Let's take this from the start. Why don't you…" Annoyed at his incessant laughter, she rapped her fingers over her gun barrel. "You done yet, Mr. Garber? Or, hell…can I call you Leon? Feels like I know you already." He'd seen her type of grin before; the type usually reserved for corporate America where boardrooms served as the battlefield. The smile of victory. And, on Keats, it looked like it tasted delicious.

"What do you want to know? If you know everything about me, what's the point?" Leon raised his hands, dropped them in his lap. *Defeat.*

Leon doubted she'd uncovered everything, certainly not his past crimes. But she knew he'd lied about his identity. Just a matter of time before everything would be revealed. With Keats' gun now in her hand, at her side, his playing the innocent card wouldn't work any longer. A foolish waste of time.

"Let's start with why you're going by 'Chris Hampton'. And where you've been for the past fifteen years."

Leon inhaled, exhaled. It'd been a long dangerous ride.

In a way, he felt relieved to put the brakes on, coast in for an involuntary early retirement. Of course he wouldn't be rewarded with a gold watch. More like a one-way trip to the electric chair.

"Detective...I'm tired. Tired of running, hiding. I—"

"Tell me what you're running from. From the moment you left Los Angeles. Left the big-ass accounting firm you were set to conquer. I'm a good listener." She punched a few buttons on her phone, clipped it to her belt. "Go."

But, behind Detective Keats, a click—a gun's antsy wink—stopped story time dead cold.

Chapter Ten

Survival mode kicked back in, something Leon'd written off. The pistol pointed at him proved pretty compelling.

"What the *hell?*" Keats turned, shocked. Her partner, Bellup, stood in the doorway, a decidedly non-police standard silencer fit on his weapon. Sweat trickled down his face, greasing his smirk. "Bellup, what the *hell*—"

"Shut up." He eased into the room with the surprising grace bestowed upon overweight men. With a honky-tonk kick, he shut the door behind him. "I *told* you to leave him alone, Keats. *Told* you to stay out of it."

"Holster your goddamn gun, Bellup. *Now.* I've got this under—"

"Shit. You don't have any idea what's goin' on, Keats." The gun volleyed between Leon and Keats.

"I was right about this guy, Bellup! He—"

Whiff. Crack. Bellup fired inches above Keat's head. A seam in the wallpaper split, the bullet buried in plaster. "Take your gun out. Two fingers. *Do it!*"

"Christ." Slowly, Keats straightened out of her squat. She pinched her gun's handle, stopped. "Don't do anything stupid, Bellup. Your pension's—"

"I don't give a rat's ass about my pension!" He wagged the gun at Leon. "*He's* my pension."

"What the hell're you talking about?"

"Your boy on the bed. Someone contacted me, someone with deep pockets. Did some favors for them in the past. They told me to look for him. You know how much green I had to lay down to find him?"

"Exactly. We're on the same side. Let's take him in and—"

"You just don't get it. Hardly the first time. Our guy here's got a bounty on his head, one that'll set me sailing off into a comfy future. Tried to get you to back off, Keats. But…no, you had to be an uptight bitch, get all up in my business. I don't know what Garber's done. Don't care. But he's mine. My backer wants him dead. Too bad you got in the way." He shrugged. "No skin off my ass."

Keats' hand wavered over her holstered pistol. Perilously indecisive. Time stopped, showdown at high noon.

The two cops had all but forgotten Leon, too caught up in each other. It would end badly, Leon knew, just a matter of who'd be left standing. He reached around for the tire iron at his back. He gauged his distance from Bellup, estimated how long it'd take to act. Bellup stood twelve, thirteen feet away, his gun arm locked on Keats. It all came down to Bellup's reflexes. Even overweight and panting, the crooked cop was deceptively nimble. Two seconds, maybe three. All Leon had.

Leon whisked the tire iron free. The sudden movement caught Bellup's eye, not yet his gun. Leon launched off the bed, dove low. His head hit Bellup's belly and he jacked up a palm beneath the cop's chin. Surprised, Bellup stumbled back.

Two shots fired. *Ffft. Ffft.* One barely cleared Leon's head, the other cracked into the ceiling. Powder flaked down upon them.

Spack. A deafening gunshot, Keats' weapon.

Bellup flattened onto the floor, Leon on top of him. Repeatedly, Leon whacked Bellup's gun-holding hand with the tire iron. Gave him a blow to the head. Unnecessary. Bellup stopped struggling, but not from Leon's attack. A blood-red butterfly sprouted wings over his chest. A fatal shot.

Leon turned, tire iron up. Smoke filled the air. Dust swirled in the fading sunlight. Keats lay on the floor. Her legs trembled, one shoe caught on her toes. She stared at Leon with terrified eyes.

Leon dropped the tire iron, no longer needed. Keats' lips bobbled, forcing out moans. Blood darkened her white blouse, her hand clamped over the gunshot wound. *Dying*, a look Leon knew well.

Disoriented—too much, too fast—Leon studied the battlefield. One dead cop, the other dying. In his room. A hopeless situation. Fleeing seemed like the only option. Keep going until he reached the Mexico border. Never look back.

But he couldn't—wouldn't—leave a good cop to die. From the bathroom, he ripped the sole towel off the shower rod. Carefully he removed Keats' hand, pressed the folded towel down onto her wound. The bullet may have missed her vital organs. *Lucky; critical, but lucky.* But light slowly dimmed from her eyes. Not much time until they went completely out.

"Keats…*Keats.*" He tapped her cheek, did it a little harder. Her eyes wandered, a drunk's lazy gaze. "Hold this. Hold it *tight.*" He pressed her hand down onto the wound. Weakly, she obliged, but her fingers slipped away. He needed to tie it.

No rope in the room, nothing long enough. Bellup lay flat, arms straight out, crucified on the floor. Quickly Leon unbuckled his belt, yanked it off his dead weight. He wouldn't need his belt, not now.

"Keats, can you sit up?" She couldn't. Just shook, tremors rippling through her. Sweat iced her face. *Shock.* Carefully, Leon raised her, slipped the belt around her. Buckled it over the towel. "Keep pressing down on it."

Dammit. He had to get her to the hospital. No time for an ambulance. But he couldn't load her into his truck, not in the daylight. With no one to help him.

He drew a hand down his face, stumped. Behind him, the door squeaked open…

Raymond ran. Weight pressed down on his chest, his lungs burned.

Son-of-a-bitch! If the little bastard stole the computer, Raymond had nothing. Leon made it clear he didn't care if Raymond ratted him out to the cops. Probably a bluff.

But what if it's not?

No matter how you sliced it, Raymond had no intention of living the rest of his life in prison. Hell, he'd already made plans to buy a luxury yacht, sail wherever the wind took him. And now…now, his dreams were drying up like a raisin in the sun.

Goddammit! From King of the World to a pauper, all in one fell swoop of fate. But one way or another, he'd have the last word yet. No one—especially not his pup of an offspring—would get the better of him. He'd knife him, that's what he'd do. Carve him up good, just like he did his wife. Wouldn't amount to a pot to piss in financially, but, damn if it wouldn't put a smile on his face. End things the proper way, something he should've attended to when he had the chance all those years ago.

His hand rode the stairwell rail, using it as a pulley. Near the top, he slowed, his legs heavy. As soon as the key tapped the lock, the door opened. *Unlocked.* And he sure as hell locked it when he'd left, no senility setting into his brain yet.

Raymond entered, fists curled. A scrawny toothpick of a man sat on his bed. Coughed into his hand by way of greeting. Then a big how-do-you-do arm wrapped around his neck and thrust him against the wall.

Attached to the arm was a mountain of muscle, hairless as a newborn babe. "Raymond Garber." A statement, not a question. Not a cop.

"Let go of me, dammit!" Raymond struggled. The bald man countered by tightening his grip around Raymond's neck. "Let me go, you son—"

Bang. Raymond's head slammed into the wall. "Raymond, I'm going to ask you a question. One question. That's all we need answered. Anything else you say is not going to help your case. If you give me the correct answer, you might live." He laid out the rules like a teacher, no nonsense. "Maybe not. It's up to you."

A younger guy, ratty the way kids dress, stepped up. "So, yo, you're the dick that killed Garber's mom, yeah?" Cock of the yard or so he acted. Guys like him filled the prisons, wasting space until shown differently. "Let me at him, I'll make him talk."

The big guy swatted him away. "Back off, Spangler. Let the professionals do their work."

"Asshole ain't gonna talk. Let's do him!"

"I said to back *off.*"

Like a pissed-off brat, the kid stalked off. The guy on the bed coughed again.

"What the hell you want with me? I'm just an old man. I ain't—"

"Ah, bullshit!" said the kid. "Dude's a friggin' wife killer!"

"Will you shut up, already? Go smoke or something! Don't go far."

"Yes, Dad," the kid groused. Gave Raymond a hateful glare on his way out of the room. Goddamn kids today, no respect.

Exasperated, the big man turned back toward Raymond. "I know who you are. *What* you are. And I don't really care. Your business. But your son's our business."

Of course, thought Raymond. No shakedown. They want Leon. *Ask and ye shall receive.* Cash register dings in his head revitalized his dreams. "What do you want with ol' Leon?"

"We want to know where 'ol Leon' is."

Happy to hasten his son's departure, Raymond had every intention of complying. But at a cost. "Well, now, just so happens I know his whereabouts. What's it worth to you?"

"How 'bout your life?"

Bedsprings crunched as the smaller man left the bed. Beneath his scraggly beard, a green smile spread.

Raymond wouldn't be intimidated; hell, he'd faced down worse men in the joint. "Looks like we're at a Mexican stand-off, amigos. I'll tell you where he is. Assumin' I'm breathing. If not…well, shit, looks like a lose-lose situation. You gimme some green, everyone goes home happy."

The big man picked up Raymond, hefted him over his shoulder.

"What the hell? Put me down, you damn jack—"

"Shut up." He slammed Raymond down into a chair by the motel room desk. Raymond's teeth chocked down, his bladder on full alert. The big man wrenched one of Raymond's arms behind the chair, clamped the other one to the chair's arm. "Bug…he's all yours."

The man called "Bug" played out a game of pocket pool in his jeans until he plucked out a golden lighter. The top snapped off, the flint wheel flicked. Mesmerized, the yellow flame danced in his eyes. It took him a minute to reacquaint himself with Raymond.

"Mr. Garber..." He cleared his throat. "Mr. Garber, I don't know if you've ever been burned before. Badly, I mean." He placed a hand on top of Raymond's. A shirt sleeve pulled up, revealing red and meaty scar tissue along his wrist. "It's... unpleasant. For most people." He actually winked. *Winked.* Raymond rocked his shoulders, but the big man held him firm. "The odd thing about burning...well...it's interesting. First you hear your skin frying. Your hair sizzling. Then you smell it. Some people say it's savory like burning beef. Others...not so much. But all of these sensations reach you first before the pain. Sort of the body's warning system that something bad's coming. And it's bad. Very bad. Excruciating. And it all happens in a second." When he snapped his fingers, they silently slid off one another. "But it feels like an eternity. And the most exciting part? You know it's coming. *Anticipation.* But let me show you. Here..."

He snatched Raymond's hand up, clamping his fist around three of Raymond's fingers. The flame started at the tip of Raymond's pinky, riding the length inward. Stone-faced, Raymond watched, unwilling to surrender. Kid stuff. Until the fire reached the webbing between the fingers.

Bug had it pretty much right. A slight snap, a pop. An awful smell, worse than scorched steak. Dark smoke rose, the smoke of his flesh. Then the pain hit. Rushing like wind up his arm, a roaming heart attack.

"Ah, Jesus Christ, goddammit, stop! Stop this shit already! I'll talk! Goddamn you, I'll talk!" Once the lighter extinguished, so did the scrawny man's elation.

Raymond sure as shit wasn't going to cry in front of these bastards. Even though it hurt like hell, he'd never shed a tear. Yet he heard someone crying. Behind him, the big man sniffed. And by God, if he didn't sob like a little girl.

"Goddamn baby! I'm the one getting his damn hand burnt off!" Raymond wrenched his hand away and sucked at the burned skin. "Shit, buncha' psychos! I'll tell you where the little pussy is. Just stop this shit!"

The large man, now wearing sunglasses, came around to face Raymond. Beneath the shades, moisture glistened on his cheeks. "Where is he, Raymond?"

Raymond spat, a perfect landing on the bald man's shoe.

The big man ignored it. "Where is he? Or do you want my friend to play with you some more?"

It pissed Raymond off to no end. In every business transaction, something needed to be exchanged. The American way. And he considered himself a true-blue American. Something could still be salvaged out of the deal. "Come on, now, fellas...how 'bout some Benjamins for my troubles?" He wiggled most of his fingers, the pinky curiously unmoving. "Just some medical cash for an old—"

"Bug?" The big guy stood aside, making way for his small shadow.

"Room 113! Christ, almighty, he's in room 113! Across the way! Just...no more!"

"If you're lying to me, old man, you're gonna regret it."

"I ain't lying! Why in hell would I lie?"

The crybaby said to his partner, "We gotta' get over there, Bug."

"What about him?" Bug jacked a thumb Raymond's way.

"Leave the kid with him."

"Think that's wise?"

"We got what we need. Besides...we'll know where the kid is. Keep him outta trouble for a while. Besides...the old man's a mother killer. I don't like people who kill...their mothers..." Sobs swallowed up his last words.

Raymond let fly another loogie, one for the road. "Goddamn sissies." Hell was his next stop, no last minute stay of execution. He'd be a fool to think otherwise, the nature of being a realist.

But he sure as hell planned on dragging his piss-ant boy along for the ride.

Sunlight haloed off the silhouette standing in the doorway. Leon raced for the tire iron. Once he heard laughter, he stopped. Wildly inappropriate laughter given the circumstances.

"Can't leave you alone for a minute, can I, Leon?" Nanette

strode in, unaffected by the cop's graveyard at her feet. If anything, she appeared tickled, envious almost, of the carnage. She uttered a wistful *tsk*.

"Jesus Christ, Nanette, you scared—"

"Come on. Let's go." With an elbow resting in her hand, she dangled her sunglasses, twirling them. As she moved her hips back and forth, her dress swayed. A tapping foot kept beat. Still flirting.

Leon didn't question why she came back, didn't care. She could help. "We've got to get her to the hospital."

She said nothing. But the glasses stopped moving. Her foot stuck to the floor. "You've gotta be kidding me. *Look* at this mess. If you want out of here, we go now. *Alone.*"

"Pull your car up. In front of my door. I'm not leaving without her." Keats stared up at the ceiling, unblinking. She murmured, possibly a prayer. Shivering as if freezing.

Nanette withdrew a knife from her purse. Small, succinct and deadly as its owner. Green gems glittered on the handle, a stylish touch. "Finish it, Leon. If you don't, I will. She knows you, seen your—"

"You're not listening to me. I'm not going to kill her like an animal. She's going to the hospital. We're taking her. Or I'll do it alone."

"You're giving me ultimatums? Should be the other way around."

"Fine. Leave."

She considered, her foot tapping again. A small grin dimpled her cheeks. With one easy flick of the wrist, she slipped her sunglasses back on. Hiding her eyes, her true intentions. "Determined. I like that."

"You gonna help me?"

"Whatever. Car's already here. But…have you forgotten your play pals across the way? You don't think this might catch their attention?"

He hadn't had time to consider it, not really. Not after his newest near-death escape. Honestly, he found it odd they hadn't been trampling down his door already. Maybe Raymond finally proved useful for something, a time killer, so to speak. But he knew Raymond would give him up soon enough.

"Let's go. Get her arm around your shoulder." Carefully they hoisted Keats up. Between them, they carried her to the running car, laid her down on the back seat. Leon kept an eye on his father's room, waiting for the door to open. He expected to see LMI men tumbling out with weapons raised in a heigh-ho fashion. Nanette hustled to the driver side, slid in.

Behind them, a voice snapped like a firecracker. "Chris? What's up?"

Leon jolted. "Gavin. Ah, hey, everything's cool." He folded his arms, covering Keats' blood on his shirt. "Sorry if we were too loud." Trying to act normal seemed ridiculous, especially with a bleeding cop in the back of the car. But he couldn't involve Gavin. "Just got a sick friend. Taking her to the hospital."

Gavin said nothing. But he looked tired and sad, frowning. Far too pessimistic for someone his age.

But after what LMI had done to his previous hotel, Leon had to cut to the chase, no time for consoling words. He couldn't live with himself if Gavin and his mother died at LMI's hands. "Hey, Gavin, do me a favor?"

"Sure, man, whatever." He dropped his skateboard to the ground, posed to take flight.

"I need you to leave. Don't go back in your room. Just go. Now."

"What? What're you—"

"Just listen to me!" Leon went to him, grabbed his shoulders, shook him. How a real father might act. "For your own safety. Get on your skateboard and ride. Don't stop 'til you hit the beach. Wait until your mom gets home. Then give it another hour."

"Chris, I don't get—"

"You *have* to listen to me. Just *go*. And...tell your mother I'm sorry. I never meant...for any of this to happen."

A flicker of excitement brightened Gavin's eyes, danger a stimulant to teenagers. Not so much anyone else. "Whoa. What're you all up in?"

"Doesn't matter. And it's not...how it looks. Just trust me, okay? I know it's a lot to ask, you don't know me and..." Leon shut up. It was all bullshit and they both knew it. Nothing he could say would change Gavin's and Terrie's minds about him, not after the dead cop was found in his room. Best to burn bridges, save the survivors. "Just do as I say, Gavin."

"Man...I don't...man..." Gavin looked down at his shadow, as long as his disappointment. Disenchantment over another adult letting him down. But Leon never asked to be that adult.

"Just...go." Leon pointed down the sidewalk. He turned his back until he heard the *chak-chak-chak* of the skateboard's wheels clattering over the pavement. "Gavin?"

Gavin's back heel hit the walk, the board tilting up. Hope lifted a smile. "Yeah?"

"You'll get to college."

"Right. Whatever." Gavin continued his departure. He lifted a hand, erecting a middle-fingered salute. "Easy for you to say. Later."

Leon wanted to call him back, talk to him. Instead, he mumbled, "Later."

In the car, Nanette tapped long fingers over the steering wheel, impatient. She rolled down the window and said, "You wanna' say goodbye to all your neighbors, Leon? Maybe go hug the manager?"

"Gotta' get my briefcase."

As Leon rushed out of his room, briefcase in hand, he glanced across the lot. His breath caught in his throat. Muscular arms draped over the railing in front of room number 242. A cigarette dangled between fingers, smoke curling up in front of the man's face. Through the smoke, a wide grin broke; roughly handsome yet childlike. *Cody.* He stood tall, flicked the butt over the railing to the cement below. Didn't budge.

Leon moved slowly, as cautious as being confronted by a rattlesnake. He knew how Cody could bite.

Cody jammed his hands into his shorts, tugging them even lower. Just casually enjoying the view.

Leon slipped into the passenger seat. As the car backed up, Leon watched Cody, waiting for him to make a move. Instead, Cody dipped his chin, a simple acknowledgement. Saying hello to an acquaintance.

Leon nodded back. Then said, "Let's get the hell out of here."

The ape and the ant barreled out of the hotel room, startling Cody. Smoke practically fumed from their asses. Ever cool, Cody turned his sudden hop of fright into an intentional hip-hop move.

"Get in there, watch the old guy," Sensitivity ordered with his stabby finger. Cody knocked his hand away. He'd seen more of Sensitivity's fingertip than he had all of Florida. He wanted to grab it, break it, make the baboon howl. One of these days.

Hell with them.

Until Sensitivity'd barked at him, Cody'd planned on telling them he'd just seen Garber. Not now, no way. Let 'em find out on their own.

It sorta surprised Cody he hadn't raised the roof over Garber's drive-by. Instead, he just let Garber go on his merry la-dee-dah way, carting off a body from the looks of things. And with the hottie maid in tow.

Garber had game when it came to hot chicks. Beat Cody to the punch with the maid. Weird when the guy had the personality of a grandmother. Still Cody honored the bro code. Killing a dude's one thing, but he'd never step on a bro's turf. Still she did wave and smile at Cody when they rolled by. Even gave a wink. A tease. Maybe he'd get the chance to find out if she could backup her tease.

Whatever. He'd let Garber slip through his fingers. Why? Self-preservation, first and foremost rule of the land. Once LMI caught Garber, Cody would be put on the extinction list. And, as always, he enjoyed the chase. He imagined it was how a vegetarian felt on a deer hunt. No fun once the meat landed on the plate.

"You hear me, Spangler?" Again, Sensitivity gave him the pokity-poke.

"Yeah, Jesus, chill. I'll watch him." Just then it hit Cody. Sensitivity opened the doorway wide, inviting Cody to perform his art. What he does best. Sometimes gifts come wrapped in ugly-ass paper. "No problem." Cody grinned, something he hadn't been doing much of lately.

"Just…don't do anything stupid," Sensitivity said as he hustled off. Even though built like a brick shit-house, Sensitivity still managed to run twice as fast as his partner. Bug clamored after him, wheezing like he had a hole in his lung. Maybe he did. Sure acted like it.

Cody didn't waste any time. He locked the room door behind him. Garber's old man stood on shaky legs, cradling his hand. He straightened and spat, "What the hell you lookin' at?"

"Shit from where I'm standin'." Cody pulled back a hand and bitch-slapped him. "That's for my boy, Leon." He did it again. *Smat.* "That's for Leon's momma."

The old man dropped down into the chair. A white lock of hair flung over his eyes, a sheepdog look. Blood colored his teeth, and behind that, he laughed. "Well, I'll be goddammed! What? You Leon's little butt buddy?"

That deserved another swat. Cody planned on enjoying this. "Shut your hole, old man. No one's manlier than Cody. Just ask the ladies."

"Hah! You probably ain't never been near a lady's teat except for suckin' on your momma's!"

As sure as a trip-wired explosion, he yanked Cody's cord. Hard. No one talked about Cody's mother. Especially the disgusting shit the old man'd said. Cody took it out in trade, hitting him again. Pounded him like pizza dough. The old man's head rocked, his hair flying. Most of what he said Cody couldn't make out, but it didn't matter. His constant laughter was easy enough to understand. Taunting Cody. He hit the old man until his hand grew numb.

"Queer for my son, that's what you are!" Garber's lip split, bleeding and puffy. And still he laughed.

"Shut up, shut up, *shut up!*"

With Cody's next blow, the chair tipped. The old man fell to the floor. Liver-spotted hands drew up in front of his face. "Whoa, hold on now! Let me get somethin' straight here…you're Leon's lil' buddy?"

Cody's fist froze in midair. He knew he wouldn't like what was coming, but he felt compelled to hear the old man out anyway. Might give his impending kill more zip.

"Then..." Garber spat blood, "...why're you and your goons fixin' to kill him?"

A question Cody'd been asking himself lately. Honestly, he'd rather hang with Garber than the LMI dicks. Maybe the old man had the answer. He waited.

"If that don't take the cake. Your beatin' the tar outta' me 'cause of what I did to Leon's momma. But you're just gonna go kill him yourself."

"None of your business, old man."

"Hell it ain't! You assholes made it my business. Let me tell you somethin' about lil' Leon...he ain't loyal to no one. Not a soul. He'd just as soon see you dead. Let you rot, one way or the other, in jail or six feet under. Ain't nothin' to him."

"Garber ain't that way, yo, he—"

"Damn, boy, aren't you about as dumb as a country bumpkin in a whore house!" Shutting one eye, he roared: *ar, ar, ar*! Give him an eye patch, Cody thought, he'd be a pirate. "He's sittin' cross the way right now, just laughin' at your pathetic ass. Why, he—"

"Shut up..." Cody stood, turned away. Defenses up. Unwanted memories sped through his mind; the good times and bad times he'd shared with Garber on the road last year. Garber could be a tool at times, but he wouldn't ever laugh at Cody. *Would he?*

"Ohhh! Hit a sore spot, did I? What's the matter, you gonna cry like your big boyfriend? That it? Boo-hoo-hoo. Jesus Christ, I'm the one bleedin' to death, you don't hear me cryin'! Buncha' little girls!" Cody heard him dragging a leg over the carpet, trying to stand up. "Yep. I know Leon, loyal to no man. Just himself. And he's havin' a hoot over you...lil' cry-baby—"

"Shut your goddamn mouth!" Cody knew Leon better than that. They were buds last year.

"You mark my word, he's gonna leave you high and dry. Make off with all his money. Let you take the fall for whatever the hell he's mixed up in." Cody turned back. Garber's old man had crawled to the bed, hoisted himself into a sitting position. Grinning through broken teeth. "Oh, yeah, I can see it on your pussy face! He's already done that! Left you standin' with your pecker in your hand while he rolled on all fancy and free. He…"

Cody didn't want to think about it, tried not to. Hell, he'd even justified Garber's behavior last year. When he'd framed Cody. Sent him to jail. While Garber flew down to Florida. Scoring babes. Living la vida loca. Garber'd framed him, plain and simple. And for what? Cody hadn't done jack-shit.

The old man screwed up his face. "Aw ha, ha, ha! I know ol' Leon, he's over there makin' fun of you! Laughing, giggling like a little girl over how dumb you are!"

"I'm not dumb…" For once, though, Cody didn't believe his own press. Maybe he'd been stupid to go to prison for Garber, not rat him out. Garber hadn't suffered, not at all. Only Cody.

"Yessir, he's slapping his leg, throwing down a real hoot at your expense. You candy-ass cry-baby!" Garber smacked his knee, growled at the ceiling like a blues singer. The kind of music Leon'd introduced Cody to. When they used to be friends. "Howdy-do, he's havin' himself a good ol' time! Makin' fun of you…the way you dress…"

Shit. How could Cody have been so dumb? Garber had made fun of Cody's clothes, looked down his nose at his personality. *Jealous.* Simple as shit, Garber was jealous. Trying to tear Cody down, the way the assholes at school, at the foster homes, used to do. *Exactly like those bastards.*

Come to think of it, Garber did think he was all that and then some. Thought his shit didn't stink, his piss didn't run yellow. Only thing yellow about him was his cowardice. *Bastard.*

"Heh hah! Leon's sittin' pretty right about now, just yukkin' it up. If I was you, I'd go over there right now and carve him a new face. Make him less of a pretty boy!"

Something gleamed on the floor, something standing out in the shadows. A message. One meant for Cody. He stalked toward it. Bent down, plucked it up. Ran a finger along the broken glass shard. Pressed hard until blood popped out. Tasted it.

"And, you, with your mommy issues. Hah! Mommy issues, for God's sake! Leon's telling everyone about it right now! What'd Mommy do to you? Pull down your britches, laugh at your lil' pecker, and—"

Cody only heard *Mommy.* Again and again. *Mommy, Mommy, Mommy…*

He didn't remember tearing across the room. Didn't remember his handiwork, the fun part. A shame. But he liked the aftermath. Quite a bit.

The old man's fingers twitched at the glass shard in his neck. With a lucky jerk, he yanked it out. Blood jetted across the room, painting the walls. The stream dwindled, picked up again. Red shadows pooled on the carpet. A bib of blood wrapped around Garber's neck. Cody caught some of the backsplash, rubbed it over his face. Tasted sweet victory.

A cooling calm enveloped him like a mother's touch he'd never known.

He sat in front of Raymond Garber, cross-legged. And watched the old man's eyes bug until he dropped dead.

And, now, more than ever, Cody knew, absolutely so, he had to kill Leon. For everything he'd put him through. But even worse, for *laughing* at him.

Cody'd heard about meditation, all that yoga stuff. Thought it was bullshit. Until now. Adrift in comfort, he enjoyed a righteous buzz.

Parts of a conversation dribbled in and out of his world.

"Jesus Christ, what a mess…"

"Hey, you said to let the kid have his fun…"

"Alright. Let's get outta' here. We don't want anything to do with the dead cop across the way. Fire the old man's room up, Bug. Make it fast. I'll grab the pain-in-the-ass…"

Someone grabbed Cody, yanked him to his feet. Shoved him through the door. Gasoline permeated his nose, strong and crude. But not strong enough to yank him off his cloud.

As he shuffled down the walkway, he heard a *floomph.* Felt heat warming his back, a cozy blanket of security.

He crawled into the car, half lucid. Reveling in the possibilities of what he'd do to Garber. Leon's father had just been the warm-up.

During the ride to the hospital, Nanette's seductively voiced

GPS (Leon wondered if it might've been her own voice) lulled Leon into a sense of false security. Other than Keats' labored breathing from the back seat, the trip was a quiet one. Solemnly so.

Leon needed the downtime to think.

He didn't trust Nanette. Desired her, maybe. Hated himself for doing so. Because he knew she'd carefully orchestrated how he felt. The way she probably had done to her victims. After everything he'd been through, it'd be ridiculous to end up as one of her homicidal statistics.

Good cops and bad cops were on his tail. Making Florida his worst possible location right now. Whether Keats lived or not, a manhunt would soon be unleashed, the intense kind cops only beat for their fallen brethren. Furthermore, if LMI had bought off Bellup, more dirty cops were probably chomping at the bit. LMI liked to hedge their bets.

Raymond was good as dead, no doubt about it. Leon'd be lying if he didn't admit to being pleased. Yet, part of him, an incessant nag of a demon, told him he should've done the deed. At times, wishy-washy thinking was easier than standing on the good side of the moral equator.

And it killed him to think of Gavin and Terry's reaction upon hearing of his next door activities. But dwelling only dragged him deeper into self-loathing.

Furthermore, he didn't know what to make of Cody's response (or rather, lack thereof) upon seeing him. He'd saved Leon's hide, no denying that. But where Cody stood now was anyone's guess.

Too much to process in too little time. And way too many dangling loose ends.

Leon longed for closure, a beautiful myth, something he'd rarely achieved in his life.

If he couldn't achieve that, he'd settle for sleep.

Keats' breathing grew deeper, a death rattle. But Leon knew she was a scrapper. He suspected she'd will herself to live until she'd brought him to justice.

Near the hospital, Leon flagged down a homeless man and paid him to escort Keats inside via his grocery cart. Keats actually managed to hobble a few steps before collapsing into the cart. Once she passed out, Leon checked for a pulse. Weak, but defiant.

Leon waited until they were blocks from the hospital to ask his question. "Why'd you come back for me?"

Nanette lifted a well-disciplined eyebrow. "It's a woman's prerogative to change her mind."

Typical. And twice as maddening. "You're not going to tell me." Leon let it rest. He didn't have the energy to verbally spar.

"'Spose not. Why'd you save the cop? Stupid. Could've been a one-way ticket to prison for you."

"Something I had to do."

"Oh, my God. You're a boy scout."

"Be prepared."

"Yeah, well, it didn't look like you were very prepared at the motel, Leon."

"I'm here. We're safe."

"Barely."

"Where're we going?"

Another smile, one plummy with wicked promise. "My place."

Nanette's "place" turned out to be a lavish penthouse apartment, no motel slumming for her. Starkly appointed in severe blacks and whites, it resembled a zebra killing ground. Slick plastic chairs offered impossible to sit upon contours. Modern art explosions hung on the walls. Glass-covered table-tops provided an obstacle course to navigate. One clumsy slip and Leon could easily imagine tripping to his death. It smacked of money. Big money. Hardly a surprise.

Seeking out a functional piece of furniture, Leon sank into a furry black loveseat. Nanette joined him. With ease, she brought her legs up, showing them off before tucking them beneath her. Even her knees looked as flawless as the European furniture.

"Nice digs."

"Not really mine," she said. "But my friend won't need the place now."

Perhaps Leon had grown accustomed to Nanette, but nothing

she said shocked him anymore. Although he couldn't help but wonder about the fate of the apartment's former occupant. He skittered out of that dark alley, a trip he'd rather not take. "Does your friend have a TV?"

She picked up a remote smaller than a baby's fist. A tap of a button and an enormous screen dropped down. The images blinked by rapidly until Leon told her to stop.

Flames flickered behind a reporter. An arc of water was snuffing out the motel fire. People gathered in front of Leon's former residence, noodling for a fleeting moment of fame. When he saw Gavin waving into the camera, Leon grinned.

"Turn it up."

"*...the fire at the Dolores Motel is now thought to be under control by the South Beach, Miami Fire Department. One man is presumed dead, the name being withheld at this time. All other residents have been evacuated while firefighters...*"

"That's enough."

Nanette flipped the TV off. "Your father?"

"No. *Not* my father. But definitely Raymond Garber. And definitely LMI at work. Their new hit men like fires."

"Sorry." She pouted her lips, a look better suited for patronizing children.

"You mean you're sorry because he died? Don't be. The man meant nothing—"

"No, no..." She placed a hand on Leon's knee. He pinched the bridge of his nose, shut his eyes in his best oncoming headache performance, trying to ward off just how nice her touch felt. "That's not what I meant, Leon. I mean...I'm sorry you didn't get a chance to kill him yourself."

He gave her a sideways glance, no longer able to ignore her hand now roaming up his leg. From blood thirst to flirtation, all within seconds. Forgoing subtlety, he picked up her wrist and dropped it to the sofa. "Is that all you care about? Killing?"

"Of course not. I like the finer pleasures of life, too."

Her red-lipped smile, richer than blood, mystified him. Somewhere along their travels, she'd changed her lipstick. He'd never noticed her doing it.

"It's getting late, Nanette. Albert said we're moving tomorrow."

She shifted, making herself more comfortable. Her hair bowed in, accentuating her smooth neck. A foot dangled over the floor, wiggling until her shoe loosened. Then the shoe hit the floor with a jarring *clump*. "It's not so late. Nightcap?"

"No thanks. I don't drink. Night." He folded his arms over his chest and closed his eyes. And waited for her to leave. She didn't take the hint. Several times he wanted to peek, surrender to temptation. A tough battle. Finally, her feet dropped softly onto the carpet. He heard the click of the lamp switch.

"Night, Leon. Sleep tight." Her hand played lightly over his cheek, the fingers drawing slowly off. He opened his eyes to darkness and watched her shadowy form disappear into an adjoining room. The door shut gently behind her.

Leon stretched out onto the loveseat, the armrest his pillow. He sank deep into the soft upholstery, uncomfortable after the hard, worn mattresses he'd grown accustomed to. Above him, the night lights of Miami sifted in through the curtains. Car horns beeped with party-time urgency. A police car's siren screamed. Miami had nothing on New York; two cities that never slept. Which is what he needed to do. But he couldn't.

He sat up. Nanette's door now stood ajar, just a crack. Unnatural orange light bobbed from within the room. Her scent lingered in the air, a light floral bouquet. He imagined her waiting in bed for him, a mythical mermaid luring him into her lair. And like a punch-drunk sailor lost at sea, he wanted to go to her.

His hand wavered over her room's doorknob, inches away from making a huge mistake. A mistake he couldn't stop. The door glided open. Candle flames waved from atop a bed board. A golden glow graced Nanette's body, tantalizingly covered by the thinnest of silk sheets. Propped up on an elbow, she grinned, victorious. A demanding finger wagged. Leon followed her direction, stripping as he entered the bedroom.

The sheet felt cool against his flesh. Nanette supplied the heat. His chest rose as they kissed, his breath hurried. She wrapped her legs around him, strong and contrary to the softness of her breasts. A surprising alley-oop and they flipped over, Nanette on top. No doubt the way she liked it.

"Nanette, maybe we shouldn't—"

A finger to his lips sealed the deal. "Shhh." She grabbed his hand, gently guiding it back toward the lattice of the headboard. Suddenly, her free hand slashed up. Candlelight caught a flash of silver. Metal clanked. Handcuffs caught his wrist.

Stunned, he jerked his hand away. "No handcuffs!"

As she leaned on his chest, she pulled the handcuffs into view. Hooking a finger around one cuff, she dropped the other with a *clink*. "You sure? Trust me…it'll be fun." She sulked, a false face he'd seen before.

He didn't doubt it'd be interesting. But he wouldn't allow himself to be chained. Especially with her. And the ghosts of her past victims haunting the bedroom. Gently, he bucked, trying to rock her off. Unfazed, she shoved him back into the sheets. The handcuffs *chakked* to the carpet, a safer place for them. "Oh well, your loss. Now…" She favored him with a full and toothy smile. *The better to eat you with, my dear.* "…where were we?"

His mind resisted. But his body was game, all-in. She released a small groan, a sign the turbulence had passed. They entered a natural rhythm, rowing their bodies together with ease.

Until her hands left his chest. He opened his eyes. Above him, she brandished a knife, the switchblade she'd shown him earlier.

"Jesus!" He reached for the knife. In a teasing manner, she raised it higher. Metal gleamed, nearly as hot as the candlelight captured in her eyes. Her laughter doused him with ice water. Survival instinct took over. He reared up, her strong thighs locked and going nowhere. "Get off! Get—"

"Relax, Leon." In her other hand, she balanced a green apple. Eve's tempting fruit. "Food and sex are perfect together." One expert slice and she slipped a piece into her mouth. The apple's juices dribbled down her chin. Then she slid another piece between Leon's lips. Or tried to. Leon whipped his head to the side, spat out the apple.

"Nanette, enough! I'm done!" He grabbed her shoulders, shook her.

Her lower lip trembled. Showing honest-to-God emotion. "I

don't get it, Leon. I thought we were—"

"I can't play these games! Not now or *ever*. Get off. *Now.*"

She rolled over, dragging a leg across Leon's body. Her toes slowed around his penis which had long given up the good fight. He couldn't take one last tease. Mercifully, she fully retreated.

Leon leaped out of bed. While it provided no true protection, he felt safer clutching a pillow in front of him.

In a cold monotone, she said, "I was just trying to have fun, Leon. I thought we both were. I wasn't going to hurt you."

"I don't *trust* you."

The candlelight danced away from her face. Shadows consumed her features, indecipherable darkness. "Pity. We... might've been able to..."

Her voice faltered. Leon wanted to jump right back in, ask her to finish her statement. But that's what she wanted him to do. He felt like a monkey trained to dance at her whim. Yet he couldn't deny they'd made a connection, something beyond sex. He realized, though, she'd never be able to strip away all of her masks, the secrets she fought so hard to keep bottled up. She'd become her alternate persona, her original identity long gone.

"I'm sorry, Nanette. Sorry for..." He swung blindly, hoping inspiration would strike him. It didn't.

A phone chirruped, breaking the uncomfortable silence.

Nanette rolled out of bed, strode to a dresser. The phone display illuminated her grimace upon seeing the caller's ID. She answered with a "Yeah?" The conversation was brief, mostly one-sided. Leon struggled to keep his gaze locked on hers and not her body. She ended the call. "That was Albert. With the time."

"When?"

"Ten-thirty." Shadows peeled off her as she shed her dark moment. Once she'd entered the full spectrum of candlelight, a smile brightened her face. "'Bout damn time, too."

Then she crawled back into bed, rolled over. "Night. Better get some sleep. Shut the door on your way out."

Leon hesitated, wondering if he owed her an apology. Then talked himself out of it. Even in silence, Nanette wielded formidable manipulative powers.

He hurried out of the room, quietly closing the door behind him.

In the living room, he rearranged some furniture, moving a large plant out of the way so he could see Nanette's door clearly from his makeshift bed. And he slept with one eye open.

Chapter Eleven

Unlike Leon, Nanette woke up brimming with energy. Back to her flirtatious ways as if the previous night hadn't happened. Her coping mechanism, Leon supposed. Which suited him just fine. They had work to do.

On their way to the auto shop, Nanette maintained a steady stream of patter, mostly small talk while dropping a few sexual double entendres. Excitement lit her eyes, blue adrenaline. Leon found it contagious; par for the course for people in their line of work.

Before Leon could rap on the garage door, it churned up, chunking to a halt. Dressed in business casual attire—khakis and a polo shirt—Gustav greeted them.

"Friend Leon!" He flung his arms wide. Leon knew Gustav wouldn't leave a hug unfulfilled, so he gave him a few quick pats on the back. "And the beautiful Nanette!" The small man studied them both with a knowing grin. "Good morning!"

"Hi, Gustav."

"The others are waiting. Come, come." He dusted his hands and scooted away. "We mustn't tarry. Things to do, evil corporations to topple."

"Wait. Everyone else is here?"

"Certainly! You're the last to arrive."

Leon checked his watch. "But it's 10:25. We're early."

"Yes, we got here a little bit before you."

"Huh." It bothered Leon the others had gathered before them. Probably discussing things they didn't want Leon to hear. Paranoid? Most definitely. Smart? Absolutely. Nanette appeared unaffected, anxious to get the show on the road. She took the lead, hurrying toward the meeting room.

"Gustav," Leon lowered his voice, "have they been talking about plans without us?"

The strong slap on Leon's back startled him. "Leon! Try not to worry so much! It's not healthy. Not everyone's out to get you, you know."

"Doesn't seem that way."

Gustav responded with a shrieking whoop, the grand maître D' of the gathering. When Nanette pushed open the door, all conversation stopped. Blank gazes met them. Except for Albert who stood at the end of the table, ogling Nanette's bundle.

"Ah! At last, the computer." He rushed over to her, hands out and needy.

Playfully, Nanette swung it behind her. "Just a minute now. Do you have what we agreed upon?"

Albert plucked out a bulging envelope from his pocket, handed it to her. "Yes, yes, of course, I'm a man of my word." As hasty as a child on Christmas morning, he shredded the trash bag around the computer. Then he held the device up toward the others as if in sacrifice. "The answer to our problems."

Bobby, again proudly sporting his flag of flannel, huffed out a snort, no room for technology in his eighteen-wheeled world. Skittish as usual, Teddy ducked his head as if afraid to look at anything for too long less his corneas burn out. He rapped thin fingers onto the table, attracting Delilah's attention. Once Teddy noticed her, she leaned in closer with a sadistic grin. Bartholomew, the Man with the Shoebox, was conspicuously absent.

Albert appeared disappointed by the lack of excitement surrounding the laptop. "Yes, well…I'll deal with the computer after you're gone."

Clearly, Albert intended on staying safely behind, a notion that didn't instill confidence in Leon.

Albert sat down, the computer in his lap. "We're striking now, ladies and gentlemen. August Schroeder lives in a small suburban neighborhood, twenty-eight miles away. We need him, willing or not. Bobby's your driver."

With hands locked behind his tree trunk neck, Bobby

chewed around a toothpick. "Damn straight. Ain't a better driver on this here—"

"Ahem, yes...I want Gustav taking the lead due to his persuasive manner."

Gustav hopped off his chair, snapping to full form. "You do me great honor, sir."

Bobby laughed and Delilah shot him a killer glare. Oblivious, Gustav continued to soak up his moment of sunshine.

"Nanette and Leon will accompany Gustav. Delilah, you'll stand guard."

"Where will you be, Albert?" asked Leon.

"Hm? Oh. Well..." He swayed his hand over the computer. "I'll be busy working on this. And Teddy has certain technical knowledge that may help—"

"Figures." Again, Bobby snorted.

"What's that supposed to mean?" asked Teddy in a meek voice.

A big shrug of shoulders. "Nothin'. You just look like a computer geek's all I'm sayin'."

As if falling into a seizure, Teddy started shaking. Bony fists slammed onto the table. He shot to his feet.

"Gentlemen! Enough!" Albert jumped up, the computer serving as his shield. "We're all on the same side."

"You sure about that?" Before going into battle, Leon needed to clarify certain matters. "I mean...you haven't told us everything, Albert. Like you don't trust us. And I think you know more than you're letting on. If I'm risking my life—while you're *not*—I need to know if you have my back. Have *our* backs." Leon gestured toward the others. "How 'bout it, Albert?"

"Of course I 'have your back,' Leon." His awkward usage of finger quotes suggested little practice with them. "I'll be here providing support. I'll call with any news. Or you can call me."

"Great. I'd feel better, though, if you went along for the ride."

"I've already explained that. I have to—"

"Yeah, yeah. The computer. Right."

From a jacket pocket, Albert tugged out a gun. The grey metal swam beneath the fluorescents, cold and shark like. "Would I give you a gun if I didn't trust you?" Slowly, he inched it toward Leon, tempting him. But Leon wanted no part of it. He despised guns. Still had nightmares from using them last year. Too impersonal, too bloody, too damned dangerous.

"You expecting trouble, Albert?" Leon kept the gun in sight but his hands far from it.

"I *always* expect trouble."

And, for once, Leon believed him. "I'm not taking the gun."

"You may need it. You shouldn't go in unarmed. Take—"

"Who says I'm unarmed?"

"Suit yourself."

"Fine." Nanette reached across the table, picked the gun up. "Buncha' boys afraid of a little gun. I'll take it." She rolled her fingers over the barrel, sensuously stroking it. She traced the contours of the gun with loving caresses. She shifted the weapon between her hands, getting fully acquainted. Another sexual tease. Until she pointed the gun at Leon. With a smile, she closed one eye, whispered, "Bang." Then dropped it to her lap, baiting Leon with eager eyes.

"Not funny, Nanette."

"Aww. No fun makes Leon a dull boy."

Leon wanted to believe her frightening display was just more fun and games. Maybe a little payback for last night. He truly hoped so. But with her, cryptic is a lifestyle.

Bobby blurted out, "Baby, I'd like to see what you could do with that hot piece of metal." A bad move.

The gun swung his way. "Maybe you'll get your chance, pig." This time the tease had vanished, no smile behind the gun. "Apologize."

"What?" Bobby looked around for male corroboration, received none.

"I said, 'apologize'!"

"Whoa, whoa, honey, take it easy. Just playin' with ya', that's all." Drops of sweat formed on his forehead. "Sorry, I—"

"And don't you ever, *ever* call me 'baby' or 'honey' or any of that sexist bullshit again! And if you ever even hint at 'playing with me' again, I'll blast your balls off into the next county!"

His sorry smile, meant to placate, made him look even more pathetic. "Point taken, ba...um, Nanette."

Leon reached over, carefully nudged the gun down. Only then did he notice the revolver shaking violently in her hand. "He's not worth your time."

Her eyes met Leon's. Anger dissolved into pain, pain so intense Leon wanted to take it from her. Then like a rubber band, she snapped back, smiling, almost a different person. "Very few men are worth my time, Leon." She added a wink, sat back in her chair, holding the gun primly in her lap like a court stenographer. "Let's get back to business, shall we?"

It took a while for Albert to gather himself. "Um, yes, well…I, ah…that's it. We need Mr. Schroeder. Needless to say, alive is the only option. And I must stress the urgency of the situation."

"Why? I mean, we've waited this long. Why the rush now?"

"Leon…if we found Mr. Schroeder, do you think LMI can be far behind?"

Rasmussen estimated nearly a quarter of a million dollars of plastic floated in his swimming pool and that didn't even take into consideration the expensive rafts and furniture pieces. Sheera bobbled about, her built-in twin life preservers keeping her afloat. Alongside his nurse, she splashed and squeaked like a dolphin. While watching the women, Rasmussen sucked a Long Island Iced Tea through a straw. Beyond the flatlands, a mountain pierced the ocean blue sky. The sun beat down on his neck, warm and tingly. Time for Sheera to supply more lotion. After a few more minutes of watching. The view was too good to disrupt.

Hell, he should've felt more alive than he did now. But he didn't feel good, not today. No amount of flesh on display could fix his ills. Rasmussen despised loose ends. And Leon Garber had proven one frazzled loose end he desperately wanted to pluck out and pitch away. Problem was, like a gnat, Garber made a helluva lotta noise without being seen. Completely unacceptable.

He boiled, hotter than the burn on his neck. Time to get proactive.

"Gaines!" He rotated his chair in a half circle. "Gaines!"

"Here, sir."

"Jumpin' Jesus Christ!" How long Gaines had been behind him, Rasmussen had no idea. Sometimes he thought Gaines enjoyed sneaking up on him, trying to give him a heart attack. But Rasmussen wasn't about to give his lackey the satisfaction of kicking off so easily. "How many times I gotta tell you not to do that?"

"Yes, sir." Gaines stood at attention, averting his eyes from the bountiful parade in the pool. Actually, Rasmussen had long suspected Gaines was asexual. Had no taste for lust. One of the reasons why Rasmussen trusted him. Like a neutered dog, he stayed loyal, not prone to carnal diversion. "Sir, I just heard from Mr. Summers."

"Well?"

"He's been in contact with our insider. Who claims to know where August Schroeder is."

"What? Augie? I thought that ol' son-of-a-bitch was dead!"

"That's what we were lead to believe, sir. But unfortunately he's still with us."

August Schroeder. Rasmussen grinned, allowing himself a rare foray into the past. Under his administration, Augie'd been one of LMI's very first clients. The times they shared were worthy of folklore. Back in Rasmussen's hell-raising days, the killer cop could drink him under the table. These days, the only hell Rasmussen managed to raise was from the confines of his chair, barely a whiff of brimstone. But all good things come to an end. Augie'd gone rogue, vanishing without a trace. Except for a last threat of blackmail if LMI didn't leave him alone. And Augie had the goods, too. Rasmussen learned his lesson, learned it the hard way. Never befriend your employees.

"So? What's the holdup? I want his head on a platter."

"We're working on it, sir. But our insider is demanding a sizable finder's fee before Schroeder's location is disclosed."

Rasmussen slashed his cane down. "Goddamn! Give 'em the cash. That ain't no problem. Then give him a quick trip six feet under. No one extorts me."

Gaines grinned. "Yes, sir. I think you'll be happy with the results. There's more, sir…"

"What is this? Some goddamn game show? Spit it out and don't be cute."

"Our informant claims Garber and several other renegades are going after Schroeder. It's a perfect opportunity to kill two birds with one stone."

Suddenly, the alcohol kicked in, a comforting sensation. Rasmussen's heart raced, a vibrant beat. He felt ten years younger; virile almost. "What're you waitin' for? Get on it! Go! Now!" The cane rapped Gaines' legs.

"Yes, sir."

Rasmussen felt his smile widen. Unusual, nearly painful. He leaned over his cane, hiding his giddiness. Wouldn't do at all for anyone to see him cut loose, not one iota.

"Girls! Do that one thing again. You know, that Ethel Merman thing."

Sheera emerged from the water, her long blond hair pinned to her shoulders. "You got it, honey."

It was good to be the King.

Sensitivity tapped off his phone, flipped it up into the air. A rare good mood. Which usually meant tears were just around the corner, more bipolar Jekyll and Hyde crap.

"That was Summers," he said to Bug. "We've got a lead on Garber and the others. And get this…also August Schroeder."

"Whoa. Schroeder." Bug sat up in bed, his eyes wide. Whole lotta' action going on with these two this morning. "Never thought we'd get him."

"I know, right?" The two goons smiled at one another, a prelude to making out or something.

"Yo, who's August Schroeder? He a big deal or what?"

Sensitivity shook his head. "Don't worry your shaggy lil' head over it, Spangler. You don't need to know. But, hey, thought you might be happy about Garber."

Garber. Yeah, Cody was happy. Excited even. Payback's coming. He'd been sitting on pent-up anger ever since he offed Garber's old man. Garber needed to pay for making fun of him, and Cody sure as hell meant to enjoy it. "Shit, boys, let's bounce." Cody rocked on his feet, eager for the hunt. This time he wouldn't let Garber slide either. Even if it meant the end of his affiliation with LMI, probably even his life. Some things are just worth it.

Every time Bobby swung into a hair-pin turn, he punched the pedal. With a rabbit-eating grin, he looked back, seeking kudos. His reckless driving ate the gas while pure testosterone fueled him. The man drove like a maniac, practically slapping an *"arrest me"* sticker on the van's bumper.

Nanette, on the other hand, had settled into quiet determination, her jaw set rigidly, eyes locked straight ahead. Unnaturally quiet.

Gustav sat in Delilah's lap. Her fingers entwined within his blond hair, combing out her doll's locks. He looked satisfied, sleepy almost, the only relaxed member in the van.

"Gus, where's Bartholomew?"

"A busy man, our Man with the Shoebox. He had a pressing engagement; otherwise I'm certain he'd be thrilled to join our party."

Party. That's how everyone treated the mission. A van full of dangerous, adrenaline-amped killers out for a good time. Not for the first time, Leon wondered about the merits of his teammates. But, as in all wars, fellow soldiers aren't chosen. They're recruited. Or they volunteer.

Leon held tight to his briefcase, his last connection to his old life. A cumbersome artifact, but one he couldn't quite let go. And he certainly didn't trust Albert to watch over it.

Another death-defying turn thrust Nanette close to Leon, her weight heavy on him. She lingered. When she dropped a hand on Leon's knee, he started. "Sorry, Leon. Call it animal attraction." Then she turned off the flirtation machine, settling back into solitude. Leon could practically see the mental wall she'd erected. Not a bad strategy.

Along a quiet residential street, not too far from the ocean, Bobby slowed the van to a crawl. Small houses lined the street, topping out at one level. Airy doorway arches suggested a Spanish Colonial flavor. Par for the course of many Florida neighborhoods built in the '30's, architects had run amok, splashing around the most ghastly array of colors available: dull aqua, sickly pink and mustard brown. Bobby pulled to the curb, killed the engine.

"That's it over yonder." Bobby prodded a finger toward a flat, orange domicile with a partial red-brick roof. A matching orange wall surrounded the property, the stucco falling off in weather damaged blotches. A very clear message hung on the wrought-iron gate: *No Trespassing.* Not exactly the most encouraging of welcomes. "I'll stay in the van, keep an eye out. If I see anything, I'll lay on the horn and y'all come running."

As Leon climbed out, Bobby grinned at him, very insincere. Nanette ignored Leon's helping hand, jumping out on her own. She untucked her blouse, stuck the gun at the small of her back. Armed with only a couple hypodermics and his briefcase, Leon second guessed his decision about not accepting the gun.

At the gate, Gustav frowned at the electronic lock.

"I'll go around back, scope things out," said Delilah. Before anyone could object, she dashed away down a narrow graveled alley running alongside the house.

Gustav pressed a button in a weather-proofed box. He turned toward Leon, hands in pockets, humming.

Finally, "Yeah?" The voice sounded ragged, full of sea salt and tar.

"Hello, my friend! My name is Gustav. Do I have the pleasure of speaking with August Schroeder?"

Silence, then an electronic parrot squawked. "Ain't no one here by that name. Just me."

"Now, Mr. Schroeder, our sources have been very careful not to make mistakes. I assure you we mean no harm. We'd just like to talk—"

"And I tole you, I never heard of no Schroeder!"

"Sir, we have something of the utmost importance to speak with you about." Gustav cupped a hand around his mouth and stage whispered, "It's about LMI."

The extended silence sliced as sharp as a sword. "Don't know what you're talking about! Leave me alone before I call the cops!"

"My friend! As I said, we—" Gustav stopped when he

realized he'd been cut off. He turned to Leon, mischief twinkling in his eyes. "Oh dear, this could've gone better."

"Well, I doubt he's going to call the police," said Nanette.

"Indeed." Gustav stepped back, looked up at the wall. "Friend Leon, give me a boost if you don't mind."

Leon thought it a bad idea, but at least it was an idea. He leaned down, bridging his hands. "Be careful, Gus."

"Careful's my middle name!" Gus clapped his hands with a joyous smack. "Up we go."

At the top of the bricked trellis, Gus scrambled, his feet wobbling over the edge before they vanished. A small thud and a grunt, then Gus appeared behind the gate. With his hands wrapped around the iron bars, he looked jailed. Something Leon hoped to avoid.

"Let me see now…" Standing on tip-toes and with a finger to his lips, Gus examined the lock. Then he punched several buttons. After a sharp *clack*, the gate popped open.

Leon stepped through quickly. Nanette followed closely, warmth radiating from her. Twin palm trees stood sentry at the side of the small domicile, their limbs waving from an ocean breeze.

Over the sighing of the wind, Leon heard something else. A clink of chains, a growl. Stampeding footsteps, evenly paced. A Rottweiler rounded the corner. Its tongue trailed between a mouthful of sharp, yellowed teeth. Bearing down on them fast. Gus squealed, hopped back. Leon froze. Nanette grabbed for her gun, swung it up.

"Go!" Leon twisted, hands fumbling at the gate. His toe caught on an ankle, tossing him into the fence. *Clunk.* The dog barreled through the yard, its growl rising. Three more leaps, it'd be on them.

"Bruno, heal!" Like a command from God, the voice came from above. Immediately, the dog stopped, sat. Its mouth closed, but the ears perked up.

Ka-chak. A sound Leon knew and hated. He looked up to where the voice originated. Atop the home's archway, August Schroeder stood on a small flat roof, shotgun pumped and aimed toward them. His muscular arms were the guns of a sailor, matching anchor tattoos to boot. When he squinted into the sunshine, he even looked like Popeye. His sun-burned skin contrasted with his bountiful mass of white hair, blood on the snow.

"You don't listen very well! I told you to get the hell off my property!" He raised the gun, eyed down the long barrel, indecisive between the three of them.

Gustav, ever the ambassador of peace, waved his hands and took a bold step forward. "Again, I can assure you, Mr. Schroeder, we come in peace."

"I don't give a good goddamn what you come in, little man! But you ain't comin' into my home. Now leave! 'Fore I let Bruno have at ya!"

As if on cue, Bruno agreed with a growl.

"We just need information, sir. No need for violence. We have a mutual enemy and would like your assistance in putting an end to them."

The gun wavered. So did Schroeder's conviction. He dropped the gun's barrel to the roof. Quietly, he asked, "LMI?"

"Yes, sir."

"If you're pulling my leg, short stuff, I'll pull the trigger."

As if it was the funniest insult he'd ever heard, Gus squealed. Bravery in the face of danger. Or naivety. "No pulling on your legs, kind sir."

"Five minutes, then you're gone. And you forget about me."

"A bargain well worth met, sir."

"Don't move a muscle 'til I get down there or Bruno'll have you for an early bird supper."

"We aim to please."

Schroeder stormed out of the house, shotgun leveled in front of him. He took a long, gaping look at Gus and said, "Circus in town or what?"

Again, Gustav chortled as if he found unexpected poetry in Schroeder's insults. "You are very too much, Mr. Schroeder!"

"Get in. Quick. Before the neighbors see you." He stood aside, allowing them entry.

Quite different from the delicately manicured lawn, a hoarder's paradise awaited them inside. Stacks and stacks of newspapers threatened to topple at a mouse's sneeze. A maze of wet, moldy boxes comprised towers. The lone, uncovered piece of furniture was a fire-engine red sofa, two oval-shaped bottom prints molded into the left side. Schroeder ordered them to sit as he stood guard. "Now what the hell's this all about? I ain't even heard the name 'Schroeder' in many a year. The man's long dead. I'm Dale Carter, retired salesman."

"I'm sure you are, 'Mr. Carter,'" said Gus with a vaudevillian wink. "Your secret's fine with us. But, to make things—how do you say?—straight on the point, we also used to belong to LMI. Now we don't."

"Huh. I ain't sayin' I know nothin' about this LMI, but just out of curiosity, what's your beef with them?"

"They've been using their clientele, us, to eliminate people for monetary and political gain," said Leon. "They've lied to us. We want to destroy them."

"Well, shit and hellfire, why didn't you just say so?"

"We've been trying to."

"All right, looks like we got us some talkin' to do." With remarkable speed, he swept the gun barrel across a stack of papers hiding a wooden chair, then sat, utilizing the shotgun as a crutch. "So...talk."

"I'm Leon, you've met Gustav and this is Nanette."

Nanette turned on the charm, this time chaste and restrained. Leon swore she even manufactured an on-demand blush to her cheeks.

"Nice to meet you there, pretty lady. Really nice." Schroeder took in the sight for a while and Nanette let him. Quite a different response than the one she'd offered Bobby earlier. "You can call me Augie. Just 'til we're done here. Then you never call me anything again."

"Understood. We know Jasper Rasmussen is the head of LMI and—"

"That ol' bastard? Huh. Thought he'd be dead by now."

"Wish he was. So...you know him?"

"Hell, yes, I know him! Or...used to, more like. We go back many a year..." His eyes turned glossy, flipping through memories. From another room, a clock ticked impatiently. A cardboard box creaked. Papers dropped like melting icicles.

Gustav cleared his throat, a small, yet polite, push. "Mr. Schroeder? Augie?"

"Hm? Oh." He squinted his eyes, brought the shotgun back up. "Who're you? What're you doin' in my house?"

"Ah, it's me, Augie, Nanette." She tapped his knee, just the right touch. The right person to bring him back to the now.

"Nanette! Of course, dear." He gave as good as he got and patted her knee back with a chesty chuckle.

"Augie, you said you knew Rasmussen."

"Yep, knew the ol' codger well, matter of fact. But there came a time when I found out he wasn't operatin' by any code. Man had no ethics. All he cared about was power. He was killin' people to make himself rich."

"That's what we found out. With your help, we want to stop him. Along with the rest of LMI."

"Damn Rasmussen. I told him I wanted out. He threatened me, threatened my kids." Lost, Augie looked around the clutter. "Where's Augie, Jr. anyway?"

"Um, not sure, Augie. But you were talking about Rasmussen." *Alzheimer's*, Leon thought. Potentially a big problem.

"Yeah, yeah." Augie's hand slashed down, wiping away his memory lapse with pained pride. "You need to understand somethin'. The guys I killed? They deserved it. Murderers, rapists, worthless scum who tap-danced around the legal system. I was still a cop, doin' my best to uphold the law."

While Augie provided a very loose interpretation of the law, Leon held his tongue. He was no better, a kindred spirit of sorts to Augie. At least they rid the world of those who deserved it.

"But ol' Rasmussen, he didn't give a damn 'bout anything except gettin' rich. And killing anyone who stood in his way. And that included me. I went underground. Years of detective work taught me how to hide in plain sight. Hadn't had a problem 'til you showed up on my doorstep, either." Crow's feet pinched his eyes as he shot Leon and Gus a stern look, noticeably leaving Nanette out of the line-of-fire.

"Augie, my friend," said Gus, "we will not pose a problem for you. We're after the same thing."

"Justice." Leon let the word hook and anchor. What he knew Augie wanted. "Problem is we can't find Rasmussen. He's invisible, off the grid."

"Well, hell, I know where he is." Augie leaned forward, expectant, happy to contribute to the hunting party. Then awareness receded. His forehead wrinkled. Clouds of confusion hovered over his dissolving grey matter. Leon kept quiet, afraid to tip the scales too far into forgetfulness. Another stack of newspapers sluiced off a tower.

Outside, Bruno barked, a feral roar. A voice shouted. Augie bolted up, shotgun rigid, eyes alert. Nanette drew her gun, firmly grasped in both hands. Gus took it all in with glee, kicking his feet on the sofa.

And then all hell broke loose.

Cody saw the tail end of a van hauling ass down the road, much too fast for a suburban soccer mom. Sensitivity's fingers tapped out the plate digits on his phone. Yet they stayed in the car. Like usual.

"What're we waitin' for, yo? You ain't gettin' any younger and you sure as shit ain't gettin' any prettier." Cody nudged the big man's shoulder.

"Shut up, Spangler. Ready, Bug?"

"Yep." Bug smiled at the box of pyrotechnics riding in his lap. "We bringing the kid?"

"Oh, hellz, yes, you're bringing the 'kid!' I got dibs on Garber! No way am I sittin' this out."

"Don't have much choice, Bug. Spangler, you don't do anything unless I say so. Stay in back, stay low."

"How come you guys are bringin' guns? Thought you said things had to look like an accident. So how 'bout givin' me a gat, yo?"

"Were you born stupid or did practice make perfect?" Sensitivity swung an elbow behind him, then pulled back. "Right now, all that matters is cleanin' up this mess. Just shut up, don't say a word, don't do anything."

"Whatever. Just as long as I get first crack at Garber's what I'm sayin'."

Outside the car, Sensitivity adjusted his sunglasses and glanced up and down the street. "Let's do it."

Cody hopped out of the car, stretched, flexed his biceps. Getting good and jacked for the endgame.

With a silencer-fit gun in hand, Sensitivity led the way. He studied the iron gate, tapped it. The gate popped open. Sensitivity slipped through the small passage, Bug next. Cody, as always, brought up the rear. His pulse raced in his ears. The sound of music.

From a distance, metal jangled. A beat box of pants grew loud, louder, ending in a snarl. A ball of galloping black fur raced toward them.

"Shit." Calmly, Sensitivity brought his gun up, leveling it at the oncoming Rottweiler.

Cody's own animal instinct kicked in. "No!" A shove took Bug out of the way. Then Cody hammered a fist down on Sensitivity's arm. The gun misfired, chuffing a bullet into the ground. Uprooted dirt spat up. Cody whirled. The Rottweiler flew by him, its maw latching onto Sensitivity's outstretched arm. The big man tumbled, the dog on top of him. His hands slipped around the dog's throat, throttling it at arm's length. Strangling the poor animal. Ropes of dog saliva spattered Sensitivity's head. His sunglasses dangled from one ear. The chain rattled, swooping up and landing like a whip.

Sensitivity's hands tightened around the dog's neck. The dog's guttural bark peaked in a squeal.

Goddammit.

Cody joined the battle. He kicked Sensitivity, did it again. The dog snapped at Cody. It hooked a tooth into his jeans, ripping a hole at the ankle. Cody tottered back, stumbling over the chain.

But at all costs, the dog's safety came first.

Cody chased the length of the chain to its tethered source. Hooked to a spike in the ground. He unclipped it, ran back with the free end of the chain clattering in his fist.

Behind the dog, Cody yelled, "Heeyah! Git, boy! Git!"

The dog ignored him, Sensitivity's meaty head clearly more appetizing. "Let go of the dog, yo! I'll get rid of it!"

Sensitivity yanked the dog forward, narrowly avoiding its snapping jaws. With a grunt, he heaved the beast. It spun in the air, its legs swimming. Like a cat, it righted itself, landing on its feet. Cody snapped the chain taut. Dragging the dog behind him, he ran toward the gate.

"Come on, boy! Go! Run!" Cody stood as bait at the gate's opening, the chain his fishing pole. Now in an insane fury, the dog clambered toward him. The animal couldn't help it, Cody knew, nothing personal.

The Rottweiler planted its front paws, then sprang up. Cody wheeled along the fence. The dog flew by him, through the gate and landed on the sidewalk with a thud. Dumbfounded, it shook its head, jumped back up with a snort. Cody slammed the gate. Paws clabbered at the bars. The dog bounced on back legs, practically climbing the fence. Cody flipped the lock, then kicked the gate. "Go! Be free!" He pointed down the road, the dog taking no heed. Behind him, Sensitivity was on his feet, shaken but not out. He shoved Cody aside. Aimed his gun through the bars.

"No!" Cody wrenched Sensitivity's arm up. The gun lifted, just barely, whiffed out a shot. The tip of the dog's tail exploded, leaving a raw nub. Not a deadly wound, but enough to send the dog yelping down the road. The chain rattled, diminishing in the distance.

Cody heaved a sigh, leaned back against the fence.

Sensitivity hadn't yet had his fill of choking things. He grabbed Cody by the throat. "You stupid son-of-a-bitch! You'll kill strippers, innocent people! But not *dogs*?"

Cody couldn't speak, but nodded. Made sense in his world.

From the house, an explosion roared. The sound shook the palm trees, echoing down the empty street. Smoke curled out of an open window. A shotgun's trunk poked out. The barrel tipped up. Something clicked, louder than a mouse-trap. With his hand still on Cody's throat, Sensitivity rolled along the fence, then dropped to the ground. Cody sprawled on top of him, an all too vulnerable shield.

Another blast blew out a crater in the earth inches from Cody's face.

Augie jagged through the house's clutter like human lightning. By the time Leon freed himself from the sunken bun imprints of the sofa, Augie'd blasted a shotgun shell through the window. Leon joined him, Nanette by his side.

In the yard, Cody lay on top of a monster of a man, scrambling to get up.

Worse, Bobby and the van were gone.

"Dammit, the bastard left us!" Leon plucked out his hypodermic. Useless, worse than a knife in a gun fight.

Augie cocked the shotgun, rocketed off another salvo. Leon waved the cloud of smoke away, looked outside. The yard now appeared empty.

"I need more bullets. Get me my damn bullets!" Augie stared at Leon, eyes wide as the moon. And nearly as vacant.

"Where are they?"

"The bullets! I need more…bullets." His voice trailed away.

"Augie! Where's your ammo?"

"Goddammit…where did I put it?" With his back against the wall, Augie slid down to the floor and sat. He massaged his jaw, his brain working overtime.

Nanette aimed her gun out the window. She withdrew her arm, shook the pistol, banged it against the wall. Her coloring paled. "It's jammed."

Leon's legs grew unsteady. Nanette dropped the gun to her side, stumped, defeated. Gus hovered beneath the window on the opposite side of the door, peeking outside. Unnerving quiet filled the house.

"Looks like trouble, my friends," Gus said quietly.

Outside, the big man had made his way to a palm tree, the trunk only covering half of his massive body. An easy target if they had a weapon.

Next to Leon's head, the window split. Glass tinkled to the floor. Another bullet whistled through the window, thwacking into the opposite wall. Leon dropped to his knees, briefcase clunking alongside him. Carefully, he raised his head and peered out the window. On the left side of the yard, a twig of a man hunkered down, slithering his way between pink plastic flamingos, seeking shelter. Working his way toward them.

A volley of bullets sprayed through the window. No gun reports; just a light rain of tip-tapping destruction. Newspapers ballooned up, floating down in parachutes.

On all fours, Leon skittered toward Augie. Retreat, their only chance of survival. "Augie...Augie! Listen to me!"

Augie's gaze travelled over Leon's shoulder, then found him. "What? What's going on? Who're you?"

Nanette shoved Leon aside. "Augie, it's me, Nanette." Tenderly, she sandwiched his cheeks between her hands.

"Hey, sugar." Whether he remembered her or not, it didn't matter. A pretty face roped him back in.

Footfalls mounted the front steps. Leon reached up, slid the door's chain lock into place. Three bullets sliced through the wood. Splinters bowed in, one flying into Leon's palm. He dropped to the floor, afraid to move.

Against all odds, Nanette maintained a calm tone. "Augie, do you have a car?"

"Sure do, sweetheart."

"Where is it?"

"Out back, of course."

"We've got to go now, Augie. LMI spooks're outside."

That was all Augie needed to jump-start his inner soldier. He hopped to his feet, pumped an imaginary bullet into his shotgun's chamber. "Let's go. Bastards'll never take me alive."

Won't take any of us alive, Leon thought.

A battering ram of a foot banged the door open. The chain snapped tight, caught, then rebounded the door shut. *Not for long.*

Another bullet almost parted Gus' hair. He jacked his arms over his head.

"Stay low!" Leon hopped up into a squat and duck-walked toward the back of the house.

Augie refused to lower, holding his own like General Custer. "Sons-of-bitches! Comin' into my house!" He aimed his gun toward the door, releasing twin, impotent clicks.

Reaching up, Nanette lowered his shotgun, whispered, "Come on, Augie. You're out of bullets."

On the other side of an arched doorway, Leon stood up in a hallway. His knees cracked and ached from his prolonged squat. He hugged the wall, thankful for the barrier. Quickly, he waved the others past him. He held his needle aloft, their last weapon. "Go. I'll follow."

Pounding weakened the front door. A lamp fixture above Leon's head wobbled from the attack, casting a swinging oval of faint yellow over the hallway.

Skrak-chak. The lock gave. *Whack.* The door slammed back against the wall. *Shush-shh-flump.* In the front room, avalanches of newspapers skied down to the floor.

"Christ, what a mess!" one of the LMI men bellowed, cleanliness apparently his biggest concern. In a quieter voice, "That side." A directive to his partner.

Leon swallowed, trying to stifle the dry gulp. Sweat trickled down his face. He wanted to scratch, needed to itch. He leaned off the wall, his briefcase tapping lightly against it. Leon held his breath. Listened. And waited.

Stealthy footfalls crept through the house. Floorboards squeaked.

Nanette and Augie had vanished. Yet Gustav remained behind, mimicking Leon's glued to the wall posture. With a smile, he offered Leon a useless thumbs up gesture.

Debris from the outer room toppled. Feet delicately tapped away trash, marking the hit men's progress. Just around the corner, Leon heard one of the men breathing. *Two men.* The hypo could take out one, not both. He'd aim for the bigger man if possible, a fist fight he knew he couldn't win. Depending on how well the smaller man was armed, he'd have to risk a physical assault with him. Pray for the best. Fickle, he knew; he only prayed whenever death loomed.

A floorboard creaked, grumbled. *Heavy weight.* Big man up first. The overhead lamp settled. A shadow stretched into the hallway, growing, stretching into absurd proportions. A silhouette of a gun ended in the shadow's hand. *Silence.* The tip of the gun prodded into the hallway, lowered. So did the shadow. The man set into a squat. Leon heard a hand gingerly rest on the other side of the wall, the stucco sighing.

The element of surprise, the only thing in Leon's favor. Fear, tempered by patience, kept him attached to the wall. But anxiety wanted to kick-start him into action. Jump out and jab. Get it over with. *Stupid.* Slow and easy wins the day.

The shadow wavered, blurring around the edges. A rush of wind. The bald man landed quietly in the hall. In a crouch, gun up. For a second, shock froze the assassin when he saw Leon. Leon pressed the advantage. The briefcase hit spot-on, batting the gun to the floor. In a wind-milling motion, Leon brought the hypo down. It hesitated at the muscle in the man's neck, then penetrated, the plunger flowing smoothly after it. The big man shot up, nearly seven feet of solid muscle. The needle dangled from his neck like a bizarre ponytail.

He regrouped fast, too fast. Arms outstretched, he came at Leon. Leon stuffed a high kick into his attacker's crotch. The contact pained Leon's ankle more than it did his opponent. Leon limped back.

The smaller LMI man raced into the hallway, forcing a sudden stop with his shoulder against the wall. The bald man looked. A fleeting distraction.

Gustav flung himself at the grizzled man, taking him down by the legs. Dumbfounded, the man fell onto the floor. Gus pummeled the man's ears in a constant speedy barrage. A bullet fired into the wall.

The behemoth turned back toward Leon with a smile. And stalked toward him, but now slowed to a drunken lurch.

Leon needed the dropped gun, no other choice. But he had to get by the giant to get it. He ran at the bald man, head down, briefcase up. Leon collided into a human brick wall. He recoiled, slamming down to the floor. A black boot lifted above Leon's head, the bottom as shiny as the man's head, a ridiculous last thought. Then, from between the bald man's straddled legs, a tiny coiled fist rose up into his crotch. Repeatedly.

Groaning, the giant dropped to his knees, hands suppliant as if wondering why his god had forsaken him. Leon crab-walked back before the big man fell on him. The walls shook at the impact. The lamp swayed again, nodding its approval. Gus stood proudly, one small Prada shoe perched on the mountain he'd climbed. Behind him, the smaller man lay unconscious as well.

"Leon, that was *marvelous*!" said Gus.

"Let's get the hell out of here."

"I am with you." Gus frowned at the fallen killers, suddenly serious. "One moment, please."

"Gus, there's no time—"

"Nonsense!" He dipped and swooped up the nearest gun. Cocked the trigger. "Time to finish this the proper way."

Last year, Leon'd made the mistake of not letting Cody kill some LMI hit men. A slow learner, but the lesson took seed. "Make it fast. Where there's one of them, there's another dozen at their heels. Besides…I know one more's somewhere close." *Cody, lying in wait like a snake in the grass.*

With the relish of a stage magician, Gus fluttered the gun, then pointed it at his bald target.

Click, click, click.

"Oh my, out of bullets." Sadness drew his mouth down, his new toy not living up to its potential. "Let's see, now, where's that other gun?"

Before Gus could conduct his search, though, voices rose outside, this time scattered with a large number of "*yo's*!"

Nanette hopped in behind the jeep's steering wheel. Augie refused to let go of his empty shotgun and clunked it against the passenger side door.

"Where we goin'?"

"Somewhere safe." She held a hand out, her fingers wiggling. "Keys."

Augie jerked as if receiving an electric jolt. He dug deep into his short's pockets, tapped his breast pocket. "Don't seem to have 'em."

Her lips grew tight with impatience. She knew Augie couldn't help his condition, empathized with him even. She'd seen the effects of Alzheimer's before, up close and personal. But with killers beating down the doors, even Jesus himself would be sorely tested.

"Think, Augie. We need the keys. Are they in your bedroom?" Not that she wanted to go back in the house. The prospect of facing gunfire without a weapon didn't fill her with joy. Bad enough they had to escape in a jeep. The canvas roof left her feeling unprotected. So flimsy, so fragile. But, here at Augie's house, they were sitting ducks.

"Keys….keys…" Augie's eyes closed. Frustrated, he whacked his fists on his knees, aggravated over things happening to him he had no control over. A feeling she knew all too well. "I don't know where the damn keys are!"

A deep breath. "Okay, Augie, it's fine. I'll go get them." If he'd heard her, he didn't acknowledge it. "Just stay here." As she stepped out, she gave him a pat on the shoulder.

"Dayummm! What up, what up, girl?" Immediately, she recognized the voice at her back.

Even though startled, she dusted off her inner cool, and turned to face the hunky kid from the motel. The hunky LMI killer kid, not what she needed now.

"Hey there. Small world, huh?" she offered with a grin.

Still working it, he lifted a foot onto the back bumper, draping an arm over a knee. Flexing for her benefit, always on. Absolutely hopeless, but she had to admit there was something endearing about his ridiculous doggedness. Something she could turn to her advantage. "Not small enough, yo. Where the hell's Garber?"

She wrinkled her face, her polished look of helplessness. The way most men liked her. "Don't know any Garber. But I'm glad I ran into you again. Been thinking about you." She zipped in close, walked two fingers up his chest. Checking him out for weapons. Clean from what she could see. And the closer she drew him in, the better. In case things turned physical and not in a pleasant way. Keep him addled.

"Yeah, yeah, whatevs. Saw you with him back at the motel hell." He dropped his leg, trying out a tough guy stance. "Now… where the hell is he? Tell me and maybe I'll let you live."

Honestly, she had no time for this clown. Not with a gunfight raging inside the house. She stepped in close, brushing her breasts against him. Slowly (never move too quickly in front of animals), she reached up, ruffled his hair. Keeping her hands in a strategic position. Lost in the moment, he closed his eyes, leaned down with "let's get busy" puckered lips. *Too easy.* Her fingers slipped to his ears. She pressed fingertips inside, grabbed on tight. Slammed his head back against the jeep door. Did it again for good measure. He jerked within her grasp, groaning. A beefy arm flopped up onto the window before he slid down.

Although clearly dazed, he laughed. "You like to play rough? You came to the right dude, baby. Cody'll show you a thing or two. Can't wait to—"

"Don't talk about yourself in the third person. It's unbecoming. So shut up." A well-placed kick to his mouth ensured he did just that. He spat blood into the dirt and chuckled. Enjoying every moment of it. *Interesting.* But she could have fun with any idiot guy at any time. Assuming she survived. "Augie," she called.

Augie jumped out of the jeep, standing alert, every bit the dutiful soldier. "Ma'am?"

"Keep your gun on this guy. Don't let him get up." A risk worth taking. The kid had no reason to believe the gun was empty. But she couldn't leave them alone for too long. In her experience, two unpredictable men left together always ended badly. And she needed to protect her precious human cargo, Augie, at all costs.

"You got it." Augie hoisted the gun up with a militaristic snap, levered it back down against Cody's head.

"Whoa, whoa! Take it easy, old man!"

Gravel spat behind Nanette, feet chuffing along at a brisk clip. The leather clad figure jogged toward her with the assured poise of an Olympian. "Nanette! Where's Gus? When I heard everything going to shit, I circled around, then came back."

"He's still inside."

Uncustomary fear darkened Delilah's usually impassive demeanor. Surprising envy struck Nanette, envy that Delilah cared about someone enough to worry. "I gotta' go find the jeep keys. Help Augie watch this idiot."

"Ain't no damn idiot, yo! And what the hell's up here? A hottie convention or somethin'?"

Both women ignored him. Delilah took off, a black-clad bullet. "I'm goin' in," she called back. "My guy's in there."

Shit. Nanette knew better than to waste her breath. Fine and fitting. Let Delilah take the risk.

"Dammit," Augie shouted. Nanette whirled to see Cody, recovered, on his feet. Wrestling with Augie over gun rights. Their hands grappled over the raised gun. Cody snatched it away, swung the butt up into Augie's chin. With a liquid-sounding *squich,* the older man dropped.

Cody stalked toward her, no more fun and games. Showing crazy eyes. No chance at taming this beast, not now.

"Nanette!" Leon stormed out of the house, running, his briefcase flapping against his hip.

Upon seeing Leon, Cody forgot about Nanette. He roared. And with his head down, took off for Leon like a ram.

"Cody?" Groggy from his fight, Leon stared at Cody as if experiencing a hallucination. But Cody came at him like an all too real jet, trailing a scream like fumes. Leon barely got his hands up in time.

"Kill you! I'm gonna kill—" The impact bashed the air out of Leon. He went down, the back of his head biting gravel. Cody sat astride him, beating him, clearly aiming for Leon's kidney. Leon rolled over, hands clawing at the ground. He saw Delilah's black leathered legs rushing toward him. Gus' feet swung in front of her belly.

"Cody, stop it! What—"

"Shut up, goddammit, shut up! I'm sick of your *shit!* How you *treat* me like shit!" A sharp uppercut to Leon's chin brought vision changing pain. Blood salted his mouth.

Leon knew he couldn't beat Cody in a fight, the past had proven that. But last year he'd forged a bond with Cody, one he thought he could use. His only defense. "Cody, I've never treated you—"

"Lies! You're a fuckin' liar! Back-stabbing sonovabitch!" Cody punched him again. "You don't jack with Cody!"

Through blurry eyes, Leon saw Delilah drop Gus. She took a wind-up step back, launched a shoe into Cody's side. Double kicked him again with both legs in the air. She landed in a squat, prepared to strike. Cody wheeled back, smacked her hard in the chest.

"*Oof.*" She crashed onto her bottom, gravel dust streaming high.

Relentless, Cody continued beating Leon.

"Cody, *why're* you doing this? We're friends! We—"

"Cody ain't go no friends, yo! Son-of-a-bitch! Dissin' me! Framin' me up to go to jail! While you—"

"And you killed my *father!*" Leon jolted up, their heads cracking together.

Cody stopped. Panting. Knuckles dragging the gravel. Confused. "He deserved it."

"But not by your hands! You *stole* that from me!" The thought came from nowhere. But it gave Leon strength. He jammed the heel of his hand up into Cody's chin. Cody gasped, went flat on his back.

Something flew by Leon's head. A loud *rnncch* split the jeep door beside him. *Gunfire.*

The smaller LMI man hurtled out the back door. Bullets sprayed haphazardly from his gun, his trigger finger jerking with each foot fall.

"Go!" Leon's command fell on deaf ears. Gus sat next to Delilah in the gravel, tending to her needs. "Gus! Delilah, run!"

Delilah shook it off, grabbed her parcel of love. She cut through the yard, dust fuming from her tennis shoes. Nanette had already put heavy tracks down the back road, dragging Augie along by the hand, twin blurs in the distance.

Cody groaned, wagged his head. Still on the ground but prepping for round two.

Leon had a different idea. He grabbed his briefcase and pulled himself up along the jeep's body. Then hobbled toward the narrow back road. Footfalls behind him picked up speed. Gravel crunched. Another bullet whizzed by his ear. He zigged, zagged, completely unintentional. His body struggled, his mind fuzzy. Down the road, wavy lines of heat lifted, devouring his escaping teammates until they vanished over a rise. The briefcase weighed heavy in his hand. His legs melted into tar.

"I'll *kill* you, old man! Comin' for you!"

Bullets zinged into the gravel. But Cody frightened Leon more. He knew what Cody was capable of.

Leon's legs refused to move faster. Uncooperative, like wading through swamplands.

From a distance, a bear growled. Eyes, glowing with sharp white light, blinked over the distant hill and dipped. A black body propelled toward him, rolling at intense speed. Clouds choked out behind it, Hell's chariot. Leon stopped, energy depleted.

The limousine crunched to a halt inches from Leon. He held up his briefcase, helplessly warding off another attack. A man stepped out of the driver's seat, automatic rifle materializing from within his black suit jacket.

"Duck."

Leon wondered why the man called him a duck. But the initial salvo of bullets in the air immediately clarified the shooter's meaning. Leon crawled toward the limousine. Pebbles tore at his hands, shredded his jeans.

The back door opened. Delilah leaned out, said, "Leon, hurry!"

Hysteria goosing him, Leon flung himself inside. And landed at the feet of his comrades.

With his fedora perched on one knee, his ever-present shoe-box riding the other, Bartholomew reigned over all of them. Carefully, he moved the shoebox to his chest, held it in the crock of his arm, and said to Leon, "We need to talk."

Then he raised his voice, calling out to his driver, "Go, Thomas. Leave a calling card."

Leon rocked over the floor as the limo lurched forward. Gravel sizzled beneath the tires, the back-end fishtailing. The driver rolled down the window and laid down a nice calling card of bullets as they sped away.

"No! No, no, no! Son-of-a-bitch!" On his knees, in the road, Cody screamed. Things hadn't gone his way. He had Garber at his mercy and the old man escaped. Again.

Revenge would be his, though, he knew it, damn near

predestined. He stood up in the swirling dust left by the limo, the eye of the storm.

One more chance, God, yo, just gimme one more chance to whack Garber. You know right's on my side.

Back in the yard, Bug sat in the grass, winded. Hugging himself like he was hurt. First thing, Cody looked—*wished*—for gun wounds. No such luck. Apparently Cody wasn't the only one with more lives than a cat.

"Yo, get up. We gotta get 'em." Cody added a light kick to get Bug's attention. Damn guy went over on his side, weaker than wet tissue. "Jesus, get up!"

The back door creaked open. Sensitivity stumbled out, tromping around like a baby taking its first steps. A fist curled up in one of his eyes. *Crying.* Just when Cody thought his day couldn't get any worse.

"My fault...all my fault...I let Mr. Ras-mus-mus-mussen down. *Again.* What'm I gonna do? I can't...I can't..."

Jesus Christ.

Cody's kick couldn't get Bug off the ground, but Sensitivity's fit worked wonders. The smaller man ran to his baby chick, wrapped a motherly wing around him.

"Shhh, shhh, I'll talk to Mr. Rasmussen this time."

"You mean it?"

"Yeah, everything'll be okay. It wasn't your fault." Bug shot Cody a look, one meant to insinuate guilt. *Whatever.* "Now dry up, big guy. We've still got work to do."

Sensitivity gulped the air like a fish at the top of the bowl. Rolled his shoulders. Put on his big boy sunglasses. Took a staccato burst of breath. "You're right. Sorry. Light it up, Bug. Make it look pretty and natural."

"The way Momma taught me." The men shared a laugh, bonding amongst freaks. "Gotta' get my gun first. Dropped it when the limo driver opened fire." Bug scoured the yard, nose down like a hunting dog. After a while he squinted at Cody. *Never trusting, these guys.* "Spangler, you seen my gun?"

"What? Hellz no, what the hell I be lookin' for your gun for? Garber or someone musta' snatched it."

When Bug turned around to continue his search, Cody dug into his hoodie pocket, ripping a hole in the lining. Discreetly, he moved the gun he stood on, stashing it deep within the hoodie.

Maybe the day wasn't a complete wash-out after all.

Chapter Twelve

"Where we goin'?" Augie slipped away again. Pretty much in line with how Leon felt.

Nanette took Augie's hand. "Augie, you're with me, Nanette. And our friends. We're going to Jasper Rasmussen's home. To destroy him and LMI." She said it as if cooing a good-night tale, one with a less than happy ending.

"Let's kick ass then!"

The soft breeze of the air conditioning caressed Leon's aching body. Still befuddled, he clung to the floor, something real to hold onto. He was afraid if he got off the floor, he'd wake up back under fire at Augie's house. Slowly, logic filtered through, puzzle pieces sliding into place. But a few were still missing.

Gus stood up, swaying as if on a bus, and extended a helping hand. Leon grasped it, climbed to his knees. Bartholomew gestured toward the empty seat next to him.

"How are you doing, Leon?"

"Oh, I don't know. Terrific, I guess."

Bartholomew flashed large ivory teeth. "What exactly transpired back there?"

When Leon finished (aided by Gustav's dramatic embellishment; his reenactment of how he took down the two hit men provided a masterpiece of minimalistic stage acting), Bartholomew tented fingers beneath his nose, sighed deeply. "There appears to be a problem."

"You think?"

"I do. One I'll deal with. Just not at the moment." The look he gave Leon chilled him, one of x-ray appraisal. "But right now we need to take care of more pressing matters." He turned to Augie. "Hello, August, my name's Bartholomew. We need you to tell us what you know about Jasper Rasmussen."

Nanette shook her head subtly, turned a commanding thumb her way: *I'll take care of it.* "Augie?"

"I know I asked this a while ago, but what're we doin' again?"

"Augie, it's me, Nanette. You remember me, right?"

"Course I do! Just wanna' know where the hell we're goin'."

August wore his pride like a badge, tarnished as it was. But sometimes strength wasn't enough. And, in Augie's more lucid moments, Leon suspected he knew it.

"Augie, we need to find Jasper Rasmussen."

"That son-of-a-bitch still alive?"

"He is. For now. We want to change that."

"Now that's somethin' I can get behind."

"Do you know where he lives?"

"Course I do! Been out to his ranch on many occasion. He used to have scarier than shit parties, full of freaks. I wanted no part of it, nosiree!"

"Can you give us an address?"

Bartholomew leaned forward in anticipation.

"Hah! Honey, he ain't got no address!" Deflated, Bartholomew sat back. Already giving up. But Augie hadn't finished quite yet. "Rich ol' bastard lives on a big-ass ranch, isolated in Montana. Practically uncharted lands. Nothin' else around but miles and miles of terrain and mountains. The way he likes it. I think he might've mentioned once he struck a deal with the local government...he pretty much owns them, pays their salaries, funds city improvements, everything. As long as they look the other way, forget he exists. Hell, he's the owner of Montana!"

Gustav couldn't contain himself. "Augie, my friend, can you tell us how to get there?"

"Little man, I don't reckon anyone'd be able to tell you how to get there. But I sure as shit can show you. I can take you there."

"Are you certain about this, August?" Bartholomew asked. "Can we count on you?"

"Course you can! Goddammit, just cause I'm forgettin' things don't mean I'm out for the count. I remember how to get there like the back of my hand!" He held his hand up, studied it, dropped it slowly as if he couldn't remember why he'd stuck it up. But there appeared to be nothing wrong with his long-term memory. Something peculiar to the state of Alzheimer's victims. "I want in on it. That son-of-a-bitch done me wrong. Been tracking me for forty some years now. I should be the man to take him out."

"August, I'm not certain that's such a—"

Nanette cut Bartholomew off. "Augie, of course you can come with us. We couldn't do it without you." Her pacifying words were true; Augie's mental map was their only hope. Leon just hoped it hadn't faded around the edges, the lines blurring with time.

"Damn straight you can't. Now, I gotta' tell you this ain't gonna be no picnic. It's gonna be hard sneakin' up on his fortress. 'Cause that's pretty much what it is. Out in the middle of nowhere, his private army standin' guard on all sides. Visibility's in their favor. They'll see us comin'. We can't just drive up, knock at the door, ask to plug a bullet in ol' Jasper's forehead."

"I was afraid of that." Bartholomew settled back again, thrumming his fingertips lightly over his shoebox. "We'll need a plan of action. No more running in without a clear course."

"Exactly," said Leon. "Which is what Albert's been having us doing." All eyes turned to Leon, waiting for him to assume the up-for-grabs leadership role. Of course he wanted nothing more than to pass the burden onto Bartholomew. Money is power, after all, and Bartholomew seemed in no shortage of it. "What do you suggest, Bartholomew?"

"We're leaving. Now. My private jet…" Gustav "oohed" and clapped his hands. "…is ready to fly out of a private airport just southeast of Miami. In more ways than one, Miami's too hot right now. Plus, we appear to be only one step ahead of LMI. For some unknown reason." He hit "unknown" hard and took the limo's passengers in one by one. Corroborating what Leon thought; a mole hid burrowed amongst them. Leon didn't escape Bartholomew's suspicious gaze, making him squirm. Guilty by nature, just not of this particular crime. "So we need to move fast. Press our slight advantage. I'm going to let Albert, Teddy and Bobby know, have them meet us in—"

"I'm *not* okay with that," said Leon. "Have you forgotten Bobby stranded us back there? And Albert! He hasn't told us anything. Just sending us in blind to our—"

Bartholomew stopped him with an upraised hand. "I understand your concerns, Leon. I do. I also have…questions. But, while Albert may be paranoid, he's shown a true aptitude at uncovering crucial information. We need him. And we need the computer he's currently in ownership of. Teddy also has talents that could prove useful. We need someone with computer knowledge and skills. And Bobby?" His neck cracked when he tilted it as if a noose had just yanked tight. "Do with him what you will. But we can't leave him behind. He's loose-lipped, petulant, the type who would contact LMI just to spite us for leaving him out. If he hasn't already." Silence pressed down on them as the weight of what Bartholomew said—clearly on everyone's mind—sank in. Casually, Leon glanced at Nanette. He didn't trust her for other reasons. And she'd been the first one, excluding Bobby, to flee August's home. But she wouldn't give everyone up. *Surely not.*

She caught Leon staring at her and mouthed, *What?* Her palms went up, testing for rain.

"Regardless," Bartholomew continued, "the question of Bobby's loyalty will surely be dealt with. In the meantime…" he snapped his wrist out, exposing a Rolex that Leon suspected would long outlive any of them, "…we're set to leave shortly. Needless to say, ladies and gentlemen, the siege on Rasmussen's ranch is going to be dangerous. We may not succeed. Or live. But, alas…" The shark smile surfaced again. "…as I stated in regard to Bobby, we can't leave anyone behind. Unfortunately, you have no choice. I just want everyone to realize what they're getting into."

Gustav led a cheer, capped by a rousing rebel yell from Augie. Delilah took it all in the way she usually did: with an enigmatic grin. Nanette remained impassive, one hand caressing Augie's back. And Bartholomew just watched Leon.

A suicide mission. Clear and simple. Leon supposed he'd always known it would come to this. Oddly enough, it felt like the past year had been leading to this moment: the escalating violence with LMI, burying his father issues, coming to terms with his own individuality. Perhaps this is what all of his training, his accumulation of knowledge, his studies of human psychology had been leading him to. So be it. There were less noble ways to die than to destroy LMI.

But he had something he needed to attend to first, one last part of his life he had to purge. He shook his briefcase, heard the wads of bills rattle. He wouldn't need the money where he was going. But someone else might.

"Bartholomew, of course I'm in. But first...I need to take care of something."

Gus said, "Leon, friend, what in the world might that be?"

"Personal business. Just getting my ducks in a row." Leon's smile felt small and false. The way he felt when confronted with the hopelessness of taking down LMI.

Bartholomew leaned over, carefully manipulating his shoebox out of damage's way. "That isn't a good idea. We—"

"I know it's not the best of ideas. But...it's something I have to do. Before we go." *Before we die,* Leon wanted to say. He locked eyes with Bartholomew. This time he wouldn't be intimidated into falling in line.

Nanette said, "Leon, I don't know what you're planning on doing. But we need to—"

"My decision, Nanette."

Finally, the Man with the Shoebox sniffed, checked his watch again. "I respect conviction, Leon. And determination. I won't inquire as to what it is you feel such need to do. But tell me one thing...will it jeopardize our mission?"

"No. Should things go badly, you know I won't give any of you up."

"I know no such thing."

"Tough. Work on your trust issues. Besides...should I be apprehended by the police, I suspect you'll find a way to get to me."

For the first time, Bartholomew's smile seemed sincere. Tough crowd. "And should LMI capture you?"

"I'll go down swinging." Augie hooted a marine's "hoo-hah!"

"Very well. It's against my better judgment, but I can see you won't be persuaded otherwise. I can delay the flight for... another hour and fifteen minutes. Will that give you sufficient time?"

"I believe so."

Bartholomew *tsked* at the shape of Leon's clothing. "You can't go like that." Leaning forward, he called out, "Tommy! Do you still have my extra suit and hat?"

An electronic window whirred down. "Yes, sir."

"Very good. Leon, what do you wear?" He sized Leon up and down, a mental tailor. "A thirty-six?"

"Yes."

"It'll be a tight fit, but I believe you can make do." Hastily, Bartholomew scribbled something down onto a piece of paper, slipped it into Leon's shirt pocket. "There's where you need to be. Do *not* be late. You won't like the consequences."

"I'm sure I won't."

"Shall we drop you somewhere?"

"Yes. The hospital."

The Man With the Shoebox instructed his driver to drop Leon off several blocks from the Westchester General Hospital. Leon's muscles protested at the two block trek, but soon he imagined his body would be getting all the rest it needed. And then some.

Bartholomew's suit fit like a shrunken glove, but the shell of Corporate America felt good to don once again. He kept the fedora at a downward tilt, shading his face, strolling along on agonized limbs, until he entered the hospital. Once there he straightened as best he could.

At the nurse's desk on the second floor, he inquired about Ramona Keats.

Clearly put out, the nurse angrily punched keys on her computer's keyboard. The screen's lights glared in her round (so round they looked like an embarrassing relic of the '80's) glasses. "Only family's allowed to visit." She scrutinized him, gave him a doubtful look. The cuts and blossoming green bruises on his face probably didn't help sell his case. "Are you family?" An eyebrow lifted.

"No. Just a friend." Better not to argue, attract unwanted attention. But for once, fate smiled kindly upon him even if at the misfortune of a patient. An electronic beep erupted through the halls. The nurse fled her station, joining several other aqua and white flashes of hustling nurses. Leon leaned over, spied the room number.

The hallway was barren, dark except for several deliberately spaced wall lights. The door to room number 242 sat ajar. He stood outside and listened. A steady beep came from within, a sighing respiratory machine. He peeked inside. Keats rested on her side, her back to him, one arm flung over her head. Tubes connected her to lifelines, but from what he knew of her, they were probably just for show. Very few flowers decorated the room, surprising for a cop wounded in the line of duty. Either she was unpopular amongst the men in blue or despised flowers. Quietly, he entered, sat at a bedside table, placing the briefcase into his lap.

"Detective?"

She whipped around. Immediate recognition jolted her into action. With a cop's instincts, she thrust a hand toward the bedside table, fingers searching. A lamp wobbled. Leon righted it.

"Doubt they let you have your firearm at bedside."

"What the *hell*?" She snatched the oxygen tube from her nose, flicked it aside. Above her, a machine beeped urgently. Leon stood, hit the kill switch. "You here to finish the job?" She kicked the covers off, scrabbling to get out of bed.

Leon grabbed her arm, gently pressing down. "Relax. I'm not here to hurt you. If you remember, I saved your life. I'm the one who brought you here."

A quick succession of expressions flit across her face: disbelief, shock, anger, finally a distrusting, yet, accepting amusement. "Seem to 'member something like that. Been wonderin' why."

Leon shrugged. "I don't hurt innocent people. Or good cops."

"Some hero." Her voice carried a tired, sluggish quality, but her eyes blazed alert as ever. On the job, even in pain.

"Never claimed to be one. Listen, I read you're gonna be fine. Back on duty in no time."

"Small miracle. No thanks to you."

Leon couldn't help but chuckle, gallows humor. "Keats, you never had anything to worry about from me. It's your partner who tried to kill you. I had nothing to do with it."

"That's bullshit. If you hadn't been lying, hiding out—"

"Then Bellup wouldn't've tried to blast you to Kingdom Come? What kind of roundabout thinking is that? Look, I didn't come here to fight. Nothing like that. Besides, from what I gathered from the media, they've accurately pegged Bellup as your shooter."

"Helps I recorded everything."

"Yeah." Leon winced. "Everything."

"Yup. Including everything about you, Garber. You got some balls comin' here, now that there's an APB out on your ass."

"Balls of brass."

"You get 'em from your daddy? The one you set on fire?"

"I...I didn't do that. That was..."

Even though it pained her, she sat up, sporting a *"gotcha"* look. "Yeah? Who?"

"I can't say, not now. Maybe someday I'll let you know."

"Lookin' forward to it."

"Anyway, back to business." Leon patted the briefcase. "I need you to do me a favor. When you're up and about, of course."

"Why in hell would I do that?"

"I saved your life. Don't make me regret it."

"That a threat?"

"Only the threat of my ever-lasting friendship."

She fought it, but smiled anyway. First time for everything. "Even from this hospital bed, I could kick your ass, Garber. Especially with the way you look."

"Don't doubt it. But you should see the other guy."

She winced, her eyes scrunched up in pain.

"Hurt when you laugh?"

"Only when I'm pissed. I don't laugh."

"You need to get out more. Anyway, here's what I'd like you to—"

"So you took me to the goddamn hospital, some act of charity. I know you're knee-deep into some hinky shit. I'm not doin' you any solids."

"And I wouldn't ask you to do anything illegal. Believe me, it's legit."

"Right. 'Cause you're such a trust-worthy guy."

"Something like that."

She glowered at him, fuming heavily through her nose. Maybe missing the life-sustaining oxygen. "Not sayin' I'll do it, but what you got in mind?"

"Tell you what, Keats. I'll sweeten the deal. Anything I may've done wrong in the past? It's over."

"Why don't you start by telling me what that is?"

"Maybe some other time. But I'll never break the law again. And you give me twenty-four hours, then you come after me. Come after me with guns a'blazin', badges flashin', bullets blastin'."

"I intend to."

"I'd expect nothing less."

Pride struggled to shove aside her righteousness, a richness brightening her cheeks. Probably didn't get too many kudos amongst her stable-mates. Honest cops these days seemed to be a dying breed, frowned upon even. "Save your shit," she said around the barest of smiles.

"But I give my word, after twenty-four hours, Leon Garber will be dead. One way or the other."

"What's that 'sposed to mean?"

"Exactly what it sounds like. Then, by all means, come after me. And if, for some unlikely reason, I'm still around, I promise I'll let you in on some insider info. Something big. About a nationwide organization, with their eye on expansion, involved in politically motivated murders. This is the kinda' case that could shoot you to the top, more medals than a Russian skater."

"A conspiracy. Secret organization. *Really*? You take me for a fool?"

"Anything but. That's why I'm telling you this."

She blinked. Repeatedly. A Morse Code message to her brain to decipher the info bomb. "Fine. Not sayin' I believe you. I don't. But I'm curious if on the rare occasion you're finally telling me the truth. So...what's this favor?"

"I want you to deliver this briefcase to—"

"Whoa, hold up. What's inside?"

Leon fidgeted with the locks, opened it. The top dropped exposing wrapped Benjamins and even more impressive dead presidents.

Even as she shook her head, she couldn't drag her attention away from the greenery. "I want nothin' to do with dirty money."

"It's not dirty, Keats. I earned all of this back in the good ol' fashioned world of high-finance accounting. Every penny. I've never taken a dollar I didn't earn."

"Again, wish I could believe you. So...what do you want me to do with it?

"Deliver it to my old neighbors at the Dolores Motel. Room number 114. A woman and her son. Terrie and Gavin—"

"Schreiber. Yeah, yeah. I know who they are. I know everything about you, hence them. My business."

"Thorough."

"Yeah, look where it got me." She waved a not-so-magical wand over her body.

"Keep hope alive, Keats."

"Why you wanna give them your money?"

Leon sat in silence, wondering how to best coat his answer. Sometimes the undiluted truth worked the best. "It's the right thing to do. I won't need it any more. And the kid should have the right to go to college. And the mother needs to get out of her—"

"Hooking. Huh. A white knight in killer's clothing."

It stung. The killer part. Still, it was also the nicest thing anyone'd said to him in a while. He brushed it off with a shrug. "Whatever. Can you do it, Keats?"

"Thinkin' 'bout it. What would I tell them?"

"Just say...it's from an anonymous donor. I, ah...don't know what they think of me now. They probably wouldn't take it if they knew it came from me. 'S why I'm not doing it myself. Tell them…it's for a new start."

She mulled it over, eventually rocking her head into an affirmative nod. "Fine. Can't see that you got anything to gain by it. But you bet your ass I'll be runnin' the serial numbers on the money first."

"So untrusting. But be my guest. The money's clean."

"I just know I'm gonna end up regretting this."

"Life's full of regrets, Detective."

"Tell it to my credit card company. As soon as I'm up, though, I'm comin' after your ass."

"Looking forward to it." He stood, pinched out the pleats of his slack-legs. "Better get going. Oh. One last thing." As he leaned over her, she shuddered beneath his shadow. Then she came back with arms up and crossed, ready to defend herself. With a heavy sigh, Leon yanked the nurse's button from the wall. "Just in case it's hard for you to tell when twenty-four hours is up."

"Asshole."

"Sticks and stones." He nestled the briefcase beside her and left her with a tip of his hat. His smile crumbled as soon as he hit the hallway. Hurrying down the stairwell, he rushed toward the side exit and into the night. Even though his body ached in every place imaginable, the dread that shadowed him hurt much worse.

Most of the money Leon held back went to buying his cab driver's silence. Once the cabbie dropped Leon off at the mouth of the hangar, voluntary blindness struck the driver as well, a freebie. He carefully avoided looking anywhere but the straightest course off the runway.

With the hangar's pink and gray painted, corrugated metal ridges arching high in the sky, it resembled the giant ribs of a prehistoric beast on its back.

Leon picked up his pace as he approached the hangar. Tires screeched behind him, echoing down the runway. He shrank into a crouch. The truck whipped toward him, the tail-end snaking about the tarmac. Three figures sat inside the vehicle, no doubt Bobby at the wheel.

Albert and Teddy tumbled out first, appearing a little unsteady from the white-knuckle express they'd just disembarked. Bobby hopped out next, hitching up jeans that resisted his formidable beer belly. Leon stalked toward Bobby, payback in mind. But a black roadrunner barreled by him, pecking her way across the runway.

Tap, tap, tip, tap, tap...

Delilah didn't stop until she kicked up her last step, planting it solidly into Bobby's crotch. From where Leon stood, he heard the sure to be crippling *thump*. Delilah's momentum brought them both down to the cement. Bobby's girth supplied plenty of cushion. Immediately, she bounced up, then spat on him. Groaning and cupping his wounded groin, Bobby rolled like a man on fire.

A light clapping rose behind Leon. "Marvelous," yelled Gustav.

Leon felt a cathartic grip of anger release, but still demanded answers. "Son-of-a-bitch! Why'd you leave us, Bobby? We coulda' died in that house! Almost did!"

Bobby answered with a series of unintelligible moans.

Albert intervened, placating hands up. Possibly fearful Delilah'd come after him next. "Yes, it was a poor choice on Bobby's behalf, but—"

"'Poor choice?' Is that the ribbon you want to put on it, Albert? You weren't there! We barely escaped! This idiot had one thing to do. *One* thing! And he—"

Bobby formed caveman words. "Saw...guys with guns. Left. Came back...but...everyone gone. Called...Albert..."

"It's true, Leon. He called me, let me know what was going on. I instructed him to go back for you. As backup, I phoned Bartholomew, asked him to look in on you. It was a bad situation. Bobby did the best he could under the—"

"Try harder next time!" Leon leaned over. "We're not going to get another chance."

"Jesus...Christ..." moaned Bobby.

Albert said, "Teddy, help Bobby to his feet."

Teddy looked up, down, everywhere but at Bobby. Uncertain, he stuck a tentative hand out toward his fallen comrade. Naturally, Bobby swatted it away.

"Get off me!"

Nanette joined the tarmac party, one thing on her mind. "Albert, what about the laptop?"

Albert's already round shoulders sloped even farther. "Ah... there were complications. I—"

"Ladies. Gentlemen." Leon jumped at the quiet voice at his shoulder. He had no idea how long Bartholomew had been shadowing him. "Let's not cause a scene. We need to depart." He led the way into the hangar, Bobby last and limping.

The Gulfstream jet was large, half the size of a commercial airliner. Standing in the open jet's door, Gus waved a half-full wine glass. "Your ride awaits, my friends."

Bartholomew's limo driver, a multi-tasker extraordinaire, sat in the cockpit. Leon knew good help was hard to find, particularly in a Like-Minded Individual's highly specialized line of work. Still their relationship baffled Leon. The pilot didn't look like a psychopathic killer, but Leon'd learned looks hardly mattered with people of their kind. He supposed Bartholomew's man, Tommy, may've just been an ordinary garden-variety sociopath with no qualms about where his paycheck came from as long as it was a tidy one. Bartholomew definitely walked the tightrope of privacy; his trust in the man apparently went far. There were many questions Leon wanted to ask Bartholomew, particularly what he carried inside his shoebox, but, frankly, he feared the answers.

Next to the pilot, Augie rode shotgun, an overgrown boy marveling over the magical panel of lights and wizardly dials. Let him have his fun, thought Leon, the man'd earned his worth of entertainment.

Brushing a crushed velvet curtain aside, Leon entered the cabin. The roomy interior displayed multiple shades of black, white and silver, very European. Ashen grey swivel chairs backed against one another, six in the main cabin. Accentuated black pillows, an intricate maze-like pattern woven into them, rested in the chairs. The black carpet mimicked the design element, angular grey squares and trails leading inward and ultimately, nowhere. A pristine and stocked bar lined one wall, a conference table anchored the back. All very sleek, extremely cold and uninviting. It looked to Leon like Bartholomew shared the same interior decorator as Nanette's late "friend," he of the luxury suite they'd stayed in: designer to the serial killers.

Bartholomew claimed a chair, hitching one leg up on the seat: a King on his throne, the shoebox his scepter.

Bobby shoved by everyone, still hunched over. He collapsed onto a curving couch. Delilah took a look at her victim, smirked. She grabbed a full ice bucket from the bar, strode toward him. Cowering, he tossed his hands up. "No! No more! I—"

Delilah dumped the ice onto his crotch, dropped the bucket, and slipped into a seat in the back. Balancing his drink, Gus crawled into her lap. Nanette sat across the aisle from Bartholomew. Like an insecure student at a new school, Teddy nervously sidled into the chair across from her. Nanette closed her eyes, leaned back, hanging an obvious message: *Do not disturb.* Teddy watched her with an oddly delighted smile.

"Tommy, let's take off," called out Bartholomew.

"Yes, sir. We've got clearance." Which didn't surprise Leon. He'd seen no other jets on the runway except for one grounded in the hangar.

Bartholomew pointed at the empty chair across from him. For unknown reasons, the Man with the Shoebox apparently had taken a special interest in Leon. One Leon wished he'd take elsewhere.

Still standing in the aisle, Albert wobbled upon take-off. His mouth opened, then closed with a dry snap. Something was on his mind.

After several minutes, the plane leveled out. The acoustics sounded unnaturally quiet, nothing more than the hum of a reliable refrigerator.

"Ladies and gentleman," Albert cleared his throat, a long grind. "I'm afraid I have some bad news...terrible news." Proactively, he patted his hands in the air. "As you well know, while you were retrieving Mr. Schroeder, Teddy and I were busy with Wyngarden's laptop." A sorrowful shake of the head. The funeral procession had begun. Leon suspected what lay in the coffin. "We did everything we could. Teddy finally cracked the security password." Teddy hunkered down, clamping his hands around wiggling knees. "As soon as we bypassed the security, I'm afraid a virus...a backup that must've always been in effect... destroyed the hard-drive. I'm terribly sorry. It was a dead end that—"

"Everything?" The question came from Nanette, eyes still closed. Other than her freshly worried brow, she appeared asleep.

"Yes, everything."

"It wasn't my fault, not my fault," Teddy blurted. "I did everything right! It was an accident! I didn't—"

"No one's blaming you. These things happen," said Albert, looking compassionately upon Teddy, a little proud even. Strangest "father-son" relationship Leon'd seen since, well, his own.

Teddy wrapped a straightjacket of arms around himself. Most of the passengers appeared to have already forgotten him. In fact, based upon the general apathy onboard, everyone had long ago given up on the computer's purported treasures. Or maybe they'd given up the fight entirely.

Humbled, Albert sat down, sliding into a deep funk. Even though he drew the window shade, his gaze never left the window.

"I take it you completed your business, Leon." Bartholomew placed his shoebox down onto the small table between them. Scooted it back and forth, squinting at the precise angle as if lining up a shot on a pool table. He scrutinized Leon with cagey eyes, waiting. Testing him.

The shoebox tugged at Leon. Part of him wanted to rip off the top of the box, find out what secrets were within. But he felt that's exactly what Bartholomew wanted him to do. Not that Bartholomew would ever let him.

"Yes. Everything's squared away."

"And how is Detective Keats?" Apparently LMI weren't the only ones with eyes everywhere.

"She'll pull through."

"Very nice to hear." Although he didn't look very pleased. "I've been giving our situation a lot of thought. We've been compromised."

"I agree. LMI's been right behind us every step of the way."

"Clearly we have a leak."

"Clearly."

"Any thoughts as to who it may be, Leon?"

"I've got a good idea." A lie to play the game. Although Bobby seemed the most likely candidate after his disappearance act at Augie's house, Leon didn't have a clue, not really. For all he knew, Bartholomew could be the traitor. Or Nanette.

"As do I." Bartholomew's suit whispered as he crossed a leg, the cuff riding his shoe in a precise cut. "The motive's harder to discern since everyone here appears to have a legitimate problem with LMI. But money can do strange things to people." Consulting his watch, he said, "Ah. It's time to uncover the culprit."

Standing, he announced, "Ladies and gentlemen, please. It's come to my attention that someone on this plane has betrayed us. It's the only possible explanation as to how LMI has known our every move."

"What're you talkin' about?" shouted Bobby, his taciturn self back to form.

"One of us has been selling information to LMI." Slowly, Bartholomew walked down the aisle, glancing down his nose at everyone he passed. He stopped in front of Gus and Delilah.

"Why, who in the world would do that to us, Bartholomew?" Gus looked pained, hurt as if his pride had been shivved. "We all have the same—"

"I'm afraid it's true, Gustav." He set a hand on Gus' shoulder. "Sad but true. Not to worry, though, I don't suspect you or the lovely Miss Delilah. You already have a healthy bank account, the second richest man on board." He sniffed with a haughty air of elitism. "I certainly don't understand your motivation, of course, for willing to risk your lives against LMI, but..." He weighed an invisible scale of justice with his hands. "...to each their own."

Gus clapped, the party back in full swing. "Of course, my friend! We are on board for wherever adventure takes us!" Delilah's lips formed a tiny smile.

Bartholomew moved onto Albert. "Albert, I've had the

pleasure of meeting you before. Our paths once crossed in the most…" Full-toothed smile. "…interesting of ways several years back."

Based on the way Albert squirmed, Leon guessed it was a tale Albert would rather keep hushed.

"You've led our little group this far, made some good decisions, some bad. I'd truly hate to think you'd betray us. Especially since LMI has been hunting you for quite some time. But you've exhibited some very curious behavior."

"What?" Albert's eyelids fluttered. "What've I done—"

"Precisely, Albert. There's been talk that you haven't exactly been very proactive. But…that's your leadership method, I suppose, for better or worse. However, there is the curious instance of the jammed gun."

"Jammed gun? The one I gave to Nanette? How could I've possibly known it was jammed? Surely, you don't think I—"

"I don't, Albert, relax." With a patronizing smugness, he patted the top of Albert's head. "I'm willing to chalk the gun up to human error."

"It's not like I've actually fired a gun before, you know!"

"Yes, I believe we *do* know." Bartholomew glided toward the back, determination in his step. "Bobby, how're you feeling?"

"Better if you'd get outta' my face."

"Always charming. Not so charming when you abandoned your teammates."

"Already explained that! I went for help! I haven't done a *damn* thing for LMI! You—" Bartholomew's finger pressed down on Bobby's lips.

"I believe the only thing you're guilty of is cowardice."

"I ain't no goddamn coward! Nobody calls me that!" Bobby sprang to his feet, fire in his eyes. Bartholomew doused his flame with a simple look. The truck driver flumped down, crossing bear arms.

Teddy's turn. The wiry man drew himself into an even more compact knot of bones. "I didn't do it, didn't do it, didn't do—"

"Calm down, Theodore. I haven't accused you of anything. Yet." Bartholomew stood over Teddy, tall and intimidating. "I find it rather disconcerting that you stayed behind from the jaunt to Mr. Schroeder's house. Also, Wyngarden's laptop was destroyed under your watch."

"Now just a minute, Bartholomew!" Albert jumped up, attempting to stand taller than Bartholomew. It didn't hold. He folded and lowered his voice. "I chose Teddy to stay with me to work on the computer. No one else had any—"

Bartholomew stuck an arm out, palm up, traffic cop style. "I'm only voicing what's been on everyone's mind, Albert."

He moved behind Nanette, his hands massaging the top of her padded chair. Over and over. Cool as a cucumber, Nanette kept her eyes closed. "Nanette, you're the hardest one to figure out. In fact, I know less about you than I do the others."

"There's a reason for that." She opened her eyes, gazed up. "I like my privacy."

"Indeed. I'm fairly certain we all do. Except, of course, for Gustav, perhaps." Gustav accepted it as a compliment, offered a humble bow. "But there've been times when your motivation has come into question, my dear. Almost as if you have your own agenda, playing your own game with some of the others." He gave Leon a hard to miss look.

"Hey, a girl's gotta' do what a girl's gotta' do. I have reasons. For everything I do."

"I'm certain you do."

"But I hate LMI with a passion. There's no way in hell I'd align myself with them. Never again."

After a beat of silence, Bartholomew smiled. "Conviction always wins the day with me, Nanette."

"Whatever." Nanette closed her eyes again, dismissing him with a flyaway hand.

"Bartholomew, are you about finished?" asked Albert. "I'm not convinced we have a traitor—"

"Your *naiveté's* showing." Suddenly, Bartholomew growled. "Eventually, that naiveté's going to cause someone's death."

"It hasn't exactly been easy. Being leader. I didn't ask for this responsibility. I—"

"No, it's true, you didn't. But at least wear that responsibility like a true leader."

"By all means, if you'd like to take over, Bartholomew, be my guest."

"Thank you, I believe I will." The true intent of Bartholomew's fishing expedition, Leon suspected. Suddenly Albert didn't seem so bad. "And as your new leader, any minute now…" Again he consulted his watch. "…we'll find out who our mole is."

The Man with the Shoebox grinned, relishing his covert victory.

"What're you gonna do, torture us?" asked Bobby. "And how come you didn't grill your lil' buddy Leon over there? Don't much care for the way he looks."

"I'm sorry if Leon's appearance doesn't…quite live up to your lofty sartorial expectations, but he's the one person on board I know is innocent."

Bobby flapped a hand, probably trying to work out the definition of "sartorial." "Bullshit. Don't trust him."

"We'll find out in a minute who not to trust. Earlier, after the Schroeder incident, I had my man…" A thumb jacked toward the cockpit. "…send a text to our mutual friend, Mr. Summers. An anonymous text. After all, Mr. Summers has been everyone's contact with LMI. Am I correct in this presumption?"

"Before I was black marked, yes," said Albert.

"Taking that presumption one step further—not my usual style, of course—our traitor must've been in contact with Mr. Summers. The text my man sent to Summers was very vague, very untraceable. It read, 'Sorry things went badly at Schroeder's house. Can't talk now. Call me at 9:00. I have more info.'" The Man with the Shoebox's grin grew.

Silence filled the cabin. Leon swallowed louder than he'd hoped to.

As if on cue, at 9:00 sharp, a tinny, muffled theme sounded. The theme to *Star Trek*. Guilty of profiling as the rest of them, Leon immediately turned toward Teddy.

Teddy scrabbled a hand into his pocket, quieted the phone. Like a pendulum, his head shook, picking up speed. "No, no, no, no…" He said it like he couldn't believe it. He wasn't the only one.

"Teddy? Why on earth would you do such a thing?" asked Gustav.

"Son-of-a-bitch!" Bobby pounded down the aisle until Bartholomew intercepted him.

Quietly, Bartholomew said, "Sit down, Bobby. I'll take care of this." Leon saw it in his eyes, too; he'd enjoy the task. "Give me the phone, Teddy."

Teddy ignored him. "It's a mistake. All a mistake. It's not true. Just an accident." He yipped like a small dog getting its tail stepped on. "It's not me, not me, not me..."

"The phone, Teddy. Hand it to me. *Now.*"

Withdrawing further, Teddy closed his eyes and tweaked his phone out.

Bartholomew examined the screen. Satisfied, he tapped it off. "It's from Summers. Pretty sloppy on LMI's behalf, I think, but I sense desperation." He whirled, his suit jacket tail flipping up. An ice pick gleamed in his hand, upraised over Teddy. "Ladies, you might want to look away."

Of course neither one did. Yet nausea flushed Leon's stomach. He didn't want to— *couldn't*—watch this.

"Before we bid you farewell, dear Teddy, would you mind sharing with those you sold out why you chose to do so?"

"Didn't do it, didn't do it..." Sobs obliterated his words. He swayed in his chair, hands clasped before him in a prayer-like gesture. Last rites. "Didn't mean to do it, didn't want to do it—"

"Why, Teddy?"

Through fogged glasses, he looked up. "Because of my mother! She's dying! I lost all my money in bad investments! I couldn't afford her operation! But I had to save Momma...even if it meant...even if it meant..."

"Dear God, Teddy. Is the cancer back?" Albert stood on shaky legs, leaning against a seat for support. "Why didn't you tell me?" Albert's connection to Teddy. For years, Albert had been seeking a cure for cancer. The warmth in Albert's eyes, the tenderness in his voice surprised Leon.

And now, more than ever, Leon wanted off the plane. Before the execution commenced.

"The cancer never went away! She's dying! But the operation..."

Teddy retreated from the battle, surrendering his explanation. Acknowledging his time was up.

Bartholomew pricked his own finger with the ice pick, admired the drop of blood with fascination. "Teddy, I'm not without compassion." But his smile sold a different promise. "I have more money than kings, of course. I'll see to it your mother gets her operation. You just won't be around to enjoy the results." Shadows darkened his eyes as he drew back his arm.

Teddy's hands jerked up.

"Wait!" Leon jumped, lassoed Bartholomew's wrist in his hand. "Stop. We can *use* him."

Bartholomew lowered his weapon. "How's that?" Instead of speaking to Leon, he addressed his question toward the pick. Offering a disappointed apology.

"Augie said we'd have a hard time getting close to Rasmussen's ranch without being spotted."

"Yes?"

"We'll use Teddy. Trojan Horse him."

The ice pick tip wheedled at the corner of Bartholomew's mouth, dangerously close to puncturing a new dimple. "I...see." When the ice pick lowered, so did his ever-present smile. "How do you propose we do that?"

"Let Teddy contact Summers. Tell LMI he broke away from us. But with me as his prisoner. I'm the one they've been chasing now. The one they want."

Bartholomew mulled it over, nodded. "I believe that's a valid plan." He stared wistfully at Teddy, the fish he wouldn't be gutting today.

With wide eyes, Teddy craned his head around. Took a big gulp. Then fled to the back of the plane, screaming.

Bartholomew sighed, sat down. "He'll wear out. Let him throw his tantrum. There's nowhere he can escape to." He had the nerve to wink at Leon.

Relieved, Leon practically collapsed into his chair. Not that he had any love for Teddy. But he didn't want to see him ice picked to death. And all the resultant blood. His stomach lurched one more time at the gruesome image, then settled. He withdrew a hypodermic and offered it to Albert. "This will calm him, Albert."

Reluctantly, the ex-leader of their siege took it, headed for the back.

A few minutes later, Albert returned, shaking in the aisle from a sudden burst of turbulence. "Teddy's asleep."

"My idea might get us in the door," said Leon. "But from there…we need a better plan."

Albert offered, "I've had my inside man working on a plan. Something that'll help us once you're inside the ranch."

Tired of subterfuge, Leon said, "And of course, you're not going to tell us. Not until the last minute."

"Ah, I'm afraid you're correct. But not because I don't trust you. I'm just…tired of disappointment." And he did look tired, sad in a wistful way. "Before I build everyone's hopes up again, I want to ensure everything stays on point with my insider." He offered a conciliatory smile, not the best door prize. But, for once, Leon understood his motivation. No need to set the others up just to smash them down again.

"Fine, Albert." Leon leaned back, massaging the bridge of his nose. "What do we do now?"

"Already taken care of," said Bartholomew. "I've taken the liberty of reserving a floor of suites at one of my interests in Billings, Montana." Leon wondered just how far Bartholomew's "interests" ranged. But the allure of one last night's sleep sounded enticing. "Everyone needs time to regroup. And it'll allow us time to recon the territory. Billings isn't too far from our target." The Man with the Shoebox had fallen into military mode, briskly snapping out jargon. "Albert, will tomorrow night work in conjunction with your plan?"

"I believe so." Excitement brightened Albert's face, happy to be invited back to the war room.

Which brought up another issue. "Rasmussen's going to have an LMI army at his disposal," said Leon. "How're we going to fight them?"

Bartholomew grinned. "I've got our needs covered." He walked toward the silver bar, tapped a few buttons. The panel slid back with a slashing *ching*, revealing an impressive armory. The latest in killing technology exhibited with a collector's touch. Proud of his display, Bartholomew stood by as the planeload of killers gathered in awe.

"Marvelous!" As Gustav reached for a flash bang grenade, Bartholomew swatted his hand away.

"Gaines, this better be damned good." Jasper Rasmussen answered the door in his leopard-skin robe. He scratched at the ants crawling over his body sensation. For the amount of money he'd doled out for the robe, he at least expected it to be comfortable. But Sheera claimed she liked the feel of it. Or used to. He'd long ago shuttled her off to another bedroom, her neediness a constant irritation. Just like his manservant.

"I think you'll be pleased, sir." Gaines paused, waiting for accolades.

"Goddammit, it's after ten. Just spit it out."

"After the, ah, rather disappointing outcome at August Schroeder's house today—"

"Enough of that shit!" He swung out, aiming for Gaines' face and missed the mark by a mile. He didn't need to hear again how badly his men had botched their job. Incompetent imbeciles. "Don't say another word unless you got Garber's dead body for me to see."

Gaines's smile burned slowly, an unsettling effect. One Rasmussen hadn't seen before. "Nearly as good, sir. Our insider has Garber. His prisoner."

"Bullshit! That skinny, creepy kid, Eddie?"

"Teddy, sir."

"Don't interrupt me! That little twerp got the drop on Garber? While our men couldn't?"

"That's what he claimed to Summers. He's been using Garber's hypodermic needles to keep him docile."

"I'll be goddamned." Rasmussen rubbed the top of his head. Crepe-like flakes of skin dropped like cotton willow. "Where are they now?"

"In hiding. Waiting to hear from us. Teddy's been a little hesitant in giving us their exact location."

Rasmussen's skin tingled again, this time in a pleasant way. He looked forward to meeting Garber. At last. And, for the first time in what seemed like decades, he intended on dirtying his hands again. The good old fashioned way.

"Fine. Can he get here by tomorrow night?"

Gaines nodded. "I believe Teddy'd be amenable to that."

"Then get Sensitivity and Bug back here as well. No one runs an interrogation like that freakish firebug. Garber's gonna give up the rest of his rebels, one way or another."

"Of course."

"And when Teddy gets here, give the boy his just reward." Of course he meant a face full of lead, Rasmussen's favorite precious metal. No loyalty in employees any more. "Then bring Garber to me."

"Yes, sir."

Excitement stirred his loins, the spirit of his leopard robe possessing him. "And go fetch my wife." He thought a little entertainment might be in order, a warm-up to tomorrow night's main event.

For once Sensitivity and Bug moved faster than lightning. One call from Rasmussen and Bug wrenched a U-turn in mid-city. Something was up, something big.

As soon as Cody saw the small airstrip, he thought his lunch might come back up. Flying meant security. No doubt the guards would bust his ass, find Bug's gun on him.

Once out of the car, Cody dragged his feet. But when they hustled him directly onto a small jet, relief peeled away like major sunburn. Cody poured himself a stiff drink, kicked back into a recliner. The gun jabbed him in the back, a secure feeling.

Cody had plans for the gun. Being a realist, it seemed unlikely he'd survive the fall-out either. Cool, cool, whatever. But he planned on going out in a blaze of glory, just like the dudes in that western Garber'd sent him in prison. Live big or die trying, the way he rolled.

Sensitivity swiped the drink from his hand, dumped it into an ice bucket. "We're on duty."

"Dayum, we on our way to Bible Camp next?"

"Shut up."

"And why're we flying in style now, brah? Why the hell haven't we been travelling this way all along?"

"I said, 'shut up'. You've caused enough problems. You screwed up the last operation by losing your shit over some damn dog."

"Dog didn't hurt nobody!" Cody's fingers dug into the armrest. Nothing riled him more than animal abuse. But attacking Sensitivity would likely result in his gun being discovered.

"Issues, Spangler? I've seen some messed up Like-Minded Individuals before, but you take the cake."

"I'm not crazy, asshole!"

"From where I'm sitting, I haven't seen much of anything but crazy. Oh, and I let Mr. R. know you derailed our mission imperative."

"Oooh, shaking in my boots." He rattled his hands, the gun at his back giving him courage. He couldn't wait to see how brave Sensitivity would be looking down the big, bad barrel.

Bug sat down next to his partner, whispering sweet nothings or some shit into his ear. But one word kept popping: *Garber*. Cody's end goal. Frankly once Cody capped Garber's ass, he didn't care what happened next. He knew LMI planned on doing him, any happily ever after a pipe-dream.

"Yo, what about Garber?"

Sensitivity deliberated, finally said, "LMI has him. Or will soon. We're going in to guarantee project completion once and for all." Cody didn't care for Sensitivity's smirk, the way he emphasized *once and for all*. Sizing Cody up for the kill.

But all that mattered? Garber'd been caught, soon to be dead. Which bugged Cody. The LMI idiots hadn't thought this all the way through. Not unusual for them, but something felt way off. By far the wiliest guy Cody knew (next to himself, of course), Garber wouldn't let himself get caught so easily. Definitely up to something. Count on it.

Cody couldn't wait. Christmas was just around the corner. And like Santa, Cody planned on bringing a sack-load of crap to the party.

An embarrassment of riches, the luxury suite defined opulence. Leon felt ashamed, really; it reminded him of the days when he rode his tidal wave of riches. Unnecessary perks such as a fur-lined bedspread, a bathtub large enough to house a family, and a fully stocked bar of decadent chocolates, oddly colored cheeses and foreign liquors turned his stomach. On the other hand, he wondered if he should splurge, a last meal for a condemned man. But the extravagant financial waste sapped any pleasure he might derive. Sometimes his inner accountant still fought to have a say in the matter.

As soon as he stripped the bed's extraneous pillows, someone knocked at his door. Even though he suspected the identity of his visitor (inevitable, really), he palmed a hypodermic and peeked through the eyehole.

Resplendent in a tight-fitting, crow-black evening gown (and where she kept coming up with wardrobe changes baffled Leon; she travelled light), Nanette stood in the hallway. As soon as he opened the door, she clinked a bottle of wine and a glass together.

"Leon, I know you don't drink, so I brought plenty for me." She sashayed past him, drifting an intoxicating scent of roses behind her.

"Considerate."

"I know, right?" She made a beeline for the sofa, sat down. Crossed her legs, the dress riding high. Calculatedly so, no doubt.

"What do you want, Nanette?"

"To talk to you. And to have a drink." Unexpectedly, she let her guard down, peeling away her mask of confidence. "Apologize to you, I guess." Sincerity filled her eyes.

"It's late. We have a tough job ahead of us tomorrow."

"More the reason I should apologize now. Before it's too late." She patted the empty cushion next to her, frowned at her hand as if it'd operated independently. Then gave him a quick smile. A frank, warm smile. One Leon found quite appealing. "Please?"

He couldn't refuse. But kept his distance on the sofa. "You don't have anything to apologize—"

"Maybe you don't think so, Leon. But, please, I have to do this. It's hard enough as it is already."

"Fine."

"I know I can come across strong at times."

"You think?"

She raised a finger, quieting him. "You gonna let me do this?"

"Yes. Please."

"I'm not making excuses. But, I thought...maybe you'd understand me a bit better if I explained." She twisted off the cork of the bottle, topped her glass. "I had a bad upbringing. For most of my life, men...took advantage of me. Men I trusted. Men I thought I'd loved. In more ways than just sexually, though that was at the top of the charts more often than not. Their taking advantage of me became habitual; so frequent, I began to think it was my fault. That I led the men on. Maybe I deserved how they treated me. Until one night...one night too many, I killed my stepfather."

She paused as if waiting for her words to sink in. But it was a story Leon knew well. Several other Like-Minded Individuals, himself included, had similarly deep-rooted issues. He nodded for her to continue, forcing his hand to not reach for hers.

"After I killed him...an inner strength set me on fire. Empowerment for lack of a better word. Oh, hell, that's what it was all right. So...I decided to take that, run with it. Get back a little bit of what'd been taken from me all of my life."

"I'm sorry."

She swallowed a mouthful of wine. "I'm the one apologizing. It was a game at first, using men to my ends, then disposing of them. Only ones who deserved it, though. And they did."

Leon considered asking how she knew her victims deserved their fate. Then decided to take her at her word. Everyone's human, after all.

"Soon it became more than a game, though. It became my career. And I became quite good at it, too."

"Not surprising."

"Shush. Anyway...I don't know what it is about you, Leon... why I'm even telling you this. But it's a compliment, you know..."

"What is?"

"That I can tell you about myself. I mean, I don't want to

sound arrogant, anything like that. But you're the first man in a long time I feel comfortable opening up to. And when things turned heated the other night..." A wicked smile, a deliberate eyelash drop. Back on point. "...well, let's just say old habits die hard."

"Believe me, I know. Worse than quitting smoking."

"Exactly." She shrugged, tipped the glass back. "Again, no excuses. But I *like* you, Leon." She paused, lost, searching for the right thing to say. "I *did* like you." It sounded like a wistful goodbye, lovers fated to never meet again. Leon wasn't ready to let her go.

"I like you, too."

"Okay. There. I said it." Emotions off, she suddenly stood, set down the bottle and glass. And walked toward the door in a hurry.

"Nanette, wait." Leon followed her. "I accept your apology. And I appreciate it. I know it's hard. Especially for people like us."

"'People like us,'" she repeated.

Leon kissed her. She didn't object, stepping into his embrace. But the previous night's passion had slipped away. Instead, they held one another. Holding on tight, afraid to let go. Finding like-minded people, a little too late. A farewell kiss.

With her head down, she left.

"Goodbye, Nanette."

Chapter Thirteen

Sleep didn't drop its veil over Leon until the early morning hours. By 6:00 a.m., Leon had enough and bailed out of bed. As the sun rose, he meditated. Quiet beauty captivated him as the colors of sunrise changed the sky outside: a bruised purple melted into a soothing pink and finally settled into burning oranges and warm yellows.

He managed to force down a bagel, courtesy of the in-suite bar. Coffee laced his stomach with acid and wired his brain. The walls of the suite caged him in, an upscale prison. Yet he couldn't leave while waiting for the expected call.

The call to arms at long last arrived in the early afternoon.

Bartholomew's suite—the "war room"—put Leon's to shame. Twice the size, a wall of mirrors made it appear even larger. The living room stepped down into well-appointed luxury.

Even though the volume had been muted, the television set entranced Augie. On the sofa, Bartholomew's Renaissance man, Tommy, sat next to Teddy, a pistol packing babysitter. But hardly a necessary one. Not in Teddy's nearly catatonic state of mind. A very disturbing place, Leon imagined. Leon worried if Teddy'd be able to pull off their elaborate ruse.

Bartholomew strolled up, said, "Don't worry about Teddy. I assured him if he follows his instructions, no matter the outcome, I've already put a plan into effect to see to his mother's operation." Crisply attired in a pinstripe suit, Bartholomew looked refreshed, no troublesome demons banging at his brain through the night. He gripped a coffee cup ("World's Best Funcle") in one hand, the shoebox cribbed beneath his other arm. "Coffee, Leon?"

"No thanks, I'm good."

Near the back of the spacious suite, Leon's team was gathered around a table. All except Bobby, who was sprawled across a recliner, one leg draped over the side, a ball cap cupping his face. His barrel chest rose and sank to grinding snores.

"Leon, my friend!" Gustav rushed away from the group, arms outstretched. A greeting he apparently never tired of. "Welcome! I hope you're well retired!" Behind him, Delilah grinned.

Leon knew what he meant but questioned how prophetic Gus' mistake might prove. He imagined after tonight, they'd all be "retired." Permanently. "Afternoon, Gus."

Albert glanced up from a blueprint. "Leon. We're making final plans."

Again, paranoia swooped through Leon. Always last to the party and the last to know.

Nanette flashed him a timid smile, then dropped her gaze back to the blueprint. Locks of dark hair covered her face. Hiding in plain sight.

A cricket chirped in Albert's pocket. "Ah! Right on time." He patted himself down until he found his phone. "Hold on one minute, please," he said into the receiver. Squinting into the phone's screen, he poked at it, technology clearly frustrating him. Finally, he set the phone onto the table. "Okay. We're all here now."

The caller said nothing. In the background, cars raced by, tires screeched, a horn honked. The sounds of a major city. "Uh...wait a minute...did you put me on speaker phone?" The familiar voice scattered into panic. "Take me off now!"

"Ah, Skeeter, we're all allies here. I've told everyone—"

"Whoa, whoa, whoa! Dude! No names, man! You weren't supposed to tell anyone about me!"

"Skeeter, I highly doubt that's your real name, anyway. And all I've mentioned is how you've been acting as our inside—"

"Enough! Take me off speaker! Now, man, or I'm out!"

Still troubled by the mysteries of his keypad, Albert eventually managed to silence the phone. A minimum of grunts constituted the rest of his conversation. Eventually, he handed the phone, along with a wary look, to Leon.

"Skeeter wants to talk to you."

On the other end, Skeeter screamed, "No names! *Dude!*"

Despite himself, Leon smiled. Skeeter'd helped him in the past on several occasions. Although scared to death of LMI's long reach, Skeeter'd been one of the very few people who tried to slip Leon some life-saving information last year.

"Skeeter."

"Jesus! What is it with you guys? No names, man!"

"Sorry. Glad to see you've joined our team."

"Yeah, well...I, ah, found out some crap I didn't really want to, you know?" Leon knew. Skeeter liked his job but never wanted to hear about any of LMI's deadlier details. He went out of his way to at least feign ignorance, keeping blood far from his keyboard. "I found out everything that happened to you, Leon. Found out too much, I guess. Figured my expiration date was coming soon. Thought I'd beat 'em to the punch. So...um, look, Leon, I don't know any of these other guys, not really. And I don't really know you, dude. But you've been pretty cool with me in the past, straight up. So, like...did I pick the winning team?"

"You a betting man?"

Skeeter's silence told Leon he wasn't, or at least, not a successful gambler. "Aw, shit. Don't look good?"

Leon turned, dropped his voice to a near whisper. "Let's just say the odds aren't in our favor. But we're gonna give it our best."

"Dammit. Crap, crap, crap..." Leon knew exactly how Skeeter felt; he'd been in his shoes for the better part of a year. Outside of the Bible, when you're David, Goliath destroys. "Whatever, man. Guess I'm all in now. Give me a call later, would ya? You know...if you..."

Survive. "Of course. And this goes without saying...if you don't hear from me, I understand the Caribbean's nice this year."

"Doubt I can escape them even there. Listen, dude...good luck. I mean not only for you, but, you know, for me, too."

"Thanks."

"And should you...you know, succeed...I don't want to know any details."

"Got it."

"And you still owe me some of those Omaha steaks at Christmastime." Leon'd forgotten the promise he'd made last year, but Skeeter hadn't. Skeeter had revealed himself as a true-blood, meat eater, loathing the fruit baskets Leon used to send.

"First thing on my to-do list tomorrow."

"Later, man."

Albert yanked back his phone, closed it with a snap, and addressed the rest of the room. "Okay, ladies and gentlemen, Skeeter came through for us this morning, sending blueprints of Jasper Rasmussen's ranch." Leon glanced at the blueprint, most of it unintelligible to him. Arrows pointed, lines crisscrossed and connected to eye straining tiny numbers. One thing became clear, though; Rasmussen had barricaded himself within a mammoth spread. "Rasmussen's compound—that's what it is, really, a ranch in name only—is located just east of the Continental Divide. Acres of grasslands surround it for miles. Which poses a problem. There's only one road leading to it, one Rasmussen built himself. Needless to say that makes visibility an issue. Also, there's a massive stone wall encircling it. A reinforced iron gate is the only entrance."

"What about the back?" asked Bartholomew. "The forests?"

"The back of the ranch does indeed butt up to a forest, the wall more or less keeping it out."

Delilah squinted at the blueprints, then placed a hand on Gus' shoulder. She turned him around to face her. With nearly glassy eyes, he nodded. A secret language between them. "If I climb the trees, bam!" she said, bringing a fist down on the table. "Hop over the gate. I'm in."

Albert bounced a pencil on the table, tap-tap-tapping. "Possibly. But, Delilah...Rasmussen has around the clock armed guards. They'll see you coming."

She shrugged, her leather squeaking. "How big's the forest?"

"Ah...approximately three miles deep, nine miles—"

"No problem. But I'd better get going soon. Use the daylight."

"While I like the idea of a three-pronged attack—in front, behind and from within, I believe the trek through the forest alone will wear you—"

"Yeah, right, whatever. Hellooo...girl scout here."

Gus stepped close to the table, his goose-egg belly riding the edge. "It's true, my friends! I'd wager dear Delilah is in better shape than any of us here."

Leon didn't doubt it; she had youth on her side, plus years of carrying Gustav had chiseled solid abs and arms.

"I agree." Bartholomew's cheekbones stretched high over a grin. "If Delilah says she can do it…I believe her." She gave him a funny look, then buried her head into the blueprints again. First time Leon'd ever seen her turn down a visual dare.

"Fine. But you'll be trespassing on Rasmussen's private property. In fact, he owns everything there, forest included. If Delilah's packed with camping gear, it might provide a cover story should she get caught."

"They won't catch me," she said. "No way. Not gonna happen."

"Splendid," said Gus. "I shall, of course, accompany my fair lady."

Albert winced. "Um, my apologies, Gustav. We've made other arrangements for you."

"For me? A special course of action tailored specifically for me?"

"You do what you need to do, Gus," said Delilah. "I'll be fine. Don't worry about me."

Excitement brightened his eyes as he took her hand in his, bestowing a kiss upon it. "My love, I never worry about you."

"Yes, well…" Albert cleared his throat, serial killer romance clearly not his thing. "…back to the matter at hand. As I said, the surrounding wall makes Rasmussen's Ranch practically a gated community. There're…at least six other houses comprised of multiple apartments where his, ah, army resides. He even owns—or may as well—part of Con Ed." Gus looked up at Delilah, puzzled. She patted his head, mouthed, *later*. "He has his own electrical facilities within the compound. We're going to take it out. Use darkness to our advantage."

"But if Rasmussen has patrolling night guards, surely they'll also have night-vision goggles," offered Nanette. The threat of impending danger seemed to reinvigorate her. Her energy nearly palpable, she swung her arms, warming up. "And taking out the power's going to be damn tough from the outside."

"Ah! Not with Skeeter on our team." Smiling, Albert consulted his watch for show. "At 9:00 sharp, Skeeter's taking down the power grid."

No one doubted the wizardry Skeeter wielded. If a computer could locate something, Skeeter could master it. Safely from his home in L.A., of course.

"Furthermore, our friend, Bartholomew, has a few tricks up his sleeve to combat the guards' night-vision enhancements."

Bartholomew tipped his head toward Nanette, ever the psychotic gentleman. Having only had a glimpse of the Man with the Shoebox's arsenal, Leon imagined it ran as deep as his seemingly endless money supply.

"But, friend Albert..." Gus stabbed a finger down onto the blueprint. "...I see right here there's a backup generator."

"That's where you come in, Gustav."

"Smashing!"

"Exactly."

Gus didn't bother with any follow-up questions. As long as he played a starring role in the suicidal run, all seemed right on his stage.

"Bobby will lead the frontal assault alongside Nanette and Tommy." From his recliner, Bobby raised twin devil's horns, gave them a little rock and roll shake. "Directly behind them will be Augie, Bartholomew...and myself." Fear set Albert's hands shaking over the blueprint. He clamped them down onto the table, steadying them. Leon understood. And he respected Albert for finally entering the front-lines of battle. "Every man's needed," Albert added in a tiny voice. "Now for the riskiest part...Leon and Teddy's entrance into Ranch Rasmussen..."

The plan sounded crazy. Insane. But, for once, they at least had a plan. Watches were calibrated, cell phone numbers exchanged with the proviso they only be used in case of emergency. Timelines were studied, dissected, discussed, and settled by jury. Throughout Albert's detailed explanation, Nanette distracted Leon. He caught her paying him serious attention, her face uncharacteristically somber.

Delilah left first, escorted by Tommy. But not before she

bid farewell to Gus. Kneeling, she tucked her head next to the small man's. They held one another, whispers traded along with kisses. For a while, they remained unmoving, cemented together. And for the first time, Leon realized, they were afraid. Gus' party-boy attitude vanished as soon as his love walked out the door.

Several hours later, when Leon left to prepare, Nanette stopped him. She glanced around to see if the others, busy over the blueprints and working out the final details, were watching. On tiptoes, she stretched up, delivered an invigorating kiss. This time, instead of saying goodbye, though, she seemed to be saying, "Why, hello, stranger!"

Some ranch, thought Cody. When he'd been told they were going to a "ranch," he expected cows and cowboys and ten-gallon hats and cactuses more prickly than the nuns at the orphanage he spent part of his childhood in. After travelling miles through dusty grasslands, he certainly hadn't expected this. The ranch turned out to be a true kazillionaire mansion in the sky.

A skyline of mountains provided the backdrop to a building that looked out-of-place in the middle of nowhere. The modern, stone-walled mansion looked like it'd been dropped down from Heaven, angelic architects putting in some real overtime. A series of arches ran along the first floor, supporting the double-sized second floor with windows so big you could land a jet inside. Six mini-versions of the main building sat alongside the God-like version, man created in His image.

Once Sensitivity drove them through the gate, things got even better. The swimming pool water glistened, alive beneath the sun's rays. But, hands down, the babes on display were the best part. More curves than the world's biggest water slide.

The Lord gives, the Lord taketh away, so the pissy nuns used to justify their cruelty to Cody.

As soon as Cody stepped out of the limo, his nirvana plummeted. Sensitivity moved like a cheetah, jacking Cody's arms behind him.

"*What*? Get off me! What're you—"

"Shut up, Spangler. Time to end your shit." He cooed it into his ear, lovingly so. His steel chest pressed up against Cody.

Lucky, smart or whatever, Cody was damn glad he'd had the foresight to stash his gun into his boot while in the plane's crapper.

Bug sidled up, bored looking, watching Cody struggle with a huge load of indifference. A troop of sunglass and suit wearing monkeys raced toward them. As if trained in Quantico, they held pistols locked in both hands, pointed at the clouds. Cody hadn't exactly expected a hero's welcome, but he thought he'd get more than this. Maybe a big old Montana steak served by a hot chick for all his troubles.

"Goddammit, get off me! I want to see Rasmussen!"

Once the woman appeared, the armed men fell silent. Even Sensitivity straightened, striking a constipated pose. The men parted, making way for their goddess. Her bathrobe swayed, billowing off her tanned, preposterous breasts. The sun hadn't been kind to her skin, but neither had her plastic surgeon. Tiny cracks surrounded her face, so tight Cody thought her skin might split in half. Not that it mattered. All he could think about was the things he'd like to do to her. The guards weren't the only ones standing stiff and tall.

"What have we here?" Behind her sunglasses, Cody thought he detected a smile, impossible to tell. When she spoke, only her lips moved. A ventriloquist's dummy had more animation.

"Yo, mama, what's up, what's up, what is up? I'm Cody, the Spangler. What say, baby, you lose your goons—"

"Shut up, Spangler! Show some respect." Sensitivity wrenched Cody's shoulders back.

"So...you're the infamous Denver Decapitator." Clearly impressed, the babe whipped off her sunglasses and nibbled at the tip, her inflated lips getting a workout.

Now Cody knew he had her. "So you heard about me, huh? Impressive, ain't I? I'm a damn artist, yo, a friggin' LMI celebrity."

"You're funny." But she didn't sound amused. Then again, who could tell? Even her voice sounded unnatural.

"Show you how funny I am when this asshole lets me go."

"One more word, Spangler, I'll break your—"

The royal highness raised a golden hand, stopping Sensitivity. "Relax, Mr. Sensitivity. I just wanted to get a good look at the young psychopath who's caused my husband such trouble over the last year."

"Wait...what? You're married to Rasmussen? He's, like, really old and shit! And if you wanna' get a better look at me, let me go. Looks are free. And I ain't psycho!"

Eh, eh, eh, a robotic laugh. "Funny *and* cute."

"Got that right, baby." Sensitivity tightened his grip like the big dumbass had a crush on the boss's wife. Something Cody wondered how he could play if necessary.

"As you now know, I'm Mrs. Rasmussen. My husband's been waiting for you."

"Yeah? Well, let me see him already."

When she pouted her balloon lips, Cody felt the earth move. "I'm sorry. He's taking his afternoon siesta."

"I don't give a damn if he's takin' a crap or not, lady, let me talk at him!"

Eh, eh, eh. Cody was killing her, absolutely slaying. But she hadn't seen anything yet.

"No manners. Tsk. And I'm afraid my husband doesn't want to see you. He wants you dead. Those are his orders. To kill you as soon as you arrive."

"Wait a...that ain't right!" The gun scratched at his leg, so close, so far. But he couldn't go for it now; he hadn't had his play-date with Garber yet. He needed to buy time. Even if he was out of barter. Always cool under pressure, though, his motto. "You can't kill me. I know Garber better than anyone, yo! You need me!"

"Now why would we need you? Garber's already a prisoner of an associate of ours. Coming here as we speak. You're moot. Frankly, I thought you've been moot well over a year ago. But... my husband makes some strange decisions sometimes."

"I ain't moot, yo! Look...Garber's got somethin' up his sleeve. He's a tricky bastard. You really think he'd just roll over, say, 'Yo, I give!'"

Cody thought she'd fallen asleep with her eyes open. Finally she said, "I considered Mr. Garber's capture may've been too easy. Contrary to Jasper's thoughts."

"You bet your sweet—" Sensitivity tightened his hold over Cody's arms again. "Ugh. Get off me already!" Cody tried stomping his captor's foot. But Sensitivity, nimble as ever, swept his boot over and back.

Mrs. Rasmussen ignored the show. "What could Mr. Garber possibly do to us from his disadvantageous situation, Cody? Enlighten me. I'm all ears." *The one place you haven't had any mad work done,* Cody nearly added.

"I don't know what he's doin'! But you know he's workin' with some other LMI freaks, right? If you want to get them, you gotta' get Garber to talk. And, trust me, dude don't give up jack! Only if you know how to press his buttons. And I got his blueprints, baby girl."

She looked at the sky as if checking for rain, then studied the sprawling mansion behind her. A click of her lips sprung like a mousetrap. "So why don't you tell me about these hot buttons, Cody?"

"What, you kiddin' me? No way I'm gettin' rid of my only leverage."

"Fine. Let's keep him around until Mr. Garber shows up. Mr. Sensitivity, please show Cody to bunkhouse number six."

"With pleasure, Mrs. R."

A group of men jostled, pushed and shoved Cody down a long marbled path to one of the smaller mansion offspring. Sensitivity nodded at one of the preppy goons to unlock a door that lead downstairs. Several other doors lined the hallway, chains sealing them shut. A prison.

As a farewell gift, Sensitivity stretched his ape-like hand over the top of Cody's head. And squeezed. Cody felt his eyes bulge, his scalp tighten. "If Mrs. R.'d said the word, I would've popped your head like a grape, Spangler. Think I might just yet. As soon as Mr. R. gets up from his nap."

"Jeezuh Crigh!" Cody didn't recognize his own voice. For sure it wasn't the way he'd meant to sound. With a shove, Sensitivity hurled Cody across the cement floor. Cody dropped hard. His ankle twisted, screaming at his brain to acknowledge the pain. The door slammed shut. Sensitivity whistled his way down the hallway.

Cody massaged his ankle, tracing the lines of the hidden gun with care.

Soon.

The Chevy bumped across the terrain. Teddy's driving was nearly as erratic as his squirrely behavior. Alternately, he braked, accelerated, the car lurching in fits and starts. Leon could practically feel Teddy's nerves emanating through the car trunk.

Leon's legs ached. He stretched them slowly so as not to push into full-blown cramp territory. Intentionally, the ropes binding his hands were loose. He tugged them tight until minor rope burn appeared on his wrists. Appearance meant everything.

Inside the trunk, darkness surrounded him. A rank smell permeated the interior, a claustrophobic coffin. Panic kept pushing, but he did his best to quell it.

As bad as Leon had it, though, Gustav had it far worse.

Leon asked, "Doing okay, Gus?"

"*Righ ah rai.*" *Right as rain.*

Even given the man's small size, it amazed Leon Gus had been able to squeeze into the tire well. Like a contortionist, Gus'd balled up, curling his body around the rim while lying on an assortment of weapons.

So much of their plan relied on sloppy luck. Not for the first time, Leon thought Albert and Bartholomew had severely underestimated their opponents.

The car chugged along. Gravel popcorned beneath Leon, indicating they were close. Sweat broke out across his brow.

Outside, voices barked. The Chevy slowed. The motor purred, vibrating into Leon's chest.

Tekkata-tekkata-tekkata…

Teddy's voice sounded like an underwater hiccup. Suddenly, the car pitched forward. The engine died. Hot metal clicked.

Denk, tic…kkik…

"This is it, Gus," Leon whispered. A soft knock-knock answered him.

Footfalls crunched over gravel. A key twisted into the trunk lock.

Kik-chik.

The trunk lid lifted. Bright lights poured in. Leon shielded his bonded hands over his eyes and blinked at a collective of silhouettes holding flashlights. Beyond the shadows, floodlights illuminated the grounds, a pale moonscape. A German shepherd approached, dragging a suited man behind him.

Chhf, chhf, chhf...

With its head hanging over the trunk's mouth, the dog sniffed. A cold, wet nose brushed Leon's hand. A low, steady growl rose into a bark, amplified within the trunk.

Guns clacked, prepped and aimed.

"*Whoa!* What *else* is in the trunk?"

"Nothing, I swear!" screamed Teddy. Behind the armed men, Teddy strained on tiptoes to see Leon. "Ah... maybe the dog smells my gun." Teddy mopped his forehead with his sweater. Then pulled a pistol out from his waistline.

"Drop the gun! Now!" Gun barrels swept toward Teddy. His arms shot up, his gun dangling by a finger.

"I'm on your side! See? I'm dropping it! Just...don't shoot!" The gun fell to the pavement. On full alert, a guard kicked the weapon away.

"Get him out of the trunk," ordered a stout man with a flat-top haircut. Ex-military, no doubt. "Search him. You two... watch the other one."

An octopus of arms reached in for Leon. As he was lifted out of the trunk, he tugged the slack rope taut around his wrists. Leon's head banged into the open lid, a sadistic cop's trick.

The Shepherd sniffed Leon's ankle, its nose traveling north. With a throaty growl, the dog stopped at Leon's pocket.

"Dammit, be careful!" yelled "crew cut." "Pat this guy down."

A guard spun Leon, facing him against the trunk. Leon dropped his hands onto Gus' hiding spot. Cautiously, the guard slipped his fingers into Leon's jean's pocket, plucked out a sandwich bag.

"What's this?"

Leon shrugged. "Beef jerky. Only thing I've had to eat in days."

The guard dropped it to the ground, not worth his time. But the dog found it of interest, digging its snout inside. Another man swept the trunk with a flashlight. "More fuckin' jerky inside the trunk."

The dog whined, sniffing at the bumper.

"Shut the trunk. Bluto doesn't need any jerky."

The jerky had been a last-minute addition, a smart one. It's impossible to fool a dog's nose. But you sure as hell can distract them.

Delilah had breezed through the forest in no time, shoving away branches while flying over the ground cover. Upon seeing the mansion, she snapped off the penlight in her mouth. On the outskirts of the forest, the moon provided just enough light.

The wall stood at seven feet tall, no clear handholds. A Douglas Fir's thick arms waved in a breeze, scratching at the wall. One stray branch reached over the wall's boundary. She scaled the tree. Not the best for climbing, by any means, but Delilah accepted the challenge. Kept things exciting. No doubt the branch would give beneath her weight, but she'd use it to her advantage, swing in on it like Tarzan.

But first she needed to recon.

From her vantage point, she spotted two guards patrolling the back of the mansion, semi-automatics propped in their arms. As expected, night vision goggles looped around their necks. Not that they needed them now. Flood lamps surrounded the ranch, the grounds brighter than a baseball stadium.

Soon it'd be time for her to join the party. From her backpack, she retrieved her goggles, slipped them on. A netherworld of green met her, the flood lights hot blinding flashes. She turned them off.

Her thoughts kept wandering to Gus. Back at the hotel, she hadn't told him about the strange rush of fear that'd nearly brought her to her knees. Fear not for herself, of course, but for her lover. Gus never lacked confidence and it seemed pointless to stick a pin in it at that point. But he'd been tasked with a giant of a job, one she hoped he'd survive. Maybe her worries were unfounded. Every challenge they'd ever faced, though, had been together.

Tears built. She closed her eyes, forcing them away. It'd been some time since she'd cried, since she'd lost control. Something she definitely couldn't—*wouldn't*—do now.

With a hand cupped around her phone's light, she checked the time. Just a few minutes, then "kerblooey".

She manned up, chuffed out a few deep breaths. And inched out onto the branch...

Rasmussen's men retreated in a shuffle of boots over gravel.

God-speed, friend Leon.

Gus unscrewed the bolt, slid the cover off and uncurled on top of the well. A knot of tension swelled in his gut. During the trip, he'd attempted to send positive vibes to his dark beauty, Delilah. Checking in with her via the psychic airwaves.

Of course it was all balderdash. But, over the years, he'd developed a mental shorthand with Delilah. They understood one another, *became* one another. To paraphrase a delightful American love film, *she completed him.* So he didn't find it entirely out of the realm of possibility to connect on some psychic level with her. But she wasn't answering.

It troubled him. They hadn't been separated in years, not for any length of time. And he wasn't about to lose her now.

Hold on, my love, I'm coming.

He kicked at the back seat. One, two, three...*clunk.* Legs first, he shoveled himself into the back seat, pulling the bag of weapons behind him.

Outside, the lights burned bright. He slung an automatic rifle over his shoulder, double-checked the bag of plastique.

He peeked over the window's rim. At least three guards had stayed behind, patrolling the vast grounds. To get inside, he'd have to take out one, possibly all of them.

Wonderful!

Leon had entered the heart of LMI. Now to stake it.

A gun barrel goosed him across sprawling marble floors

and through a series of elaborately decorated rooms. Ancient weaponry and mounted animal heads on display confirmed what Leon'd already suspected about Jasper Rasmussen: he thrived on violence.

Behind Leon, Teddy constantly asked about his fate, attempting to write his own happy ending. "Rasmussen's going to pay me, right? And let me go? Since I brought him Garber, right?"

The armed guards kept their mouths shut but their guns ready to talk.

A winding staircase delivered them upstairs. Their footsteps echoed down the hallway: *click, clack, click.* Near the end of the hallway, the guards stopped in front of twin Oak doors.

The lead guard rapped his pistol against a door, then opened it. Leon snuck a glance at his watch. Only minutes away from show time.

As Leon entered the room, he tightened the loose ropes within his fist. Played his fingers over them like Rosary beads.

Leon'd been in many boardrooms in the past, but none like this. The expansive oak table, shinier than a newly minted penny, ran the length of the room. Numerous leather chairs gawped with open-mouthed seats. Stained glass windows, an odd choice, stretched to the high ceiling: Church of the Damned.

Jasper Rasmussen sat at the opposite end of the table, a withered raisin of a man. The two killers Leon'd tussled with before bookended Rasmussen—the sickly looking small man and his giant of a genie partner. Rasmussen jabbed a gnarled finger toward the chair nearest Leon.

When Teddy stepped into the room, Rasmussen sputtered, "Not him, dammit! Take care of him as I told you!" The man Rasmussen directed the order to—the sort of nondescript accountant type Leon had met many times before—smiled. A man who loved his work.

Teddy grabbed the doorjamb, holding on tight while guards tugged at him. "No! No, you promised, promised me—" He flew out the door. And fell abruptly silent. Guilt hit Leon, a burst of unexpected empathy; he hadn't extended Teddy's life by much.

Two guards stayed behind, attached to the wall. Fully locked and loaded. The odds didn't look good.

"So you're the troublemaking little pest. Don't look like much to me," hissed Rasmussen.

Leon nudged a chair out and sat. With his hands below the table, he loosened the ropes. "Looks can be deceiving."

"Oh, horse shit! I've had better men than you take a swing at me."

"None of this ever would've happened had you left me alone. But, I'm grateful in a way...otherwise I'd still be killing people for you. Innocent people."

The old man's hand slashed down. "Again with the bullshit. You can color it anyway you like, Garber, but you're no better than anyone associated with LMI. You're nothing but a goddamn crazy killer. I have goals in mind, directives that—"

"Directives that line your pocket. I know what you're about. And it's over."

Rasmussen laughed, a horse's neigh. "You're done. Finished. Dead. You're just too stupid to realize it yet. But I'm gonna make you suffer 'fore you get there."

"I may be done. But so are you."

"You're hardly in any position to make threats. You cost me a shit-load of money when you destroyed the L.A. headquarters. And for what, exactly?" He spread trembling hands. "You really think a splinter in my paw's gonna take LMI down? Hell, we're already reforming L.A. Been meaning to clean house there for a while anyway. You can't kill the beast. Son, our overseas contingent is just gearin' up, ready to—"

"Don't call me 'son'."

"Heh. Your daddy issues. Big man still suckin' at his dead daddy's teat."

The words stung Leon. But he couldn't lose his head, not now. "Any issues I've had are resolved. Now all I care about's taking you down. Regardless of what happens to me. And you're going down. Any minute now."

Leon scooted the chair back. He pressed down on his toes, raised his heels. Preparing to act. Mentally calculating the location of the men behind him. He'd have to move fast.

"You believe the balls on this bastard?" The two killers

roared over their boss's question, business as usual at LMI.

Then the lights went out. So did the men's laughter.

As punctual as a Swiss watch, the floodlights died at 9:00. Throughout the mansion, all lights blinked off.

Gustav felt like a spy on a death-defying mission. Earlier, he'd even considered wearing a tuxedo, but the trip in the car well would've left him looking anything but debonair.

He left the car (the *James Bond* theme looping in his head) and flicked on his night-vision goggles. The green spectrum disoriented him at first, made him a tad nauseous.

A guard stood by the front door, struggling with his own night wear. Gustav raced toward him, his favorite killing knife ("Percy") extended like a rhino horn.

Gus' feet hit the pavement. The guard wheeled around. Gus swung his knife up and dug it in deep. The guard's belly unleashed a torrent of blood.

As much as Gus would've loved to take time to admire his handiwork, he only had minutes before the generator kicked on. A twist of the door knob met with resistance. *Locked.*

Behind Gus, a voice rose, heavy and out-of-breath. "Stop! Put your—"

Gus freed the gun from his back and rattled the gun in a wide arc. Bullets cut through his opponent's midsection. The guard collapsed with a groan, then a jangle.

A jangle? Keys!

Not too far away, Gus heard men screaming, running in his direction. He hopped down the steps, dropped down on all fours. A ring of keys splayed out on the dead guard's belt loop. With a slice through the loop, "Percy" cut them free. Gus held the rings up, shaking blood from them.

So many keys, so little time.

The sky cracked. Above his head, a bullet chocked into the door. More gunfire exploded behind the mansion.

Delilah.

Gus laid down a cover of bullets. Fireflies flashed from his gun.

The first key failed. In his hand, the key ring shook. The

second key slipped in, turned. Cool air kissed him as he entered the mansion.

Inside, two armed men chugged down a hallway. Gus fell on one knee, no time to take aim. Didn't have to. Pebbles broke away from the stone walls. A last reflective trigger pull by one of the dead men fired a bullet over his head.

Something deep groaned in the belly of the mansion. Sudden light blinded Gus, hot fire in his goggles.

The generator.

He'd missed his time window.

But, like the best cinematic secret agents, he meant to fulfill his mission by any means.

Bobby drove the last mile of hard road without headlights. Nanette held on tight, riding shotgun and holding a shotgun. Tommy, Bartholomew's aide, sat silently in the back seat. Leaving Nanette alone with her thoughts.

Voices crowded her head. Her id urged her on, stroking her self-confidence with rallying *hollahs*. But her stepfather's voice— vile and poisonous—kept trashing her self-confidence. Calling her a stupid and weak girl, useless in a suicide mission. Unless, of course, she died.

She evicted the voices—tried to, at least—and moved to the here and now. The only time period that mattered. No sense wallowing in the past. She wondered if she even had a future. Bobby's dangerous driving didn't exactly boost her estimated life chances.

Right on time, the lights went out at casa de Rasmussen. A fireworks display of gun flashes cut through the darkness. Bobby flew off the road. The SUV's tires spit up grass as they raced parallel along the ranch's protective wall.

The back window whirred down. Calmly, Tommy tossed flash bang grenades up and over the wall.

Explosions rattled the car windows. Nanette's earplugs provided little soundproofing. Artificial lightning lit up the sky. Across the grounds, voices cried out.

Clearly in his element, Bobby whipped the SUV into a loop. He floored the pedal. Taking them straight into the gate. Nanette braced her arms against the mantle.

Grrrnnch. Spang!

Sparks sprayed off the vehicle. Metal tore and folded. The left section of the gate crashed back. The SUV tilted, righted itself. Nanette banged her head into the mantle. The seat belt bit into her shoulder, her stomach. The vehicle nosed up, finally stopping on top of the downed gate.

Her muscles ached. White noise buzzed in her head. Voices sounded urgent, yet far away. Not far enough away.

Nanette kicked open the door. Bobby, battling his seat belt, shook his head. Tommy'd already bolted from his backseat vantage point. He leveled his automatic over the roof of the vehicle and fired. Guards dropped.

Behind them, the second SUV zoomed up, headlights doused.

Nanette heard Augie scream, "Take that, you sons-of-bitches!"

Bullets chunked into the SUV's driver's side. Nanette hefted her shotgun up. A shadow dodged to her right. She pulled the trigger, nailing her target.

Gunfire flashed in her goggles. At her shoulder, Bartholomew stood, impervious to the flying shrapnel, tranquilly firing a pistol. Never losing his delicate hold on his shoebox.

Then the world went white.

Nanette ripped the goggles off and blinked at the electronic sunrise.

As soon as the lights went out, Cody jumped to his feet, his bad ankle forgotten. In the distance, gunfire blasted. A kick-ass sound.

"Yeah, baby!"

Garber's here.

But no one had invited him to the party. He pulled the firearm from his boot. Carefully, he patted down the wall through the dark cell until he found the door. A couple steps back and he lowered the pistol toward the lock. Then fired.

Crunch. Zinggg. Splack.

"Jesus!" The bullet ricocheted, whisking by his ear. From the ground, he shot again.

Spang. Zzzzz-Crack.

Hopeless.

Set into the door, a panel slid back. Pale light swept in. Then a dark figure obscured it.

"You done yet, tough guy? You can't shoot through metal."

Mrs. Rasmussen. "Lady, let me the hell outta' here!"

"Fine. On one condition…"

"Yeah?"

"When play time's over, you don't forget who let you out."

Cody crawled to his feet, smiled. Women always found him irresistible. "Got no beef with you lady. 'S cool, yo."

A chain rattled. The door opened. A flashlight's beam fell on him. Behind the flashlight stood an armed man. But she drew his attention. A flimsy nightgown barely covered her curves and valleys. Her sexy grin strained through the plastic.

"Well," she said, "what're you waiting for?"

Once Cody had his eyeful, he brushed by the duo.

"Wait."

"Baby, I gots bidness to take care of."

"You might want to use these." She tossed him a bundle.

In the dark, it took him a minute to figure out what it was. But once he strapped it on, toyed with a few switches, the world turned green.

Kick ass.

Like a cat, Delilah dropped off the branch and landed in the yard on all fours. Then the lights came back on.

Gustav's in trouble.

So was she. Men rushed her from three directions.

Bullets spit up grass at her feet. She twisted, tugging at the gun on her back. Defiantly, the strap held. Another bullet *spacked* into the wall behind her.

One more wrench and the gun freed. She flipped it into her arms, cocked and ready. And let it rip. The guy to her left buckled. Constant gunfire shook her arms, the gun jacking into her chest. Number two crashed down.

But the third man had vanished.

The goggles hindered her. She yanked them off, letting them dangle around her neck. Looked around her.

She waited a beat. Then, at a sprinter's pace, she hurtled toward the back patio.

A whistle by her ear. Grass chuffed up behind her.

Phtt, phtt, phtt. A hidden assailant with a silencer, twice as bad.

Without slowing, she turned, firing haphazardly. She hit the bottom patio step, flew up to the next.

Crack, spick, dikka-dikka…

She wove between patio furniture. Bullets launched the chairs. A glass table cracked, then fell. A folded umbrella toppled in front of her. She hopped over it, stretched her gun arm behind her and fired. Blindly, desperately.

If she could only *see* her shooter, *hear* him…

Behind her, glass tinkled. A broken window. Her way into the mansion, her only hope.

With her elbow, she shattered the rest of the window. One last volley of bullets for cover. Then she didn't stop. She kicked a leg up and over the sill. Ducked her head and rolled into the house, landing in a squat. Outside the window, she heard the man mounting the patio steps. Delilah aimed for his shadow. Whispered, "Surprise."

Kak, kak, kak… Dropped him like a lost call.

Voices shouted above her, from the second floor. Gunfire cracked. Smoke filled the hallway. Several doors lined the hallway. First one: *locked.* And the second, and the third…

Footfalls clambered around the corner. No time to make it back through the window. Trapped like a cornered fox.

She tucked into a narrow door frame, held her breath. And waited.

The first guard crashed into the hallway. The doorjamb hindered her aim, her bullets cracking into the walls. Foolishly, the man dropped into a crouch, an easy target. She took him out. Then she raised the gun to head level. With a sweep of her arm, she cut through the next two guards as soon as they rounded the corner. And kept the hits coming. Until her gun *clack-clack-clacked.*

Out of ammo.

Bodies lay in a pile at the end of the hall. Smoke rose from her now worthless gun. But she couldn't hear any more approaching guards.

Except for the man behind her.

Shit.

The bullet tore into her. She twirled, less than graceful. The pain didn't matter so much, at least not the physical pain. The man who got her, though? That *sucked.* Comical in his dumbfounded look, he gaped at her. A frightened mouth breather. Probably a newbie; green around the collar, even greener around the gills.

Which sucked even harder.

She fell to her knees. Held out her index finger, thumb up. Dropped the hammer.

"Bang," she said.

He winced. Actually *winced.* She went down, her body burning. And she still managed a chuckle.

Then she thought of her lover, how she'd miss him.

Gus...

Inside the mansion, splendid confusion ruled. Footsteps trampled overhead. Gunfire blasted, voices cut off in mid shout. It reminded Gus of a bowling alley. Only these "pins" stayed down.

But the explosions concerned him. Explosions from outside, where Delilah was. He intended to complete his mission, then find his love.

Two guards barred Gus' path to the cellar. He opened fire. The gun's whiplash jerked him to the floor but not before it tore open a guard's chest. The second guard jumped over Gus, ignoring him; a soldier trained not to be distracted, Gus supposed. His mistake. Gus ran after him, slashing "Percy" wildly. He lunged and chopped down the back of the guard's legs.

"Shouldn't have underestimated me, my friend," he said before finishing the job.

Cool to the touch, the cellar door opened quietly. Gus flicked on the light at the top of the stairs (no sense in being discreet about it now) and descended. He trailed a hand across fabulous rows of wine bottles (which he hoped to explore further at a later date), marveling at the lack of dust. Anything to keep his mind off Delilah.

He counted off his steps until he found the generator. The green box rose before him, chugging with artificial life. Between a series of triangular grates, lights sparked. Gus found where the machine churned the loudest and attached the plastic explosive. Seemed much too easy.

Unsatisfied, he considered the remaining explosive in the bag. Tossed it back and forth between his hands. Even though Bartholomew had instructed him to apply only half, he shrugged, stuck the rest on. No one would accuse him of doing a half-glass-empty job. The timers slid in easily. As an afterthought, he cut the delay by fifteen seconds. Trying to make up for lost time.

Gus ascended the stairs. First, he heard the tremendous explosion. Then he felt it. An onslaught of heat rolled at his back, a God-like shove. For a minute he flew, an exhilarating feeling. Then the kitchen stove ended his flight.

Chank!

Leon thrust the chair back into the guard behind him. In the dark, he lunged for the second man, grappling for his rifle. His hand located the barrel. With his other hand, he grasped the guard's throat. He levered the gun barrel across his shoulder, aiming it back toward Rasmussen. Leon squeezed the guard's trigger finger.

Krak. Spack. Tinkle...

"Jesus *Christ*," Rasmussen croaked.

Bullets zagged through the room. The gun's charges exposed the other guard coming Leon's way. Leon jerked the gun toward the guard and fired. With a grunt, the man slammed into the wall.

Leon heard the three men at the opposite end of the room scrambling. A squeak of a wheelchair's metal, a whirl of a small engine. And something being snapped together, interlocking metal parts. A weapon.

Click, snakt, chok...

One thing at a time. Leon tussled with the guard he held to the wall. Fingernails clawed Leon's cheek. Tobacco pungent breath panted into Leon's face. Leon's elbow went up, chopping into the man's throat. With a wheeze, the guard released the gun and went down.

"Get him, goddammit!" Rasmussen's voice sounded distant, muffled. *In another room?* But the stealthy quiet of the two killers concerned him more.

He needed night-vision goggles. A hasty retreat outside, pillage a dead guard.

Leon groped around, found the slumping guard's collar. He yanked him away from the door. Footsteps approached behind him. Leon released another short round.

The brief light show spotlighted the big man diving beneath the table. Too close for comfort. Leon wrenched the door open and dodged into the hallway. His feet tangled, tripping over something. When he went down, his trigger finger jumped, illuminating Teddy's dead body. Teddy's eyes and mouth gawped open. Bile rose in Leon's throat. He crawled away, quickly working his way to his feet. Bursts from his gun provided the only light at the end of his tunnel.

Behind him, the boardroom door opened. Suddenly, the hallway lights snapped on. Bright stars circled in his vision.

The rangy man stood in the hallway, holding a weapon that looked heavier than his entire ninety-eight pound wet body. Something composed of metallic boxes, parts, and canisters. Just below the weapon's barrel tip, a flame danced. Sparkling in the carrier's eyes.

A stream of white-hot fire spat out from the flamethrower's mouth. Leon dropped, his gun spinning away from him. As the fire drew closer, he screamed.

Albert took his failure personally, he always did. For years, his therapist had told him to knock it off, he couldn't control everything.

"Yes," Albert had responded, "but I *should* be able to control everything." Which had been his driving force—his motto, if you will—ever since his beloved Gretchen had passed. It's what had moved him to find a cure for cancer, an essential tribute to his late wife. No matter the cost. It frustrated him he couldn't wrangle the insidious disease, tame it. When things continually slipped out of his control, he sank into a deep depression at the unfairness of it all.

And, now, it ate him up inside—his own internal cancer—that his plan had gone completely off the rails. Rasmussen's lights were supposed to have remained off, giving Albert's team a shock and awe advantage.

From where he stood—in the middle of a surrealistic war of guns, completely uncivilized—shock and awe had subjugated him.

Next to his outgunned peers, he sought cover behind the shrapnel of the SUV they'd rode in on. Although he had a rifle, he'd yet to use it. Odd, where he drew the lines. Of course he'd taken lives before. But that had been in the name of science, bettering mankind. Belatedly, he questioned his involvement in this entire fiasco.

He should've questioned the issue earlier.

"Albert! Help us!" Sweat glued Nanette's hair to her face. Panic fed her clear desire to live. Something Albert needed a good dose of. "Shoot!"

He stuck his gun up, squeezed the trigger willy-nilly. Hoping a stray bullet might land. As long as he didn't have to witness the fall-out.

If he believed in Hell, surely he'd landed there. The surrounding tableau looked like the remains of a war-ravaged country.

Rasmussen's team appeared to be growing, organizing and inching closer to the SUV's body. Worse, more voices rose behind them, rallying. Trapping them in the middle.

Bartholomew seemed oblivious to the danger. He stood tall (as tall as any man Albert'd ever seen), nonchalantly blasting his pistol. Grinning through it all. At one point, Bartholomew'd said, "This is…interesting." Without a doubt, Albert knew the Man with the Shoebox was the most insane of their collective of loosely wrapped people.

Albert again doubted every decision he'd made regarding their siege against LMI.

Rasmussen's men had the clear advantage, knowing the

terrain. They dove behind giant boulders in the rock garden, seeking refuge behind trees. Strangling Albert, bit by bit.

Suddenly, Tommy dashed away from the SUV and ran toward the mansion. Bullets lit up his trail as if his shoes left behind sparks. A foolhardy move. Or perhaps he meant to draw fire away from his master, Bartholomew.

Takka-takka-takka.

Tommy reached the marble steps. Not fast enough. Like a marionette, he jerked, his arms flailing. Once he fell, his gun ripped a farewell salute into the sky.

Bartholomew shrugged. Then kept firing.

Bobby managed to crawl into the backseat of the SUV. He tossed an object up, caught it. "This'll show the bastards."

Only then did Albert realize what he intended to do. "No! Bobby, don't—"

Bobby ignored him, hurled the flash bang.

"Everyone get down!" Albert hit the ground first, not that it mattered much.

The sky opened up with a chilling sunrise. Intense even through closed eyelids. A massive thunder cloud crashed around them. The ground trembled. So did Albert's ribcage. Next to him lay Nanette, her face buried in the ground. He reached for her hand, held it. Little comfort during Armageddon.

Albert's head pounded. As soon as he climbed to his knees, he retched. Violently.

Stunned, Bobby sat up next to the car. Nanette's mouth opened and closed, presumably yelling at Bobby. But only an intense buzzing filled Albert's ears.

But since they had earplugs, it had to be far worse for Rasmussen's men. A second wind invigorated Albert, brought him up on unsteady legs.

"Let's press the advantage!" At least that's what Albert thought he'd screamed. Funny not being able to hear your own scream.

Nanette nodded, apparently astute at reading lips.

Albert hustled into the front yard. No looking back. Taking control. He tested his gun. After the first few rounds, the gun felt comfortable in his hand, an extension of his newly found courage. He plucked off a writhing guard (most of them on the ground from the explosion already), then another. Line 'em up, shoot 'em down.

Augie fell in line behind him, his military training a boon. With an indecipherable battle cry, Augie shot his way through the guards on the ground. Nanette and Bartholomew followed. Pride swelled in Albert. Even given a hiccup, he'd force his plan to work.

Then another explosion ripped through the mansion. And the fates unplugged the lights again.

"Oh…" The only thing that came to Albert's mind. Change never set well with him, scientific constants his preference.

He wrestled with the goggles, yanking them on, adjusting them. The strap bound him too tightly, crunching his nose. His glasses fogged up. He couldn't breathe, feeling absolutely miserable. A flick of the on-switch came a little too late. Only then did he spot the band of amassing shadows approaching from behind.

"No!" He fired his gun in a very orderly manner, straight line, move it over an inch, repeat. He barely noticed the first bullet rip into his stomach. But the second one? The one tearing apart his chest? That one he noticed.

He lay down, taking his time. No sense in rocking the apple cart now. Had he been a religious man, he would've comforted himself with the notion he'd see Gretchen again. Alas, as a man of science, he waited to greet never-ending nothingness. And wondered if it was too late to convert.

The explosions didn't bother Cody, no big deal. The fact he was missing out on the fun, however, provided a real buzz-kill. Especially if someone had offed Garber before he had his chance.

As he left the prison cottage (or whatever the hell they called it), the lights had come back on. Minutes later, they went out again. Some kinda' party. But with the goggles, he was fully prepared to crash the party.

Outside, he stopped, trying to piece together what he saw. Two teams were trading bullets, bodies dropping everywhere.

Instantly identifiable in their yuppie-wear, Rasmussen's goons comprised the team nearest him.

Cody stayed to the shadows. He jogged toward Rasmussen's men, dropping every few feet. The first body he nearly tripped over had been gutted. He traded up guns with the dead dude, an automatic much more fun.

Most of the men at his feet were dead. If not, they killed it at playing possum. He considered spraying them with bullets just for the hell of it, but he had his eye on the big prize. The mansion. Without a doubt where he'd find Garber.

He ran, staying within the shade of the large house. Several people hunkered down in the grass were shooting at the LMI army. Outgunned, big time. Cody couldn't tell who they were, not even with the goggles. But hotness of white light stood out in one curvy figure. The babe from the motel. When he heard her screaming voice, something he was familiar with, that confirmed it.

He crept closer, listened. Four people: the chick and three dudes, none of them Garber. Call him a sucker for a pretty face, or maybe he just couldn't stand unfair fights. Or maybe he just hated Rasmussen's gun-toting yuppies. But he might as well even the score a little. Hell, he hadn't had this much fun in a long time anyway. And he hadn't yet fired the automatic.

In a squat, he ran beneath the mansion's darkened windows. Near the front door, a cluster of trees formed. A perfect spot, his grassy knoll.

The hottie's team gave as good as they got, holding Rasmussen's team at a standstill. But it wouldn't last. *Numbers win wars, yo.*

Cody barely contained his excitement. The automatic ripped in his hands. He expelled his breath, almost as good as sex.

"Eat it, beeyotches!" The men danced beneath his bullets. He didn't get them all. No need to. At least he gave the babe a fighting chance. Sassy chick like her deserved it.

Before he tore into the ranch, he yelled out to the stunned foursome, "Yo, you're welcome!"

The flame kept coming. So did the small man with the crazy

grin. Fire licked the stone walls, charring them black.

Leon spotted his dropped gun, a foot away tops. Not much but a deadly margin.

Bursts of fire roared over Leon. Close enough for him to smell the burning cotton of his shirt, hear it hissing like a snake. Clearly, the man was toying with Leon, taking his time until he decided to put Leon on the spit.

An explosion shook the floor. A mechanical screech rose, then dwindled. The lights shut off. With the bright white light of the torch still imprinted in his mind, Leon scrabbled toward his gun.

The small killer stood still. The torch diminished, nothing more than an orange-blue flicker.

Leon found the gun, aimed for the lamp. Without hesitation, he pumped lead into the madman.

The flamethrower dropped first, the flame fizzling out with a *tmmp*. The man toppled. Instead of a grunt, an agonized cry, anything expected, he simply said, "Crap." Then silence.

Except for the feet beating up the stairs. Leon hurried toward the downed killer, gave him a blind man's pat-down. Around his neck, he found goggles. Liberating them from the hitman's head proved easier than Leon thought; the thinnest sheath of skin over bone patched the man's head together. Leon enlarged the goggle's strap, slipped it over his head, thankful for Bartholomew's lessons.

Rasmussen. From within the boardroom, Leon'd heard his voice come from another room, an adjoining room. With gun in hand, he raced toward the next door. At his back, the boardroom door yanked open. The big man clomped out.

But the bald killer was too busy to pay attention to Leon. He crashed onto his knees, crying over his spilled partner.

Nanette never expected a gift like that, particularly one wrapped up in Cody's hoodie. She didn't question it either.

A few yards away, she spotted a tree, her destination. She ran, firing until the gun quit spitting. Rasmussen's few surviving guards either cowered on the ground (sitting targets) or high-tailed it in the other direction (smarter targets). Augie stood by her side, blasting away with experienced aim.

"Haven't had this much fun in a long time," he screamed over the gunfire.

But the person really enjoying himself appeared to be Bartholomew. With no seeming rhyme or reason, he pivoted in a circle, indiscriminately firing. Remarkably, returned gunfire avoided him, an invisible shield up. Even more remarkably, his shoebox never left his grip.

Smoke twisted off Nanette's empty gun barrel. She listened. A few dying groans. By the pool, a lawn chair collapsed. Other than that, the calm after a storm. "Think we got it under control. Now we go in."

As if forgetting something, Bobby stuck a finger up. "Hold up. Need reinforcements."

"Bobby, wait! We've got to move now," Nanette called after him. But he ignored her, chugging toward the SUV, his flannel shirttail waving. He dipped inside the shattered vehicle, leaning over the front seat.

From a broken window, he yelled, "Yeah, baby, that's what I'm talkin—"

Fwoomph.

The SUV's interior lit up. Flame engulfed Bobby. His shriek rode down Nanette's spine. Then the automobile exploded.

"Look away," shouted Augie.

But the warning came too late. Intense light filled Nanette's night vision, searing a path from her retinas into her brain. She fell to her knees, dizzy.

Once the ground quit trembling, Bartholomew offered her a hand up. Into her ear, he said, "Boys with their toys." With a parent's amused exasperation, he gave a slight head shake.

"You all right, little lady?" asked Augie.

"Will be."

The SUV burned. An appropriate funeral pyre for Bobby, dying behind the wheel. Tired of being blinded, Nanette ripped off her goggles.

Just in time. The lights in the mansion popped back on. Another volley of bullets sounded from within.

"Let's go." Nanette reloaded her rifle. "Leon's still in there."

Augie led them to the front door. Cop style, he gestured for silence as he hugged the door. After he nudged it open, he dropped into a squat with his gun poised. He gave them a thumb meeting index finger o.k. signal and they entered the belly of the beast.

As if swimming out of a murky pond, Gustav slowly rose, breaking the surface of consciousness. Undoubtedly, he'd died. Because he stared up into the face of an angel.

"Delilah? Am I….am I in Heaven?"

Delilah chuckled. "No. Doubt you'll be going there. But it's not your time yet." She had his head cradled in her lap, stroking his cheek. But something also licked at his cheek, something wet and warm. A dark wet stain formed on Delilah's leather jacket. Blood oozed from her wound.

"You're hurt!" He shook off his own intense pain and sat up.

Only when Delilah grimaced did he realize the extent of her injury. Before, she'd always seemed impervious to pain.

"It hurts, Gus. I'm gonna beat you to Hell unless we do something about it."

In protective mode, he bounced to his feet. "Can you walk?"

"I can try." A small shrug, not her usual full-on shoulder heave.

He wanted to help her up, tried tugging at her arm. Payback for the many times she'd taken care of him. Before he'd never had a problem with his diminutive size, always rising above whatever limitations life had doled out to him. But he felt powerless now, cursing his size. He'd do anything for her. *Anything.* To keep her from dying.

Every small movement doubled her over. "It's…bad…"

"Delilah, you've got to try!" Near tears, he grabbed her wrist. Pain marked her face, pain he caused her. "Please! *Try…*"

"I'm trying, dammit." She made it to her knees. Raised shaking hands. Then slid back down and curled up. Groaning, but not crying. *Never* crying.

Desperate, Gus looked around. If he were a full-sized man, he could carry her to safety. Carry them into a long life together. "My darling…I'm sorry…so sorry. I've let you down. If…"

"Never. So…shut up." She extended her hand. He gripped it, held on. And he felt ashamed. She lay dying at his feet, yet she still had the inner strength to comfort him.

He manned up, six feet tall inside. "I'll get you out of here. One way or the next way."

She smiled, but dropped it just as quickly.

Dead guards littered the floors. From the nearest, he liberated a gun. Brought back the hammer with a satisfying *clack*. *Lock and load them*. If he had to, he'd force someone at gunpoint to carry her out to safety.

At the kitchen door, he listened. Footsteps quickly approached. He flung open the door and sprung out. His finger nearly closed on the trigger until he recognized the intruders.

"My friends! You are needed!" He wanted to envelop the three of them in a hug, but social niceties would have to wait.

White as paper, Nanette dropped her gun. "Gus…glad you're still alive."

"Indeed. But I'm worried about Delilah."

Nanette gave Delilah a quick exam, her bedside frown hard to miss. "Delilah, just…hold on, okay? First, we need to find Leon…finish this. Then we'll come back for you."

Gus wouldn't have it. "No! Delilah comes first. Please! She risked her life for the mission!"

"I don't know, little feller," said Augie. "Seems to me—"

"Unacceptable! I'll drag her out of here myself if I have to!"

Bartholomew exchanged a quick glance with Nanette. Then sighed. "Call me a fool for love. I'll help." To Nanette, he said, "I'll be back in a minute. Are you okay to go on?"

Nanette nodded.

Sudden guilt ate at Gus. "I'm sorry I'm unable to finish this, friends. Truly sorry. But…" Choked up, he spread his hands toward Delilah.

Nanette dropped into a squat. "It's okay, Gus. You did great. Just…take care of her. And yourself." Nanette straightened, hustled out of the kitchen, Augie at her heels.

Bartholomew scooped up Delilah and placed the shoebox onto her chest. He stared at the shoebox, hesitated. Frowned. He whispered something into Delilah's ear. Gently, she placed a hand on Bartholomew's treasure, securing it.

With a smile, Bartholomew said to Gus, "Let's go."

At the still intact SUV, Bartholomew carefully tucked Delilah into the passenger side. Then reclaimed his shoebox. He held it up to the sky, an offering to whatever gods he worshipped.

Gus appropriated a wooden crate full of weapons from the back, dumped the contents and slid it into the driver's seat.

Bartholomew jangled the keys in front of Gus, doubt in his eyes. "Are you certain you can drive, Gustav?"

Gus dismissed the notion with a wave. "My friend, this is my long leg." He held up the rifle next to him. "Plenty good for brakes and gas. I can manage anything."

"I'm sure you can." The Man with the Shoebox reached into his pocket, withdrew a business card. "Call this man as soon as you reach town. He'll tend to Delilah."

"Thank you, my friend." Delilah nodded her thanks as well, all she could manage. "Good luck inside the mansion. And… look after Leon."

No more time for goodbyes. Gus slammed the gear into reverse, crammed the rifle down onto the gas pedal. "Ready, my love?"

"Always…"

The lights coming back on paled in comparison to the real problem.

Leon had entered a study, full of bookshelves and a well-stocked bar. And in one corner, a safe room. A goddamned safe room, no doubt where Rasmussen had buried himself while the sky fell around him.

The steel reinforced door looked impenetrable, the only thing adorning it a boat's wheel and a keypad. A green light blinked above the door: *occupied.*

Leon buckled to his knees, staring at the fortress, worse than a dying man's desert mirage. He'd come all this way, fighting for his life, to ultimately be flummoxed by a steel door. Inches away from Rasmussen. It may as well've been a different continent. He could huff and puff all he wanted; nothing could blow Rasmussen's little house of steel down.

A bittersweet ending.

Out in the hallway, the large man continued to bellow. In seconds, he'd be exacting revenge on Leon.

But someone else entered the fray. Screaming louder than the bald man.

Cody.

Of course.

While racing through the mansion, Cody destroyed everything in his path, living or inanimate. On the first floor, he hurdled over dead bodies while adding more to the count. Vases shattered in his wake. Windows exploded. He'd never taken out so many people at once before. *Way cool.*

But above all the commotion, Cody heard Sensitivity scream. *Upstairs.* Where he knew he'd find Garber as well.

His heart pounding, he mounted the steps two at a time. At the top of the stairs, Cody caught his breath and stopped. Sensitivity stood in the hallway with his back to him. His shoulders rose with shuddering sobs. Standing over his dead partner, Bug.

"Time for payback!" Cody couldn't help it. All the kick-ass movie heroes always have a catchphrase. But it cost him. Sensitivity whirled and fell into a crouch. Startled, Cody fired, the kickback lifting Cody's aim over Sensitivity's head. Way off.

"You little shit!" Head down, Sensitivity charged.

"Whoa!" Cody tried to take aim. But Sensitivity moved faster. His head cannon-balled into Cody's stomach, bringing them both down. Cody's gun went high, bullets *crick-snak-zinging* into the ceiling. A giant hand gripped Cody's throat, the other pummeling Cody's gun arm. Pain desensitized Cody. His hold on the gun loosened.

And the hits kept on coming. Cody's eyes blurred, his face numb. Sensitivity wheeled back, holding his fist in midair as if summoning more strength.

"You stupid son-of-a-*bitch*! I should've *killed* you when I had the chance!" The blow to Cody's face dimmed his vision. Cody dug his heels into the carpet, trying to push away. He grabbed

Sensitivity's hand, trying to wrest it away from his throat.

"All this trouble…Bug's *dead*! Because of *you*!"

Tunt. A jab to Cody's ear.

"Psychopathic *shit*!"

Chumpf. Bones broke, soft tissue tore in his nose.

The world brightened, colors heightened. Sound swept away. Thoughts dissolved into abstraction. Cody never realized death would be so peaceful.

"Stay down, Cody." Little more than a whisper, but Cody recognized the voice. *Garber.*

For a blessed second, Sensitivity stopped pummeling Cody. Cody lay back, strangely tranquil.

A string of snaps followed. Above Cody, Sensitivity jerked his arms like an orchestra leader. Red circles grew across his white button-down chest. His eyelids drooped. But not before releasing one final tear, warm when it dropped onto Cody's cheek. Sensitivity slid sideways, quietly. Not the big death Cody'd expected from such a massive man. Somehow, the quiet thump of his body to the carpet sounded less than satisfying.

Then, above him, Garber loomed. Anger brought Cody back. Energy surged. He shoved Sensitivity aside, reached for his gun.

Garber kicked it away. "*Stop*, Cody. Just…stop it."

"No fuckin' *way*! You're *dead* old man, *dead*!" Cody swung a weak fist at Leon, missed him. He followed it with another failed attempt. "Teach you to dick with me…make fun of me…"

"Cody, aren't you tired of this? You can't fight now. Don't. And I don't know what LMI's been telling you about me, but I never—"

"Gonna kill you…"

"Listen to me." Garber dropped into a crouch, his gun within Cody's reach. "I've never belittled you. Last year…we were…if not friends exactly, I got to know you. Liked you, even. Hard as that is to believe. We were like Butch and Sundance…"

The old man rambled on, not a lot of it making sense. Something about the movie Garber'd sent him while he'd cooled his heels in prison. A western.

"I don't get close to anyone, Cody. But against all odds… especially since you were trying to kill me, frame me…I found myself caring about you. I'd never do anything to hurt you."

Placating words, nothing more. Trying to throw Cody off balance. Never again. "Bullshit, old man. You…you…" Cody's brain clouded. It hurt too much to think. He couldn't remember why he wanted to off Garber, not really. Something Garber's prick of an old man had said. Something… "Your father tole me you were draggin' my name through shit. You were—"

"And you believed that bastard? Cody, he never spoke a word of truth in his life. You know me. I don't lie. I…wouldn't hurt you…"

Cody closed his eyes. He couldn't listen to it any more. Couldn't take it. Because it sounded like the painful truth. He'd been duped. Again. Worse, his purpose had been stolen from him. He had nothing left, his life nothing but a waste of space.

Cody snaked his hand out, grasped Garber's rifle. Pulled the snout to his forehead. Ready to feed it. "Do it, Leon. Just…do it. Pull the trigger."

"No…"

"Just *do* it, old man!" Cody never thought this encounter would end in tears. Especially his own. His shame buried a little more of his soul. "Just…do it. Kill me…I've got nothin' left. Nothin…Put me down. I'm fucked up…"

"We all are, Cody. Some of us more than others."

Cody's hands slackened. Gun metal, cold and smooth, slipped between away from him. Just like everything else in his life.

"Kill me….please, Leon?"

The gun rose. The barrel shook before Cody's eyes. A click, the last sound he'd hear. And he welcomed death to take him away. But apparently death had other plans. Leon sat, set the gun across his lap, flung his legs out.

"I can't…I just…"

The croak in Garber's voice amazed Cody, absolutely astounded him.

"Jesus, old man, look at the two of us…"

Leon chuckled, dry and dusty. "Yeah…aren't we something. And don't call me 'old man'."

"Yeah, speaking of old men…sorry I did yours."

"Don't worry about it. I'll return the favor someday."

For a moment, Cody forgot where he was, forgot the urgency of the situation, forgot his embarrassing loss of cool. Just laughed even though it felt like his ribs might collapse.

Storm-trooping footfalls and cocked triggers ended the short reunion.

As soon as Leon saw Nanette and Augie, he thought the cavalry had arrived. But the cavalry had their hands raised, conspicuously empty of weapons. Armed LMI guards stood behind his teammates. And even though she trailed the gathering, the blond woman in back clearly reigned as the pack leader. With a snap of her fingers, the men cleared a path for her.

She flounced Leon's way, a swivel to her hips that could slip a disc. Extensive plastic surgery diminished her smile, bare to begin with. "Well, isn't this sweet?"

Leon didn't know how to respond. But Cody had plenty to say. "What's up, baby? We're on the same team, 'member?" In one quick swoop, he dashed away his tears, replacing them with his familiar—and oddly comforting to Leon—arrogance.

"That remains to be seen. Up on your feet, boys." She gestured toward the safe room. "Let's finish this."

Leon offered Cody a helping hand up. No surprise, Cody brushed it away with a snarl. Using the big dead man's body for support, Cody somehow hobbled up into a crooked stance.

The gun lay on the floor not far from Leon. With one dive, he could grab it, open fire. But, without a doubt, it'd end with Nanette dead. One way or the other, they'd all be dead soon, a no-brainer. But, frankly, he didn't have the strength left to go down swinging.

Rasmussen's men corralled the hostages into the room. Last to enter (but always making the biggest entrance), the blond walked toward the vault's door. She punched a series of keys. The light transitioned to red.

Behind the door, Rasmussen cried out, "Who is it? I've got a gun, goddammit!"

The woman said, "I know, dear. Everything's under control. It's safe to come out."

"Bullshit! Prove it to me!"

"Gaines and the guards have the captives in hand. Come out, Jasper."

A small, unassuming-looking man (presumably Gaines) verified what she said. "It's true, sir."

The door inched open. A gun barrel noodled out like a periscope. Then Rasmussen's liver-spotted head appeared, his eyes blinking like a newborn's. "It's over?"

"It's all over, dear." The woman patted Rasmussen's head. With her other hand, she easily snatched away his gun. "No need for that anymore. But, my dear, I'm afraid it's time for you to retire." She turned the gun on the old man.

"What the hell're you doin', Sheera? You're my goddamn wife! Quit screwin' around and put that down. Stop this horseshit!" Clearly Rasmussen didn't take his wife's surprising turn seriously. But Leon did. And he wondered why they'd been allowed to live to witness it.

"Always an asshole, dear." She jammed the barrel into Rasmussen's large ear. He swat at it like a horsefly.

"I swear to God, Sheera, if you don't put that down now, you're outta' here!" He turned to Gaines, said, "By God, show this woman who's boss 'round here!"

Gaines inhaled through clenched teeth. "Sorry, sir, no can do."

"What? What the hell is this?" Rasmussen sputtered, waiting for someone to come to his aid. His late and not-so-loyal team hemmed and hawed. Some offered satisfied smiles, indicating just what kind of boss Rasmussen had been.

"I swear to God, Jasper," said Sheera, "you're too full of yourself to realize what's happening. I'm the new boss."

"You're out of your—"

"You signed everything over to me."

"Impossible!" Rasmussen banged his fists on his wheelchair's arm pads. "I'd never do any—"

"I'm afraid it's true, sir," said Gaines, relishing the moment with a grin. "I always told you to read papers thoroughly before you sign them."

"I'll have your head, Gaines! All of yours!" A root of a finger swept the room. "You've got one last chance to—"

"Oh, dear, you're so tiresome. Time to finish this." Sheera extended her arm, the gun leveled at her husband's face.

"Hold on, sugar, hold on." Augie stepped forward. "Would you wanna' deprive an old man of his last wish? How 'bout you let me take care of the ol' coot."

Squinting, Rasmussen leaned forward. "Augie? That you?"

"Sure is, you ornery bastard."

Sheera let the gun slip, dangling it by the trigger guard. "So, you're August Schroeder."

"That I am, ma'am." Augie's face brightened.

"Heard a lot about you. Fine. Make it quick. Make it hurt." She handed Augie the gun.

Augie took it, admiring its beauty. "Thankee kindly."

"Wait a goddamn minute! Augie, we go way back! You can't just shoot me!"

"Shoulda' thought of that before you turned on me, Jasper." Augie gripped the wheelchair handles and spun him around, facing the safe room. "Ladies, maybe you shouldn't be witness to this." He winked at Nanette, favored Sheera with a second one. As he rolled Rasmussen back into the bunker, he said, "Nice wheels, Jasper. I'll be needin' some like 'em soon, I 'spect."

From the safe room, Rasmussen's voice struck helium-inhaled heights.

Crack.

Leon jumped at the blast.

Augie strolled out, his smile speckled with blood.

"All right, enough fun." Sheera looked at Leon. "Mr. Garber, I have a business proposition for you."

Not much of a fan of Sheera's last business transaction, Leon said nothing, quietly waited. She opened the negotiations after all.

"How would you like to be the new CEO of Like-Minded Individuals?"

Rationality left the room. Leon'd heard her, just couldn't fathom the idea. Nanette tossed her arms up, for once as befuddled as Leon.

"You've got to be kidding me."

"No joke," said Sheera. "In fact, the idea's been percolating for a while. Not only with me. But with our overseas affiliates as well. It's clear you have a real aptitude for this line of work. You know how to get things done. And your corporate business background is a true bonus, something Jasper never had a knack for. Not to mention your…instincts, your determination. Singlehandedly, you've decimated two of our previously impervious foundations. You—"

"Yo, I helped!"

"Shut up, Cody." She glared at him, a stern mother. "Leon, I understand you haven't been happy with LMI's business model."

"Nice way of putting it."

"I promise you, you'd have free reign to run the company as you see fit. After one stipulation, of course." She waited for the hook to take hold.

Leon chomped at the worm. "And what's that?"

"Nothing, really. Nothing more than any large corporation would expect. You need to keep turning a profit, keep us in the black."

Leon didn't buy it, not for a minute. Her words sounded as phony as her facial reconstruction. But the ludicrous idea set his mind's gears in motion. "What about you? I thought you were the head of LMI now."

"In name only. I don't have a mind for business." Her lips turned up a sneer. "Such nasty business." Leon withheld a sarcastic laugh; a minute ago, she'd been ready to excavate a new mouth in her husband. "I'd prefer to stay out of it. I'm a simple woman with simple needs. Money suits me just fine."

That Leon believed. "What if I stop the political end? No more killing for political purposes."

"Fine. I never bought into that part of the business model in the first place. As I said, I'm perfectly content with money, not power. Besides…money is true power."

"No more innocent people die at Like-Minded Individuals' hands. From now on, I pick the projects. Only people who deserve it."

"Acceptable. As long as you keep us financially growing, you can do as you please."

Leon considered. Absolutely ridiculous. But he knew the only other option was eating a meal of bullets. And, as Sheera and her late husband had said, LMI didn't stop at the walls of a Montana ranch. Not even at the US border. "Overseas affiliates" she'd called them. To truly destroy LMI, it'd have to be an inside job. Infiltrate, unplug. *Bury.*

A shadowy figure lurked just outside the door. Tall, thin, something tucked beneath his arm. The Man with the Shoebox. Leon couldn't tell, not absolutely, but it looked like Bartholomew shook his head. A quick, solemn swipe. *A warning?* One blink later and Bartholomew just as quickly vanished.

Leon glanced at Nanette for a visual clue, advice of some sort, anything. What he saw worried him. *Disappointment.* But this was his chance, the first good one he'd been handed since the entire debacle began. To destroy LMI, sacrifices would have to be made.

"I pick my team." Leon eyed Gaines, a man he already didn't trust.

Sheera shrugged. "Of course. Within reason."

"Starting with Cody."

This time Nanette couldn't hold her tongue. "Oh, come on, Leon!" She hitched a thumb toward Cody. "You can't be serious. He's completely—"

"Hey, watch it, yo! I gots mad skills, baby!"

Sheera silenced him with an upraised hand. "While I happen to agree with your friend's doubt regarding Mr. Spangler, let's call this a goodwill gesture, Leon. He's on your team."

"Damn straight, yo." Cody straightened out of his battered hunch, smoothing out his hoodie. He tossed around a handful of haughty nods to his new subordinates, the armed guards in the room. Immediately Leon wondered if he'd just made his first mistake in the new world order.

"And everyone that's helped me. Nanette, Augie, Gus, Delilah, Albert…" Leon stopped cold when Nanette shook her head. Her eyes glistened, the message clear. Leon'd already lost some of his team. His boldness faltered, legs threatening to follow. He felt responsible in a way; he'd started all of this. Well, at least he'd responded after LMI's initial salvo. More the reason to take them down. For his fallen comrades. He'd mourn them later. Privately. Breaking down in tears was no way for a CEO to lead by example. "No one touches…everyone who's still alive. You understand me, Sheera? They're under my protection. And I want it in a contract. I know LMI loves their contracts."

"Of course. Do we have a deal, Mr. Garber?"

Last chance. His only one. "Yes."

Sheera smiled, not exactly filling Leon with confidence. "Splendid. Welcome to your new kingdom." She waved her hands, fairy princess style. "What's left of it anyway. I'll have contractors out here first thing in the morning. After we clean up the bodies, of course."

"Of course." Still dazed, Leon left the room. Before he toppled over, he stumbled into the boardroom next door. He assumed the head of the table, the deep leather welcoming him like a glove. And looked around at his new kingdom.

It felt good to be the King.

To be concluded in:

KILLER KING

Killers Incorporated, Book 3

.

About the Author

Stuart R. West is a lifelong resident of Kansas, which he considers both a curse and a blessing. It's a curse because…well, it's Kansas. But it's great because…well, it's Kansas. Lots of cool, strange and creepy things happen in the Midwest, and Stuart takes advantage of them in his work. Call it "Kansas Noir". Stuart writes thrillers, suspense and horror, both for adult and young adult audiences. Stuart spent twenty-five years in the corporate sector and now writes full time. He's married to a professor of pharmacy (who greatly appreciates the fact he cooks dinner for her every night) and has a twenty-six-year-old daughter who's still deciding what to do with her life. But that's okay. It took him twenty-five years to figure that out.

Curious about other Crossroad Press books?
Stop by our site:
http://store.crossroadpress.com
We offer quality writing
in digital, audio, and print formats.

Enter the code FIRSTBOOK
to get 20% off your first order from our store!
Stop by today!